THE GIRLS OF SUMMER

THE GIRLS OF SUMMER

Katie Bishop

ST. MARTIN'S PRESS
NEW YORK

First published in the United States by St. Martin's Press, an imprint of St. Martin's Publishing Group

THE GIRLS OF SUMMER. Copyright © 2023 by Katie Bishop. All rights reserved. Printed in the United States of America. For information, address St. Martin's Publishing Group, 120 Broadway, New York, NY 10271.

www.stmartins.com

Designed by Gabriel Guma

The Library of Congress Cataloging-in-Publication Data is available upon request.

ISBN 978-1-250-28391-7 (hardcover)
ISBN 978-1-250-28392-4 (ebook)

Our books may be purchased in bulk for promotional, educational, or business use. Please contact your local bookseller or the Macmillan Corporate and Premium Sales Department at 1-800-221-7945, extension 5442, or by email at MacmillanSpecialMarkets@macmillan.com.

Originally published in the United Kingdom by Bantam Press, an imprint of Transworld Publishers, a Penguin Random House company

First U.S. Edition: 2023

10 9 8 7 6 5 4 3 2 1

To my parents, for teaching me to love to read

THEN

*I*t's too hot to be outside for long. Sweat is starting to dampen my scalp, thickening in the roots of my hair and pooling in the crevices of my collarbone. My T-shirt sticks to my spine and my arms are tinged pink, an ungainly line of skin beginning to blister along the top of my thigh. I curl my toes into the damp sand and feel the sharpness of a small shell against the sole of my foot.

Please, don't let him have left without me, *I think.* I'll do anything. I need him to come for me.

From my spot on the sand, I can just make out the dock. Rising out of the sea is the rickety wooden platform where I disembarked months ago, seasick and tired. A small boat is tethered there, bright blue and bobbing in the slow swell of the tide. It will leave in ten minutes, and I am supposed to be on it.

When I arrived here this morning, the dock was quiet. Now there is a bustle of activity, a queue of impatient tourists ready to embark. The waves edge close to my legs and dampen the ground beneath my heels. I shiver as saltwater laps the tip of my toe.

Just a few more minutes. Just a few more minutes and he'll be here.

"Rachel!"

Someone is waving one arm in my direction, their figure silhouetted against the brightness of the sky. I lift one hand to shield my eyes and see that it's Helena. She's walking quickly, half jogging, and as she collapses down next to me, her chest heaves, her breath tangled up in her throat. Her hair is damp, and salt crystals are beginning to form and glitter at her neck, a white and grainy sheen that edges in one long streak from her jaw down to her collarbone.

"They came for him," she says, her voice ragged and airless. "This morning."

I'm already shaking my head, clambering to my feet.

"No," I say.

"They didn't find him. He'd already left. He got away."

It takes a moment for me to find the words, for the shapes that Helena's mouth makes to form into something resembling meaning.

"He can't have."

"I've been to the house. Everything's gone."

"You're lying."

"We knew this would happen, Rachel. We knew they'd come for him, in the end."

I gather up my bags, staggering in my hurry to get away. She opens her mouth as if to say something before I go, one arm raised up as if to catch me, and then seems to think better of it. There's nothing she can say to stop me now.

My things are too heavy as I tumble up the beach. My shoes catch in the sand and I bend down to tug them off. I throw them onto the ground so that I can dash to the road, away from Helena and toward him. I flag down a car, a local man who pulls up looking concerned at me, barefoot and weighed down by too many things. I splutter out an address and then hold out a wad of notes, my entire boat fare.

"Please," I say. "I'll pay you."

He shakes his head, obviously misreading my distress as something more sinister. It takes me a moment to remember that it is.

"No money," he says. "I'll take you home."

As his car veers up the hillside and away from the dock, I try to compose myself. I take deep, desperate breaths, sucking in air through my nose and exhaling in long, hard gasps. My face is wet, and when my tears reach my lips, they taste as salty as the sea. As the driver wrenches the steering wheel in a way that only someone who has grown up around these vertiginous roads can, he glances anxiously in the rearview mirror.

"Everything OK?" he asks.

I nod. "It will be," I say. "It has to be."

How many times have I climbed the hill to this white-painted house, spent the night, left early in the morning with my head spinning? I remember the first time, when he sent a car to pick me up and I wore the nicest dress I could find. It was flowing and white, and I felt like a Greek goddess. But then, of course, that was before. Before the whispers started to curdle the summer air like an impending rainstorm. Before police descended on the island, their uniforms oppressive and dark beneath the midday sun. Before the body washed up, broken on the beach. I heard she had been there for hours by the time they found her, her skin swollen by the sea, her face no longer recognizable.

"Here?" the man says.

I nod and wipe my sodden cheeks. "Here."

I abandon my bags at the roadside and rush toward the wooden door. I can already see that it is open. He would never just leave it like that. He worries endlessly about locking up the bar at night. I call out his name as I step into the cool shade of the entrance hall. At first it looks the same: the wrought iron statue on the side table, the white rug at the bottom of the stairs. Yet his keys are missing from the bowl next to the door, his jacket no longer hanging and ready for him to throw on against the evening chill. I dash upstairs, still calling out for him.

I'm sobbing by the time I reach his bedroom; guttural, animal-like noises. The wardrobe doors are thrown open, shirts scooped off their hangers as if by someone who left in a hurry. Sheets have been torn off the bed, and a fallen lamp sits in pieces on the floor as though whoever broke it didn't have time to clean up. A door to a balcony has been left ajar, and thin curtains drift lazily in the breeze, their movement absurdly calm against the chaos he has left behind.

For a moment it feels like everything should stop. The world is still spinning. The sun is still shining. But he is gone. I lie stomach-down on his bed and try to capture the smell of him. I breathe in, hoping to find the remnants of his aftershave, a small part of him still left behind, but the white expanse of the mattress only smells of detergent. I wail into a discarded pillow, not worried about who will hear, my body arching into the bed. Around me the house remains cavernous and still, as though nobody has lived here for years. As though none of us were ever here at all.

NOW

The heat is unbearable.

It crawls into my lungs and knots itself in the damp folds of flesh beneath my clothes. It slickens against my skin and leaves streaks of sweat on the backs of my thighs. I waxed my legs in anticipation of this holiday, conscious of how my pale skin would look in the sunlight. Perhaps I was conscious of more than that, hoping this trip would reignite some of the heat that has been missing from my marriage. Instead I look across at my husband and feel faintly repulsed. His underarms are damp and staining the shirt he put on especially for our last night here. He's staring out at the sea, but I know he isn't seeing it the way I do. To him it could be anything. Any view, anywhere. To me the swell of the tide speaks of secrets, the salty air smelling irrevocably of promise.

The sea always reminds me of that summer. How the entire world had seemed within reach back then. I remember sitting with my toes in the sand, the vastness of an ocean stretching out before me, and feeling as though the whole universe was mine to be had.

"Shall we order more wine?" Tom asks.

I shake my head. "I'm actually pretty tired. Let's get the bill."

He nods and beckons the waiter over. He always does what I want him to. I used to like it, years ago. It used to be a relief, after every-thing. Now I wish that he wouldn't. That he would have his own thoughts and things to say. That he would tell me no. I think I am starting to be scared of what I might do if he doesn't.

"Ready?" he says.

I'm too young to be feeling like this, I think, but I nod and bend down to gather my bag. There are a lot of things that never get said between us. There may as well be one more.

We trudge back to the apartment block in silence. The strip that lines the beach is quiet at this time of night. The families who fill it in the daytime have already vacated the shops selling inflatable rafts and the restaurants that stock cheap wine and child-friendly pizza menus. The pavement is scattered with the remnants of days out, leftover sandwich packets, and abandoned bottles of sun cream. This part of town is the domain of tourists, of cheap package holidays and sun-worshippers. The coastline that was once quiet is now bloated with hotels and neon-fronted bars, concrete structures that threaten to obscure the peaceful slope of the town into the island's hills.

When Tom promised he'd book somewhere nice for dinner on our last evening, I had hoped we'd go anywhere else. Perhaps to one of the inland restaurants that cater to the sprawling villas that cling to cliff faces and hillsides far away from the town, dimly lit and de-murely designed to fade into the scenery. We've already spent most of the holiday meters away from here, stretched out on beach towels and stopping off to stuff ourselves with salty olives and feta on the way back to the apartment. When I realized that we were heading in this direction, my hand clutched in his and slightly clammy, I had clenched my mouth into a smile.

"I love this place!" I had enthused, and deposited a neat clean kiss on his cheek.

He had looked painfully pleased with himself, and I found myself wishing that I hadn't bothered wearing my favorite summer dress, its thin straps chafing against my sunburned skin.

The island has changed, but then so have I. Memory is funny like that. It weights places with a significance that slowly gathers pace over time. As I got further away from that summer, my recollections of this place became imbued with magic. I remembered arriving here by boat, the harbor bathed in a syrupy early-evening glow and my shoulders slumping beneath the weight of my backpack. I remembered the taste of the local alcohol as I danced until my bones ached and my body felt weightless. I remembered the taste of his mouth, the heat of his skin, the feeling that if I didn't belong to him then I would die. The further away I got, the more mythical the island became in my imagination, a world where emotions were heightened until they almost hurt and every day was tinged with promise.

"You didn't think I'd forgotten, did you?"

I'm so caught up in remembering the past that I've barely noticed the present. Now that I look at my husband, I can see that he's delighted by his surprise. He peers at me eagerly, waiting for my reaction.

"This is it, isn't it? The bar you used to work in?"

I recognize it at once, of course. It's still as ramshackle as it used to be, a tumble of wooden steps leading up to a squat building wrapped in a winding terrace. There's a lithe blurriness between the outdoors and the in, tables spilling onto the deck and the sound of the sea echoing off the walls. The doorway is ringed with fairy lights now, flower garlands hung up in a feeble nod toward some unidentifiable tropical theme. It used to be shabbier and busier. It used to feel bigger, as though it were the center of gravity itself, the place the entire world orbited around.

I nod. "Yes, but . . ."

"Well, you didn't think we were going to go the entire holiday without stopping off for a drink, did you? I'm surprised you weren't up on the bar our first night here, downing shots like nobody's business."

He nudges me gently, and I can feel how hard he's trying.

"Honestly, Tom, I'm really tired . . ."

"Oh, come on. You've been telling me about this place for years. You think I'm going to let us go home without one drink?"

I look at him, and I see how desperately he wants me to be happy. He knows I've been despondent all holiday, even though he hasn't commented on it. We're not good at talking about how we feel or what we think. He looks hopeful, as though this surprise might be the thing that fixes everything. I let out a small sigh.

"All right, one drink."

It didn't used to be a cheap bar in a tacky tourist trap. Sixteen years ago this island was tucked away, reachable only by boat. It was frequented only by the money- or time-rich: people who could escape from reality in holiday homes high up in the hills or stop off on their backpacking trips. Before anyone caught on to how the sea was the perfect kind of warm and the food was cheap and good, before the apartment blocks began to clamor for coastline and tourists began to demand pints of lager for a euro, this place felt secret and special. I used to know which tables got the coolest breeze and which sticky cocktails were the best value. I used to be able to reel off what beers we had on tap like a nursery rhyme and persuade anyone who'd listen to buy one of the pricier bottles of wine. I used to be a different person entirely, not somebody's wife letting herself be guided into a bar that she does not want to go to. I wonder vaguely if my dress is too short as the wicker chair scratches the backs of my legs. I'll be thirty-five in a few months. I was ridiculous for thinking that coming back would make me feel seventeen again.

"What can I get for you?"

A teenage girl with her hair tied up in a scrunchie thrusts a bowl of salted peanuts down between us. She wears a black T-shirt and her limbs are long and tanned.

"Wine?" Tom asks.

I shake my head. "Tequila."

I'm looking directly at the waitress, daring her to smirk at my drink choice, but I can still feel Tom raising his eyebrows. When you've been with someone for ten years, you don't need to see their face to know exactly what they're thinking.

"Tequila it is!" he says.

"Two?"

"Four," I say, and the waitress nods and turns away.

Tom lets out a low whistle and leans in, even though there is barely anyone here and he could speak as loudly as he wanted to without being overheard.

"Thought you were tired?"

"Call it a nightcap."

"Fine, fine." He leans back again, a small smile playing at his lips. "So. Go on then. Tell me all about your wild summer working here."

And so I tell him all the things that don't matter, all the stories I've polished like sea glass over the years. I tell him about arriving here with my best friend Caroline, the summer before our A levels. We were supposed to be island hopping for the summer before returning to college in September, but I stayed on. I tell him how this was the backpacker bar, the dirtiest drinking spot for those of us who passed through and ended up lingering, entranced by the slow and consuming charms of island life. I tell him about getting a job here, about how I had to make a Long Island iced tea as a test and mixed one so strong I almost choked on it. I tell him I fell in love and I let him think I mean with the island. He doesn't need to know about him. He doesn't need to know what I did.

"Four tequilas," the waitress says as she places them down on top of napkins.

They come without lime or salt. We would have got hauled up for that, back in the day.

She slides the bill onto the table, scribbled in red pen on a torn till roll. Tom pulls out his wallet and counts coins into her hand. She nods in thanks and doesn't offer to bring him back change.

"Well, cheers. Last night of the holiday and all that."

Tom holds up his shot to tap against the side of mine and then throws his tequila back with a grimace.

"Ooft. Been a while since I've had one of those. Takes me right back."

He turns the glass upside down on the table as if we are teenagers playing at drinking games. We never knew that part of each other. We had already seen too much by the time we met to be looking for fun. Our relationship has always been characterized by a kind of seriousness that I used to think made us solid, dependable. As though we had been together for years before we even began.

"I need to go to the bathroom," I say, my chair scraping against the stone floor as I stand.

"Not chickening out, are you?"

I pause to meet his eye and slowly lift a shot glass to my mouth. I throw the drink down without breaking his gaze. It burns all the way to my stomach.

I don't need to ask anyone where to find the ladies'. I know this place better than anywhere. I spent months living here and then years imagining it, my mind roaming back to the places my body could no longer go.

The toilets have been done up since then, the small and slightly dingy cubicles replaced with chrome and black-painted wood. It feels impersonal and wrong, an attempt at trendiness that is out of place. As I wash my hands, I catch a glimpse of myself in the revamped mirror. There's a vague pulse of surprise that is becoming increasingly familiar with age, a tantalizing moment when I don't quite recognize myself. Somehow the shock of seeing I am getting older never seems to fade. I know I'm still young, really. Thirty-four is not old. And yet each barely there line beginning to claim space at the corners of my eyes, each gray hair that I find first thing in the morning and screech at Tom to come and pluck out, reminds me of the stasis that my life seems to have slipped into while my body starts to change.

"Is this it?" I say to the mirror.

The woman who stares back is silent. The last time I would have looked at my reflection in this room, a very different person would have returned my gaze. A bit drunk, perhaps. Blissfully happy. Enviably young.

"Is this what?"

Over the sound of a toilet flushing, a woman blusters out of one of the cubicles. She's about my age, faintly smiling at this madwoman talking to herself in the bathroom as she plunges her hands beneath the tap.

"Nothing," I say, suddenly embarrassed. I busy myself gathering a wad of paper towels to dry my hands. They never had hand dryers in here back then either. "Just talking to myself."

The woman looks up to meet my gaze in the mirror, and as she does, her smile freezes. Her eyes widen and her lips part as though her words are stuck in her mouth.

"Rachel?" she manages. "What the hell are you doing here?"

✳

W e're leaving."

Tom looks up from toying with his phone in surprise. "Right now?"

"Now."

I hurriedly down my second shot and gesture for him to take my hand so that I can tug him away.

"But we only just—"

"*Now*, Tom."

As always, he doesn't say no. We walk back to the apartment in silence. I found it on an online booking site, back when I was sick with enthusiasm about this holiday. It had been Tom who had suggested that we come here. It was a few months ago, an evening when we had sat in the garden in silence over dinner.

"You've obviously been down lately," he had said gently. "It might cheer you up."

At first I had pulled a face. The island was mine, sacred in my memory. I didn't want to share it with Tom. For years I had carefully curated my recollections of the place, held them so close to me that the thought of going back had felt unimaginable. Sometimes the idea of returning would come to me, perhaps after a couple of glasses of wine or a hot, hazy evening when the scent of sun cream momentarily made me yearn for that summer. When it did, I would quickly suppress it. I worried that seeing the island again would chip away some of the perfection I had assigned to it, that a rogue misremembered road or rubbish-strewn beach would knock the shine from its carefully sculpted veneer. Worse, perhaps I would see other girls, infallibly young and impossibly beautiful, and be reminded that I wasn't the person I was when I was there last. Of the things that had forced me to leave.

Yet Tom's suggestion seeded a strange kind of hope deep within the pit of my stomach. I *had* been feeling down lately. Not myself. Maybe going back was what I needed. Maybe it was what *we* needed. Maybe being back would make me into the person I was sixteen years ago, the kind of person who loved fiercely and who ran into the sea at midnight just to see how it felt. I began to search flights, marveling at how easy it was now and shaking my head in disbelief at the range of accommodation on offer. I settled on a simple self-catered place five minutes from the beach.

"We can afford somewhere nicer," Tom had said bemusedly.

I had shaken my head. "This is perfect."

We had somewhere nicer at home. We had saved and saved for our house, for an upholstered bed and a sofa you could sink so far into that you'd never want to move. Of course we could have stayed somewhere nicer, some all-inclusive resort that only touched the edges of island life. We could have drunk canned cocktails so sugary they hurt our teeth, and I could have come back without ever stepping outside a hotel. But I had wanted to recapture some of the simplicity of my first trip here, when I stayed in a hostel where the water only ever ran freezing cold or scalding hot. I felt, somewhere deep inside me, that if we had fewer things, then maybe our feelings would have more space to exist. There seemed so little room for them around mortgages and coffee machines and work emails.

When we booked the trip I had been excited, dizzy with the thought of revisiting those precious months. Yet as soon as we checked in I found myself avoiding the bar. I skirted around the streets I used to walk down and dodged the places I used to know. There was a sickly sense of fear whenever I imagined seeing that place again. A strange and unsettled feeling that raged somewhere taut and implacable. A tightening of my throat made me stay away, even though I had truly thought I wanted to go back. A terrible knowledge that it would only remind me of how much time has passed since then. Of the disintegration of the girl I used to be.

"Do you want any water?" Tom asks.

"I'm OK."

I close my eyes and feel the weight of him lower down beside me, the mattress groaning in protest. For a moment he is still, the sound of his breath stirring the humid air. Then he reaches over and places one hand on my hip, skimming the light cotton fabric of my dress.

"Did you take your temperature?" he asks.

"This morning."

"And . . . ?"

"Not yet," I lie.

He pats my thigh and then plants a light kiss on my cheek before pulling away.

"OK, babe," he says. "Just thought it was about the right time. But what do I know?"

Then he clambers to his feet and I hear him potter to the bathroom. The extractor fan splutters and whirs to life, noisy and clattering with effort, and the bright white strip light hung above the sink bleeds out into the bedroom.

As my husband hums to himself while he brushes his teeth and unbuttons his shirt, I lie quietly and wish I were anywhere but here. That woman in the bar knew my name and my face, but she wouldn't have recognized anything else about me. I didn't even know anyone had stayed behind. I thought we had all escaped, that we left our lives here still hopeful for a future brimming with the same kind of excitement we had grown used to. But of course, we had learned that excitement emerges from the unknown, and with the unknown comes terrible secrets. The kind of secrets that made it hard to stay.

Tom ambles out of the bathroom, pulling off his shirt, and flops onto the bed beside me. He lies flat on his back so that I can feel the expansion of his breath against the bedsprings, smell the sourness of sweat cooling against his skin.

"You know," he says, "we could anyway."

There is a silence broken only by the extractor fan, still trying valiantly to pump the damp and decay out of the aging bathroom. It smells slightly moldering, in spite of the air freshener the owner has dotted about in an attempt to hide how the apartment is crumbling behind its freshly scrubbed tiles and neatly ironed sheets.

"I'm tired," I say at last. "And we've got to be up to pack tomorrow. Sorry."

"You don't need to apologize to me," Tom says. "Are you ready to sleep then?"

I nod and wait for him to reach across me to turn out the light. I lie motionless as his breathing slows into snores, still in the dress I had picked out hopefully for our last night in paradise. I try to stay awake to listen to the sounds of the island one more time, but all I can hear is the noise of a distant motorcycle revving up and some drunken girls singing songs about love. I fall asleep imagining the sound of the sea instead.

THEN

W e're here."

I open my eyes to see Caroline grinning down at me. She reaches out a hand to tug me up from the floor of the boat. I've been lying there for the last hour, the wooden deck slightly damp against my back, but anything was better than sitting up while the sea rocked violently around us.

"Get up and see paradise!"

Caroline has barely pulled me to my feet before she's dashed away, hoisting her backpack on and fighting to be the first to disembark. I take a moment to steady myself, resting my hands on my thighs and silently pleading with the world to stop swaying just long enough for me to stagger ashore.

When I finally straighten, slowly and with a deep inhale for good measure, I see the truth in Caroline's words. We got the last boat over and the sun is low in the sky, casting shades of amber and aureolin across the bay. The island stretches out before us, a cluster of white-painted buildings vying for space along the coast and a sprawl of ragged hills rising up behind them. The village is glittering and pale, glowing in the burnished shades of sunset. It really is paradise.

I take a deep breath and the air is clean and fragrant, the smell of the sea sharpened by the salty scent of fish frying somewhere. My stomach emits a small shudder, and I'm relieved to find that seasickness hasn't stopped me from being hungry. I would eat my way across Greece if I could.

"Not got your sea legs yet?"

From one of the long benches that line the boat's edge, a girl throws a sympathetic smile, adjusting the straps of her own bag. I hadn't noticed her before—the boat was crammed with backpackers, with barely enough space to sit. She looks effortlessly cool, long brown hair spilling down her back and woven into elaborate braids decorated with brightly colored threads. She wears a tie-dye crop top and harem pants printed with parades of white elephants. One ear is lined with an entire row of delicate golden hoops that snake from lobe to helix. It's a look that Caroline tries to emulate, buying floaty smocks from tucked-away marketplaces and wearing tiny studs in her nose. She never quite seems to pull it off. But then, four weeks into traveling, I still look like I'm going for a picnic in the park, in my white floaty vest top and denim shorts. I'm hardly one to talk.

"Not quite," I say, straightening up.

"Well, you're here now."

"Yes." I take a deep breath. "I'm here now."

Caroline is already talking animatedly to a trio of girls on the dock, waving her arms as she points toward me. I trudge down the gangplank to meet her, my legs still braced against the unsteady rhythm of the waves.

"There are only a couple of hostels on the island," Caroline calls out to me. "This lot are going to show us the way. Come on!"

It was Caroline's idea to go traveling the summer before our A levels. I'd been less sure, my parents frowning and saying that I should wait until next year.

"You're not even eighteen yet!" my mum had harrumphed in our suburban kitchen. "What are you going to do out there, exactly?"

What we were going to do didn't seem to matter at the time. All that seemed important was the possibility of being far away, some-place where the sun would bleach my hair and the mundanities of life back home would be easily forgotten. I was bored of days portioned out by sixth-form bells and long, cold corridors. I was entranced by the pictures that Caroline pointed at in a well-worn travel magazine as we stretched out on her bed after school, our skirts hitched up over our thick, regulation tights. As a gray sheen of rain ran down her bedroom window, we looked at pictures of sun-soaked shores and whitewashed buildings glinting with heat. I could almost feel the warmth radiating from the glossy pages. We frayed them with our touch and turned their corners over with excitement, a promise of summer hidden behind the name of every town. I imagined holiday romances with young men with long, tangled hair, and nights spent dancing under the stars. The extent of my travel experience was the one package holiday my parents insisted on every year, but that did little to deter me. I had savings stored up from a year working at a DVD rental shop that I'd been carefully putting away to buy a car. We booked a plane ticket the next day.

"Island hopping!" Caroline had declared, thrusting a brochure into my suspicious-looking mum's hand. "Seven weeks. We'll be back by mid-August. Completely safe, and anyway, the flight's only a couple of hours. You've got nothing to worry about."

Ever since then, Caroline has led the meandering path that we've drawn across the Greek archipelago. She's always been better with people than me, blond and preppy and effortlessly likeable. She would corner new friends in dorm rooms with her teeth bared into a grin and scribble down the names of mythical-sounding places, nodding absorbedly.

"That sounds *exactly* like what we're after," she'd pronounce happily. "So how do you get there again?"

This place had been my idea though. We were over halfway through our planned trip, and party resorts crammed with backpack-ers were starting to wear thin. While Caroline slid into new friend-ship groups easily, energized by the never-ending rotation of people,

I found myself nervous and tired. The constant circus of smiling and trying desperately not to overthink my every word, of painfully navigating in-jokes while Caroline laughed along, was exhausting to me. As we pored over brochures, I had imagined myself sun-kissed and glowing. I had envisaged some part of myself left behind with the cold English weather. A whole new person rising with the temperature. I hadn't counted on still being just as shy and awkward out here, the shadow behind Caroline's blazing sun.

"Let's go somewhere properly remote and lie on a beach for a week," I had pleaded.

Caroline had nodded and shuffled her notes. As much as she tried to give the impression that she simply floated between places, turning up wherever a good recommendation carried her, she was a prolific planner.

"OK, there's this one place that sounds great. Teensy. Only one town and then loads of beautiful beaches. It's a bit of a nightmare to get to, but I'm up for it if you are."

We sketched out a winding route, catching buses and boats that grew increasingly smaller and more sparsely filled. Now that we're arrived, guided to our hostel by our new friends, we calculate that a private room works out almost as cheap as two beds in a dorm. The room is basic, with thin sheets and a cracked mirror hanging askew on the wall. In the bathroom, a wisp of black mold coils out from between tiles and a still-sodden bathmat wilts on a rusted radiator. A window looks out onto next door's air vent, and the twin beds sag in the middle when we sit on them. In a half-hearted tribute to our destination, someone has hung a print of Santorini above one of the narrow beds, the shades of blue too bright and the whites of the buildings graying.

"Imagine making Santorini look ugly," Caroline muses, as though she is an expert on the place, not someone who'd taken a single day trip to its whitewashed streets two weeks ago. "Anyway. Shall we go out and get some food? I'm starving."

We find a tiny taverna right on the beach and order souvlaki and beers. Caroline slurps her beer down before the food arrives and orders another. She stretches her arms above her head and grins, her face radiant in the early-evening light.

"This place! Great idea, Rach."

I sip my beer and bite into an olive. It tastes salty and slick in my mouth, its oily juices so sharp I almost wince.

"Wait, is that . . ." Caroline squints at something behind me. "It is! Hey! Over here."

She stands up, waving her arms above her head.

"The girls from the boat I met earlier," she explains, beaming as she collapses back into her chair. "We can probably squeeze them in, can't we, if we just pull that table there over . . ."

Three girls pile into the taverna, grinning and hugging Caroline as though they've known each other all their lives. It's one of the things I've found interesting about traveling. Intimacies seem to arise from the smallest encounters: a single night out, a shared dorm room. Strangers become your best friends for a few days, an attachment that feels intense and electric, and then you never speak to them again. Or at least they become best friends with Caroline. I've always made friends slowly, careful of any assumed confidence and wary of sharing secrets. Even my friendship with Caroline was birthed from our mothers' closeness, formed at a prenatal class and followed up with playdates and cups of tea at our kitchen table while their husbands worked.

"We've literally known each other our whole lives," Caroline will often tell people, for once not being overly liberal with her use of the word.

I smile and say hi, and they exclaim that that was me, the girl on the boat who lay on the floor the entire time. I nod and laugh and help them to drag chairs over.

As I move my beer aside to make space on the table, Caroline is already reeling off the places we've been to so far, counting them off on her fingers.

"And then Zakynthos, which was great. So much fun," she babbles. "So, after here, who knows!"

A waiter places laminated menus on the table as our new friends murmur appreciatively about how cheap it is in Zakynthos, how great the sunsets are.

"Wait!" one exclaims. "We haven't introduced ourselves properly. I'm Helena."

I find myself shaking hands with Helena, Kiera, and Priya in an elaborate imitation of adult rituals. None of us are old enough to have ever really needed to shake anyone's hand or enact any kind of formality before. Yet out here, ordering beers and forgetting to call our parents, we all feel endlessly grown-up.

"So where are you off to next?" Caroline takes a sip of her beer.

"We're actually staying here for a bit. Working. Saving up some money for the next few months," says Priya.

She seems to be constantly playing with her hair. It's entrancingly dark and glossy, and she toys with long strands as though she knows exactly how mesmerizing it looks. She twirls it around one finger, tosses it back over her shoulder, shakes her head so that it tumbles down the length of her spine.

"Here?" Caroline raises one eyebrow. "Doesn't seem like there'd be that many places looking."

"We've already got something lined up." Kiera places her menu down on the table. "Girl we met back in Athens sorted it. She'd just left and said they were always looking."

It's the first time she's spoken. Of the three of them, Helena seems to dominate the conversation. Her body claims the same kind of command, tall and willowy, her eyes an unnerving gray that makes it hard to look away. In contrast, Kiera is slight and delicate, almost birdlike in her proportions and the distracted way she plays with the corner of a menu. Her hair is a golden-brown shade that reminds me of honey, of sand, of the early-evening light. It's cut bluntly above her shoulder blades so that it brushes along a smattering of freckles that rise up her neck. They embellish her collarbone and her jawline, almost as if the sun has claimed her skin as its own.

"Bar work," chips in Priya. "Easy money. Then we're going a bit further afield. Are we ready to order?"

Caroline neatly skirts around how long we've got left on our trip. Most of the other backpackers we've met have already finished sixth form and are stretching their wings beyond the few weeks we have remaining. While we're studying oxbow lakes and *King Lear*, they'll still be exploring the real world, and I can already sense Caroline prickling with envy.

We stay at the restaurant until the sun has slid beneath the horizon, casting the world with shades of pink, and then orange, and then finally a deep and bloody red. Night tiptoes into the edges of the sky, and the air cools slightly against our skin. I've never quite got used to the lingering warmth of the nights out here, the promise of being able to stay out late that it brings, the way you can look up and see the stars without needing to plead for a jacket. The heat sings of possibility, and I can feel it creeping around the cracks in our inhibitions as we down the dregs of our drinks. The empty beer bottles tinge the evening with a kind of honeyed glow, the lights strung up around the taverna's terrace becoming faintly magical. Being drunk is an almost entirely new experience for me. Back home I'd only experienced the occasional Smirnoff Ice, smuggled from Caroline's mum's cupboard and drunk furtively in a park or bedroom. My parents would only ever let me have one glass of wine with special dinners, and even then I would glug it back resolutely, keen to show them I was mature enough to enjoy it. The revelation that nobody out here seems to bother with IDs was unexpected, an entire world of adult delights opening up a year early.

"We're going to check this place out where we're working," Helena says eventually. "Wanna come?"

I can see Caroline's eyes start to glitter already, her speech becoming more rapid and high-pitched. She grins.

"Definitely! You're up for it as well, right, Rach?"

I nod and mimic her falsetto enthusiasm. "Definitely! Let's go."

*

The bar is tucked away on a side street just back from the main strip. You can hear it before you see it: a babble of laughter, the pulse of a bass line trembling down the cobbled road. The boundary between where the party starts and the street ends is blurred by crowds that spill out onto the pavement, smoking and brandishing plastic pint glasses. Women who look like they've just rolled in off the beach perch on the edge of a terrace, and couples writhe in time to a trancelike beat. We've arrived late enough that tables have already been pushed to the sides of the single room, a makeshift dance floor forming in the space they left behind. A crowd jostles for space at a long bar staffed by girls a similar age to us. They're all dressed in shorts and slim-fitting T-shirts that show off the hard, flat lines of their stomachs. They weave around each other as they scurry to pour drinks, to take handfuls of change, to replace bottles on shelves lined with spirits, their order undefined and haphazard. I'm immediately fascinated by them, their tanned skin and ease of movement as they navigate the small space. It is almost as though they are performing an elaborate dance, a ritual of motion as their bodies slip around each other in perfect synchrony.

"This looks great!" Caroline exclaims. "I had no idea there'd be clubs here."

"It's not exactly a club," says Helena. "It's a bar, really. But it's so popular, and if people want to dance . . ." She spreads her hands wide in a gesture of *what can you do.* "Come on then. Let's get a drink."

Caroline clutches my hand as we slip through the thickening crowds. We stake out a spot at the bar, and Helena suggests getting tequilas, shouting out the word like a battle cry. I nod, even though shots still make me feel sick, and count out coins. Traveling has been much more expensive than I anticipated, and I experience a sharp jolt of worry when I realize there are no notes left in my purse. I had carefully calculated my budget for the week, promising myself I'd be careful with it this time.

"Cheers!" exclaims Caroline, holding her shot aloft.

We all whoop and clink our glasses. I throw my drink back and wait for the heat to extend outward, to blur my brain and to expand into the tips of my toes. I see Kiera wince, holding her hand to her mouth as if she isn't used to taking shots.

"Let's dance!" Priya says. She's glassy-eyed, wiping the corners of her mouth with the back of her hand.

The dance floor is hot and sticky, and I stumble as I try to keep up with the other girls' moves. They sway seductively, their arms extended and their hips moving in time to the music. I usually feel awkward dancing, but the tequila is doing its work and I stretch my arms skyward and close my eyes. When I open them, Caroline is laughing, reaching out to clutch my hands and pulling me close so that our bodies are entwined and our pelvises press into each other. She's caught someone's eye and is doing her best to impress them—I can feel her glancing over my shoulder, grinding close to me as she makes sure they're watching. She's always commanded the attention of boys, flirting in the hallways after school and pouting with her gloss-slicked lips. She balances her body in front of men like a prize while I wish somebody would look at me the way they do her, that hungry and carnivorous gaze that promises you are worthy of desire.

I've never quite managed to mimic her confidence, her assumption that she will be wanted. More often than not, my own body feels like a thing I haven't quite grown into yet, a new outfit I still need to expand out to fill. I don't look around to see who she's got her eyes fixed on. I just wrap my arms around her and try to keep up, the beat quickening and my movements out of time.

"I'm going to sit down for a minute," I shout into Caroline's ear, my voice hoarse as it competes with the pulse of the music.

She nods, smiling, and I'm not sure if she's heard me. I pull away from her anyway. I head back to the bar and wait until I can squeeze onto one of the stools lined up against it. I ask for a water, my mouth dry. The server fills a tall glass with ice, and I vaguely remember my mother warning me not to drink the water abroad, promising me bouts of food poisoning. I throw it back anyway, the ice clinking against my teeth. The air is so warm that I can immediately see the solid cubes start to disintegrate and slip into small slivers. I take one in my mouth and feel it slide into nothing against the damp heat of my tongue.

"Vodka?"

I hurry to swallow, press the heel of my hand into my lips to wipe them. They are already dry beneath my touch.

"Water. It's so hot in here."

"Let me get you something stronger."

I survey the man leaning up against the bar beside me. He's much older, maybe in his early thirties. I note that his jaw is shaded with stubble, faint and wiry as though he shaved this morning. The boys at school hardly have tentative lines of upper-lip fluff, a shaving rash from skin that barely needs to see a razor. He has a slight East London accent, and his shirtsleeves are rolled up. In spite of the scent of sweat that is beginning to permeate the room, his clothes look crisp and fresh. I feel a dull tug of disbelief that this man—grown-up and attractive—is offering to buy me a drink. Telling me that he will buy me a drink. As he leans closer I smell the tang of aftershave on his skin and feel an unexpected pull of lust.

"Thanks," I say.

He flags down one of the girls and she comes straight over. As he asks for two vodka and Cokes, her gaze slides across and she seems to weigh me up, her eyes narrowing. I look down at my glass.

"What's your name?" he asks, bringing his mouth close to my ear, even though it isn't so loud over here, away from all the speakers.

"Rachel," I say. "My name's Rachel."

And I know before I even ask his that I will never forget it.

NOW

I always wake before Tom. I prefer it that way. Even at the beginning, almost a decade ago when everything was new and exciting, I treasured that tiny sliver of the day alone. I would wake without an alarm and try to slide out of bed without disturbing him. I'd make a cup of coffee and go and sit in the living room, or out on the balcony of our first tiny flat if it was warm enough. In summer the sky would still be dark, and I would watch it mottle into light, flecks of blue and white and yellow spreading upward and outward, until they cast the horizon in a bright and hopeful glow. I would feel like I was the only person alive, even as the world around me started to stir, the distant growl of traffic beginning to clog the arteries of the city and sirens left over from the night wailing sluggishly in the distance. I'd let my coffee go cold and throw the dregs down the sink. Then I'd climb back into bed and coil my body into Tom's, feeling him judder into consciousness and letting him sleepily kiss my neck. I'd feel a small and secretive pleasure that before his day had even begun, I'd had my favorite part of mine.

But on the last day of our holiday Tom wakes me, humming tunelessly from the bathroom. Without air-conditioning the room always seems to get stifling overnight, the smell of our bodies and the density of our sleep filling the air. Blearily, I roll out from under the sheets and tug open a window. The outside is sharp with heat, smelling faintly of petrol and dust from the road that runs beneath our room. For a moment I stay leaning on the sill, my best summer dress now creased. I wait for a breeze but find that the air is still and heavy, the languorous weight of summer barely stirring against my skin.

"Dressed already?" Tom rounds the door holding armfuls of clothes. He bundles them into a suitcase laid out open on the floor.

"I was wearing this last night," I say. "I must have slept in it."

"Were you?" He shrugs. "The boat leaves in a couple of hours. I thought we could go for breakfast first?"

There's no hot water, and I find myself washing beneath an icy stream, my body recoiling to the edge of the shower stall. I never used to mind things like this. It made me feel like I was living a new and wholly unpredictable kind of life that was a million miles away from my parents' yellow-tiled bathroom with its white, fluffy towels and reliable water tank.

As I lather my hands with bodywash, I remember my encounter last night. The woman in the bar knew me. She had perhaps thought of me often over the years, in the same way I had thought about her: slipping around the sides of memories, always in the background of moments that felt soldered onto my soul. She hadn't expected to see me back here. And why would she? That summer was a seismic shift in both of our lives, the kind you turn your back on and try never to speak of again. You can always go home and get a job and get married and forget any of this happened. You can mention the months you spent traveling to anyone who asks in a vague and distant manner. You can joke about finding yourself while all the time knowing you lost a part of yourself that you can never get back. You can slip into anonymous lives where nobody knows what happened. The woman in the bar might have recognized my face, but she doesn't know anything about the person I am now.

I brace myself to rinse the soap from my skin as I remember her wide eyes. Her evident surprise. I've spent all holiday avoiding the bar, and yet the thought of boarding the boat without seeing her again feels unbearable. It's as though she was there for a reason. As though the Fates have placed her in my path. For the first time in years, there's an itch in the seat of my stomach, an urgency to recapture the things I left behind.

※

D o you mind if I go for a walk?" I ask Tom. "On my own."
He blinks at me dressed in leggings and a T-shirt, ready for our flight, my skin still damp from the shower.

"If you want to, babe," he says. "Everything OK?"

I nod. "Fine. I just . . . just want to be alone for a bit. Before we leave here for good."

Outside, I pull on a pair of sunglasses and head in the direction of the sea. It feels good to be on my own. With Tom alongside me wondering aloud where we should go for lunch or whether it was time to top up our sun cream, it was easy to forget why we were here. Without him, the streets seem singed with my seventeen-year-old self. Alone with my thoughts, every place I pass is permeated with ghostly presences. A shuttered-up house that was once our closest shop. The narrow road leading straight to the beach that the tourists didn't know about. The house where we once lived, now converted into a much more upmarket hotel. On every corner I see Kiera crying with laughter over something Helena said, curbs where someone was sick after a night out, places where he kissed me and it felt like the beginning of everything.

If I really focus, if I'm careful not to glance down and see that my less lithe body no longer belongs to a seventeen-year-old, I can almost imagine I'm back, half a lifetime ago. I can pretend I'm on my way to work, that it's my turn to open up the bar and that I'll arrive to the remnants of the previous night, bottles to be cleared away and countertops to be scrubbed. I'll open the shutters and let daylight invade, the morning sunlight hollowing out the corners people hide in and the tables people dance on. For a few hours the entire place will be mine, and I'll feel a possessive sense of pride at being trusted with turning the ruins of last night into the brightness of a new day. I'll imagine who might meet the love of their life tonight, or fight with their best friend, or sing until their throat hurts. I'll feel a secret warmth, knowing that in some small way I will have played a part. I can almost feel the weight of the keys in my pocket now.

I turn in to the same small backstreet I've walked down dozens of times before, and my illusion immediately flails. Instead of a quiet residential road with a nameless bar on its corner, the street has been transformed along with the rest of the island from remote getaway to tourist attraction. Signs advertise holiday lets, and a house that used to belong to a family who would always complain about the noise in broken English has been turned into a tourism office. Its shuttered windows are wallpapered with posters about boat trips and excursions to a lagoon on the other side of the island. We all drove there once and spent the day lounging beside the warm and inert pools, the bright blue water and muddy depths making our skin feel oily. I picture the secluded dirt road that we navigated down now clogged with tour buses, the marshy ponds thick with crowds dive-bombing from rocky platforms, the murky and mysterious quiet disemboweled with fights over the most photogenic spots. I had thought I could recapture something of how I felt all those years ago by coming back here, but it has only served to remind me how slippery and impossible it is to summon the past. Perhaps this is simply the nature of growing up. Of growing older. Perhaps I will never feel the same again.

The bar itself has a name now, printed onto a sign that swings from the side of the building. I can't believe I didn't notice it last night. *Helena's Hideaway*, it announces in childishly painted print. With a deep inhale I brace myself to see her again. I'm not a teenager anymore. Whatever I might find inside doesn't scare me.

"We're closed," the same girl who served me last night announces in a bored voice as I mount the steps. She's sitting at one of the tables, her long legs perched on a chair set up opposite her, a laptop resting on her thighs. In the daylight she looks exactly like her mother used to.

"Come back later," another voice calls from the back of the room. "We open at three."

Helena hasn't even looked at me, bent over the bar as she scrubs it clean. She wears a baggy shirt, her hair tied untidily back into a bun. I cut my long hair off years ago, opting for a sensible bob that skims my shoulders, but she has kept hers long and wild. It always was her best feature. Her arms are dark with years of sun, and her sleeves are rolled up as she rakes a sponge down the long surface. It seethes with soapsuds, and I can smell its lemongrass scent as I near her.

"I came to talk to you, actually," I say.

She glances up in surprise, and I'm close enough to see her eyes widen in recognition. In a face that has changed with time, weathered with the heat and slackened around her jaw, her eyes have stayed the same shade of gray.

"I didn't think you'd come back," she says.

"Neither did I."

✳

She sends her daughter to the shop, telling her they need fresh lemons.

"I'm *busy*," the girl protests, gesturing to her laptop, but the promise of a few euros to spend on herself seems to placate her, and she takes the proffered money and leaves with an emphatic slam of her screen.

Most of the chairs are tidied away and upturned on tables. Helena drags a couple down and gestures for me to sit.

"Can I get you anything?" she asks. "Coffee? Beer?"

I glance at the clock hung up behind the bar. "Coffee, thanks," I say.

I can see she is self-conscious, rolling down her sleeves and then pulling them up again, faffing with finding clean coffee cups and setting up the machine. The front of her shirt is wet with soapy water, and she rubs at the damp patch on her stomach as though she could dry it just by will.

"Sorry, I obviously wasn't expecting anyone," she says, searching for the milk. "Although I guess I look a bit different to you anyway these days."

"It's OK," I say. "We're all pretty different now."

Coffee slops over the rim of the cup as she sets it down, and I see that her hands are shaking. She doesn't fetch herself anything to drink. She perches opposite me and ropes her fingers together so that her hands are clutched into a fist on the table.

"It was a bit of a shock to see you last night," she says, her voice even. I can feel how hard she is fighting to stay level, the catch of her breath behind every word. "I haven't seen any of the old lot for years. I'd almost forgotten about you all."

I take a small sip of my coffee, even though it is still too hot and scalds my tongue.

"Me neither," I say. "Maybe I should have expected it, coming back out here. But I really thought everyone had left."

"They did," she says. "Everyone but me. At first I just thought I needed a bit more time. But then it was months and I still hadn't left. And then this place came up for sale and . . ." She shrugs in a way that speaks of a silent history that needs no words.

"Has anyone else been back since?" I ask.

She shakes her head. "No. Who would want to?"

"You did."

"It's different. I never left. Sometimes I wish I had done. But I don't think I'd quite understood . . ."

She doesn't finish. She doesn't have to.

"I know," I say. "I was lucky, I suppose."

Helena frowns. "Lucky?"

"Well, that I never got caught up in it all."

There is a beat when Helena just looks at me, and then her face shifts into an expression of pity. I've seen her look at me like that before, only this time is much less terrifying than the first.

"Oh, Rachel . . ."

"Change!"

Helena's daughter slams a handful of coins onto the table between us, juddering my coffee cup in its saucer. Helena seems dazed at her sudden presence, standing up slowly and then hovering as if unsure whether to follow her as she strides toward the bar, the bag of lemons swinging from her hand.

"That was quick . . ."

"It's only across the road, Mum."

Helena's daughter deposits her purchase on the counter and then launches herself up onto the bar stool. She pulls an iPhone out from the pocket of her shorts and seems immediately absorbed in it, her thumbs twitching at lightning speed as she taps on the screen.

"It's made me think," I say to Helena as she lowers herself into her seat and glances nervously back at her daughter. "Seeing you last night. Being here again . . ." I take a deep breath and feel my stomach tightening. "I think I want to find him. You bought this place. You must have talked to him, then. Do you know where he is?"

Something flickers across Helena's face: a clenching of her jaw, a creasing of her forehead.

"Why do you want to . . . ?"

"Please, Helena. Just tell me if you know."

Back on the island, he feels within reach again—a lifetime of possibilities only just out of grasp. He's no longer confined to the past, a distant memory that belongs to another time, another person, another incarnation of myself. The walls of this place vibrate with him, corners where I felt his eyes tracing the lines of my body, hidden spots where I longed to steal a kiss. The familiar heat reminds me of his touch, his skin, his taste. The feeling of want is no longer vague and chipped away by time. It has suddenly transformed into something visceral and powerful, an ache that starts in my chest and expands outward until I can't feel anything else. I can't leave here without at least trying to find him.

"I don't know . . ." Helena is frowning. "I don't know if this is a good idea."

"So, you do know, then?" I can hear the want in my voice, urgent and strained. "You know where he is."

"I know, but I don't think—"

"Helena, please."

I reach out and my hand finds her wrist. She flinches at the contact, my fingers clutching at her so that I can feel the fragile hardness of her bones. My need for him feels primal and urgent, and I'm terrified she'll tell me to leave without sharing what she knows.

"Please," I repeat. "Why won't you tell me? I need to talk to him, Helena. I need to find him."

"OK, OK." Helena seems desperate to quiet me as she pulls her arm away. "Fine. But just . . . just don't tell him I told you." She holds out her hand. "Give me your phone."

I push it toward her, and she sets it down on the table beside her own, opening up her contacts and glancing between them as she types.

"He's back in the UK. In London. Don't ask me how I know." She hands back my phone and I notice that her hands are shaking. "And promise me you'll really think about it before you get in touch with him. About if you actually want to talk to him. I don't think I would, if I were you."

"Thanks." I start to stand, tucking my phone into my handbag. It feels like the most precious thing imaginable. "I should go. My flight home is today."

"You haven't finished your coffee."

"I know, sorry. It was good to see you though. Maybe we should keep in touch."

"Maybe." Helena gathers up my coffee cup but makes no move to suggest that we share numbers. "Maybe."

As I descend the steps back to street level, she stands at the end of the terrace, watching me go.

"Rachel," she calls out. "That man you were with last night. Is he your husband?"

I turn around to see that my cup is still clutched in her hand.

"Yes," I say. "His name's Tom."

She nods. "He looks like a nice guy," she says. "You should be careful. I'm just not sure you know quite what you're getting yourself into."

THEN

The next night we get ready in our cramped hostel room. Caroline shotguns the first shower and takes longer than is fair, warbling cheerily to herself as I perch on the bed hoping that the hot water doesn't run out. I can already feel myself growing nervous, a white-hot swell of anticipation writhing beneath my rib cage.

"It's not anything fancy," he had said as he helped me down from the barstool, still slightly dizzy. "Just come as you are."

Yet in spite of his words, Helena had clutched my arm when I weaved back to the group to tell them.

"Those parties are a big deal," she enthused. "Our friend back in Athens told us all about them. I can't believe you got an invite already!"

I shrugged and felt myself flush red. I was as bemused as Helena seemed to be that I'd somehow been the one plucked out of the pack, that I was the one told to bring my friends to an address scrawled on my arm in blue ink.

We hadn't talked for long. It had been just enough time for him to buy me another drink and tell me he had somewhere else to be, his eyes lingering along the length of my body as though he was loath to leave. I had felt my chest ache with disappointment until he turned at the last minute. Asked me if I had any plans the next evening. Told me about a party being held by his boss, so casually I'd had to purse my lips tight to hold in my excitement.

"You can definitely stick around if you keep on landing us golden tickets like that one," Priya had announced when I made my way back and gleefully shared the invite. "What was the name of the guy again?"

Lying on my narrow hostel bed, I find myself mouthing it, testing how it tastes on my tongue. Alistair. I've never met an Alistair before. It sounds impossibly glamorous and worldly. I try out our names together to see how they sound. *Alistair and Rachel.* Then I shake myself, feeling stupid with my own thoughts, and roll off the bed to find something to wear. I've never been much good at packing, mostly relying on my mum to do it for me, and all the clothes balled up in my bag are crumpled and stained. I uncoil a dress that I last wore back in Corfu and gingerly bury my nose into its deep folds. It smells salty and slightly sour, the legacy of being hauled off sea-damp skin and then buried deep in a stuffy backpack. My cleanest item is a bright pink tie-dye dress, but when I hold it against myself, I worry that it makes me look young, my cheeks clashing horribly with its fuchsia swirls.

"What are you wearing?" I ask Caroline as she parades out of the bathroom draped in just a towel and flops down onto her bed.

"I don't know. Something posh. Well, as posh as I've got. Maybe that long dress I bought back in Athens?"

I regard the pile of clothes strewn across my bedsheets for anything that could be remotely regarded as posh.

"Look, just borrow something of mine," Caroline says with a small eye roll. "It's not like any of your stuff is nice enough."

She's been quietly irritated ever since I won the much-lauded invite. It seemed to elevate me to a higher level of interest among our new friends, and Caroline had looked slightly put out as they gushed about the party. She had spent all day lying alongside me on the beach, her sunglasses pulled down low on her nose as she complained of a headache and insisted that we not talk much. I didn't mind. I stretched out next to her and nursed the secret special glow that had taken root when Alistair had touched my arm, his fingers hot against my skin. Her offer to loan me something sounds more like a mild taunt than generosity, but I ignore the edge in her voice and kneel down next to her backpack.

"Don't mess anything up," she says, wrapping her hair in a towel to dry.

It turns out that her bag is even messier than mine, and yet somehow I manage to locate a long white dress that is relatively smooth and sweet-smelling.

"Planning your wedding to Alistair, are you?" she says.

She catches my eye and then seems to soften, perhaps seeing my embarrassment.

"Fine. Wear it. It'll look nice on you actually."

As soon as we meet up with the others, I know that I have overdressed. They're wearing strappy tops and shorts, already slightly tipsy from sharing a bottle of ouzo in their dorm room. Caroline pretends not to mind that we have tried too hard in comparison, sticking her chin out and linking arms with Kiera.

"Well, what else do we get to dress up for these days?" she demands.

I tug at the bright white skirt of my dress and feel self-conscious. We pile into a taxi with no seat belts, Priya perching on Helena's lap. The two of them are talkative and loud, alcohol eroding the edges of their inhibitions, while Kiera squeezes in beside me. Caroline takes the front seat and twists her whole body around to face us as if afraid of missing out, singing songs and snorting with laughter. I catch the eye of the taxi driver in his mirror and see that he looks tired. I wonder how many other girls like us he has ferried to parties up in these hills, excitable and balancing dangerously close to the cusp of adulthood. I wonder if he has daughters of his own, if he warns them to stay away from the girls who have started to come here from another world.

The car slips up the narrow roads that line the mountainside, its swooping headlights illuminating rock faces and cliffsides. I grip the seat in front of me and take deep breaths. The sharp corners make my stomach clench. Every so often we glide past villas, their exteriors illuminated by spotlights. They grow larger as we drive farther away from the main town, edging up the hillside with their windows facing out to the sea. The view must be spectacular in the daytime. The driver catches me staring.

"Millionaires," he says in thickly accented English. He jabs a finger at one of the houses. "They come here, build houses. Visit for the summer and then gone the rest of the year. Poof. Disappear."

He shakes his head, seemingly exhausted by the thought of it. It occurs to me that the rhythms of island life might be less gentle than I had imagined. Everything seems so easy to an outsider: the long lunches and hot, idle days. But then I think of him working all night in summer, saving up to see himself through a winter when the island empties. Staying out until dawn to have enough money to send those daughters of his off to college and release them from a life that relies on the whims of visitors who come and go with the good weather. I resolve to tip him, and then remember my near-empty purse.

The car pulls to a stop, gliding into an enormous driveway. Alistair had told me his employer's name as though I should recognize it, each syllable weighted and suggestive. Henry Taylor. Helena had squealed when I repeated it. Whoever Henry Taylor is, he must be important—I've never seen a house quite like this before.

"Is this it?" Helena breathes, leaning close to the window to peer out. "Jesus. It's massive."

She turns to grin at me as she pulls open the taxi door, eager to climb out.

"Nice one, Rachel."

I feel a jolt of pride so satisfying that I don't mind when they all pile out of the car without paying. I press coins into the driver's hand, embarrassed by his curt nod when he counts out the exact change, and shuffle across the cracked leather seats to clamber out. The villa is white-painted and sprawling, columns lining the exterior in a nod to Ancient Greek architecture, spotlights casting long shadows against the high walls. The others are already striding toward a pair of enormous wooden doors and I have to hurry to catch up.

"Henry Taylor is mega-rich. He owns loads of property and stuff, I think," Priya is explaining. "And he throws these massive parties that are *famous*."

Kiera nods excitably. "Our friend back in Athens went to one and she said it was amazing," she enthuses. "Loads of free booze and—"

The doors swing open before we even reach them, music bleeding out into the night air.

"You made it!"

It's Alistair, dressed in a bright white shirt with the sleeves rolled up. He's grinning, holding out his arms wide to all of us, but it feels like he's looking straight at me. I hadn't noticed before how green his eyes are. The way they fix on me makes me painfully aware of myself. My hair isn't quite tamed, still static from the sea, and even though Caroline carefully daubed a sheen of smoky shadow onto my eyelids, I can't help but think she painted on her own with much more precision. She squeezes my hand now, her perfect eyeliner creasing as she grins at Alistair.

"Just about!" she announces, letting go of my hand to stride toward him.

I feel a flicker of annoyance. His eyes settle on her, and I think of how she must seem next to me: taller and skinnier, her hair half tied up to show off her sharp cheekbones.

"This place is insane!"

"I'll give you the grand tour," he says. "But first—drinks!"

He holds the door open for us and Caroline parades inside. I'm still a few steps behind, but just when I think I have lost him, I feel his eyes linger in my direction and my skin vibrates with his gaze.

✳

The air is dense, and my limbs feel slightly out of sync with each other. I lift my drink up to my lips and find I have moved my arm too quickly, so that the slim rim of the glass collides with my teeth. Kiera laughs at my surprise as I blink down at my own hands, not quite able to fathom how I managed to splash half of my vodka and lemonade down myself.

"You," she says, taking a neat sip of her own drink, "are a sloppy drunk."

She's talkative now, the charge of alcohol making her more outspoken than I've seen her so far.

"I'm not *that* drunk," I say.

She shrugs as though it doesn't matter much to her, and then leans one slim arm against a balcony railing. We bumped into each other in the queue for the toilet and then paused at the top of the stairs. It's the perfect place to take in the view of Henry Taylor's villa. When Alistair guided us through the front door, I found that I was holding my breath. The house is the kind of place I've only ever seen before in films or on television, vast and high-ceilinged and modern, too many doors that lead into too many different rooms to count. The interior walls are the same pristine white as the exterior, dotted with abstract and expensive-looking prints painted in vivid colors. In the hallway there is an enormous metal sculpture that seems to take up too much space. It feels frighteningly grown-up and glamorous all at once, an entire world away from the sensible red-brick house where I grew up with its magnolia paint and neat wooden fittings.

Henry Taylor's house is so slick that I'm almost scared to touch anything, terrified of spilling a drink on the floor or the matching ivory furniture. It doesn't feel like the kind of place that's designed for children, or for teenage girls who have had a bit too much to drink. It's for people who can confidently sip red wine without worrying about upturning their glass over one of the plush and perfect rugs, or who have interesting things to say about art. As Alistair poured us drinks, I felt a shudder of excitement that he considered us adult enough to invite.

The enormous curved staircase that Kiera and I peer over suspends the second story above the first, leaving a vast belly of a ground floor. From up in the shadows, we can see the party taking shape. A cluster of guests are already beginning to dance, their blood too charged with the vodka being passed out at the door to stand still, while others linger at the island that sections off the slick kitchen, all silver cabinets and stone countertops. A glass wall opens up the rear of the property, a pool lit up a chlorinated blue beneath the craggy side of a cliff face. I can just make out the partygoers who have migrated outside into the nighttime air, hear a whoop and a splash as someone plunges into the water. Being in water would feel so good right now. I imagine the lubricous weight of it sliding around my body and take another gulp of my drink.

"God, are we going to need to rescue Helena?"

Kiera nods to a vast sofa positioned artfully in the middle of the room. Helena is leaning against a much older man, her skirt riding up her legs as she laughs at something he says. I can see that she's drunk, her body too close to him as she brings her mouth to his bearded face and speaks into his ear.

"I don't know," I say. "Are we?"

Kiera shrugs. "Maybe in a minute. Helena always seems to need getting out of trouble." She glances sideways at me. "Daddy issues," she deadpans. "You know how it is."

"What do you mean?"

"You know. Dad was never there, mum was an alkie, stepdad was . . ." She looks at me again, seeming to remember herself. "Don't tell Helena I told you anything, yeah?"

"Anything about what?" I say.

For a second she frowns. When she catches on, a smile spreads across her face. "Right. Exactly. You know what I'm saying." She takes another swig of her drink and then turns to head back downstairs. "But just keep an eye on Helena. I could do with someone else making sure she's not getting herself into trouble."

She holds out a hand for me to take, looking back at me over her shoulder. When I reach out and clasp her fingers between mine, she smiles, her hair reflective in the swirling, sparkling lights. I hope vaguely that Caroline might be watching from somewhere, filling up her drink or flirting with someone in the hall. Before we can go and drag Helena to the dance floor, a hand brushes against the small of my back.

"I've been looking for you," he says, his breath hot against the side of my face.

Kiera looks back with a knowing smile and her grip loosens from mine.

"Don't worry," she says. "I'll catch up with you later."

I know I'm blushing when I turn toward Alistair. I've always been bad at hiding how I feel, my face betraying me before I can arrange it into an expression of easy indifference.

"Come on," he says. "Let's dance."

With his hand still pressing into the curve of my spine, we follow Kiera downstairs. He takes my drink out of my hand, setting it on a sideboard as we pass so that he can loop his arms around me, pressing into my hips as he begins to sway me in time to the music. At first I'm not sure what to do with myself. I've danced with boys before, at parties and at school discos. They would always stand an arm's length away, their hands planted firmly on my waist as though my body was a thing to overthink. Alistair holds me against him like I'm supposed to be there, as if my bones were created to fit into his. His fingers linger against my hip and then stray up to my neck. He feels in control in a way I have never experienced before. It's surprisingly easy to relax myself into him, to feel the tension of his pelvis against me, to let his hands tighten to the curves of my body as I press back. I have had sex a few times, but this simple act of contact feels far more erotic. The way other boys touched me felt clumsy and hurried, but every move Alistair makes is deliberate and unrushed, as though my skin is something he has been waiting a long, long time for and wants to enjoy.

He shifts his head so that it rests in the side of my neck and his mouth is close to my ear.

"It's hot in here," he says. "Do you want to get some air?"

I nod even though I had forgotten that I could be too hot, or that I could have any needs beyond wanting to feel him close to me, to feel the friction of his body against mine. He leads me outside and we sit opposite each other on sun loungers, my bare legs almost touching his. Inside the house the heat was artificial, the press of too many people competing with the crispness of the air-conditioning, but out here it is damp and organic, the sluggish warmth of the night clinging to our bodies and dampening the crooks of elbows and knees. The air smells of chlorine and the light is aqueous and dim, the green glow of the pool illuminating my skin. Somehow, I have a fresh drink. I'm thirsty enough to gulp it down, and then he is passing me another. Someone has closed the screen doors so that the music inside is faint and distant. Instead crickets create a symphony for us, a creaking, rhythmic composition that drowns out the strains of the sound system.

There are a few partygoers dotted about still, couples weaving their bodies around each other and bubbles of laughter drifting in the lethargic breeze. A woman swims languid lengths of the pool, her hair fanning out in the water and her body pale and glittering beneath the surface. I am reminded of the sea nymphs that we learned about in school, Amalthea and Thetis and all the others with names that felt magical and strange at the time. Now I feel as though I am creating my own mythology, as though moments that should belong to another time of war and love and tricks played by distant gods are coming true.

"Did anyone ever tell you," he says, "that your eyes are the exact same color as the sea?"

His words knock any intelligent response out of me, any notion I might have had to flirt or to say something to impress him. It's so far from the compliments the boys at school use, the monosyllabic categorizations that they pass between them or shout across the classroom. *Fit. Hot.* Stripped-down versions of sexuality plastered onto our bodies as we pass by them in the playground. But Alistair thinks I have eyes the same color as the sea. He half smiles, looking faintly embarrassed by himself.

"God, listen to me," he says. "What do I sound like? It's just that when I saw you back at the bar it was the first thing I thought. I thought that I had to talk to this girl with eyes like the sea. It's not just the color either, it's . . . the depth of them. It's like looking right into an ocean."

"No one's ever told me that," I manage.

"No?" He takes a long swig of his drink. "Good. I like being the first."

I don't know how to respond, so instead I duck my head and toy with my drink, running my finger against the edge of the glass.

"So, Rachel," Alistair says.

I wish I had a more interesting name than Rachel. Rachel seems too out of place against the magic of the night. I should have had one of those ancient names we learned about, an amalgamation of syllables that would evoke mystery and beauty. Yet somehow, Alistair wants to talk to me. Just Rachel. His eyes linger on mine as I wait for him to speak. I'm not sure anyone has ever looked at me this way before, with that simultaneous longing and ease. I'm used to quick appraisals before the boys at school turn their attention to Caroline. To being discarded after one hurried glance. To almost-men who haven't quite figured out the boundaries of desire yet, who prefer pornographic bodies on a computer screen to the girls right in front of them. I am suddenly painfully aware of the slight shadow of sunburn on my shoulders, the artless application of my makeup. When Alistair's gaze lifts high enough to meet mine, it is as though it is cutting straight through me.

"What brought you out here?"

I take a sip of my drink to steady myself. "My friend Caroline, really," I say. "This trip was her idea."

He nods. "I thought that might be it. When I saw you the other night, I could tell you weren't the same as all your friends. You get so many backpackers here to have a good time, but I always think you could just do all that partying back in London. You looked different. Thoughtful. Like you actually want to experience something new. Something different."

I set my drink down on the floor. One corner of his mouth twitches upward, one eyebrow lifts.

"You look embarrassed now," he says, and there's a teasing edge to his voice. "Have I embarrassed you?"

I shake my head. My cheeks are hot and I can tell I'm blushing.

"No, no. It's just . . . is it that obvious?"

"Is what that obvious?"

"I . . . I think I feel a bit out of place on this trip, actually. Caroline's much more outgoing than me. I'm always just her friend. Always the quiet one."

He looks straight at me, as though he can see into my soul, and I feel another spasm of longing somewhere unlocatable inside me.

"You know," he says, "that used to be me too. I used to hate it. But now I think it makes me interesting. It's always the quiet ones. That's what they say, right?"

I let out a small, involuntary hiccup, the drinks I have downed starting to catch up with me. My hand flies to my mouth and he laughs.

"Don't worry, it's cute." He takes a swig of his own drink and then looks back toward the house. "So, tell me about your friends."

"My friends?"

"Yes. All these people who are so much more outgoing and adventurous." He gives me a lopsided smile that sends a pulse up my thighs. "*Apparently.*"

He's drinking something straight in a lowball glass, and I can see the dark hairs on his arm. I sit up straighter, wondering how I look in the iridescent gleam of the pool lights.

"Well, there's Caroline," I say. "And then Kiera. She's the one I was with inside just now. And then Helena, she seems nice, but you know. Daddy issues."

I say it mimicking Kiera, with the same knowing drawl and shrug, and immediately feel self-conscious. The words don't sound right coming from me. They're too high-pitched, a weak imitation of worldliness.

"Daddy issues?"

"Forget it," I say, slightly too quickly. "I wasn't meant to tell anyone."

"Hey, it's fine." He reaches out to touch my thigh, and I am surprised that my skin doesn't blister beneath his. "I'm not really that interested in your friends anyway. I'm interested in getting to know you."

"Me?"

"Don't sound so surprised." His hand is moving now, his thumb rotating in slow circles. "I want to know more. I want to know all about you, Rachel."

The sound of my name on his lips makes my stomach tighten. Before I can stop myself I'm imagining him on top of me, inside me, my name being whispered in my ear as he presses his body against mine. I bat the thought away and duck my head to hide my embarrassment.

"There's not much to know," I say weakly.

"There's everything to know," he says. "I can already tell."

He leans forward, and for a moment I think that he might kiss me. Then he stands up and stretches himself out, his arms reaching toward the star-speckled sky.

"It's getting cold out here," he says. "Shall we go back inside?"

I've lost all my words, the delicate heat of anticipation still caught in my throat and vibrating against my lips. He's not looking at me, already glancing back toward the party, the music a tantalizing beat. It's as though he has held something mouthwatering and brimming with promise in front of me, some morsel dangled so close to my tongue I can almost taste it. The party that seemed so glamorous and adult just an hour or so ago now seems staid and restrained. Why be around other people when I can glow beneath Alistair's eyes, balance in that space where everything is magic and unrealized promise? He glances back toward me, and I see his face shift into a smile as he notices my hesitation. It's indulgent, and when he speaks, his voice comes out as a coo, a teasing depth that makes me feel small and precious.

"Don't look so forlorn," he says. "I just want to get us another drink. We can talk more inside."

He places his hand in the small of my back, and all of a sudden going inside doesn't seem like such a bad idea anymore.

As we head back to the party, I notice for the first time that Caroline has been outside the entire time, watching from across the pool. She doesn't move as we weave toward her, but her eyes stay fixed on us. I see something in them that I don't recognize at first, but as Alistair leads me to the dance floor, it clicks. She was looking at me with jealousy. I'm surprised to find that it feels good.

NOW

It's the height of summer, and yet the sky back in London heaves with rain. I peer at the rivulets running along the ridges of pavements and wonder if I should make a dash for it. I had agreed to meet my best friend Jules near the Underground station, but I forgot to bring an umbrella and my ballet pumps are already sodden.

"Don't just *stand* there." An elbow makes heavy contact with my back as a man in a shiny suit barges past, opening up his own golfing umbrella with a furious backward glance.

With a defeated sigh, I pull my blazer up over my head and start to jog toward the inviting yellow glow of the pub.

It's the kind of place that once would have been a shabby local boozer, all sodden beer mats and sticky tables. Yet as corners of London have started to crystallize cash, council flats being bought up and renovated into swish apartments for couples to spend their parents' money on, it's been updated into the kind of place where people hold Thursday night post-work drinks and go on Tinder dates. Trendy real ale taps are adorned with cartoonish logos and cast-iron industrial lighting makes a half-hearted nod toward a personality.

Jules is already seated at a dark wooden table paired with studiously clashing leather chairs, two wineglasses placed in front of her. She stares down at her phone, transfixed by the bright light of the screen, and doesn't see me approach. I find myself smiling, remembering how anti-technology Jules was for years, refusing to get a smartphone and declaring that social media was only for people who didn't have anything to do in real life. As soon as she got one, admitting defeat when it became clear that an Etsy shop probably actually was the best way to sell her homemade homeopathies, she became an addict, as though making up for all the lost time we'd spent swiping through Instagram while she had adventures.

"Sorry I'm late." I pull my blazer off and drape it over the back of a nearby chair, my arms icy with the rain.

"You're soaked!"

"Have you seen it out there?"

I lift up my glass and take an appreciative slug as I settle into my seat. Among all the other shifts in my life, my friendship with Jules has always stuck. In some ways it's surprising, when you consider how much our lives diverged over the years. While I found a steady job and got married, she traveled the globe, disappearing for months on end, only to resurface at the end of a scratchy line on a long-distance phone call. She had flings with men who were her whole world until she dropped them to move to another continent, and took up jobs in places I'd never heard of. She came back tanned and begging me to come out with her next time, even when she knew I had determined to stay.

When she met someone and moved to London a few years ago, it felt like a relief, a reassurance that most people settle down in the end. I hoped it would stop me waking up in the middle of the night with a rising panic that I was wasting my life as Tom slept next to me. If even Jules could end up in the suburbs, then surely it was simply the nature of things. We visited her and her new fiancé with a nice vase and some flowers to put in it, and I was surprised when the sense of want failed to dissipate over takeout curries and the expensive wine Tom and I brought with us.

"How's work?" she asks.

"Oh, you know."

Although I like my job, I know Jules isn't especially interested. She asks because she cares, but she's never been one for museums. She prefers things in real life, things that happen before her eyes and at the speed of the present. I'm more one for the past, so my role as a museum educator suits me. I like to see schoolchildren imagining mythological places for the first time, hearing stories about gods and goddesses and seeing tiny fragments of a civilization that foundered into jewelry behind glass and dusted-down carvings. I remember learning about mythology for the first time at school and feeling enchanted by stories that have lasted for thousands of years. Of course, the section on Ancient Greece is my favorite. I like to think the islands haven't changed so much over time, that the women of Ithaca and Delos would look out at the same glittering blue seas that I did, their wrists clattering with the bracelets that today we display alongside neatly typed notes and vaguely asserted dates.

"Busy?"

"Always. How's Eli?"

"Let's not spend the entire night talking about our husbands." Jules drains her glass and stands up to get another. "Let's get pissed. Shall I get a bottle?"

We drink until the rain that pours down the window feels almost magical, as though the whole world outside is water. We talk too loudly and check our phones at irregular intervals. I fire off a misspelled message to Tom to tell him I'll be home late and to have dinner without me. My stomach wheedles, and we buy an overpriced packet of crisps from the bar and another bottle.

Two girls who can only be in their early twenties slide into the table next to us. I see them make pointed sidelong glances as I snort with laughter at something Jules is saying and feel self-conscious and silly. They probably think we should be at home by now, tucking children up in bed or drinking cups of tea in our dressing gowns.

You'll get older too, I want to tell them, and you'll feel exactly the same, only sadder. Only fiercely conscious of time in a way you can't imagine when you are only twenty-two. Preoccupied with the way it seems to go faster every year. How that sense of endless possibility disappears, and the sensation that life is an adventure waiting to be had gently splinters into late nights at the office and long commutes and portioning out your year by the long spaces between holidays and special occasions. How you become someone you never would have recognized before, the kind of person who worries about sodium content and sleep quality. The kind of person who would never drop everything to embark on a trip that could turn their world upside down.

"They're judging us," I hiss, interrupting Jules mid-speech. "They think we're too old to be having fun."

Jules glances behind her and then shakes her head.

"You are obsessed with what everyone thinks of you," she says. "And you're obsessed with getting old. You're still so young! *We're* still so young!"

"Tom wants us to go and see a doctor," I say, setting my glass down heavily on the table.

"What kind of a doctor?"

"You know. A fertility doctor."

"Seriously? How long have you guys been trying now?"

"A year? A bit longer maybe. I haven't really been keeping track."

"But he has."

"I guess so."

There's a pause, and I can tell she's waiting for me to say something more.

"I just don't think we need to force it," I say. "If it's supposed to happen, then it will. Maybe we can go and see a doctor at some point. But now? It still feels too soon . . ."

Before I can continue, Jules has reached across the table and is squeezing my hand.

"I get it," she says. "I know."

After that, I find I don't want anything else to drink. I'm tired. I have work in the morning, and I know I'll feel dreadful. Tom will probably be annoyed with me by now. I imagine him stretching cling film over a plate to leave for me in the microwave, the meal he has prepared wilting beneath its plastic sheen.

We walk to the tube in silence, and when we go our separate ways, Jules pulls me into a hug so tight I can feel the long, hard bones of her rib cage pressing into me.

"It'll be OK," she says. "Promise."

I sober up as I clatter back toward the suburbs, the dense heat of the Underground seeming to sweat the alcohol out of my system. I stare at my reflection over the heads of late-night commuters as they go home half asleep. I look pale, my skin dull and greasy, the bones beneath my eyes seeming to sink. You'd never think I'd only just been on holiday, spending a week lying in the sun and chasing my teenage dreams.

Without even thinking, I find myself pulling my phone out of my handbag, my fingers illuminating the screen. It's an instinctual gesture, a modern impulse made out of boredom and a discomfort at the threat of my own thoughts for the entire half-hour journey home. A picture of Tom and me flushes the background, our heads pressed close together, smiles beaming. It was taken years ago, back before we even got married. We look desperately happy and hopeful. I'm not quite sure why I haven't updated it.

There's an unread message from Tom festering in my inbox and a profusive scramble of emoji hearts from Jules. I swipe both away and open up my address book. I've looked at his name and number more times than I can count since Helena added it. It still makes me shiver slightly to see it there, the tangible line of text in the same phone that tells Tom to go to the shop to get dinner, or dutifully dials up my mum for our fortnightly phone call. His name, and a way of finding him. I could call him right now if I wanted to. All it would take would be the tiniest movement of my thumb, a heart-stopping moment while our phones connected across a city. Ten seconds or less to collide my past and my present. Ten seconds or less, perhaps, to find out he hasn't thought about me once over all these years. I lock my phone and tuck it back into my handbag.

※

can smell Tom's specialty pasta dish before I even reach the kitchen, lashings of white wine and cream. The garlicky scent has gone stale in the air, and the lights are all off downstairs. His dish is neatly washed up and placed beside the sink to dry, and there's a bowl covered over in the fridge for me. I eat it cold, cramming the congealed and hardened spaghetti into my mouth faster than I can chew. I leave my plate dirty on the sideboard.

"How was your night?" he calls out as I'm only halfway up the stairs.

I immediately feel guilty as I see him peer around the bedroom door, laptop still clutched in one hand.

"Fine."

"Jules OK?"

"She's fine." I peck him on the lips and am aware that I must still taste faintly of wine and prawn cocktail crisps. "She asked us over to dinner sometime actually. Maybe in a few weeks?"

"Sure." Tom slams his laptop shut. "I'll check my calendar at work."

He sits on the bed as I take out my earrings and undo my hair. It used to be one of his favorite things about me. He used to bury his hands in it and make me promise never to cut it short. It takes me a moment to realize I'm not remembering my husband.

"How tired are you?" Tom says, and I know what he's asking.

"I'm OK," I say. "Just give me a second."

I shut the door to our bathroom behind me. We had added en suites to the long list of things we wanted in a forever home, along with outdoor space and a spare bedroom. Tom had looked at me hopefully when he'd tentatively suggested that we'd need a two-bed, and I had agreed with him. It was normal, wasn't it, for couples who had been married for a few years to be thinking about the future? To imagine multiplying into tiny parts of each other, to be filling up rooms and painting walls white and yellow in anticipation? As I sit on the lowered toilet seat, I try to remember when we stopped talking about other things. When en suites and color schemes became more important to us than each other. When Tom started to talk about babies more and more often, to look doe-eyed at small, round-faced creatures pushed about in prams at the local park and then squeeze my hand and smile.

I turn the taps on full blast to disguise any sound and then slide a cosmetic bag crammed with tampons out from under the sink. I dig my hand between the slippery plastic wrappers until I find what I'm searching for. It's the last place Tom would look, somewhere there's no risk of him stumbling across the innocuous pink packet. It feels reassuringly familiar in my grasp as I slide it out silently, my routine well practiced. The plastic buckles as I press against it, a gentle give so that a small pill drops into my hand. And then it's gone, slipped atop my tongue and swallowed down in a second. I don't need to swill it away with water. I've been taking them for long enough, my body ready to dilute the tiny tablet into my bloodstream, a ritual of womanhood that has followed me since my early twenties. Since before Tom and I met and all the way through our marriage. It's the easiest thing in the world. It's the biggest lie I've ever told.

I zip up the bag and tuck it back beneath the sink. I wash my hands so that they're convincingly damp and turn off the taps. I can hear the creak of springs as Tom settles back on our bed, the bathroom door the only thing between him and a deception that would tear us apart.

After that I crawl into bed beside him. Perhaps in a gesture of guilt I've already undressed, and I see the dilation of his pupils as he slides his hands down to feel the hard ridge of underwire against my rib cage, the tension of thin lace against skin. He tastes of toothpaste, and I feel myself relaxing into his familiarity and cleanliness, the motions of intimacy I know by heart. How he will kiss along my jawbone and then down my neck. How his legs will press mine open gently and preemptively as he lifts up my arms to wrap around his neck. He's always so careful with me now, each time we have sex seemingly weighted with possibility. When he pushes up inside me, he looks me straight in the eye and smiles, and I crane my neck up to kiss him so that I don't have to meet his gaze. He feels like safety and suffocation all at once, and I push my face into his shoulder as he moves above me and imagine other places and other men.

"I love you," he murmurs, his mouth close to my ear.

I press my hips up and say it back, and it's easy because I do. Just not in quite the same way.

THEN

At first, I convince myself that I have misread Alistair's easy confidence as flirtation. After the party I lie awake in my hostel
bed, sheets thrown off and my body slick with sweat, and re-
trace our first meeting. Perhaps he'd meant to talk to one of the other
girls. Perhaps he was just speaking to me to fill time before someone
more interesting came along. Perhaps he was using me to get closer
to Caroline—something that has embarrassingly happened to me before on at least two occasions. I have to remind myself that he took
my number. That he promised to text me later. That it was me he
chose to talk to, when it could have been Kiera or Helena or Priya. I
thrash against the mattress in an attempt to find a cool stretch in my
single bed and burn for him to have kissed me, unable to figure out
why he didn't. I fall asleep with my phone clutched in my hand, solid
against the slippery contours of dreams.

By the time I wake up, he has messaged me. I present the text
with ceremony to the others as we gather for breakfast in the hostel's
decrepit dining room. Our limp slices of toast and saccharine jam
are abandoned as they lean over my phone and dissect his message
in reverent tones.

"Alistair is *so* fit," Priya breathes. "God, I'd jump if he asked me out."

"He's not asking me out," I tell her, feigning nonchalance even though my insides fizz with excitement. "We're just having a drink."

I only half believe myself. The fact that his first message is so straightforward, so assured, feels dangerous and exciting. I'm used to seeing girls at school go through the elaborate and agonizing rituals played out by boys our own age: the will-they-won't-they dance of wondering whether a guy will make a move and, if he does, what it means. Alistair's message is so simple, just a few words that I want to read over and over again.

Hey Rachel. We should grab a drink. Are you free later?

I press my phone again so that the message flashes bright. I'm usually never the center of these kinds of discussions, the giddy analysis of another person's interest. I feel myself puff up with self-importance as Kiera asks me whether I've responded yet. Before I can answer, Caroline interrupts.

"Don't you think it's a bit creepy?"

It's the first thing she has said to me all morning. She sits back, her arms folded and her mouth a hard line, a cup of instant coffee cooling in front of her. She stumbles when none of us respond, when Helena and Priya don't rush to support her.

"He must be nearly twice your age," she says, but her voice already sounds too high-pitched, prim and prudish.

"But he's not exactly some ugly old guy, is he?" Helena says, before I have time to speak. "Anyway, my mum and stepdad had a ten-year age gap. It's not even that unusual."

Caroline opens her mouth as if to answer and then seems to think better of it. Instead she tosses her hair and pouts. Helena redirects the subject, and yet I can still feel Caroline's eyes fixed on me, furious and cold, the bite of rage in her voice hovering between us. I choose to ignore it. Instead I pull my phone back toward me and enjoy the hum of anticipation as I lift it to respond.

﹡

Alistair and I meet in a tucked-away cove just around the bay. It would be more private there, he told me. A better place to watch the sunset. I felt the weight of his words, the implication that we would need privacy, and was thrilled.

Beaches often remind me of stilted seaside trips taken with my parents when I was younger. Strips of graying sand and greasy fish and chips turning pallid in their paper. Fighting to find a place to sunbathe as crowds battled to make the most of a rare day of sallow sun. But this place is different. It feels quiet and untouched, the ground smooth and blank where the tide has washed it flat, the sand bleached white. The sun is warm on my legs, and Alistair cracks open bottles of beer, the yeasty taste of alcohol turning sweet in the breeze. I feel myself getting tipsy quickly, the drink lending a celestial quality to the late-afternoon heat, the kind that makes colors feel both brighter and softer. I cast aside the cardigan I brought with me in case it got cold, my limbs bare, the skin on the tip of my nose starting to peel.

As the heat seeps out of the day, we talk. He asks me about myself in the most abstract of ways, about my thoughts and feelings rather than anything concrete or logistical. Why I wanted to travel. How I feel being out here. It makes it easy to avoid bringing up the particulars of my home life, the fact that I'm still in sixth form and that my flight back home looms just a couple of weeks away. I ask him about himself, and he tells me about his work for Henry Taylor.

"Henry just likes things done his way," he says, seeming to weigh up his words. "I make that happen."

"What kind of things?"

"Oh, you know. The bar is his main thing on the island, but he owns property out here too, so I do a lot of taking care of that. Doing his books. Looking after his business interests."

I don't dare ask him what business interests he means, afraid of sounding young and foolish, not sure what the right questions are.

"He's away a lot," he says. "He has clients all over the place. Property ventures, investments. This place is his escape. Where he comes to get away from it all. I get to live up in his house for free so someone's there to take care of it when he's not here. To take care of everything for him while he's away. It's a better way of life than I used to have. Simpler."

"So you get to live here all year round?" I ask.

I look out at the sea as I speak, hardly able to believe this place could be somebody's home. The sky has begun to tinge into dusk, sweeps of pink and violet mirrored by the ocean. The shadow of the moon hangs pale and promising, almost out of sight. The island feels so magical it's difficult to imagine that it could ever be mundane and everyday. He laughs at my disbelief.

"All year round," he says. "Makes the job worth it."

"Don't you like working for Henry Taylor, then?" I ask.

"Oh, of course I like it," he says. "I met him back in London, a few years back. I was in an office at the time. It was all-right money, but I was sick of it. My firm worked on a contract for Henry, and we got on. He showed me another side of life, one where you aren't just tied to a desk all day, spending hours stuck on the tube, getting by but only just. All of a sudden there were these parties, trips. He offered me a job, told me he needed somebody to take care of his place out here. Run this side of his business."

He takes a long swig of beer and then stretches his palms out toward the horizon.

"How could I say no to this?"

I faintly marvel at the fact he's lived enough of life to get sick of it. To have had an entire era in one place and then years in another. I look at him and see an entire universe of possibilities, a worldliness I can hardly hope to attain. I'm not sure what to say back to him, so I close my eyes and turn my face to the sky. I pretend that I'm enjoying the moment, chasing the last embers of heat and light from the corners of the day. The sun is imprinted on my eyelids, flickering white and then a pulsing, bleeding red. I try to focus on it, to keep it there for a moment longer, but my vision betrays me and it fades into nothingness.

"Stay still," he says. "Just like that."

I feel the corners of my mouth lift, the give of sand beneath me as his body shifts over mine. I open my eyes just before he leans in to kiss me. It's brief, as though he barely needs to touch me at all, the lightest tracing of his lips against mine. His own mouth is slightly chapped from months of sun and salt water. I remember the baby-soft faces of the boys from school and feel a judder of pleasure at the weather-beaten feel of him, the sensation that summer is beneath his very skin. He sits back, his eyes never leaving mine, and lifts a sandy bottle to take a sip.

"You'll get me in trouble," he says with a small smile.

It's the kind of comment that makes me feel like someone else entirely, tempting and dangerous. All day I've felt utterly helpless, checking my phone every five minutes to see if he's messaged and desperately trying to summon topics that might capture his attention, but his words make me feel powerful. As though I have the potential to cause the kind of desire that gets grown men into trouble. I smile back in what I hope is a flirtatious way, lowering my gaze and then looking up like I've seen Caroline do a thousand times. He laughs.

"Seriously," he says, setting his beer down on the sand. "I won't hear the end of it if Henry finds out I've been picking up girls at the bar. I'm meant to be working. He's not big on mixing business and pleasure. Obviously when I saw you I couldn't help myself . . ." He pauses and his gaze dances up the length of my body. "You haven't told the other girls that we're spending time together, have you?"

"No," I lie. "I haven't told anyone."

He nods and slides one hand on top of my leg.

"That's good," he says. "We have to keep this a secret for now, OK? We have to make sure Henry doesn't find out."

"Why can't he find out?"

Alistair skips a beat, looking out to sea for a second.

"Henry's great. Generous. But you have to play the game his way. Stay on his good side. Keep work and life separate." He takes a swig of his beer. "You're friends with some of the girls at the bar. I'm their boss. I have to keep things professional. No favorites."

"Would he really care?" I ask. "You're my friend's boss—not mine."

"You don't know him. He's particular. He puts a lot of value in loyalty. And if I lose this job, there's nothing else out here for me. Henry has given me everything I've got. The least I can do is follow the rules."

"But," I say, "you're still here."

I'm emboldened by the fact that he would break the rules for me. That he is willing to take the risk. He leans forward and kisses me again, slowly this time.

"Just trust me on this one," he says. "It's not worth him finding out for now. Not yet. And besides, you don't want the others being funny with you about it. It's better if it's just between us. More special. Our secret."

For a second the words sound strange. Heavy. Not all secrets are good, after all. But then he lifts a strand of my hair and leans forward to kiss my neck, and he smells as sharp and clean as the sea on a summer's day, and I remind myself that he wants me. That this could be the start of something. That some things are worth keeping secrets for.

NOW

'm on my lunch break when he calls me. I've spent all morning with year-fives from a North London comprehensive, trying to conjure up some interest in Ancient Roman life with papier-mâché pots and PVA glue. I tap at my keyboard to jolt my computer into life and, as if by instinct, type the same words into Google that I do at least once a week. It's almost mechanical, my fingers thrumming across the keys, finding the letters that will spell out his name, *Alistair Wright*. I pause and then, for good measure, add *London*.

Did you mean Alastair Wright? Google chirrups back at me, unhelpfully offering up staff profiles of lecturers, someone who works at an architect's firm in Farringdon, a teacher who has won an award. I scroll down, methodically scanning and then disregarding each. I glance past LinkedIn profiles and local newspaper stories and then sit back in my chair, breathing a sigh of part disappointment, part relief. There's nothing new. Nothing that might provide any clue as to what happened to him. Yet this time my search is different—I'm no longer reaching out into an ungiving expanse of endless people, thousands of cities, and millions of faces. This time, I know exactly how to reach him.

"There's a phone call for you." An assistant whose name I can't remember leans her head around the door.

I see her gaze sweep my office before she ducks out again, taking in the yogurt pots strewn across my desk and the pile of papers balanced in a precarious stack on a spare chair. I know I'm lucky to have my own room, even if it is a windowless space lodged beneath a set of stairs in a part of the museum that everyone forgot, but I don't seem to be able to keep it tidy. My lack of an office-mate only encourages the ever-expanding sprawl of mess, mind maps from weeks ago still stuck up on the walls, and tens of tabs I'll never read opened on my computer. Mine and Tom's home is always immaculate, the cupboard under the sink stocked with bleaches and polish, potions that promise to keep sinks limescale-free, and sprays that smell of soap and citrus. It sometimes feels comforting to come into work and be briefly surrounded by my own chaos.

I dig around the pile of unsorted shoes and cardigans bundled beneath my desk to find my handbag. I pull out my own phone and see the urgent list of notifications filling up the home screen. Five missed calls from Tom. I scramble to my feet, hurriedly hitting redial. It goes straight to voicemail, jammed to my ear as I dash down to the main office.

"Sorry, sorry," I hiss as I pick up the handset held out to me. "Tom?"

There's a pause before he speaks, long enough for me to have imagined a million scenarios that might have happened to him. Then his voice, as calm as always and immediately reassuring.

"Hey—sorry, I tried calling your mobile and you didn't answer."

"I wasn't at my desk. Are you OK?"

"Yes, I'm fine. Well, not *fine*. I'm at the hospital, actually."

"At the *hospital*?"

"Don't worry, I'm fine. Well, fine-ish anyway. Broken leg."

"Broken . . ." I hunch over, lowering my voice in spite of the apparent indifference of anyone in the vicinity. "What do you mean? What did you do?"

Tom works in technology, something with computers at a finance company that I've never quite bothered to grasp. When we first met, back when I was in my mid-twenties, I would thrust broken laptops and unconfigured phones at him with alarming regularity, and he'd laugh and say that wasn't really what he did but then sort it out anyway. I let him solve my problems, and it felt like a relief to be able to do so, to relinquish the parts of my life that made me feel helpless and hand them over to him to be fixed. By the time we moved in together, our work conversations mostly revolved around office politics and promotions. He told me vaguely about projects he was working on, and as he progressed up through the company, he seemed to spend more time in meetings than tinkering about with technology. The thought of him being involved in some kind of workplace accident seems absurd.

"Bad tackle at the work five-a-side," he says.

"Five-a-side?" I lower my voice. "As in . . . *football*?"

"Yeah." He has the decency to sound sheepish. "I've been playing on the work team. It's just a bit of fun but—"

"Since when?"

"Since last year. After work, mostly, but this meeting got canceled earlier, so we just thought we'd have a kickabout and—"

"Which hospital?" I interrupt him. "I'll come and get you."

When people worry about their husbands keeping secrets from them, I imagine they think of hidden text messages and clandestine affairs. The absurdity of Tom's deception takes me by surprise. As I clamber into a taxi and we slide through the streets toward Guy's and St. Thomas', I try to remember late nights and excuses. I can't think of a time when he messaged to tell me that he was working late, or said he was at after-work drinks when he might have been trundling around a football pitch trying to keep up with younger colleagues. Maybe I never asked where he was. Maybe I just wasn't paying any attention.

When we pull up outside A&E, he's waiting, crutches propped

beneath his arms and a cast strapped onto his leg. He must have already been seen by the time he called me. I hurry to open the door as he hobbles toward us, wondering what kind of wife makes her husband feel like he can't call her on the way to the hospital.

"What the fuck, Tom?"

That kind of wife, I suppose. He winces as he shuffles himself into the backseat, easing his leg into place and wielding his crutches at me to take. I climb in after him as he gives the taxi driver our address.

"Glad you're all right too, Rach."

He sounds spikier than usual. It's a tone I'm not used to from him, and I find myself frowning as I scan the extent of his injuries.

"Well, what do you want me to say? There's me thinking you haven't played football in about ten years, and then I get called out of work for this?"

"Jeez, Rachel, give it a rest." He leans his head against the window and gazes fixedly out at the gray streets and clusters of pedestrians clamoring outside the hospital gates. "These pain meds they've given me are about to knock me out. Can we just talk about it later?"

"No, we can't talk about it later. At least tell me what the doctors said."

"It's just a stress fracture," he says, his voice sounding thin with exasperation. "I'll be out for six weeks. It's not a big deal."

"It is a big deal," I hiss, aware of the taxi driver glancing at us in his rearview mirror. "Thirty-eight-year-old men don't get stress fractures playing football, Tom. They don't *lie* to their wives about it."

He shuts his eyes. His entire body is leaning away from me.

"I didn't lie, Rachel," he says. "I just didn't tell you."

Back at the house Tom insists that he needs to nap, worn out from the pain. I help him up the stairs, him sitting down on each step and hauling himself backward with his leg stretched out beneath him. He lies on our bed still fully clothed and closes his eyes before I can say anything else. I know that as soon as I leave the room he'll be on his phone, scrolling through Twitter or BBC Sport. Still, I manage to play the caring wife for just long enough to close the door gently behind me and tiptoe downstairs. I make myself a coffee and perch at the kitchen counter with the mug clutched between my hands.

Our house is silent, the distant hum of the main road at the end of our residential street the only sound. When did Tom stop telling me things? We used to tell each other everything, the minutiae and mundanity of our days inextricably linked, woven into anecdotes about work and fired out in endless back-and-forth messages. There's an intoxicating excitement when you first meet someone, an obsessive kind of fascination with what they had for lunch or how they spend their weekends. I would have viewed Tom's love of football as something that showed he had his own interests, a promise of space on a Saturday afternoon. Maybe I would have gone to watch him play and caught his eye from the sideline, a flicker of flirtation between us. Although when I really think about it, I'm not sure Tom and I had ever shared blistering glances across a football pitch, or anywhere else for that matter.

"This doesn't mean anything," I remember telling him the first time we slept together, pulling my T-shirt off over my head without ceremony.

It hadn't taken me long to discover that he was the kind of person who didn't do meaningless. When I declared I didn't want anything from him, he had turned up with dinner and invited me out with his friends. Before I knew it, I was meeting his parents, who smiled benevolently and told him how lovely I was. I had surprised myself with how much I liked it, how easy things could be if I simply sat back and let life happen to me. All I had to do was not resist as he took my hand and grinned in response. I was twenty-five, and after years of puzzling over how other people made relationships seem so simple, I found myself moved in with him within months. It seemed that I hadn't decided on any of it, and sometimes I would wake up not remembering where I was and panicking about how I had got here. When I came back to myself, Tom's gentle snores stirring me to reality, I would feel instantly calmed. There was a consuming and imperfect relief in letting every decision be taken out of my hands. There was a comfort in having him sleep next to me.

I take a sip of my coffee. The countertops are gleaming, the breakfast dishes already washed up before we went to work. We used to lie in bed eating takeaway pizza and getting grease on the sheets. Tom used to tell me everything. For a moment I let myself feel furious with him for keeping such a meaningless secret, but then I remember all the things I've never told him. That same omission I make every single day. It turns out our marriage is full of secrets. His is far smaller than most, but perhaps that's why it hurts. We've reached a point where we simply don't bother telling each other things. Where hiding the truth from each other feels like less effort than talking about it.

I reach for my phone and swipe away the missed calls from earlier. Then I click on Alistair's name and find that my fingers are typing so furiously I've tapped out a message before I've even had time to think about what to say.

Hi. It's me. Rachel.

I stare at it for a second. It's hardly poetry, but there aren't really the words to map out the expanse between us, the sixteen years since we saw each other last, all the things I have wanted to say to him since then. I wonder if he'll start when he sees it and recognize my name at once. If he'll be transported back to the taste of sea salt on my mouth, cheap tequila, the undulating heat. If he'll remember the hardness of my seventeen-year-old body, sunburned skin on sunburned skin, me telling him I loved him with the waves lapping against our feet. Or perhaps there have been other Rachels since me. Other women he's made the same promises to, whose bodies he's made vibrate with longing. Maybe I'm not the only past lover who still daydreams about him. Maybe there's somebody who doesn't need to daydream, who shares his bed and makes him cups of tea and fights about doing the school run. Alistair has always belonged to such an impalpable time that it seems impossible to imagine him doing normal things—washing up and getting the tube to work. But now I have his number. Now he is a real person, distilled into something as tangible as a text message.

Before I can change my own mind, I tap send and watch my message turn from a half-formed draft into existence. Somewhere in this seething mass of a city, his phone will be lighting up, a piece of me waiting to be discovered by him. We met before smartphones, before our devices became demanding and petulant things, streams of messages betraying whether we'd read them and expectant of an immediate response. It seems strange that I don't know whether he's the kind of person who will reply at once, or leave me on read, or have messages lingering in his inbox for hours unopened. They seem like details I should know about someone I've thought about almost every day for over a decade, and I wonder if I've made a mistake. Maybe I've imagined the bond between us, as distinct as a long thread stretching across the city, weaving from my life to his, wherever he might be. Maybe it was broken back when he left me behind. Maybe time and distance are far bigger forces than I imagined.

I stand up, the stool I've been perched on scraping across the kitchen tiles, and empty my coffee into the sink. My blood already feels charged with adrenaline, a pulsing and nervous energy flickering just beneath the surface of my skin. I've barely turned back to the table when I see my phone light up out of the corner of my eye, a glimmer that causes my heart to jolt. For a moment I stand completely still. It occurs to me that this could be the moment that changes everything. My past could be about to collide messily with my present, invading the edges of my neatly arranged kitchen. Or it could be obliterated, all the moments I've clung to for all this time discarded with a single dismissive text. I'm almost compelled to fling my phone across the room, to shatter it before I can see what he's said, to stay balanced in this precarious state of possibility for just a little bit longer. But the temptation proves too much. It always did when it came to him. I snatch up my phone and tap the message open hungrily. These will be the first words he's said to me in sixteen years. I want to absorb them, to soak in them, to memorize them and repeat them to myself over and over again. Five words, simple and unrevealing, and yet I stare at my phone for so long that he may as well have penned me an essay.

I place the phone back down on the counter. They're not the words of someone who sounds happy to hear from me. They're the words of someone who disappeared years ago and didn't look back. Briefly and without meaning to, I'm taken back to why he left. The secrets I kept for him. But my mind instinctively scurries to block it out. *Think of Tom upstairs with his broken leg. Think of how furious you are with him. Think about work, and how you really should call and tell them you won't be back in today.* My hands are gripped so tightly my nails have left crevices in my palms. I rub the reddening flesh to ease away the tension, but it's settled somewhere unplaceable inside me that can't be massaged out.

I drift upstairs and switch on the shower. It's something practical that I can do. Something necessary and thoughtless. I strip off my work clothes and leave them in a pile on the floor. I turn the water up until it's too hot, almost unbearable, and lean my head against the tiles as my mind goes blurry from the steam and the heat. It feels good, as though I'm slipping away from myself, shedding my skin and becoming someone clean and new entirely. I shut my eyes, and as I do, I see the message again, the typed-out words that have transported me back. I whisper them to myself, water running into my mouth, and as I do I can almost hear his voice speaking to me like he never left.

How did you find me?

THEN

S till here?"

The decking gives as someone collapses down next to me. It's Helena, her T-shirt riding up to expose the tight indent of her belly button. I'm sprawled out on the cushions scattered across the bar's terrace in an effort to tempt daytime custom. It's unsuccessful enough that no one seems to mind me spending all afternoon here, cadging occasional beers off whoever is on shift.

"Nowhere else to be," I say. "Are you finished?"

Helena nods. "All done for the day. Thank God. You should have seen the state of the toilets, good luck to anyone who's on shift next and has to clean them." She pulls a cigarette packet out of her denim shorts and pats herself down, hunting for a lighter. "No Caroline again today?"

"No." I take a cigarette from the carton she proffers. I've never smoked much before, but it feels easier out here to simply do the things you are offered than to say no. "She's down at the beach, I think."

Helena takes a long drag of her cigarette.

"No Alistair today?"

Her voice sounds level, a throwaway remark. I have to glance sideways at her to see if she knows. If she can tell.

"No," I say. "I haven't seen him all week."

It's strange how easy it is to lie about it. In reality I've seen him almost every day since our first kiss. I tell Caroline I'm out with Helena, Priya, and Kiera. I tell them I'm with Caroline. Alistair and I meet in secret, on tucked-away beaches and sometimes at bars too expensive for the others to visit. He's kissed me so many times now that my lips feel singed with him, that I can almost summon the taste of him in my mouth. I'm getting used to it, the feel of an adult face against mine, the graze of stubble against my cheek. At first I was clumsy and unsure, but my confidence has slowly grown, my movements matching his. I'm so aware of his age that I expect him to try and progress things quickly, yet somehow our relationship fails to move any further. I wait for him to invite me up to Henry Taylor's house, to pull me behind some rocks on a secluded stretch of sand, but he never does. We only ever spend an hour or two together before he tells me he has to go, and I'm left wondering whether he wants me after all.

Whenever he's too busy to see me, I distract myself with nights out, my tongue thick with the taste of cheap vodka and my throat hoarse with singing at the top of my voice. As the afternoon gives way to dusk, the beach turning cold and the air thickening into the promise of evening, the bar tempts us in with the warmth of alcohol. A thrum of bodies pressed together. The hum of the sound system and the possibility of an entire night opening out ahead of us. Even though Alistair manages the bar, he rarely seems to be there. Kiera, Helena, and Priya mention him in vague snatches that I cling to—when he messages them to arrange their shifts or when they wonder when he'll pay them. I go out hoping to see him. I spot a dark-haired man across the room, the flash of an expensive watch, a smattering of stubble, and my heart leaps, even though it's hardly ever him.

"You're quiet." Helena blunts her cigarette out and flicks the smoldering stub away from her. "Daydreaming about Alistair?"

"Alistair and I are just friends."

"Course you are, babe." Helena smiles. "He'll miss you when you're gone."

I haven't told anyone that my flight back home leaves in a couple of days, and I skip a beat at Helena's words.

"Gone?"

"Yeah." She pulls herself to a seated position, leaning back on her long arms. "I saw Caroline at the beach yesterday. You guys are off home in a few days, right?"

"Yeah," I say. "I guess I am."

Until we arrived on the island, I had felt ready to go home. I was painfully aware of the figure in my bank account teetering dangerously low every time I checked my balance, the initial excitement of independence beginning to wear thin. But now, with thoughts of Alistair never far from my mind, days portioned out by school bells and the same five weeknight dinners, rotated over and over again, are beginning to seem like a less tempting prospect. I would go home and show my parents overexposed photos of the Acropolis. I would head up to my room and stretch out on my single bed to dream of Greek sunsets. I would go to school and be ignored, my friendship with Caroline now frayed perhaps irreparably. I would sit on the edge of the schoolyard, my back against the hard brick of the sixth-form wall, and wish that my classmates could see me for who I was out here. Out here I am interesting. My skin is turning golden and my hair is burnishing at its tips. My body seems desirable for the first time, and yet I am going home to tuck it back beneath a polo shirt and sit behind a desk learning about life from textbooks.

"Have you thought about staying?" Helena asks.

She's playing with a strand of her hair, weaving it into a tiny plait, not really paying much attention. She says it so idly, as if it would be simple. As if I wouldn't have to deal with furious parents and a phone call to my school. As if it wasn't what I wanted more than anything.

"I can't afford it," I say.

"Why don't you ask Alistair if he can sort a job out for you at the bar? They always seem to need more of us."

I look over at my new friend and feel a pulse of longing for the ease with which she imagines that I can leave my life at home behind, even if only temporarily. Priya and Kiera are both on a gap year, a university place already deferred and awaiting them next September, but Helena is distant and vague about her own plans. The hints of her life that Kiera spoke of at the party have since been elaborated on in only the most sketched-out and indistinct ways, and I have started to understand that Helena is much more rootless than the travel companions she's collected. Once, after too many tequilas, she told me that she hasn't spoken to her mother for eighteen months, that she'd spent the year before she came out here sleeping on sofas and working late-night shifts to save money.

"It was worth it though," she said, glassy-eyed. "It was that or keep on working in shitty bars in the back end of nowhere forever. Why rot in a dead-end job when you can be out here having *fun*?"

When she speaks, I wish that I were as boundless as she is. Not having anything to go home to feels enticingly glamorous, astonishingly freeing. I imagine working here, measuring out shots and berating customers for having one too many. I imagine moving into the house Helena has recently relocated to, a sprawling apartment complex Henry Taylor keeps to help out the bar staff newly arrived and needing somewhere to stay. I envisage myself living with a crew of girls my own age and with no other purpose than enjoying their summer of freedom. I've seen them dancing together at the end of the night, arms wrapped around shoulders and faces split with smiles. I've heard them make in-jokes and groan about the early-morning cleaning shift. I've watched as they flirt with Alistair from behind the bar and felt a tug of jealousy at the closeness that seems to come from scrubbing down tables and drinking together after lockup. Then I think of Caroline and how furious she would be with me if I stayed. My parents. A lost year of school.

"I can't," I say. "I have to go home."

"You should talk to Alistair about it," Helena says again. "I have a feeling he'll want you to stay."

※

The day before I am due to leave, Alistair finally asks me to the house.

The message arrives early in the morning, as Caroline and I silently navigate around each other in our hostel bedroom. The tiled floor is taken up with open backpacks, piles of clothes, toiletries waiting to be sorted and packed away. Alistair's texts usually arrive with an infrequency that feels taut and precious, as though every message has been earned, every pixelated kiss perfect. They make me long for the reams of IMs that Caroline would receive from boys back home, smiley-spangled minutiae and late-night typo-ridden texts asking her what she was doing. She spits toothpaste into the sink as my phone vibrates, and I snatch it up from my bed before she can ask who it is.

Henry's going away tonight, it reads. You should come over.

I suppress my excitement as I fold floaty T-shirts and still-damp bikini bottoms, my heart thundering. It's the confirmation I've been waiting for. The thought that an older man could be interested in me when I barely summoned the attention of schoolboys back in England had felt faintly unbelievable until now, a tempting kind of danger a million miles from my life at home. I think of teachers and family friends in their thirties and cringe at the thought of them touching me, their coffee-scented breath and the inevitable need to explain away any hint of flirtation. But here, everything is different. I am different. The heat seems to crawl beneath my skin and invade my imagination. It stops me sleeping and makes everything feel possible, permissible. An older man. A summer romance. The complete and utter disintegration of my inhibitions.

"I think I'll go out tonight," I tell Caroline when she flops onto her bed, her packing complete.

She just shrugs and stares at her own phone. Over the last few days the already palpable tension between us has tightened. Alistair's attentions had elevated me to the coveted status of cool girl among our new friends, a shifting of my social standing that Caroline has found hard to navigate. There is a secretive pride in my effortless absorption into the team, a sense of wonderment that after years of wanting desperately to be liked and feeling hopelessly grateful for Caroline's friendship, it has only taken the approval of one man to make me worthy.

"Don't be loud coming back in," she says, her voice brisk and tight. "I don't want to be tired on the flight tomorrow."

※

He sends a car to pick me up, all leather seats and blacked-out windows. I sneak a sluice of Caroline's favorite red lipstick, blotting its sticky traces with my fingertips as the driver glances back at me in his rearview mirror. I have to steady my breathing as the slant of the road heightens, a vertiginous shift in the world that suggests we are nearing Henry Taylor's villa. I stare at my faded reflection in the car window, a wide-eyed girl looking pallid and frail against the backseat of one of Henry's cars.

I know what Alistair will expect from me tonight. After all, he's an adult. A grown man in his thirties. The fact that we'll be alone in Henry's house without the worry of parents coming home early is unusual and enticing. I sit up slightly straighter and remind myself to act appropriately adult. To let him know I'm ready for it. To pretend I know exactly what I'm doing, when really I'm hoping he'll take the lead and leave little room for guesswork.

He pours me a drink as soon as I arrive, an ice-cold glass of wine that cuts through the humidity of the night. We sit next to each other on Henry's sofa, the few inches between us feeling vast and insurmountable. I don't know how to initiate things. How to show him that I want him. In the end, I don't need to worry about it. Everything happens more quickly than I expect it to, our drinks barely touched, our clothes discarded on the living room floor. He takes me up to his bedroom, one hand in mine as he tells me to lie down on his blank white bed. He seems transfixed by my body in a way that feels entirely unfamiliar to me, circling my hips with his hands and marveling at how slim they are, laughing at the ghost of a bathing suit sketched out in pale lines of flesh. He raises one thumb to wipe at a place where Caroline's lipstick has clotted against the corners of my mouth like sweet-smelling blood.

"You don't need that," he says. "All that stuff."

I reach up to swipe the remnants away with the back of my hand.

"Caroline lent it to me," I tell him. "It's not mine."

"Well." He leans down to kiss me. "You're not like the other girls. You don't need all that crap."

I vaguely remember something Caroline said once, some derisive drawl about how it's not really a compliment, to not be like other girls, and then quash it. I've spent my whole life trying to be like other girls. The opportunity that Alistair presents to me, some unfamiliar option to be beautiful and desirable without trying to be somebody else, feels like a relief.

He puts his mouth close to my ear, and I can feel the weight of his longing as he exhales heavily.

"God, you're so young," he says.

It sends a shiver that starts in my pelvis and radiates outward to the very edges of my body. I imagine myself as he must see me, the tightness of my body, the smoothness of my flesh, the lack of complication compared to the women his own age. It bolsters me slightly, this sense that I'm something precious and new, that I don't have to be anything other than young. I don't need to worry that I'm not interesting or confident or sexy—the very quality of my age is enough. My legs are clamped tight with nerves, but he kisses all the way up them, easing them open with one hand as he slips the other beneath my hips.

"Relax," he says. "Just let yourself go."

I shift slightly to slow the strokes, edging his hand farther back down my body. I want him, but I want this more. To stay in this exact moment, this cusp where desire radiates from him and I can feel how much he wants me. I want this in-between place where everything is possibility and longing. I notice that I am already wet, my body responding more quickly than my brain. He makes me feel helpless like that, as if I am out of control. The power that he has over me both excites and terrifies me, as though I can't trust myself to know what I will do with him.

The act itself is more bodily, more real. His eyes fog over and his desire transforms into the logistics of completion and the mechanics of intercourse. Afterward, he sprawls out on the bed, his breath slowing, his eyes closed. When he opens them, he is looking at me as though I am an entirely new person now, his eyes tender and still half glazed over.

"Hey, you," he says.

"Hi."

He leans across to kiss me on the temple.

"I'm just going to jump in the shower," he says. "Make yourself at home."

I wrap myself in a thick white dressing gown and pad downstairs, my footsteps disturbing the vast silence of the house. I pour myself a glass of water and sit on Henry Taylor's sofa. I imagine that Alistair and I live here. I see us having friends over and drinking champagne at the sweeping kitchen island. I imagine Caroline coming to stay, wide-eyed and impressed. I imagine my parents visiting and then shake off the idea. The thought of them, socially awkward and with my dad out of his depth without being able to discuss which motorway they took to get there, makes me cringe.

I go to another of the marble-tiled bathrooms and splash my face with cold water. When I look back at myself, I'm surprised to see how small I look. There's still a stain of scarlet smeared at the corner of my mouth, shadows of mascara smudged from screwing my eyes tight shut. I look even younger than I am, a girl who will be back at school in a few weeks. A child playing dress-up with her mother's makeup. I take a wad of tissue paper and scrub every trace away until I am bare-faced, my skin pink and new.

When I emerge, he's already in the living room, a towel wrapped around his waist, topping up the glasses we discarded earlier.

"That's better," he says when he sees my makeup-free face.

He passes me my wine. It tastes too dry and heavy for me, but I take a sip anyway.

"So." He perches on the back of the sofa, and it strikes me how at ease he is everywhere he goes. "I saw Helena earlier on today."

I wait for him to continue, his statement seeming to hover between us.

"She told me that you're leaving," he says. "Tomorrow."

I feel my skin flush.

"She said that?"

Somehow I can't quite imagine Alistair and Helena talking about me when I'm not there. I think of Helena's easy confidence and immediately feel young and stupid. I wonder what they say about me, whether Alistair has noticed how much prettier Helena is than me, how self-assured.

"You are, then?" he persists.

"I . . ."

It's as if I've managed to separate Alistair and my plans to leave in my imagination. Out here everything is still fantasy and illusion, a few magical snatched weeks a million miles away from my life back home. The fact that I will have to go back to my parents' house has sat like a weight at the end of my time here, an ugly and inevitable drawing back toward myself. But then I remember how Alistair looked at me earlier and I wonder if perhaps I am more myself out here. If the version of Rachel who can entice older men and make friends easily might actually be the real me.

"You should stay," he is saying before I can speak. He says it so easily, as if the idea has only just occurred to him.

"I can't," I say, my voice reluctant. "I have to go back. Caroline will hate me if I stay."

"Caroline? Your friend with the blond hair?" He looks at me as if he can't believe what I'm saying. "You know that she'd do the same, don't you? That she'd drop you in a second if she'd met someone out here. If someone asked her to stay?"

"I don't know . . ."

"Don't worry about Caroline." He takes a swig of his drink, businesslike in spite of his bare chest. "The other girls like having you around. *I* like having you around. You can work at the bar. Move into the house down in the town."

He reaches out and takes my hand, and I can feel myself relenting.

"Caroline holds you back, Rachel," he says. "Everyone does. They don't see you like I do. They don't know your potential. Remember what you told me when we first met? About how out of place you felt?"

He leans his face so close to mine that I can smell myself on his skin.

"You're not out of place here, Rachel," he says, his voice wheedling and low. "You're exactly where you need to be."

NOW

On the tube I paint on lipstick, a peachy, velvety shade that I immediately worry makes my lips look thin. I hadn't dared to put it on in the house, nervous that Tom might glance up with a frown and ask me who I'm dressing up for. I'm being paranoid, of course. As I pecked him on the cheek, he just smiled and told me I looked nice. If he noticed my most expensive perfume, spritzed liberally on my collarbones and dampening the insides of my wrists, he didn't say anything. He didn't comment on the outfit I had agonized over, eventually settling for skinny jeans and a camisole top. Nice enough to make me feel attractive, casual enough to suggest I haven't spent the last decade and a half imagining this meeting.

"Say hi to Jules from me," Tom said mildly, picking up the remote and flicking through television talent contests and Saturday night game shows.

His leg was propped up, a stool I'd fussed over getting at just the right angle beneath it. I'd lined up beers next to him and laid out a sheaf of takeaway menus within arm's reach. After a week of being dimly irritated by his slow hobbles around the house, of fetching him glasses of water to swill down his painkillers and feigning patience as I hovered below his slow crawl up the stairs, my lies seemed to have sparked a guilty kind of tenderness. I paused at the door to the living room, looking back at my husband. Isn't this what everyone wants, someone reliable and kind to come home to? When I return later on this evening, everything will be different, but he'll still be there, his empty beer bottles deposited into the recycling bin and the takeaway menus tidied away.

"Sure I can't get you anything before I go?"

He had looked somehow frail sitting on our vast sofa, his leg subsumed by the largeness of his cast.

"I'm all right, thanks." He placed down the remote, having settled for some eighties action film being repeated on a backwater channel. He'd never ask me to watch something like that usually, knowing how much I'd hate it. He always lets me choose what we watch. "You just have a good time."

Sitting on the tube with the world rattling around me, the thought of having a good time seems absurd. This isn't supposed to be merely enjoyable. It isn't the Saturday night out with Jules that Tom imagines. This is supposed to be world-altering, life-changing. I've always quite liked the idea of fate, the thought of a roster of gods making choices that are entirely out of our control, sending our stories spinning in unexpected directions at an imbalance of their whims. I imagine that the carriage thundering beneath the city, carrying me toward Alistair, is somehow supposed to be there. That this journey was mapped out long before I tracked down his number or decided to send that text. It's a vaguely comforting concept, and I can see why ancient people went in for Zeus and Aphrodite so much.

I drop my lipstick back into my purse and glance up at the map above me, counting out the stations left to go. He chose the location, somewhere in central London two changes away from me. As we draw nearer, the names of familiar stops marking out my proximity to him, I start to feel like I'm seventeen again, that same heady mixture of nerves and excitement vibrating somewhere deep inside me.

By the time I arrive, my nerves have transformed into a raging, writhing thing in my stomach. After my first message I had asked him to meet for a drink. It had taken him over a week to respond, an agonizing and terrible ten days before a message materialized reeking of a confidence that felt familiar and new at the same time.

How about dinner?

The restaurant he chose shrieks of a similar assurance. He hasn't tried to select anywhere trendy or self-consciously cool. It's the kind of establishment that must have been here for years, embedded into the city like it belongs. Where business deals might be struck, or men who know about wine might take their wives for their anniversary. *Where men might meet their mistresses,* I think, without meaning to. The interior is sleek and understated, booths tucked into tiled walls and waitresses gliding between tables holding gilt trays of oversized glasses.

"I'm meeting someone," I say to the maître d'.

He's young and attractive and I wait for him to appraise me, for his eyes to slide along the lines of my body in the way women become accustomed to from near childhood. Instead he fixes his eyes firmly down on the opened-up book before him, reservations listed in thick black ink. It's the kind of place that would never replace a decades-old system with an iPad.

"Name?"

"It would be . . ." I hesitate. "Wright? Alistair Wright?"

He nods, looking uninterested. Saying Alistair's name out loud feels like such a monumental thing that I almost expected a reaction, yet to him it's just any name, any person.

"Please," he says. "Follow me."

I give him one last chance to take a look at me and feel myself deflate slightly when he doesn't, simply extending one arm and waiting for me to follow. It's been a tense dissonance of aging to feel those sidelong looks disappear, to notice that you no longer catch the eye of strangers in the same way. It always used to make me feel uncomfortable, the unabashed weighing up of my physicality in my teens and twenties, the positioning of my body as something to provide gratification, if only for a few moments. I didn't think I would miss it when it became less frequent. I assumed it was an integral part of womanhood, and yet it had petered out much sooner than I had expected. I sometimes wondered, with a faint horror, whether it wasn't simply my appearance that drew men's eyes but the unrelenting appeal of extreme youth. If my body had been at its most vibrant when it had been skinny and barely formed. If the contours of adulthood had sapped something away from it.

I see him before he sees me. He's at the most tucked-away table, angled from the entrance so that we have to take an elaborate route around other diners to reach him. I know him at once just from how he sits, his legs spread out and one arm propped up on his thigh as he browses the menu. He would always command space without asking for it, an easy acceptance that the world would accommodate him. It was exactly why he could always fit in anywhere, whether it was at a ramshackle bar fifty feet from a beach or in the kind of restaurant where waiters set ice buckets on stands alongside the table.

He wears a white shirt still, the neck more open than is strictly fashionable these days. I notice with a glimmer of longing that his chest hair is dark and visible at the deep V of his collar, and I remember the length of his body above me brown with the sun. The waiter is still nearing him with a harried pace, and I have to keep up even when the world is slowing around me, even when every part of me is screaming to stop. To turn around before he even looks up. To scurry back home, all two changes and countless stops on the tube, only to curl up next to Tom on the sofa just like any other Saturday night. I could tell him that Jules canceled last minute. That she had a headache. That I have a headache, and he will make a fuss of me and limp to the kitchen to fish paracetamol out of the medicine box and make me a cup of tea. Yet the waiter strides over as though he isn't leading me into the biggest decision of my life, and I have to follow him.

He looks up right at the last minute, just as the maître d' pulls out my chair for me, his face expectant. His eyes are still so green, still so similar to how I remember, that something catches in my throat, some irrepressible drawing of breath out of my body. And then, of course, I notice that they're not the same at all. That they droop slightly at the edges. That a certain slackening of his eyelids has re-shaped them. That there are the whispers of lines at the corners of them, faint patterns of age that coil out toward his temples. That his dark hair has lightened and started to gray at the roots. That his jaw is less square, his shoulders slightly rounded. The chest hair that just a moment ago sent a pulse of desire through me looks absurd all of a sudden, wispy and overexposed.

I lower myself into the proffered seat and blearily accept the waiter's offer of water, my eyes never leaving Alistair's. It strikes me that the last time I looked at him like this I was still eighteen. I was kissing the lines of his jaw and holding him close, two bodies tense with fear. I was hopeful and foolish, imagining that the next time I saw him would be the start of everything. I couldn't possibly have dreamed how different we would both be. The things that would happen to us between now and then. On the table between us is a single white rose encased in a slim glass vase. I can't stand roses, the sickly sweet scent of them, their delicate perfection. The smell makes me shudder, although Alistair doesn't seem to notice.

"I bought champagne," he says, gesturing to the ice bucket be-side us.

The waiter goes to serve me and Alistair waves him away. Alistair's glass is already full and an empty flute is waiting on the table before me. He brandishes the bottle and I obediently hold out my glass. The bubbles writhe and seethe, almost spilling over the edge as he pours too generously. I have to lift it to my mouth to take a sip before it overflows. I glance up over the rim of my glass, half embarrassed, waiting to see if he's watching me with a familiar amusement and tenderness, but he's already looking away, putting the bottle back down. The way he used to want me was so indescribable, so vast and unrelenting, that I had assumed it would transcend decades and distance. Yet here we are, sitting opposite each other, his eyes looking toward his menu as though I were just anybody. I'm suddenly conscious of the swell of my stomach tight against my jeans and my hair tied up into a sensible ponytail. The champagne tastes acidic against my tongue, and I swallow before it goes flat in my mouth.

"The steak's good here," he says, and I nod, at a loss for what to say.

Around us the restaurant rattles, the sound of plates being set down on tables and the muted chimes of a piano playing somewhere out of sight. It would be an exaggeration to say I've imagined this moment every day, and yet he has somehow slipped around the edges of my life, the thought of him coming to me often and at the most important moments. When I arrived back in England. When my parents divorced. When I stood in a sunlit room in a white dress waiting to marry Tom. I imagined Alistair reaching across some table somewhere indistinct, taking my hands as I told him everything. How he changed me. What I went through after he left. The things I did for him. The lies I told. He might be angry at first, but then he'd stroke the side of my hand the way he used to. *It's OK*, he'd say. *What else could you have done?*

"So." He sets down his menu at last. "I wasn't expecting to hear from you. It's been a long time."

I take another sip of champagne to delay my response. My heart is thundering so hard I don't quite trust myself to speak.

"I know," I say at last. "I wasn't really expecting it either."

He nods. His hands are toying with the corner of the menu, folding and unfolding the creamy card. A single petal sheds from the rose between us, unceremoniously settling on the table. Alistair swipes it away immediately.

"You went back?"

"Yes. For a holiday."

The words sound weak coming from me, a desperate woman wanting to rekindle a teenage crush. I meet his eye and I long for him to see me. *This isn't me*, I want to tell him. *I'm still the same girl I was back then.* The waiter comes back to take our order and Alistair speaks for us both without asking. Two steaks, his bloody.

"You still like steak, right?" he asks me after the waiter has left.

If it was anyone else, I would have hated the presumption, but then he is smiling at me in a certain lopsided way that suggests he's done it on purpose: a reconciliatory gesture; a sign that he remembers, even now, even after all this time. He isn't overlooking my preferences but recalling them, reminding me of how well he knows me via the elaborate medium of food orders and faintly woven memories. He's remembering the same night I am, the time he took me to a restaurant up in the hills and ordered me steak and champagne because I'd never had either before. The bubbles made me light-headed and the steak was tender and beautiful all at once, a sensation so perfect and consuming that it was like a first kiss. He laughed when I took a mouthful, wide-eyed with delight. I find myself smiling back at him, a moment of joint history that we both still recognize. There's an intimacy in shared memories that I've missed. I study his face again and he isn't so different. Of course, he's older. But he's still attractive. He still has that same look about him that probably makes women go crazy. I still find myself tucking a loose strand of hair behind my ear and touching my fingertips to my lips, self-conscious beneath his gaze.

"You look good," he says, reading my movement immediately. He always used to tell me that he knew me better than I knew myself.

"Thanks," I say. "I must look different to how you remember."

He shrugs. "Different isn't a bad thing."

We meander around tentative topics after that. He asks about how the island has changed, and I ask him why Henry ended up selling the bar. He just throws back the dregs of his drink, the same easy decadence that used to seem daring and new.

"Henry died years ago," he says.

"I'm sorry," I say, even though I'm not sure whether it's the right response.

Alistair waves my comment away and asks me what I do for work now. I tell him about the museum. Our steaks arrive before I can ask him the same question and mine is pinker than I would have liked, rust-red juices weeping into my asparagus and forming bloody pools at the edge of my plate. He slices straight into his, prodding the undercooked meat appreciatively with his knife.

"And what about life outside work?" he asks. "Married? Kids?"

"Married. What about you?"

He shakes his head, spearing a potato.

"Never felt like the right time, you know?" He shovels the food into his mouth and chews slowly, swallowing with exaggeration. "So, what does your husband think? Of us meeting up like this?"

I place my fork down and take another gulp of champagne. He's seamless when it comes to refilling my glass, topping it up every time I set it down. He gestures for another bottle, and I hope he'll be paying for dinner. My salary barely covers my half of the mortgage, and Tom's scrupulous with checking our joint account. Not that he suspects anything. Tom's trust in me has always been unwavering. He's simply one of those people who likes order, who got excited at the introduction of banking apps and sets saving goals.

"He doesn't know," I find myself saying, even though I know at once what Alistair will think.

I'm surprised when he doesn't ask me why. He simply raises his glass, that same half smile playing at the corners of his mouth. There's something familiar about it, some almost imperceptible sense of déjà vu that makes me want him all over again.

"To secrets," he says, and I find myself clinking my glass against his and smiling back.

THEN

The day after I first sleep with Alistair, there is a storm.

Most days, when the island prickles with heat, it is impossible to imagine rain. The thought that the bright blue skies might coil and curdle into cloud feels absurd, the idea of thunder like a whisper of a distant myth. Yet on the day when my holiday should end, the heat wave temporarily breaks. The air becomes dense and sultry, the humidity so heavy that my skin feels damp when Alistair drops me off outside my hostel. The clouds haven't given way yet, but they teeter above me, a great blank slate as the world cowers a putrid and violent yellow below. In a place where nobody ever seems to be in a rush, people hurry past, their necks craned as their eyes twitch skyward, eager to beat the deluge.

"So you'll tell her?" Alistair says. "Right away?"

I nod and he looks pleased with me.

"I'll meet you at the bar later," he says. "Bring your bags."

When I get to the room, Caroline is already dressed in a cotton sundress and an oversized straw hat, her backpack propped ready beside the door. She snorts in disbelief when she sees me, still in my clothes from last night.

"I knew you were going to see him," she says. "Come on, we need to get going soon."

She turns to haul her backpack on, not offering to help me gather the clothes still strewn out on my bed. I stay still as she fusses, adjusting her straps, still not facing me. When she spins around and sees me motionless, her face drops. We've known each other for so long that I don't need to say anything. My lack of words is enough.

"You're staying, then."

"Alistair's sorting me a job at the bar."

Her lips purse. "But what about school?"

"I'll go back next year." I bend down to scoop a handful of clothes into my backpack, unable to look at her for any longer, desperate for something to do with my hands. "People take gap years all the time. I'm just doing mine a year early. It's not a big deal."

"Are you insane?" Her voice is high-pitched and I can tell she's trying to fight back tears. "Your mum will go crazy. *My* mum will kill me, leaving you out here."

"So?" I say. "I'm eighteen in a couple of weeks. Legally an adult. There's nothing they can do."

It's not like me to stand up to Caroline, but I'm emboldened by Alistair's belief in me. Maybe Caroline does hold me back. Maybe this is who I am when I don't have her weighing me down. When somebody actually sees my potential.

"Are you kidding?" She lifts one hand to scrub a furious tear threatening to spill. "Staying here just because some guy's shown a bit of interest in you? I mean, seriously, Rachel. And don't tell me there's nothing going on, I'm not an idiot."

She shakes her head.

"You have no idea about men, Rachel. No idea. You never have. He'll drop you, sooner or later. What do you think some old guy like him wants with someone like you? We're kids to him."

My chest tightens and I fasten the buckle on my backpack.

"You don't know him," I say. "You're just jealous. You hate that someone wants me and not you."

"Fine," she says. "Stay here. Just don't come crying to me when it all goes wrong."

"What could possibly go wrong?" I say.

But she's already gone, the door slammed behind her, and I'm left in our crumbling room alone. As her footsteps reverberate on the corridor outside, I reach down to pull my backpack on, ready to make my way back to him.

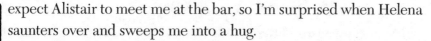

I expect Alistair to meet me at the bar, so I'm surprised when Helena saunters over and sweeps me into a hug.

"You're staying!" she says. "I'm so glad."

She takes me to the house Henry Taylor owns, just a few streets from the bar. She tells me he had bought it with plans to renovate, to tear out sloping stairwells and stacked-up rooms and turn them into something new. Instead the bar has bled down the street and filled it with life. Helena, Kiera, and Priya are already settled alongside eight other girls, backpackers and young women with thick accents who descend on the island for a summer season of work and then drift away with the heat when winter comes. The front door swings open before we can even reach it and Priya is grinning out at us, her lips painted bright red even though she is still dressed in pajama shorts.

"You made it!" she exclaims. "I thought I was going to miss you. Me and Kiera are on shift in . . ." She glances at her wrist and then starts. "Shit. Ten minutes. I gotta get going."

She kisses me exaggeratedly on each cheek as I descend to her level, and I feel the imprint of her lips sticky against my skin.

"See you both later though?"

Helena guides me past her and into the kitchen. It's early evening, the one small window casting the room over with the amber glow of dusk, a promise of the night ahead. Three girls are perched around the kitchen table, a folded-up flyer wedged beneath one of the legs to stop it from wobbling. They are clearly at vastly different stages of their day, one wearing an oversized T-shirt as a nightie with her hair escaping from a bun on top of her head while the others are dressed to go out, a cheap bottle of wine on the table between them.

"Are you sharing, then?" Helena tugs open a cupboard and passes a glass to me.

It's a chipped tumbler, not right for drinking out of, but one of the girls shrugs and sloshes out a generous measure. It tastes sweet and cheap, yellow in color and slightly warm in temperature.

"Work or play?" Helena asks.

"As if there's any difference with you girls." The woman who is dressed for bed clambers to her feet and gestures for Helena to take her seat.

She speaks with a European accent I can't place, her vowels thick and rounded. She looks older than us, although her striking face makes it difficult to guess her age—she's all cheekbones and a square-set jaw. She sighs and drains the glass of water in front of her. "Sit, sit. It's fine. I need to get ready, anyhow."

"You're an angel," says Helena, sweeping in to take her spot. "Thanks, Agnes."

Agnes doesn't respond, but as she leaves, I catch her glancing back at me, her eyes slightly narrowed. I feel the intensity of her gaze even as she turns to go, catching the door against her hip to swing it shut.

"She comes back every year, apparently," Helena hisses as soon as she is out of earshot. "She's a right moody cow though. Can't be bothered with us lot."

"Every year?"

The idea of the island existing beyond this year feels almost un-imaginable. It hardly occurred to me that for some people it could be a place they returned to, as rhythmically as the tide.

"Yeah. Her and Henry have a history, apparently. They've been working together for years. Don't worry about Agnes though. She's fine, as long as you don't bother her much. Now, wait until you meet the others . . ."

In another place the house might have seemed decrepit, with its chipped paint and doors that don't sit right in their frames, yet the occupants fill the rooms with life. Throws decorate the walls, and a hum of noise filters through the house. A constant rotation of women swing in and out of the kitchen, complaining that their shift is due to start or asking who borrowed their hairbrush. Girls hitch themselves up on countertops or perch on the floor with their legs stretched out on the linoleum.

Helena introduces me to a parade of names and faces, hurried explanations of gap years and working summers. I try to remember as many as I can. Eloise, a girl with a crisp London accent and long hair so blond it is almost white. Amy, who drags me into an overexuberant hug when Helena tells her that I'm staying, as though we've known each other all our lives. I get lost after that, syllables and excited introductions blurring together.

"So, what do you think?" Helena asks me once the room begins to empty out. "There's a room free—you could move in straightaway?"

I call my parents that night to tell them about my plans to stay, their protestations coming out broken and distant.

"I'm just doing another couple of weeks," I lie, the line crackly. "I'm only missing the first week of school. Honestly, I'm fine."

I hang up with my mum still asking questions—where I'm going to stay and what I'll do for money. It is the first time I have lied to her, but as the dial tone hums, I feel a certainty that I have done the right thing. In just two weeks I will turn eighteen, and everything will be out of her control. While my parents hunch over their staid suppers every evening, packet-mixed puddings followed by the *News at Ten*, I will be on the other side of an ocean. I will stay in bed until noon and spend the long hot days lying on the beach with friends. I will be with Alistair, sleeping beneath crisp white sheets and waking up with his hand heavy on my waist.

＊

My absorption into the group of girls who live in my new home is easy. Our days wind around each other intricately and intimately. We take the shots that people buy for us, dance in the stock room together when a good song comes on, slack off from scrubbing tables to lie out on the terrace and smoke. There's always somebody awake in the kitchen and ready to pour you another drink, to stock up on bread and milk and swap shifts with. We bring other eager travelers back to the house for late-night parties after closing time and show off our home as though it were the Elysian fields. We feel disproportionately proud when they ask:

"So you *live* here? On the island?"

And we nod and show them there's a way up onto the roof, as long as you don't mind shimmying out of Kiera's window and grasping onto the ledge above. As long as you can haul yourself up to chest height until you are high enough to sit and see the sea, broad and perfect as it stretches away from you and blurs into the sky. We spend hours up there after our shifts, the night air cooling our skin and seeping the alcohol out of our systems. Sometimes we doze off, the flat roof hard against the length of our spines, and wake up with the sky turning golden above us. We open our eyes to the heavens, tempering pink at their edges and turning stars into faint sketches of themselves against the dawn light. When the sounds of the morning stir us, the occasional car rolling sleepily on a street below or shop shutters sliding open with a clatter, we roll onto our sides and pull ourselves upward, rising to meet the day. We clamber downstairs more slowly than we came, our bodies heavy with sleep, and crawl back into the closest bed we can find. We don't always sleep in our own rooms—somebody usually has someone back, or has fallen asleep in the wrong place. Instead we slot into empty sheets like an elaborate jigsaw puzzle, sometimes curling two bodies into one narrow bed. We drift away like that with our arms and legs wrapped around each other, and when we wake up, we do it all again.

I feel as though I have somehow transcended my parents' expectations and been thrown into an entirely different orbit to the one that was planned for me: Finish my A levels. Go to university. Move to a city and get a job. Meet a nice young man with a safe and stable job and wear white on my wedding day. A mortgage and two children. Instead I fall into the rhythms of island life, the ever-changing circle of a new set of friends, the possibility of adventure always temptingly within reach.

And then there is Alistair. He sometimes shows up during my shift at the bar, some unspecified business calling him in as I spill drinks and get nervous about whether he's watching. Occasionally he comes and talks to me, his voice low against the music until the other girls yell at me that there's a wait and I should start serving.

When I'm not working, the need for secrecy makes him more sporadic. He sometimes visits the house, to drop off money or to ask somebody to do some errand up at Henry Taylor's villa or an extra shift at the bar. He doesn't come to my room and I don't ask him to. If we cross paths in the kitchen, he'll say hi, my name falling from his mouth as if it belongs to anybody. It's only when we're alone that he says it like it is dripping with liquid gold, his mouth tracing the lines of each syllable. It makes me hungry for the attention, desperate for the next time we're alone together. It makes me want him in unspeakable ways, a force that tears through me from deep in the pit of my stomach.

He always seems to have some job Henry wants him to do— somebody he needs to call to discuss unspecified business, a flight he has to book, stock he has to order for the bar. We only meet in secret at Henry's vast villa. With the owner away, we drink ice-cold wine with our feet dangling in the pool and have sex in showers tiled with marble. When he touches me, I think back to all the times Caroline and I would loiter at the edge of some sixth-former's football game, hoping to catch his attention as he shot dismissive glances our way. I think of all the times I cadged a cigarette off one of the boys at the park, holding smoke in my mouth before I spotted him snatching sidelong stares at Caroline as she inhaled properly and threw back her long hair so that it fell over her shoulders just right. Then I look at Alistair and I see someone who wants me and only me, who wants to lock the door to the rest of the world so that we can lie down with one body alongside the next and consume each other.

✳

One morning, after Alistair drops me off at the house, I find that I don't want to sleep. After I've spent the night with him, I always feel vibrant and alive, my mind spinning, my body bruised by his touch. I turn away from the apartment block and walk in the direction of the sea as if my body is a compass that swings me toward it. The early-morning light slicks the streets with a shade of bronze and the crisp promise of another day. At the harborside, fishing boats are beginning to leave for sea, small painted platoons bobbing in the waves. There is a slow bustle of activity, nets being sorted and café owners setting up tables overlooking the ocean. This time of day is for the island's residents, the people who were born here and will die here with the sea air in their lungs. They prepare for the day while tourists sleep in their beds. We will all leave eventually and they will stay, watching us come and go as surely as the pull and flow of the tides.

The sea is drawing out now. Salty lines etch along the beach to show its steady progress. I find a place to perch, the sand still wet beneath me, and just for a moment I am still. It's strange how infrequently we allow ourselves to stop. Most of the time it's only then that I feel how dynamic the world around me really is, the constant movement of the sea and the sun, the shifting of the sand, the gentle hustle of people going about their day. It makes me feel very small.

A woman approaches from along the shore, silhouetted against the half-light of dawn. Meters away from me, her face breaks into a grin and she raises an arm to wave.

"It's you!" she says.

It takes me a moment to place her. Her long hair is caught in a lopsided bun that balances precariously atop her head, and her face is streaked with the remains of what must be last night's makeup, thick smudges of mascara around her eyes. She cocks her head to one side.

"The girl from the boat?"

That's when I remember her. The girl who pulled me up from the floor of the boat on my very first day here. My eyes dart to her ear, and I see the same row of piercings glinting in the sunrise, the same braid tangled in her hair.

"Oh, yeah! Yes, it's me. Hey." I hurry to stand up, brushing sand from the palms of my hands.

She turns her face toward the sun and squints out to sea.

"Isn't it the best at this time of day?" she says. "It makes you feel like anything could happen."

I follow her eyeline to where the sun catches against the horizon, scattering light like gold dust on the vast expanse of silvery sea.

"It is," I say. "It really is."

"So." She turns back to me, the corners of her mouth upturned. "Looks like you were out late last night as well then?"

"Something like that."

"I met this guy." She mocks fanning herself with her hand. "The stamina. Seriously. I'm knackered."

I laugh. "So what are you still doing out here?"

"Me? I'm actually working out here for a few months. Teaching some kid English whose parents holiday out here. Seriously, easiest money I've ever made. And their *house*." She shakes her head. "I mean, these people are rolling in it. I'm meant to be there in a few hours actually. I know, I know."

She glances at her watch.

"I should make a move. It was good bumping into you though . . ."

"Rachel."

"Rachel. Nice to meet you again."

She turns to walk away, back toward the cluster of the town. The peace of the moment feels broken, and I roll my shoulders to shake off the night, ready to go home.

"Hey, Rachel." The girl turns back toward me. Her voice drifts slightly in the breeze, my name sounding as though the wind could wash it away. "Have you eaten yet?"

I shake my head. "Not yet, no."

She smiles, and looks mischievous and kind at the same time.

"Breakfast?"

※

We go back to the apartment she is staying in. It's on the ground floor of a house close to the beach, an ashtray and a set of empty glasses perched on steps up to the front door. There's a young man in the kitchen, bare-chested and bashful when we enter to catch him drinking milk straight out of the carton.

"Animal!" the girl declares. "Rachel, this is my flatmate Jack. Jack, Rachel."

We smile shyly at each other, and he asks if I want coffee. I never used to drink coffee before I came out here, but Alistair makes sweet, dark cups every morning and I have become used to the taste. It makes me feel grown-up to sit and sip from pristine white mugs as the light filters gently into the house.

"Yes, please," I say.

Jack sets a pan on a dilapidated stove while the girl bustles about him, pulling bread from a cupboard and cheese from a fridge.

"Come on," she says. "We can sit outside."

She drags a kitchen chair out and uses its seat as a makeshift table. She loads it up with bread and cheese and tomatoes, a butter knife that is slightly dirty. We perch on the white stone steps, and she stretches her legs out and turns her body toward the sun.

"Dig in," she says, making no move to do so herself.

Our slapdash setup directly faces a small street leading straight down to the sea, and so our view is unbroken, a cluster of houses forming a frame. I tear off a piece of bread, unsure of what else to say.

"You're staying here awhile as well then, are you?" she says.

"I think so."

"You know, you didn't strike me as the type." She shoots me a short sideways glance. "On the boat. I thought you and your friend were just here on holiday."

"We were," I say. "She's gone now. I just got some work out here and decided to stay a bit longer."

She nods. "It's beautiful, isn't it? Something about it pulls you in. I don't know how I'll ever leave."

Just then Jack comes outside, nudging the door open with his hip and clutching a tray of mugs. We take one each from him and he sets his own on the floor. He sits down beside it and leans his long back against the wall of the house. I take a sip of the coffee and am surprised to find that it's strong and good.

"So where are you working?" she asks.

"Just at a bar, back in the town."

"Oh?"

"You'll probably know it," I say with a pulse of importance. "Henry Taylor's place?"

There's a beat of silence so small you could almost miss it. Perhaps I would have if I didn't catch a tiny dart of movement. Jack's head glancing down reflexively, the girl's eyes flitting up to exchange an almost imperceptible look of recognition.

"Oh yeah?" Jack says, his voice level. "Cool place."

"Have you been?"

The girl screws her nose up.

"Not really," she says. "We don't go out that much."

After that there's a shift in the atmosphere. Jack makes noises about having to get in the shower and disappears inside, and the girl drains her coffee and says she should probably get ready for work. I clamber to my feet, dusting bread crumbs from my thighs.

"Well, thanks," I say, thrown by her sudden coolness. "For the food. And the coffee."

"No problem," she says, already bent over and clearing away the uneaten meal.

When she straightens, we are eye to eye. I hold out my coffee cup, and she hooks it beneath one arm to hold, her hands already full of almost untouched food.

"I'll see you around then," she says.

I nod.

"And hey—Rachel?"

"Yes?"

"Be careful of that place. Henry Taylor's place. A lot of us try not to go there. The locals say it's bad news."

In the distance a wave crashes onto the shore, a creaking, sweeping noise that soundtracks every interaction out here.

"What do you mean?"

"Just—" She backs toward the doorway. "Just be careful. And hey, if you ever need somewhere to get away from it all, even just for a bit. Well, Jack and I are here. You can always come and hang out."

"Thanks," I say. "But people must be getting it mixed up. Seriously. I really like it there."

She shrugs. "Well," she says. "The offer stands."

She's halfway inside the house, edging the door shut with her foot, when I realize that I don't even know who she is.

"Hey," I say. "I never asked. What's your name?"

She pauses, and her eyes glint again in the same inviting way they did back at the beach.

"Oh yes," she says. "Can't believe I didn't say. My name's Jules."

NOW

When I have sex with Alistair, it is not how I remember it.
There used to be a sheen to my experience, a gloss of naivete and the compelling promise of adulthood. Our bodies were different, both taut and ribbed with desire. Our actions were weighted with possibility, each touch a whisper of something more to come. I so badly want it to be the same. I want to close my eyes and be eighteen again. I want it to be perfect. I want the last sixteen years to disappear when he kisses me, for the rest of my life to become dim and indistinct, pressed to the corners of my consciousness by his hands on my hips, my thighs lifting up to meet his.

We go back to his flat in a taxi, perching at opposite ends of leather seats. The driver asks where we're going and Alistair tells him an address. After that we sit in silence. The heat of the restaurant seems to have stretched out to an unexpected flatness, a loss of words as we loop past late-night kebab shops and Tesco Metros. I must have taken hundreds of taxi journeys across this city over the years, crawling home after parties and Tom's work events and anniversary dinners. I often get sleepy and curl into Tom in the backseat, my body heavy as his stays upright, his hand absentmindedly stroking my shoulder. There's a tension between Alistair and me, an uncertainty about whether we should be here. After all those years of wanting him, I wish I could slow the speed of the car, to stay suspended in this moment of possibility when I am both a faithful wife and a woman who goes back to other men's homes late on a Saturday night. Then I remind myself he isn't just another man. Not a stranger I've picked up at a bar, or found online for an illicit tryst. This is *Alistair.* My very bones seem to belong to him, and his body feels indistinguishable from my own in its familiarity. We were always supposed to be here. In fact, we should never have been apart. His hand is supine on the seat, and I reach out and touch him. He glances at me in surprise, but then he squeezes back.

He lives above a takeaway in some high street I've never heard of. I peer up as he pays the taxi driver, a neon sign illuminating bare brick and plastic-framed windows. It's so far away from the white walls of Henry Taylor's house that I'm only half convinced he's serious.

"This is your place?" I ask him.

"I know," he says. "It's temporary."

It's nicer than I expect it to be inside. It's clean at least, and surprisingly large. London can be deceptive like that, property prices driving people into high-rises and former storerooms. He goes to get me a beer, and I perch on the sofa surveying his space. I know I'll relive this night over and over, and I want to take everything in. I want to know him again by the rooms he lives in, the beer he chooses to drink, the smell of his sheets. I study the prints hanging on the walls and find them inoffensive, something chosen by a landlord who had no idea who would be staying here and for how long. A black-and-white London scene blotted by a bright red bus and a chirpy affirmation scrawled in an almost indecipherable script. There's nothing here that reveals the person he has become since we were last together, no books left on a side table half read or keepsakes from exotic trips displayed on the empty shelf above the dining table. The carpet is smattered with wires from an enormous television crammed directly opposite the sofa, and a console table by the door is strewn with un-opened post.

"Here you go." He holds out the beer toward me, the glass wet and slick.

He swigs his own standing in front of me, one hand dug into a pocket. His eyes never leave mine, even as he tilts his head back.

"You're still so beautiful," he says.

Then he is beside me, kissing me, the bottle cold in his hand as it presses into the back of my neck. I feel my body responding to him at once, my arms lifting up to wrap tightly around his neck, my hips rising to accommodate him on the small seat. The muscles along the length of his shoulders are still there, still tense beneath his shirt, still broad. He smells different, but only just. He used to smell slightly salty, as though the sea were in his skin. Now he smells of aftershave, the same one that used to sit in a bright blue bottle on his bedside table.

Wanting someone is a slippery and indefinable thing. With Tom it's about familiarity. It's about the comfortable feel of someone you know, the scent of their body in the bed beside you, the security of knowing how their muscles will respond to your touch. With Alistair it's about wanting something else entirely. As he pulls off my jeans, his lips trailing down the inside of my thigh, one hand deftly ca-ressing a sensitive spot at the back of my knee, I'm not quite sure if I want him or if I want to be the person he knew sixteen years ago. That summer. Those weeks when the world felt perfect. He tugs my top off over my head, and I lie back on the sofa with my eyes closed. Suddenly, I'm a thousand miles away more than a decade ago. He's in control and I can just let it all happen to me, let the entire thing wash over me like a wave breaking on the shore.

I'm not sure that sex is ever really just about sex. It always seems to be a thousand other indistinct things at once. The feeling of being desired. The longing for someone to see you, for your body to be something sacred and perfect, if only for a few moments. The hope that this is only the first time. The fear that it might be the last.

"Bedroom?" Alistair murmurs close to my ear, and I find myself nodding.

The room is dark and he flips on a lamp. It only half illuminates the space: an unmade double bed, a mismatched dining chair stacked with discarded shirts. I'm reminded, uncomfortably and briefly, of home, Tom waiting for me on an expensive sofa, the washing neatly tidied upstairs. I bat the thought away as Alistair fumbles in the drawer of a bedside table.

"It's OK," I say to him. "I'm on the pill."

He's the first person I have told. It feels odd to impart my secret so casually, to see him just nod and then lower himself down next to me, pulling my face close to his. If sex for me is about a thousand other things, then for Tom it has become about just one of them. It didn't used to be that way, but recently he has had a singular focus, one based on timings and anxieties. He's hopeful whenever my period is late, while I know every time we have sex that I am going to disappoint him. As I run my fingers through Alistair's hair, I feel myself relax into him, a pulse of yearning I had almost forgotten I could feel. He says my name and it makes me want him more: a reminder of my existence, a promise that I haven't become invisible.

Somehow, I have forgotten to ask why he left all those years ago. I thought tonight was about the past, about a time that would be impossible to recapture. Somebody who found it easy to abandon her life to embark on something new and strange and unexpected, who would stay out all night and not worry about telling anyone where she had been—I thought that person was somebody I had lost, a whole other being that had disappeared along with the hardness of my teenage body, the lengths of hair Alistair used to tangle his hands up in. But when he looks at me, the Rachel I thought I'd lost doesn't belong to the past at all. She's here in the room with us, touching him, wanting him. Wanting this moment to last forever. Suddenly, the reason Alistair left doesn't feel important anymore. For the first time in years, I am too consumed by the present to care.

Afterward I take a shower, careful not to use any of his body-washes, which claim to smell of bergamot and woodsmoke. It strikes me how easy it is to become a woman who lies to her husband, covering up her tracks by making sure her hair doesn't get wet and she doesn't come home with a different scent. Tom's five-a-side football games somehow don't seem quite so terrible anymore.

Alistair offers to call me a taxi, but I tell him I'll take the tube. I want the time alone, to walk down a street I don't know and calculate a route back to more familiar stretches of the city.

"I'll message you," he tells me at the door, and he kisses me so gently that he feels like a different person to the man who was bruising my lips with his mouth just half an hour ago.

It's before midnight, and the streets feel as though they are still warming up for Saturday night. Gaggles of girls in tight-fitting dresses screech and pose, their arms linked as they scurry for a bus, and a busker gamely strums a guitar outside an off-license, hoping for late-in-the-day tips. I pull my jacket more tightly around myself, trying to remember the last time I was out with friends this late. Jules is the only person I see regularly now and we squeeze our nights out around busy work schedules, pleading tiredness by ten o'clock and talking teasingly about the days when we'd be out until dawn crept up over the city.

Of course, we're romanticizing. It wasn't like that really. At least, not right away. I was a mess when I got back from Greece. At first I wouldn't go out at all, lying on my side in my childhood bedroom and feeling as though the world were ending. When I finally did move to London, the years of my life when I should have gone to university and made friends and had flings and indulged in all the other preoccupations that are supposed to consume our late teens and early twenties somehow having got lost, I was determined to make up for missed time. I moved into a run-down house-share and went out every night.

I brought home men whose names I didn't know and hated them for not being him. I was asked to move out after I came home too drunk to remember the pan of pasta I'd left boiling on the stove and started a fire in the kitchen.

My one saving grace was my job working in the museum café. I had been there for three years when I met Tom. On my lunch break I would see women I went to school with on Facebook, posting about moving in with friends and announcing promotions with brandished glasses of prosecco, and then I would go back to deep cleaning the coffee machine and updating the specials board. I would often go straight from work to house parties in the depths of London, where I only vaguely knew the host and sticky punch laced with rum was dished out in plastic cups. Someone would always suggest going out afterward, and I would close my eyes on the dance floor and feel the music pulsing through me and dream I was anywhere else but here.

I met Tom at one of those house parties. It was one of the rare occasions when Jules was back in London. Somebody she'd met in Australia had decamped to the city, inviting Jules to their new flat in a crumbling Victorian terrace. Jules had disappeared almost as soon as we arrived at the party, absorbed into excited circles of friends exclaiming about how good she looked, how tanned she had stayed while their skin turned pale from the English weather. I managed to find the alcohol supply and installed myself in the kitchen, leaning against the sideboard and sipping a vodka and Coke, not really caring whether anyone talked to me. Tom was the only person who did in the end, everyone else too wrapped up in their drinking games to take any notice. We left as the party was beginning to empty out without really defining where we would go, ambling around dimly lit streets convinced that a taxi would eventually roll into view. When my shoes started to hurt, we sat on the curb and talked. We were waiting for a taxi, but it almost felt as though we were waiting for morning, for the baby-blue glow of the sky that was beginning to unfurl from behind a cluttered skyline to intensify, and for the thrum of 5 a.m.

buses to begin their rounds. When a car eventually drew sleepily into sight, Tom flagged it down and told the driver his address. I liked the certainty of it, the fact that the decision was taken out of my hands.

He's still up when I get home, the living room illuminated by the cyber-blue glow of the television screen, a half-finished beer in his hand. He reaches for the remote when he hears the click of the front door.

"Good night?"

"Fine."

"Jules OK?"

"She's good," I say. "I'm just going to go and jump in the shower."

"Sure. I'm coming up to bed when I've finished this." He pauses to look at me, and as he does, his eyes narrow. "You OK, babe? You seem a bit . . ."

He shrugs, half searching for the right word and half relying on the elaborate language of married couples, the unfinished sentences and the fact that I know what he means before he says it most of the time. It's an intricate rhythm between us, entire conversations that can be construed from exchanged glances, jokes that we make by meeting each other's eye across the table at a dinner party. I feel a short tug of guilt.

"I'm just tired," I say.

He seems to consider me for a moment, his eyes lingering instead of turning back to the television. It occurs to me then how terrible I am at being loved. I never did quite seem to get the knack of it.

"You go get some sleep then," he says. "I'll be quiet when I come up."

I shower again, this time in cold water, clenching my teeth against the chill. I feel as though my skin has been scarred by Alistair's touch, traces of him lingering in the curves of my hips and the crevices of my body. I've relived being with him so many times that it feels discordant to have a new memory to replace the hundreds of old ones. I place my hand on my stomach and remember how it felt that summer, as if all the possibilities in the world were inside me, secretive and vast.

I turn off the lights and lie on the bed still wrapped in a towel. Downstairs I hear Tom performing his usual nightly routine, checking that the back door is locked and switching the dishwasher on. It takes him longer than usual, his broken leg making him move about the house below me slowly. I listen to his progress with my head pressed into the pillow, hearing the familiar sounds and footsteps that make up our life together. I could fall asleep forever like this, the motions of our marriage playing out around me, predictable and safe. When he reaches our room, he shuffles to the bed without turning on the light and lowers himself down gently as I let my breathing become shallow. He's asleep before I am, and as he shifts beside me, I tell myself that the man I am meant to be with is already here. I will never see Alistair again.

THEN

When I've been working at the bar for a couple of weeks, Alistair invites me up to the house late. We drink an expensive bottle of wine sitting at a dining table designed for far too many people, the emptiness of the house feeling more pronounced with vacant chairs on either side of us.

"Henry's back on Friday," Alistair says.

"This week?"

He nods, and all at once I see the private enclave we have carved out for ourselves being taken away. The house I almost felt was ours filling up with people, and my fragile illusion of adulthood teetering and being trampled on by too many feet on the pristine stone floors.

"So you won't be able to see me for a bit?" I ask, my throat suddenly tight.

"What? No, what makes you think that?"

It's a genuine question, but it feels almost rhetorical. After all, Alistair makes the rules.

"I just thought . . ." I shrug. "You know. That you'd be busy."

"Well, yes." He lifts up the wine bottle, already half emptied. "But Henry enjoys having company. Actually, I was thinking maybe you should come over here. Bring a few of the other girls. Have some fun."

"But then won't they know about us?" I ask.

He reaches over to top up my wine, his arm brushing against mine. "They don't have to," he says. "Not if you don't tell them."

※

The next morning I watch him drive away, sick with the thought of inviting the others to Henry Taylor's house. I don't want to share Alistair with anyone. I want to be enough for him. The first time we slept together, he made me feel like my age was something special, but now I wonder if I've started to seem young and uninteresting to him, if he'd prefer Helena's loud confidence or Kiera's quiet beauty. If he'd like someone older, perhaps closer to Agnes's age.

But in the end, I can't say no to him. Priya is working, so I ask Kiera and Helena to come with me. Alistair sends a car to pick us up, and when we go outside, I am surprised to find Agnes already waiting. Her face is blank and bored-looking, and she just shrugs when Helena asks almost defensively how she managed to get an invite.

"Henry always invites me to these stupid parties," she drawls in her densely accented English.

We wait for the car in silence, Agnes's presence darkening the excitement that usually accompanies a visit to Henry Taylor's house. Of all the girls, she has been the most difficult to get to know. For the rest of us, intimacies spill out of sharing the same space, of borrowing hair straighteners and debating hangover cures. Agnes is different. She works longer shifts and stays in her room. She isn't a backpacker on a brief sojourn from her life, and has no immediate plans to leave. I once asked what brought her to the island, searching for conversation when we shared a quiet shift, and she told me that she can make better money out here than she can back home. Later on that night I found myself riffling bemusedly through my purse and counting out handfuls of change. Our pay never seems to go quite far enough to cover the drinks we're constantly buying on nights out, the way we often end up spending all the money we earn back at the bar. Agnes just shrugged and told me she makes good tips, and I resolved to flirt more, to wear my hair down like she does, to smile at the older customers, and to spill fewer drinks.

When we arrive at the party, the atmosphere is unstructured and relaxed. A handful of guests hover, holding drinks or clustered at the kitchen island. I notice that almost all of Henry's friends are men. They're much older than us, all at least in their forties. Alistair is making drinks at the counter, low tumblers filled with large ice cubes. Helena bowls straight up to him, the rest of us trailing in her wake.

"Make us one, will you?" she demands.

He looks up and smiles at her, hardly seeming to even notice me. I'm used to it by now, the nonchalant feigning of indifference in front of other people. It makes me ache for the next time we're alone together.

"Coming right up," he says. "You girls too?"

He's already taking glasses out and lining them up on the sideboard. He doesn't ask us what we want. He just sloshes a dark liquid into each tumbler without measuring it out.

"So." Helena throws hers straight back and leans against the counter. "Seems pretty chilled here tonight."

"Henry wanted a quiet one," Alistair says, holding out a glass to me. "Intimate."

He refills her drink straight from a cut-glass bottle, a larger measure this time. I'm struck by how at ease Helena seems.

"Intimate," she repeats. She takes a long slow swig, seeming to roll the liquid about in her mouth. "Sounds . . . interesting. So where is the famous Henry Taylor?"

Her eyes are scouring the room, and I find that I'm also itching to finally see the man whose house I have spent so much time in.

"He's about," Alistair says. "Probably upstairs. I'll introduce you when I next see him."

"You should," she says. "I can't wait to meet him."

My face feels hot and I take a sip of my drink to cool down. The liquid is sweet and sharp at the same time. It burns in my chest and makes me splutter. Alistair and Helena turn to look at me and the moment between them is broken.

"Baby's first whiskey?" Helena says, her voice silken, and she laughs as she reaches out to pat me on the back. "You'll get used to it."

"I don't blame you, I hate this stuff." Agnes grimaces as she sniffs her own drink. "I'm going to go say hi to people."

"Great, thanks, Agnes." Alistair sets the bottle back down on the counter. "I told you girls that you're working tonight, right?"

"Working?"

"I must have forgotten to mention. It's double pay though, don't worry."

"So like . . ." Kiera glances between Alistair and Helena in confusion. "Making drinks and stuff?"

"If people want them, yes. But more just making people feel comfortable. Milling about, chatting to the guests. That kind of thing." Alistair catches my eye. "Hey, don't worry. You can still have fun. Help yourself to drinks, have a nice time. These guys just like having nice-looking young girls around. You know what they're like. And we really want everyone to have a good night tonight. Henry has a lot of business interests here at the minute. We want to keep them happy, feeling relaxed. Are you girls OK with that?"

"Absolutely." Helena turns to scan the room. "Just tell me who to talk to first."

Alistair smiles and my insides turn. I clench my jaw and throw down my entire drink.

"Definitely," I say. "I'm definitely good with that."

※

The rest of the night seems to unfurl with a blurriness, lithe and indefinable. I initially feel awkward, tagging along behind Helena as she infiltrates conversations and sprawls on the sofa like she belongs there. I perch on the edge of a cushion, clutching my drink and smiling politely. Someone tells me that I look beautiful, and my eyes seek out Alistair. I see that he's still leaning against the sideboard, in conversation with a man in a bright blue suit. He doesn't catch my glance.

Our drinks seem to be constantly topped up. Kiera thought we might be making them for other people, but we don't even have to fetch our own. There's always another bottle being placed on the long coffee table, another fresh glass being pushed into my hand, someone offering to get more ice. I drink neatly and efficiently, aware of how the whiskey slides between me and my self-consciousness. I take short sips at stoic intervals and am surprised by how quickly my glass empties. Another refill. I laugh at something that somebody says. Someone else rests a hand on my hip as they slip past me, and I don't really mind. I look for Alistair and see that he has disappeared. He never did introduce us to Henry Taylor, and I wonder if he is one of the people I have already spoken to, each crisp suit and open-necked shirt blurring into one. I take another sip. I glance up at the clock that dominates the far wall and see that we've somehow been here for two hours already. My glass is almost empty again. Helena is snorting at something that some man is saying, playfully drinking straight out of a bottle. Someone asks if I'm having a good night, and I feel my face turn pink beneath his gaze and stammer through my response.

"Get this girl another drink," he booms. He turns back toward me. "Are you always this quiet?" he asks.

"I guess so."

His eyes slide up and down, seeming to take a measure of me.

"That's OK," he says. "We'll have you feeling comfortable in no time at all."

As it gets later, the weight of our inhibitions begins to dissipate.

People disappear into other rooms, the cluster of company in the living room breaking into smaller groups. I go to the bathroom and find a scattering of white powder on a shiny countertop. I press my finger into it and bring it up close to my face. It's crystallized and bright, like tiny diamonds. I wipe my hand on a towel and then sit down to pee, the sounds of the party seeping through the door and over the rush of water.

When I return to the living room, Agnes is lying with her back on the floor. A man is stretched out beside her, both of their eyes closed as they talk. Helena is no longer on the sofa, and I lower myself into the indent she has left behind. A half-empty bottle still sits on the table. I lift it to my lips and take a swig, just like I saw Helena do. The taste has become less powerful as the evening has progressed, the warmth of the whiskey in my chest now feeling vibrant and smooth. Someone puts on music and Kiera starts to dance, two men urging her on. She sways with the music, her arms stretched out above her head. She looks beautiful, her sandy blond hair brushing against the blades of her shoulders, her limbs the color of burnished gold. When she stumbles from the drink, they catch her. They're all laughing, urging her to sit down.

"You can sit here," I say.

As I stand up, the room swells slightly, my brain not seeming quite able to catch up with my movements. Everything feels a little bit more opalescent, a little bit more glowing and perfect. I find that I don't really mind where Alistair is. He'll be back for me.

"I'm just going to get some fresh air," I murmur, but nobody is listening.

Kiera has sunk into the sofa in my place, men firmly planted on either side of her. I have to step over her outstretched legs to get to the glass doors that lead out to the garden, and as I do, her eyes slide up to meet mine. She reaches out one arm and her fingertips brush against mine.

"Don't go," she whispers.

Although her expression is bright, her voice is soft and imploring.

"I'll be back in a minute," I say, and she nods and closes her eyes.

Outside the air is dense and warm. Without the crisp freshness of air-conditioning, the atmosphere feels slick and damp, a mugginess that promises the relief of rain. The only light comes from the muted underwater bulbs of the pool, the pump of a filter sending reverberations across the surface and scattering their greenish glow. It makes the garden feel almost swamp-like. There's moisture in the air and my movements are slow, as if I am trudging through mud. I take my shoes off and perch at the edge of the pool, sliding my feet beneath the surface. They are sore from wearing a pair of shoes borrowed from Helena, and it feels good to lower them into the coolness of the water, to feel their sudden weightlessness beneath me. I stay there for a few moments, closing my eyes and listening to the sound of insects protesting in the heat and the strains of music still playing in the living room. The alcohol has filled me with a sense of peace, and with the lights turned down I know that nobody will see me out here. I could sit here all night. I could stay out here until morning. I could wait for Alistair to miss me and come out to find me.

When the ache has eased from my feet, I lift them out of the pool and pad over to a waiting deck chair. I stretch out, my skin still damp, and turn my face up to the sky. Clouds are gathering, and yet the moon is perfect and pale, still steely and bright above me. The air is so thick it feels almost like being underwater, and I'm so sleepy from the alcohol that I could just close my eyes, just for a minute, just to rest them. With the sounds of the party as an obscured lullaby, I feel myself drifting gently away. There's a tantalizing moment between sleep and wakefulness, a second of balance when I could drag myself back, and yet instead I let myself topple over the edge.

※

The first thing I notice when I wake up is that it is raining. Perhaps that's what stirs me, the sensation of water breaking against my skin. It takes a moment for me to place where I am. I am outside. The bed I am lying on is scratchy and tense against my back. But then, of course, it isn't a bed at all. It is a sun lounger, and I am beside the pool at Henry Taylor's villa exactly where I fell asleep. Except that now it is dark. Even the moon is blotted out by cloud. The lights in the pool have been switched off and the living room is black. My brain tries blearily to calculate how I got here. I only meant to close my eyes for a second, but I must have been asleep for much longer. My mouth has the distinctive sour and dry quality of a hangover, and the world feels sharp and less magical than it did when I fell asleep. The shower must have only just started, the cautious and sparse kind of rain that paves the way for an abrupt and near-tropical downpour. As I gather myself, it transforms into a deluge, the sound of the water beating down against the mountain toward me. Then it is torrential, a clatter of raindrops against the pool sending splatters of water skyward. I raise my hands over my head and run, wrenching the patio doors and saying a silent prayer that they are still unlocked. They glide open and I launch myself inside, my skin icy with water and a puddle forming at my feet. The house is dark and silent. I reason that everyone else must be asleep and then feel faintly annoyed that nobody came looking for me. I'll have to sleep in Alistair's bed. It'll be his fault if anyone finds me there. He should have noticed I was gone.

My dress is soaked and my hair sticks to the side of my face. I need a towel. A hot shower. To get out of this dress. I've been here enough times to know the layout of the house even beneath a dense coat of darkness, and I pad across the cool hard floor toward the stairs. I must be leaving a trail of water behind me. I'll have to come back and clean it up later before anyone else wakes up. Unless I'm too late—I notice a dim glow from upstairs, a light easing through a door that is slightly ajar and a murmur of voices. They sound urgent and low, a heated conversation straining just out of earshot. It comes from a room at the far end of the corridor. I'm almost ready to ignore it when I hear a short and high-pitched sound. It's almost like a sob, half formed and guttural. Then I hear a girl's voice I immediately recognize, a scrabble of sounds and a clatter of movement before the door swings open and illuminates the corridor. Kiera is silhouetted in the doorway clutching her shoes in her hand. She freezes when she sees me, and as my vision adjusts to the new half-light, I notice that her eyes are wide and stark, her irises consumed by the black orbs of her pupils.

"Kiera, are you—"

She rushes toward me and snatches up my hand.

"Let's go." She tugs me toward the staircase, her hand hot and clammy in mine. "Come on. We can call a taxi downstairs."

"What are you—"

"Rachel, please."

"Kiera, *stop*." I drag her to a halt.

She turns to face me, and I see that her lip is broken from biting, leaving cracked skin and a delicate line of blood where her mouth joins. Her movements are twitchy, her hair sticking to her collarbone.

"Are you high?"

"What do you mean, am I . . . ?"

"You are, aren't you?"

I've never seen anyone on drugs before, but my voice rises in confidence. The white powder downstairs. Her agitation. It all fits together.

"I . . ." She glances behind me, her eyes wild. "Yeah, I took something earlier. Just a bit. But that's not what—"

"You need to calm down."

"Rachel, *please*." Her voice is desperate now. "I need to get out of here."

"I'm soaked, I need to dry off."

She grips my hand more tightly. "You can dry off back at the house. Just . . . I really want to go."

second I hesitate. But then I let go of her hand.

"I'm staying," I say. "You go."

"Rachel—" she starts.

I turn and let myself into the bathroom, locking the door behind me. Instead of switching on the shower, I wait for a moment, standing close to the door and listening. At first there's no noise. Then there's a man's voice and a shuffle of movement, the sound of footsteps on the stairs. I find that I've been holding my breath and let it all out in one long exhale. I've never seen Kiera like that before. She's usually so quiet, so reserved. She looked completely different tonight. She looked like someone I don't know at all. Behind the drug-induced haze, there was something urgent and wild, something I can't place. It takes me a moment, until the sounds from downstairs fade and my breath has slowed, to recognize that the unidentifiable expression was fear.

NOW

ave you got the wine?" Tom asks, just as the cab pulls up outside Jules's front door.

"I thought you had the wine?"

"You're joking, right?"

I look sideways at him. "It wouldn't be a particularly good joke,
would it?"

Tom exhales through his teeth. "I got that one especially . . ."

"Jesus, Tom, it's only fucking wine."

I pull open the door of the taxi and haul myself out. We fought
earlier in the day, an argument about nothing in particular that felt
like it was about everything, and the tension has bled into the evening. We took the taxi journey in near silence, Tom grumpy about
how expensive it would be to get to Jules's place now that his leg has
rendered him incapable of taking the tube, and me snapping that he
should have just let me invite them over to ours instead if all he was
going to do was complain.

It has been a week since I saw Alistair. A week of shredded nerves
and sleepless nights. At first I was sure he would message me, that
I would have to gather the strength to respond and tell him we had
made a mistake. When I didn't hear from him, I found that he filled

my thoughts with an urgency I couldn't suppress. Could it be that he didn't want to see me? That he regretted what had happened? What if it didn't mean anything to him? A dinner with an ex, sex simply because I seemed up for it? I went to work and stared at my computer screen. I came home and sat in front of the television in silence without taking in anything we watched. When Tom asked me what the matter was, I told him I was just feeling run-down. Exhausted.

"You need a break," he said. "Maybe we should go down and see your mum next weekend? Get out of the city."

I nodded mutely, knowing that I wouldn't. I suddenly felt irrevocably tied to London. He was here—he had been here all this time. The invisible thread that stretched between us felt more visceral than ever, and perhaps if I went away it would snap.

Jules answers the door while Tom is still hobbling down the path behind me.

"You're here!" she exclaims. "You two are always so punctual."

"Thank Tom," I say, letting her pull me into a tight hug. She smells earthy and familiar, a tang of incense and woody perfume. "I'd never get anywhere on time if it wasn't for him."

She holds me at arm's length to smile sympathetically at Tom.

"Look at you! Let's get you inside and comfy, you poor thing."

After all her adventures, Jules has somehow ended up settled into suburban life. She reminds us to take our shoes off and leads us barefoot through to their open-plan kitchen extension, where her perfectly welcoming husband is stirring a casserole at their eye-wateringly expensive new counter. She fusses over finding the perfect wineglasses and pours us all a glass of red, finding cushions so that Tom can settle onto a sofa.

"Looks pretty nasty, mate," Eli says with a shake of his head, a tea towel slung over his shoulder that suggests how at home he is in the kitchen. *No gender roles here*, their setup seems to scream, as Jules jokes about how lucky we are that Eli's cooking.

When Jules first met Eli, I had been relieved at the thought of

dinner parties like this. After years of catching Jules between con-
tinents, our lives would finally align. Our partners could be friends.
We could see each other with the kind of convenience that didn't
mean trying to find common ground when I was booking house
viewings and she was booking flights. Now, as I accept a drink and
Tom asks Eli about his new job, it makes me want to scream. In the
same way that you might imagine veering off into the median when
driving down a motorway or diving from a tall building when at the
top, a brief moment of madness that reminds you that you're alive, I
want to drop my glass onto the pristinely white floor tiles and yell. *Is
this it?* I will demand. *Is this what it was all about?* Jules hasn't even
touched her wine, sniffing it appreciatively and then setting it down
on the side. To make up for her, I drink mine in two large gulps and
then ask for another.

I know that I'm getting drunk before dinner is even on the table.
Eli and Jules are languorous in their preparation, the perfect hosts,
drinks constantly topped up and olives duly circulated as food bubbles
on the stove. On the counter is a vase stuffed with roses, bloody and
brilliant red against the crisp white countertop. Eli puts on easy jazz
on a smart speaker, inoffensive elevator music, and Jules talks about
how well her online business is going.

"People are getting so into alternative remedies now," she explains.
"People used to think it was this weird hippie-dippie shit, but it's
gone completely mainstream. I was really lucky with it, to be honest.
Right place at the right time."

Instead of waiting for another top-up to be offered, I wander to
the sideboard and pour my own, ruby-red droplets scarring the iridescent faux marble and matching the crimson shade of the roses. I
find myself plucking a single petal and crushing it between my fingers, the scent waxy and sickeningly sweet.

"Just popping to the loo," I say, but nobody is really listening. I
pick up my wineglass to take with me.

A lamp has been left on in Jules and Eli's bedroom, and I follow its dim glow inside. I set my glass down on a chest of drawers and perch on their bed. My head is starting to throb, a dim ache beginning to radiate from my temples. I shut my eyes and lie back on the bedspread, the mattress drooping slightly beneath me.

I see him everywhere now. Flashes of that night. The electric pulse of his hands against my skin. His eyes watching my every move. When I left his flat, there had been a tinge of regret, a certain guilt, a notion that I should have left the past in the past. My appetite for him and all the things I had imagined he might be had been sated. But now, with seven days of distance between us, I feel like I am starving again. Recall has glossed over my uncertainty, reshaping it into something precious and still. The way he remembered about the champagne. How he listened attentively as I talked, how it made me feel captivating, mesmerizing, sexy. How, as he laid me back on the bed, it seemed as though my life didn't exist outside his flat. As though the world had slowed and dissipated and everything was loud and quiet at the same time, deafening and silent. As though I was the person I used to be back when I was seventeen.

I lie there for longer than I mean to, lost in a woozy haze of too much wine and too little sleep. Chatter drifts from downstairs, the occasional laugh, the clink of cutlery being set down on a table. *I am supposed to be here*, I tell myself. Not with Alistair. Not even thinking about Alistair. With my husband and my best friend on a Saturday night. All the people who are most important to me are in this house. Yet I feel as though I am somewhere else entirely.

"Rachel?"

Eli's voice cuts through my thoughts and I sit up too quickly. The room spins and I have to close my eyes for a second.

"Sorry." I peel them open gingerly, waiting for the burst of light that has erupted behind them to fade again. "I just sat down for a second . . ."

"Well, I've been sent as the search party. Dinner's nearly ready."

"Thanks." I stand up and reach for my wineglass. "I'll be down now. I just lost track of time for a minute there . . ."

I wait for him to tell me not to worry about it and leave me alone again, but instead he steps closer to me.

"It's a great picture of you girls," he says.

He's looking down at a long dresser that spans the length of one wall. I hadn't spotted the photograph before, boxed into a battered leather frame. I didn't even remember any photographs being taken back then. It always felt like we were too busy living life to capture it, too early for smartphones and the careful documenting of every moment. Yet there we are, Jules and me all those years ago. I had almost forgotten how young she used to look. How young we both looked. After all, that summer made me feel impossibly old.

"You must have been—what there?" Eli picks up the picture. "Nineteen? Twenty?"

"Eighteen." I hear my voice as though somebody else is speaking. "I was eighteen."

I don't remember the picture being taken, its grainy quality suggesting the flash of a disposable camera, but I do remember that night. None of us would ever forget it. Jules and I are baring our teeth at the camera, my eyes bright and hopeful, day-glo face paint daubed across our cheekbones. I had convinced her to go out, a full-moon party Alistair had dreamed up, hoping we could draw more people in, that the bar would go down in history as the place that launched a party island. But Jules had left early. She hadn't been there when it happened. She didn't see Agnes run down onto the beach. I've never heard anything like it, that scream. It still sends me cold when I think about it.

"It was a long time ago," I hear myself saying.

"Jules still talks about it," Eli says.

For a second, I wonder how much she's told him. I wonder if he knows. I've always been so protective of that time that I forget other couples talk about these things. That they lie awake late at night with their bodies curled toward each other and share the parts of themselves that shaped them into who they are today.

Rachel never got over it, I can imagine Jules saying. *And who can blame her really?*

"Anyway." Eli claps his hands together and we're back in London, a thousand miles away from that place. "Are you hungry?"

Of course I'm not hungry. Not after that. My stomach feels curdled from the wine, uneasy from the sharp shock of seeing a photo from the night I have spent years trying to forget. But I slot into my seat at the table and watch as Jules ladles out spoonfuls of stew and nods emphatically at something Tom is saying. How can she possibly look at that picture every day? Surely she can't have forgotten what happened that night? I take another gulp of my drink and find that it tastes sour in my mouth.

"So, we're thinking of going to see a specialist," Tom is saying. "Not that we're worried particularly, but we just think we may as well get things checked out. Make sure everything's running smoothly down there."

Jules nods. "Makes sense, makes sense."

"What are you guys talking about?" I ask, even though I already know the answer.

Tom reaches across and slides his hand onto my thigh. He gives it a gentle squeeze, a signal of solidarity in front of Jules and Eli.

"The fertility stuff," he says. "You don't mind Jules and Eli knowing, do you, babe?"

Without waiting for me to respond, he turns back to them.

"There's such a weird taboo around it, you know? I just don't think people need to keep it so quiet. Me and Rachel want a baby. Most couples do, right? So why be secretive about it?"

"I'm not sure that's strictly true."

Tom turns back to me, his brow furrowed. "What?"

"Well, that most couples do. Want a baby. I mean, people assume they do. I bet you guys are constantly getting it now you're married, right? *Are you trying? When can we expect to hear good news?* When actually people have no clue what's going on. Whether people really want a baby. I think the whole thing's a load of crap, personally."

There's a short silence around the table. Tom's mouth opens slightly as though he's going to speak and then thinks better of it. He doesn't get it, of course. He never will.

"Well, I guess it's the patriarchy," Eli chips in, leaning back in his chair unconcernedly. "People assuming that women's *purpose* is tied up with childbearing. It's obviously an outdated concept."

Eli doesn't know me well enough to understand how out of character even a small outburst is for me. He doesn't pick up on the tension thickening between Tom and me. He isn't watching me with a cautious sadness like Jules, or a wary confusion like Tom.

"Well, fair enough," Tom blusters. "But the point is that we *do* want a baby. Have done for a while. And now that it's the right time, it doesn't seem to make sense to delay getting some answers . . ."

"*You* don't think it makes sense," I retort. "I never said I'd see a doctor. I said maybe, and you assumed I would."

Even Eli is silenced now, his eyes darting between Tom and me. I take a deep breath.

"I don't want to see a doctor, Tom, and I don't want to *talk* about it all the time, all right? Now, please. Can you just leave it?"

"Rachel—"

"I'm serious, Tom. Just leave it."

There's a stunned pause, a moment when nobody talks or moves. Tom seems ready to storm off, pushing his chair back slightly and then remembering that his leg is still fractured and won't take him far fast enough to be effective. Eli glances at Jules as if looking for some indication of what to do or say. I pick up my fork and shovel mashed potato into my mouth.

"And you know I hate roses," I say to my best friend. "Why would you get roses, of all things?"

I notice that my voice is tight, as though I am ready to break into tears. I lift up my wineglass to swill my food down. Jules just looks back at me like even she doesn't know who I am.

✳

We don't stay for long after that. We eat quickly, choking down beef and red wine jus as Jules and Eli make muted small talk with Tom. I don't speak much. Instead I just fill my wineglass up over and over again. I notice the drops that form on the inside of the glass, running in slow, thick rivulets. I watch them collect at the rim and then slide all the way down again, pooling back into a scarlet ocean.

Eli calls us a taxi almost as soon as we've finished eating, and Tom limps toward it before I've even had time to put my shoes on. At the door Jules pulls me into a tight hug, her arms fierce around me.

"I know what this is about," she says into my hair.

I pull away from her. "What do you mean?"

"It's about Alistair, isn't it?" she says.

I don't respond. Instead I stare straight at her, waiting for her to speak, daring her to utter those words. Sometimes I think I've imagined it. I look at Jules, my jaw tight, and wait for her to say it. To turn the storm inside me into syllables and shapes of her mouth. To make it real.

"It's about . . ." She glances behind me, making sure Tom is safely seated in the taxi. "Rachel, is it about the other baby?"

That's all I needed. I step away from her, the relief of hearing it like water breaking against my skin. Like plunging into the sea on an achingly hot day and feeling the release of the waves against my skin. She doesn't have to say anything else. It's enough to bring back the hard swell of my stomach. How the contours of a body I was just beginning to understand were reshaped. How I traced its new lines with wonderment, hardly able to believe what I had created.

"Of course it isn't," I say mechanically, the level arch of my voice hiding the hammering of my heart. "That was years ago. There never was a baby. Not really."

Her lips purse. Sympathy is etched all over her face. In that moment I can see her remembering all of it. Me turning up at her apartment howling, bent over double, saying his name over and over again. The flight home. The clinic. The weeks I spent staying at Jules's parents' place. Looking at Jules now, I wonder if we'd have made it if it weren't for that month. If we'd even still know each other at all.

"Bye, Jules," I say. "I'll text you."

She stays there for a second watching me. She doesn't shut the door until I've reached the taxi. She'll go straight to Eli, of course, pour another glass of wine, crawl into comfier clothes, and agree to leave the washing up until morning. They'll curl up on the sofa with their feet beneath them and dissect the night with disbelief. Perhaps they'll speculate on mine and Tom's marriage. Maybe Jules will say she never did see it working out. Maybe she'll be right.

I open the taxi door and lean down so that I am at eye level with my husband.

"I'm going to stay here a bit longer," I say to him. "You go. I'll see you back home."

He peers up at me, frowning. "We need to talk about this."

"We will." I straighten up. "Tomorrow."

Without giving him a chance to protest, I slam the car door shut. I wait for him to open it again, to clamber up and fight it out in the street. But of course, Tom isn't like that. There's a brief pause, and then the engine grinds into action, the click of a gear, the splutter of the ignition. I wait until the car rolls out of view; then I pull out my phone and tap in the number of a different taxi company. When they ask for the address, I give them Alistair's.

He opens the door dressed in gray tracksuit bottoms and a T-shirt, frowning with confusion.

"Rachel—" he starts.

Before he can say anything else, I reach up to kiss him, taking the words out of his mouth. It feels daring and uninhibited, action unframed by the complexities of our history, or the fact he hasn't texted me since I saw him last, or the rules that segment the ways women are supposed to act after they sleep with a man. It feels raw and primal, and I am triumphant when he kisses me back, his hands reaching around my waist.

"Take me to bed," I say.

And he does.

There are a million ways that mine and Alistair's relationship is complicated. The way things ended. The unspoken chasm of time between now and then. The baby that barely existed, until it did and then it didn't again. There are so many reasons why I shouldn't be here. Why I shouldn't want him as much as I do. Yet when I kiss him, none of it seems to matter. When I kiss him, I am eighteen again and all the complexities of life are untouched and undiscovered. He pushes up against me, and for the first time all week I think only of the moment I'm in. It's as if Tom and Jules and the whole terrible evening never happened. It's as though the last sixteen years never really happened at all.

THEN

The morning after the party, I wake up to Alistair shaking me. The pillow beneath me is cold and damp, my hair still spanning out in wet fronds around my head.

"You can't be here," he says as I squint in the half-light of dawn. "Henry will kill me if he knows you stayed."

"What do you mean?"

"You were supposed to be working," he says. "Not sleeping in here with me. Come on. I'll take you back."

I pull on my dress from the night before and drag myself up out of the warmth of his bed. As I fasten my shoes at the front door, Agnes emerges, her hair wet and wrapped in a towel.

"Are you getting a ride?" she whispers. "Give me a minute, I'll come too."

She scurries back upstairs to dress, and Alistair and I wait, leaning against the kitchen sideboard. He toys absentmindedly with a whiskey glass waiting to be cleaned and avoids my gaze. My head feels knotted and thick, and I'm not sure if it is entirely the hangover. Kiera's wild eyes and urgent voice bled into my dreams last night, alcohol-induced hallucinations that didn't quite make sense and flitted from world to world.

"Ready, ready." Agnes piles down the stairs sounding out of breath. "Let's go."

Agnes slides into the front seat of Alistair's car as if she belongs there. I climb into the back feeling vaguely disgruntled and rest my head against the dark leather. I'm irritated that she has stayed over too, and by how relaxed Alistair seems to be about her presence when he had scolded me for slipping into his bed. I am still always slightly self-conscious around him, overthinking my every move. I briefly hate Agnes's comfortable indifference, the way she rests her feet up on the dashboard and plays with her phone as though Alistair and I aren't even there. I have to remind myself it's me he wants, even if I'm shy and strange and quiet. None of that seems to matter to him. Alistair cares about me, even if he won't show it in front of Agnes.

We are silent as the car loops down now familiar roads, Alistair taking the sharp turns in the route with ease. Agnes winds down a window, and her auburn hair whips in the breeze, a halo around her head. She rests one arm on the open frame, white and slender. The months she has spent here don't seem to have invaded her body in the way they have mine, her skin staying pale, her cheekbones defined, while my own face fills out with too many beers and too much cheap Greek food.

Alistair drops us a few streets away from the house. Before we leave, he reaches into his wallet and pulls out a sheaf of crisp notes. He hands us a few each without counting them, although I notice that Agnes's stack seems thicker than mine. I try to catch his eye, but he's already pulling sunglasses on, turning the key in the car's ignition, his thoughts somewhere else entirely.

As we walk down the last stretch of road to the house, I see a figure up on the roof, sitting in the same spot where we go to watch the sun come up. They are partially hidden from the road, obscured by the lip of the room below them, yet as I shade my eyes and lift my face I can see that it is Kiera. Her body is silhouetted by the glow of the sky, her legs dangling above the short drop. Instead of looking out at the sun, her body is bent forward, her head ducked down as though she is looking straight at the ground. Agnes follows my stare, her lips pursed.

"I'll go and check she's OK," she says. "You go get some rest."

But instead of going to my bedroom, I head into the kitchen. It has the distinct air of someplace only recently vacated, the remnants of an after-party littering the counters and tabletops. Half-drunk drinks and a shambolic ring of cards sticky with spilled alcohol are arranged around a plastic beaker filled with an unidentifiable liquid. There's a handbag discarded atop the fridge, the scant remains of a makeshift meal burned to the bottom of a pan. The morning light makes a faded tableau of the night before, a ghost of drinking games and dares and kisses shared with strange men. In spite of feeling smug as I slipped out of the front door last night and into a waiting car, I find myself wishing I had stayed. That I'd gone to the bar and danced until my feet hurt. That I'd protested when the lights were switched back on, and then sloped back here late with anyone who still had another drink left in them.

Slowly I begin to clear away all traces of the night before. I empty glasses out into the sink and gather up vodka bottles to be thrown away. I scrub discarded plates and soap down the sideboard, streaked with splashes of sugary drinks that leave viscid marks behind them. By the time I am finished, my hands are pink, the skin of my fingertips creasing with water. I sit down at the kitchen table and breathe in the citrusy scent of cleaning products. It reminds me of home. It's Sunday morning, and my mum will be in the midst of her weekend ritual by now. She'll be turning the house upside down, running a hoover along the hallway carpet and doing endless loads of laundry. Usually I would be up in my bedroom doing homework due the next day, the roar of the vacuum drowning out the sound of the radio I got for my seventeenth birthday. It feels like another lifetime entirely. I can't imagine going back to it.

"Did you just get back?"

Helena's voice makes me jump. She wanders over to the fridge, disguising a yawn with one hand. She wears an oversized T-shirt as a nightie, so her legs are long and bare. Her hair is scraped up into a ponytail that trails halfway down her back.

"About an hour ago," I say. "I was just cleaning up."

"Cool party," Helena says. "I mean, a bit tame. But I don't really mind doing that kind of thing, if the money's good."

"When did you get back?"

"I don't know, maybe about two thirty? I thought you'd already left." She closes the fridge, her inspection seeming to have elicited nothing of interest. "Those guys are such creeps though, right? Henry's friends."

I shrug. "I thought they were fine."

"I mean, they're *fine*. They're not bad guys or anything. They're just like any other guy that age with money. At least, in my experience."

She flops down into a chair beside me and spreads her forearms out on the table, resting her chin on them.

"So. What's happening today?"

Sunday afternoons are the only time the bar is closed and none of us are working. We spend most of the morning sleeping off hangovers, making occasional trips to the kitchen for glasses of water and to exchange disbelieving stories about the night before. But late in the day we will emerge sleepily from our rooms and come together. Someone will cook a vat of spaghetti and we'll take bowls up to the roof to eat, or we'll trudge down to the beach with bottles of beer to catch the last dregs of weekend sun. Someone will have slept with someone last night, and we'll tease them about it endlessly and demand excruciating amounts of detail. Someone will be leaving to go home or move on next week, and we'll toast them with ouzo in an otherwise empty café.

Before I can respond, Helena is standing up and peering out of the window.

"Priya was saying she'd heard about this place with a great view, up on the cliffs? Perhaps we could go up there later? Watch the sunset?"

In spite of myself and the hangover gathering pace, I find myself smiling at Helena's enthusiasm.

"Sure," I say. "We should watch the sunset."

We head up together, a slow migration of girls heaving crates of beer and blankets. We take turns at carrying them, one at each end of a box as we navigate the steep cliff steps and shriek that someone is going too fast or not bearing her part of the weight. The path up to the top is narrow and worn. While the rest of the island's slow rise is gradual, this is sudden and ungainly, an unlikely crease in the surface of the world that creates a sheer drop above the broad flats of the sand below. At the bottom of the climb, the sun is just hidden, the early evening casting long shadows across the ground. As we climb, it emerges above the hilt of the hill, a large and deep orange orb. I notice that Kiera and Agnes are walking together, at a slight distance behind the rest of us. They look deep in conversation.

"Keep up, you two!" Helena calls down to them, and then she bounds ahead with her arms filled with clutches of blankets.

At the top, the path trails into nothing. We line the scrubby grass with blankets and collapse down onto the hard earth, baked and cracked from months of sun. We only have one bottle opener, and it is passed around, followed by the crisp crack of beer exhaling into the air. There's a bubble of laughter that teeters along the edge of our conversation, a contented exhaustion as we lean back on our elbows and turn to face the sky. The sea seems to stretch out all the way around us in every direction we look, vast and still. Someone puts on some music, and the sound is tinny and distant against the span of our surroundings, clashes of drums and the strum of a guitar half carried away in the breeze. Priya stretches out on her back alongside me with her eyes closed, a beer loosely resting beside her. Soon enough she starts to snore gently, her breath rhythmic and gentle. Helena is cross-legged as she sits in front of Eloise and spins her hair into long plaits. Agnes and Kiera sit close to the edge of the cliff, seemingly still locked in intense conversation, their heads close together. I clamber to my feet to join them, leaving Priya snoozing on the ground.

They have monopolized the best view. A gentle give of land just before the drop reveals a panorama of sea and sky. The sun is starting to sink below the horizon, and I know that soon it will be gone. Sunsets here are rapid and unexpected, painfully slow until all of a sudden it is night. I try to remember if I had ever really watched a sunset before I came out here. There must be somewhere back home where the sky falls into darkness like this, perhaps with the right drinks purchased in the right rooftop bar. Yet when I think about it, I can only summon images of suburbia, the sky hedged in by neat red roofs, the tempered endings of days wiped out by streetlights and church spires.

As I collapse down next to them, Kiera and Agnes fall quiet. Agnes stares fixedly out to sea, and Kiera looks down. One of her legs is folded beneath her while the other dangles over the cliff edge. She swings her foot gently from side to side, and as I follow her gaze, she dislodges a small rock. We watch it plummet downward, bouncing off the jutting edges of the cliff face before crashing onto the ground. It joins a pile of stones that have fallen before it, fragments of rock that have broken away with time. A dizzying vertigo hits me, and I edge slightly backward, letting the ground wriggle out of my eyeline.

"You got back OK last night, then?" I ask.

Kiera nods but doesn't respond. A wave crashes somewhere distant and far below us. Agnes's gaze doesn't waver from the horizon.

"Did you have a good time?"

Even as I say it, I can hear that my voice sounds weak and insipid.

Unbidden, I see Kiera as she was last night, wild-eyed and nervous. The image is jarring up here against the spacious peace of nightfall. Even the most beautiful places have secrets.

"Yeah," she says almost mechanically. "It was good."

For a moment nobody says anything. Agnes sips her beer. Kiera stares down at the ground where the rock has fallen, and I look fixedly at the ebbing sun. There's a tension I can't quite identify. Sure, Kiera might be annoyed at me. But Agnes? Didn't Alistair and I bring her home this morning? I'm just about to give up and retreat back to Priya when Kiera speaks up.

"Rachel." She turns to look at me, her eyes slightly dazed from the brightness of the sky. "Do you think they're good people? Alistair? And Henry Taylor?"

I remember what Jules told me a few weeks ago. *Be careful of that place*, she had said. *The locals say it's bad news.* Then I nod.

"Yes," I say. "I do. They look after us, don't they? Give us somewhere to live. Make sure we have plenty of work. Why?"

Kiera ducks her head again. "Just wondered," she says. "That's all."

"Kiera just had a bad night," Agnes says levelly. "It's nothing. You need some sleep."

Kiera nods. "Maybe that's it," she says, her voice uncertain. "Maybe I'm just tired."

We stay there until the day seeps out of the sky, the sea turning blank and empty before us, and then we go back to the house. The walk seems to take longer in this direction, sleep already creeping into our limbs and slowing our pace. We arrive back with an end-of-the-night relief, yawning and claiming exhaustion. Some of the others stay up in the kitchen, boiling the kettle and making cups of tea, but I go straight to my bedroom. As I undress and brush out my hair, Kiera's words dance in my mind, the same few syllables feeling just out of reach.

Do you think they're good people?

I catch a glimpse of myself in the mirror and find myself smiling.

Sometimes now, when I look at myself, I see what Alistair sees. I find myself beginning to like it. Of course they're good people. This is the best I've ever felt. The most perfect version of myself I've ever been. All because of them.

Just outside the window, the roof beside Kiera's bedroom is visible. Right before I climb into bed, I pull down the blinds so I can't see her up there again, silent and still, staring out to sea.

NOW

"Amber? Amber? Hey, *Amber*?"

Our newest administrative assistant pulls an earbud out of her ear and shoots me a disgruntled look.

"Can you call someone to clear up the discovery room? Some kid spilled paint all over one of the craft tables."

Amber pouts and picks up the telephone on her desk. Her acrylics clatter against the dialing pad, and she glances over at me disparagingly as I hover in the doorway.

"I'm doing it?" she says.

"Fine, fine. I'll—I'll leave you to it. I'll be in my office if anyone needs me."

It's been an exhausting morning of shepherding a rowdy class of year-sixes around the Egyptology section, before trying to coax them into painting their own hieroglyphics. This afternoon I have an event to plan, a lecturer giving a talk on Ancient Chinese artifacts. It means a few hours alone in my office, and I've been desperate to crawl back to the privacy of my own space all morning. Since Jules's disastrous dinner party, our house has been steeped with tension, a claustrophobia and quiet rage that knots the air between us. Tom was awake when I arrived home, lying still and silent, his body rigid as I lowered myself down next to him.

"Did you mean that?" he asked the darkness. "About not wanting to see a specialist?"

I lay flat on my back, my eyes fixed on the ceiling as I answered him.

"I don't know," I said. "I really don't know what I want right now."

We were due at his parents' for a Sunday roast the next afternoon, an occasion we navigated by slipping around the sides of each other, sitting at opposite ends of the table while Tom made conversation with his brothers about the football score and I feigned interest in his sister-in-law's pregnancy. Tom is one of three boys, and with all the siblings and their partners in attendance it is always easy enough to stay in the background of family gatherings, accepting top-ups and emptily offering to help with the washing up, knowing full well that his mum won't let anyone raise a finger. It was one of the things that drew me in at first, the easy coziness of his family life in the suburbs. It was so different from what I had grown used to.

Of course, I didn't meet his family straightaway. For three months after we met, we had circled each other, never making any commitments. I saved him in my phone as "House Party Guy" and it became an in-joke between us, a beam in the intricate structure of a relationship that would stay there until we were engaged. It was only then that I updated the contact, typing in his name and finding myself slightly surprised to see it every time he messaged me.

The pseudonym was just one of many stretches of distance I carefully laid between us. There hadn't been anyone since Alistair. One-night stands and ill-thought-out flings, of course. But anything more would have felt like a betrayal. I still fantasized that he would come back for me as I made watery cappuccinos and grilled paninis in the museum café. I would occasionally call his phone, only to be met with a droning voice telling me that the number had been disconnected. I clung onto the thought that I would glimpse him across a tube carriage or see him wandering around the galleries one day. I held onto the belief that what we had had been perfect and special, our relationship holding a sanctity that would outweigh all the other terrible things that had happened. If Alistair and I were real, then everything else was a lie. If Alistair and I were real, then everything I had done for him was worth it.

Yet while I waited for Alistair, there was Tom. I would message him when I was drunk and on my way home from a party to see if he was awake, and he always was. He would open the door to the flat he shared with two guys from work and hold his finger up to his lips as I stripped off my stilettos and asked if he had anything to drink. He would have sex with me with such deliberate care that I would dig my fingernails into his back and tell him to go harder, to choke me, to care less. I was used to people who would roll off me as soon as they came and pull their boxers back on, or clamber off to go for a smoke without worrying whether I was finished. Tom was different, and I was entranced and horrified in equal measure. Yet I still kept coming back for more. He asked me out for dinner and I asked him to come over to my latest house-share instead, opening the door in underwear and a T-shirt with a wine bottle already unscrewed on the kitchen counter. He met me at work on my lunch break and we sat through an awkward coffee date, me staring at my fingernails and trying to figure out what exactly he wanted from me. I would tell him to meet me at clubs, and he would come in the middle of the night, sober and sleepy, and take me home.

Later on, when we would talk about those first few months after we met, I would realize how much he had misread me.

"I was so intimidated by you!" he told me. "You were so aloof. You didn't seem to care. And you just seemed so *interesting*. Like there was no knowing where you were going to call me from or what you were going to do next. It made me want to know more about you."

He had spun his own narrative of me, mistaking self-loathing and despair for mystique, spinning a story of the archetypal cool girl who he had managed to capture. He hadn't seen me scrolling through my contacts and then calling him because I had nobody else who wanted to be around me. Justifying to myself that it was all right to be drunk on a Monday night, as long as I could find somebody to drink with me. Waking up next to Tom and just for a moment thinking the long, broad stretch of him in bed beside me was Alistair. When I realized, I would tell him I had somewhere to be and that he had to leave.

I moved in with him when we were only sleeping together, a quirk of circumstance when my tenancy expired before I could be bothered to find somewhere new to live. Jules was out of the country, and so I crashed at Tom's place. It was only for a week at first, a week that slipped into a month of his housemates rolling their eyes in the kitchen and asking if I was going to start paying bills. When Tom casually told me he was thinking of moving into his own place, I just shrugged and said he could do whatever he wanted to. We were only having sex, after all. I was going to start looking for somewhere as soon as I could string together the cash for a deposit. It wasn't until I unpacked my things in the tiny flat he had found in the far reaches of East London that I realized my stay with Tom had somehow morphed into us living together without me noticing the shift. We went to his parents' place that weekend, and even though Tom introduced me as his friend, his mum made a fuss of me, insisting that I have another serving of her signature shepherd's pie and asking me what I did for work.

"I'm still deciding that," I had told her, toying with a forkful of mince.

Instead of looking disapproving, she clucked and told me I was still young, that you had to take your time figuring out these things, and should she do some coffees to go with dessert?

Tom and I never really talked about me moving in until it simply became accepted wisdom that we lived together. I came home and complained about work and quizzed him on how he had known what he wanted to be. He seemed impossibly grown-up to me, with his work laptop and his company bar tab on work nights out. I tagged along to them and felt self-conscious in front of his friends who had real jobs.

"Rachel works in catering," Tom would say proudly, and people would rarely probe much further.

After a while it was a given that we were a couple, although we never discussed the transition. With him at home, ready with a take-away and a glass of wine after a hard day, I was going out less. Our living situation meant that neither of us was seeing anybody else, and I had already met his family. The shift to being somebody's girl-friend, a role that had eluded me for most of my adult life, seemed strangely seamless. What's more, it felt good. There was a relief to it, a relaxation almost like lowering myself into a warm bath after coming in from the cold. It was so easy to be Tom's plus-one at family weddings, and to spend all Sunday lying on the sofa with him, and to send Christmas cards signed from both of us. I was surprised to find that I liked the stability of knowing who I was coming home to. Turning down invites because we were going to Tom's brother's place for dinner. For years I had defined myself by those few months on the island. Then one night I woke up with Tom's arm cupped around me and realized I hadn't thought about Alistair for weeks. Falling in love with Alistair had been intoxicating and sharp, like plunging from a fifty-foot building and hoping he would catch me. I fell in love with Tom in the same way you fall asleep—slowly and unknowingly into a blissful oblivion. It was only after we were married that I discovered how badly I wanted to wake up.

It was Tom who suggested that I go to university. In all the chaos that had accompanied my return from the island, I had somehow missed the chance. The next few years had passed in a blur, and when I looked around, I was twenty-two and all the girls I had known at sixth form had already graduated and moved on with their lives. It was Tom who found the Open University course in museum stud-ies, who encouraged me to temp as a classroom assistant at the local school to get teaching experience, who bought a bottle of champagne on the day I got the job and toasted to how far I'd come.

I glance down at the date on my computer screen and feel an involuntary twang of dread to see that that day was almost six years ago. How excited I had been to secure this job. How proud Tom had been of me. I'm not sure what we imagined the next few years would look like, but surely we didn't see this.

I pull a sandwich prepared at home from my handbag and peel away the cling film. Alistair has messaged me already this morning, his interest seemingly sharpening since my surprise visit on Saturday night. I've arranged to see him after work on Wednesday, and my stomach is already knotted with anticipation. I know I shouldn't be this excited about him, a man who broke my heart, but the muscle memory of my feelings seems to have melded back into shape at once. I've heard women say it before, giddy from a flush of new love, declaring that they "feel seventeen again!," but I really do. Even the thought of Tom and the wilting cheese-and-tomato sandwich he made for me this morning in spite of our argument does little to dampen my excitement. I take a bite and load up my screen for a cursory lunchtime scroll of the day's news.

A celebrity marriage has broken down. Some new arts center is opening up in South London. I click through, only vaguely scanning the stories. Some minor member of the royal family making a public faux pas and a new drugs trial proving successful. With my Wednesday night rendezvous already planned, everything feels bland and ordinary, a colorless background to the vividness that Alistair has given back to my life.

I type the Facebook URL into the search bar and click on my saved log-in to access the site, a mindless distraction from the workday. The page loads and I click into my notifications. It's unusual for anyone to message me, and yet there, alongside a glowing red friend request, is a new contact. I recognize the sender at once. She beams out from her small display picture, her face pressed up close against the same dark-haired teenager I saw back in Greece only a few months ago. The familiarity makes me swear under my breath.

1 new message from Helena Riley.

After all this time, and from thousands of miles away, she has decided to find me.

Hey Rachel, the message reads. It's Helena. I'm going to be back in the UK in a few weeks. My daughter goes to school in London, and I'm coming over to stay for a few days to visit her. Seeing you at the bar made me realize how long it's been, and I'd love to properly catch up, if you'd like to? I feel like we've got a lot to talk about.

The message is so innocuous. So casual in tone. Anyone else reading it would think we were just two old friends. Two women who haven't seen each other for years who will go for a cocktail to make stilted conversation before going our separate ways again. My hands hover over the keypad and a thousand unsaid things hover between us.

Hi, I type.

Then I pause. I look at the picture again, the crease of Helena's eyes and the swoop of hair shading her face, and it immediately takes me back to that night. The last time we were really together, before everything fell apart.

I don't know if I can meet up right now, I type. Sorry. It was just such a long time ago that I left.

I hit send and sit back heavily in my chair. The message is read at once, small gray ticks appearing beneath it. And then, straightaway, a glimmer of motion on the screen to indicate that Helena is typing. My sandwich sits uneaten as I watch the flicker of her thoughts forming, suspended somewhere between now and then. The message appears framed by a cartoonishly bright speech bubble.

That's true, she has written. It's a shame that not everyone got to leave.

My breath catches in my throat. For a moment, I'm transported away from my office. The smell of the sea is powerful, overwhelming, metallic. The sound of seabirds, their screeches like a battle cry. Instead of feeling like freedom, the sand beneath my feet weighs me down, makes it impossible to run. I imagine sinking into its silt-like heaviness, trying to dash toward the shore and not wanting to look back. Before I can gather myself, before I can even think about formulating a response, Helena is typing again.

Wow! she writes. Sorry, that was heavy!

Her message is followed by a smiley face emoji, inappropriately coy and flush-cheeked.

I don't mean to freak you out. I would just love to see you. For old times' sake. We have something in common that I don't think anyone else can understand. Seeing you back here made me realize how special that is.

I lift my hands to respond, knowing that she is waiting, watching the screen with the same anxiety that bubbles in my chest.

Have you spoken to any of the others? I type.

I hover over the enter key for a second, and then instead I press down hard on the backspace. If Helena's going to play games with the past, then I may as well ask what I really want to know. I delete the message and then type, Have you spoken to Agnes?

No, she replies. Just you.

My spine is hunched over the keyboard, my jaw clenched so tight it is beginning to spasm. It's incredible how visceral my response to Helena's words is, even now. I close my eyes and lean my elbows down on the desk, lowering my head into my hands. I shouldn't see Helena. Of course I shouldn't. I've worked so hard to move past what happened. I've just found Alistair again. But then I remember the heat on my skin. Helena in the kitchen on the day I moved into the house, hugging me tightly to her. Helena dancing on the bar, always laughing, always up for a drink. I've missed her over these years. There's a tiny part of me that wants that back.

When are you here? I write.

End of the month. I'll be in London for a few weeks, but I don't have anything specific planned. I can be free whenever you are.

I take a deep breath and wonder if I will regret this.

Fine. We can go for a drink?

There's a pause in her response this time, long enough to make me check whether she is still online. A green dot glows next to her name, a promise that she is still there.

That would be perfect, she writes. I'll message you when I know where I'm staying.

Then she's gone, the dot next to her name extinguished. I log out of Facebook and drop my sandwich into the wastepaper basket. I somehow no longer feel like eating.

THEN

The party is going to be the biggest the island has ever seen, a blowout to remedy our tiny world emptying out for winter.

Alistair tells us about it excitably at the bar. It's a quiet night when only Priya and I are working, counting stock and cleaning out beer taps.

"We'll set up on the beach," he says. "Have a massive firepit, a few different bars. It can be an annual thing. Turn this place into a party island, put it on the map."

Priya raises one eyebrow. She's drying a glass slowly, a washcloth circling its edge.

"Now?" she says. "When everyone's leaving? Who's going to show up?"

"People will show up," Alistair says. "We'll put on boats from the mainland. And anyway, so what if they don't? That will make it more exclusive. A talking point. People will hear about it and then want to come back next year. It's all about the long-term plan, Priya. You've got to be ten steps ahead in this business."

Priya shrugs. She's leaving at the end of the week, and her enthusiasm for her job at the bar and patience with Alistair both seem to be thinning.

"I think it sounds great," I say.

Alistair puffs up at my words. "That's what I like to hear. Right, I have to get going. Rachel, you're coming to help out later, right?"

I nod. We've already agreed that I'll tell the others Henry Taylor needs me tonight. It's the first time all week that Alistair and I will have been alone, and I'm already counting down the hours until the end of my shift.

"Great. I'll pick you up after you finish," he says. "Bye, Rachel. Priya."

Priya is setting a glass down with her back to him and doesn't turn around. We were supposed to be open late tonight, but we haven't had a customer in over an hour and Priya is already talking about shutting up early. When I arrived on the island, I hadn't imagined how quickly the sheen of high season would begin to rust. I had deferred my spot at college imagining that I would stay here all year, but now it is almost October and the air is starting to cool, my summer wardrobe beginning to feel inadequate.

It's only been two months since I first disembarked the boat, and yet the beach is already sparsely populated, straggles of tourists trying to capture the last remnants of heat and backpackers making the most of slashed prices as the locals try desperately to extend the summer season. Some of the other girls are getting restless, their plans to spend the winter in hotter and more distant climates or to go home in time for Christmas edging into sight. For the past week, the realization that I don't know what to do next has sat like an itch against my skin. I don't have the money to keep traveling, and the thought of going home to my parents—a year with no job or college enrollment stretching endlessly ahead—makes me feel desperate. Then there's Alistair. Even imagining leaving him behind feels unbearable. He's become everything to me so quickly that I feel defined by him, as though without him I am not sure who I am again.

I pick up a glass and absentmindedly wipe it down, and as I do, I think of my missed period and the anxious ache that has gathered pace in my chest over the last few days. I had been so caught up with everything here that I hadn't noticed, and once I realized that I hadn't needed to buy tampons this month, it felt too long since my last period to calculate. Last night I stood in front of the cracked mirror in our communal bathroom and placed my hand just below my waist. Outside, a bubble of activity was audible. Someone was playing music, and the pulse of water in aging pipes groaned from the effort of filling up the kitchen sink. The stairs clattered as people piled down for the start of the evening shift and a flicker of laughter rose and fell down the corridor. Someone hammered on the door and asked how long I would be. Was it possible that among all of this Alistair and I had created something new? My stomach felt flat and taut beneath my palm, and yet for the first time since I had realized that this summer would soon come to an end, I felt a warm glow of possibility.

Of course, I haven't spoken to Alistair about it yet. Pregnancy tests seem difficult to track down among the island's scant collection of shops, and a trip to the decaying doctor's surgery that nestles in the center of town feels too dramatic. It could just be one missed period, after all. Maybe two. Every day I tell myself that if it hasn't arrived by tomorrow, then I will go to the mainland to find out. Every day I inspect the thin cotton of my panties, waiting to see a brown streak of blood. Every day I go to work, message Alistair, and wait all day for a response, hang out with the other girls, and tell myself that I will give it just one more day.

In the meantime, I have found a distraction in Jules. I had left our cobbled-together breakfast thinking I wouldn't see her again, yet not long afterward I found myself heading down to her apartment on an afternoon when my bedroom felt stifling and the house was unusually empty. Jules was sitting out on the stoop, an open bottle of wine beside her as she painted her toenails in rainbow colors. She smiled as if she had expected to see me and went inside to fetch another glass.

Since then I'd visited her regularly, squeezing myself in around the hours she worked and catching her before my shifts. At the start of the trip, I had found myself struggling to make friends, overshadowed by Caroline and her magnetism, but it turned out someone like Jules was what I had been missing. She didn't seem interested in the other backpackers who hopped between islands in search of the cheapest beer, the strongest ouzo. She was interested in tucked-away places and historical sites. She told me about Greek mythology, about islands where gods and goddesses were born. She knew the names of different flowers and pointed them out as we walked from her apartment to the beach. She never seemed perturbed by me turning up at her apartment at irregular times, always greeting me with a broad grin whenever I showed up. It was refreshing, to be with someone who didn't know Alistair at all. To not have to worry about someone catching wind of my feelings for him, or flirting with him in front of me, or asking me what I was doing when I had plans to sneak up to Henry Taylor's house.

"Are you guys open?"

A boy hovers in the doorway, looking uncertain as he glances around the now-empty room. Disco lights swirl across the floor, and the music is muted, turned down low without a crowd to shout over it. Priya glances at her watch.

"We're open," I say before she can respond. "What can I get for you?"

He sits up at the bar and asks for a beer. Priya disappears into the stock room as I snap the cap off a bottle, conscious of his eyes on me. He must be about my age, maybe a year or two older. His hair is slightly too long and he still wears beach shorts.

"Is it always this quiet around here then?" he asks.

I shrug, setting his drink down in front of him. "It's a Wednesday night. And summer's almost over. You should come back at the weekend, it'll be busier then."

"Are you trying to get rid of me?"

I start to protest, but then see that he's smiling, teasing me, one corner of his mouth upturned. He's attractive in a way I'm not used to, and it strikes me how long it's been since I had a conversation longer than a drink order with a boy my own age. I suddenly feel self-conscious, and I pretend to busy myself finding him a beer mat, wiping down the bar in front of him.

"Have you been out here long?" he asks.

"Not too long. A couple of months."

"That's pretty cool. Are you staying?"

I shrug. "Probably for a bit longer. I haven't decided yet."

He takes a sip of his drink, and I notice how fine the hair on his arms is, how his torso hasn't quite filled out with muscle yet, how his limbs still seem slightly too long for his body. I didn't realize how men grow into themselves until Alistair.

"Me neither," he says. "I'm meeting up with a bunch of friends I met back in Mykonos out here. They arrive tomorrow. We were thinking we'd see what the vibe was like, decide where to go from there."

I don't respond. Just a few weeks ago I would have tried to convince anyone who would listen how perfect the island was, how there's no other place like it. Now, with the summer season slipping away, I feel desperately protective of it, as though the magic of it must be shared among anyone who stays, and I want it to be all mine. My lingering presence here has started to feel as though the entire situation requires some kind of complicated explanation. So I live here? All year round? And what do I do once the tourists leave? I avoid the questions, knowing I don't have any of the answers.

"We were actually thinking we'd go down to the beach tomorrow night. Get a firepit going. Have some drinks," he says. "Maybe you should come? You know. Give us some of your top tips about the place. It'd be fun."

It takes me a moment to realize he's flirting. There's a subtlety to it that takes me by surprise: a slightly raised eyebrow, a suggestive wheedle to his voice. I'm so taken aback that I find myself imagining the scene. The warmth of a fire. The heat of his body beside me and the suggestion of it moving closer as the night wore on. How perhaps, as the evening started to cool, he would offer his hoodie, the scent of youthful skin still lingering in its folds. I find myself thinking of first kisses, new friends, travel plans that would take me away from here. How easy it would be to go to a party with a boy I didn't have to pretend not to know. I see an entire relationship unfold before he's set his beer back down, his eyes still on me. Then I think of Alistair waiting up for me back at Henry Taylor's house and know that I could never settle for anything less.

"We close in fifteen minutes," I say. "You should drink up."

※

By the time we leave, Priya is restless, complaining about how tired she is.

"Do you have to go up there?" she asks as we lock away the till. "Can't you just come back?"

"I want to go," I tell her, and she shrugs and says it's up to me.

I doze in the car up to Henry Taylor's house, the turns in the road only just keeping me balanced on the edge of wakefulness. They morph into the edges of dreams—of falling into great cavernous spaces and sailing a boat out into fluid and amorphous seas. When we pull up outside the villa, the place has a dreamlike quality to it, the kind that emerges from the emptying embers of sleep. The lit-up facade of the house seems to gleam an ethereal white, the glow that it projects soft and perfect. I had already told Alistair I was on my way, and he is there to let me in, to chuckle at my sleepiness, and to kiss the very tip of my nose. When I go to say something, he holds one finger to his lips.

"Henry's here," he says; then he beckons me into the kitchen and hands me a drink. "Let's go and sit outside."

I hesitate. "Is it OK for me to be here?"

"He's sleeping," Alistair says. "And besides, I told him I'd get one of the girls here to help out with some stuff. Don't worry about it."

We perch on the edge of the pool, our feet in the water as we sip whiskey. I thought I had got used to the flavor, but there's a slightly salty taste I wasn't expecting. Still, it slides down easily. I remember how I had choked on my first mouthful and feel grown-up as I take a delicate sip, my eyes meeting Alistair's above the rim of his glass. The glitter of the water, luminescent and lit up from below, seems to beam in a way it never has done before. I find myself transfixed by it, staring as the taste of alcohol dissipates across my tongue and heats my belly. Everything feels so perfect, and Alistair and I are together, and he is stroking the length of my spine so gently I feel like the most precious thing in the world. At some point we migrate over to the sun loungers. There is more whiskey. Alistair lifts a strand of my hair and kisses my forehead lightly. His mouth is hot and I feel as though my skin could buckle beneath his touch. I am so tired that staying awake almost hurts. It wouldn't be the first time I have fallen asleep out here.

Alistair goes inside to get another drink, and I place my fingertips against my stomach and remember the secret I am storing up inside me. The idea that I could be pregnant still feels absurd, impossible, and yet as I press my palm against my belly, there's an undeniable sense of power, as if all the world could be there beneath the span of my hand. The thought flattens my fears about being too young for Alistair, sharpens the possibility that our relationship could be something real and adult, something made out of flesh and bone.

Of course, there's no use telling him. Not yet. It's probably nothing. And yet still I feel a flicker of excitement at what we could have created together as I watch him retreat toward the house. Briefly, I think of the boy in the bar, the slight tremor in his voice, the roundness of his jaw, and find myself smiling. To think that he imagined I might want him when I have this—this grown-up, meaningful thing that elevates me a million miles above the backpackers who come for a few days and then leave. I belong here now. I belong with Alistair.

My eyes are closed when I hear his footsteps across the stone floor. I keep them shut, not quite able to will myself to open them, hoping he'll kiss me as he draws closer.

"Rachel," he says. "Hey, Rachel."

He shakes my arm, the tenderness of just a few moments before broken.

"Henry's awake."

I struggle to sit up, and as I do, I find that I'm somehow tipsy already. My vision doesn't quite catch up with my movement, and the world feels slippery and elastic.

"Do I have to leave?"

"No, you're good," Alistair says.

He draws down so that his eyes are level with mine.

"Henry says he can't sleep. He actually asked . . ." He pauses and I catch something unidentifiable in his voice. "He asked if you can go and keep him company. Take him a drink and sit with him for a bit."

"Me?"

"Yes. He's heard about you. How hard you've been working for us. He wants to meet you. You won't have to do much, just serve him a couple of drinks, listen to him talk about whatever he wants to talk about. You know, like you did with those other guys at the party?"

"But . . . it's like . . . it's like two in the morning?"

"I know, I know. It'll only be for half an hour, until he gets tired again. We need to keep him happy. He's my boss, Rachel. Yours too. And it's his house, after all. It's only half an hour."

There's an edge of exasperation to his voice, an urgency that makes me stand up. My legs feel unsteady beneath me.

"OK," I say.

Alistair takes hold of my upper arm to guide me inside, his grip insistent.

"I'll be in the bedroom when you're done," he says. "We can sleep then."

In the kitchen he hands me a decanter and two glasses. He doesn't offer to help, and I have to clutch them in the crook of my elbow, heavy and cold against my skin. Henry Taylor's bedroom occupies a wing of the house I have never been into, a flight of stairs and a long, dark corridor to be traversed before I can reach him. I walk slowly and carefully, painfully aware of the weight of the whiskey bottle against my hip. Alistair strides a few paces ahead of me, glancing back impatiently and hissing for me to come on under his breath. There's something different about him, a tension that seems a thousand miles away from his usual laid-back demeanor. But then there's something different about the entire night, a nebulous and intangible quality that blurs my vision and keeps me padding a few steps behind him. I'm too exhausted to even be irritated by Henry Taylor's late-night demands. I feel like I'm dreaming as I drift toward the door, the straight edges of walls and ceilings swaying as though my desire to sleep has invaded my consciousness, until all I can do is follow Alistair toward Henry's room.

Alistair knocks on the door and then pushes it open without waiting for a response. He steps back just slightly to allow me to pass, and as he does, our eyes meet for a moment before he looks away.

"I'll see you soon," he murmurs.

Then he nudges me in the small of my back. It's a gentle push and yet it propels me forward with force. I hardly feel as though my own legs are moving, but rather that the world is moving around me. I try to calculate how much I've had to drink. Surely not enough to be feeling quite this woozy? But then I am face-to-face with Henry Taylor for the first time, and I don't have the chance to figure out how many glasses of whiskey I drank, or whether I was slipped an extra beer in the bar that I'd forgotten about.

Henry Taylor's absences at his own parties and in the house Alistair and I have treated as our own have created a vast space for him to fill, an imposing and faceless figure that my mind has only faintly sketched out, some vague impression of sharp suits and expensive watches. Perhaps that's why it takes a second for my imagination to catch up when I see him. He's sprawled on a vast bed that thrusts out into the center of the room, his frame smaller than I expected, his dark hair graying. The wall directly behind him is made of glass, opaque and mirrored. He is wearing only a pair of boxer shorts, and I duck my head, embarrassed by the dual reflection of his legs stretching out on the sheets, pale and covered in thick dark hair. There's a slight paunch where the elastic of his underwear meets skin, stubble shading the line of his jaw.

"Rachel!" he says. "I wasn't expecting you up so quickly. I should be wearing something more suitable."

His voice is deep with a cut-glass accent, raspy from the sleep that he claims is eluding him. I stare down at the floor as he pulls on a dressing gown.

"Don't be shy," he says, and he pats the stretch of bed beside him. "Come and sit with me. Have a drink."

I stumble slightly on my way over to him. A glass drops from my grasp and shatters on the floor, shards flying across the polished tiles.

"Whoops!" Henry laughs and pulls me down next to him. "Butterfingers."

"I can clean it up . . ."

"No, no need. Never mind. We can share a glass."

I almost protest. I could insist on going down to the kitchen, on finding a dustpan and brush and cleaning up the mess. By the time I was done, perhaps the surreal quality of the night would have faded, swept away with the broken glass and the inane practicality of clearing away my mistake. But now that I'm here, the bed feels irresistibly comfortable, my head impossibly heavy. One drink here, just while I pull myself together a bit, just until Henry Taylor's had enough, and then I can crawl into bed with Alistair and sleep. *Sleep*—even the word seems to have a wondrously svelte and inviting quality. I can almost imagine the swoop of its letters, the glide of the *s*, the pillow like a pair of *e*'s, the final *p* that would plunge me into oblivion.

Henry Taylor is talking, and I realize I haven't been concentrating. He's holding a glass out to me, and I know that if I take a sip he will nod with approval and satisfaction. That's the thing with men like him. They only really want somebody to listen to them. To feel important. To have someone sit in their bed and pretend that person really wants to be there, and isn't simply on their payroll. I press back against the mirrored wall and think how pleased Alistair will be with me. How highly Henry Taylor will speak of me. We are a kind of team, Alistair and I, working together to keep his boss happy. A real couple who support each other. I nod some more and pass the glass back to Henry, but he shakes his head and asks me if I'm tired. I tell him I'm fine, and the words feel strangely sticky in my mouth, as though my tongue can't quite form them. I try again, slowly and carefully, *I'm fine, I'm fine, I'm fine*, but I'm not sure anymore whether I'm saying it or just thinking it, and then Henry Taylor's telling me that it's OK, I can close my eyes for a minute if I want to. Just a minute. Just to rest them. And it feels too easy to do what he says. To stop resisting. To let my body give in and relax into the bedsheets. As I close my eyes, I notice the sharp scent of his aftershave, and it smells impossibly grown-up. Nothing like the chemically sweet fragrance of Lynx Africa or the cheap shower gels the boys at school wear. Unfamiliar and intoxicating and wrong.

Then I feel as though I'm waking up, even though I can't be. I was just awake. I only closed my eyes. Yet somehow the room is darker than it was only a few seconds ago, and I'm lying on my front, my chin resting against my forearm. There's a dazed and dizzying second when I try to calculate how I got here. My body feels heavy and tired, as if it would be a tremendous effort to move it. It would be easier to just stay still. The bed feels so good beneath my body, the flat of the mattress seeming to embrace me. I could just close my eyes again for a minute. Alistair won't mind waiting up for me.

Then, in the mirror in front of me, I catch a flicker of movement. It's so brief that it takes my mind a second to catch up. I lift my eyes, and the reflection of the room is all shadows and blurred angles of darkness. Yet the same movement is still there, a rhythmic motion cutting through a thin shaft of light like a pendulum. My thoughts move slowly as my eyes adjust to the darkness. It must be a ceiling fan, mechanical and constant. Then, as the shadows form into shapes, I feel my breath catch in my throat. I can just make out a man kneeling above my inert body, his legs astride me on the bed, the twin splay of his thighs and the jerking motion of his arm. There's a gentle pant of breath as I hold my own, a rapid and desperate motion, a rising sense of panic in my chest. It feels too late to roll over. My body is too heavy to follow commands. Instead I close my eyes. I can still hear wet, urgent gasps, feel the gentle give of the bed beneath me pressing back up into my stomach with every stroke, imagine that clenched fist beating up and down. My teeth are gritted so hard that my jaw hurts. I wonder if I can say something, to feign a yawn, to pretend to be only just waking up, but when I try to form shapes with my mouth, it refuses to comply. I purse my lips together, but no sound emerges. It is only when I give up that I know what I am trying to say, the pressed-together *p* of *please* almost taking shape on my lips.

At the last minute I open my eyes again, just as he emits a groan and the entire length of his body seems to shudder. Watching this thing happen to me in the mirror, it is as though I am watching it happen to someone else, as though I am observing this terrible action from a distance. As his body buckles, I catch sight of his face for the first time. His mouth is slack and gawping open and his eyes are blank, as though the body beneath him is inanimate and inhuman. He exhales and collapses down on the bed next to me, and my back is wet, but it doesn't seem to matter because I'm not quite sure that I am even in my own body anymore. I am somewhere else entirely as I listen to the heavy lurch of his breathing even out, completion softening the tense weight of his bulk beside me.

NOW

That week I take Tom's advice and telephone my mum.

"I'm thinking of coming to visit," I say to her. "Are you free?"

Down the phone there's a pause punctuated by the droning sound of Radio 4 in the background, a kettle boiling in the next room.

"What kind of a question is that?" she says tersely. "Of course I'm free, Rachel. I've hardly got a thriving social life, have I?"

I take the train to her that weekend, the urban tangle of London fading into suburbia and then graying countryside. My parents divorced not long after I first moved to London, my mum keeping the house while my dad moved away. Going home is always strange, the same small, red-brick house that I grew up in now feeling cavernous with only my mum to fill it. While Dad remarried—a woman he met at work—and bought a new house in a tucked-away village, Mum made it her business to stay single and stubbornly resentful of him for leaving her. Tom and I usually visit her two or three times a year: a Sunday lunch, a birthday meal out, a stilted Christmas Day spent bingeing on television specials. The journey back to London always feels like a relief, Tom catching up on work and me quieter than usual.

Mum sniffs when I open the door, her eyes sliding up and down.

"No Tom?"

"Not today, no."

"Well, where is he?"

"Busy with work."

Mum seems to accept the answer with a curt nod, stepping back slightly to let me into the hallway. Ever since Dad left, she's carried a deep-seated suspicion of men. I half expected her to dampen my relationship with Tom with the same distrust when she first met him. By then we'd been together for two years. Although our weekends were regularly punctuated with visits to his parents' place, I had managed to keep my own mum at arm's length. When we finally turned up, a New Year's Eve visit that coincided with a graying sprawl of snow that meant crawling back to my childhood home at a snail-like pace, she had opened the door to us, beaming. She demanded to know what Tom's favorite foods were so that she could cook them for next time and insisted he had one of the beers she had purchased especially, neither of us telling her that Tom was really more of a wine drinker.

"You need to hold on to him," she told me in the kitchen, her voice self-important as she fussed to find a bottle opener. "He seems to like you, thank goodness. I never thought you'd manage to find a nice man like him. Not after . . ."

She never finished her sentence, of course. Mum was always one for thinking that all the unpleasantness of life was better off tucked away under a nicely turned duvet or hidden behind a good pair of net curtains. We never talked much about that year. I suspect she did a much better job than me of managing not to think about it altogether.

Mum boils the kettle as soon as I arrive, two mugs already lined up on the sideboard. I tell her I'll go and take my things upstairs. I already feel preemptively exhausted by the thought of being here, a weekend of long silences and disapproving glances stretching out ahead. I can hardly remember the last time I came here without Tom. I had forgotten how much easier it is with him. He always has the right things to say, asking polite questions and remembering what local traffic scheme

Mum is currently furious about. It had been he who suggested staying home this weekend, telling me when he brought me coffee on Thursday morning as I fussed over finding train times on my phone.

"I think you should go on your own," he said. "You seem stressed out lately. I think it would be good for you to have the break. Decompress a bit."

I paused my search abruptly, my thumb hovering over the option to purchase two seats on a train departing early Friday evening.

"A break from you?" I asked.

I only had a few minutes before I had to leave for work. It's unlike Tom to start a big conversation at a time like that. He's too thoughtful, too sensible. He cares about me too much. We're not the kind of couple who have rows at seven in the morning in our pajamas.

He shook his head.

"Not as such, no. Well, not like that anyway . . ." He glanced at my undrunk coffee as though he was trying to decide whether we should have this discussion now or save it up. I sometimes wonder how many marriages have a bank of unsaid things like ours does, a stagnant storeroom of conversations it was easier not to have. "I just think . . . well, that thing at Jules's the other night. You seemed really stressed out. I'm worried the baby stuff is getting to you."

"It's not getting to me, Tom. We're fine. We haven't even been trying that long. You're the one getting worked up about it."

"Well, regardless. I think you should just have some time with your mum. Take a break from it all. Not have to worry about anything."

For a moment I just looked back at him. There are a thousand unspoken things between us, a million ways our conversation could have ricocheted into a fight, a confrontation, a reconciliation. But if we didn't leave, we'd be late for work. If we didn't leave, then we'd have to discuss all the things neither of us wants to say. Sometimes it's easier just to leave things be.

"Fine," I said, and I refreshed my search and bought a ticket for one.

He spritzed on aftershave and bent to kiss me goodbye.

"It'll be OK," he told me. "It'll all seem worth it in the end."

When I stand in my childhood bedroom, the disconnect between us feels vast. Surreptitious doctors' appointments for repeat prescriptions and slipping a single pill into my mouth every morning felt surprisingly straightforward. At first it didn't even really feel like I was lying to him. After all, I didn't actually have to do anything differently—I just had to keep doing exactly what I had always done. Exactly what I had been doing for years. It is only now occurring to me that in Tom's head we are engaged in a great battle against nature, a team whose only focus is to create a new life. He sees every hope he has as joint, every disappointment when I get my period shared. It's funny how separate the exact same experience can feel to two different people.

And yet, while he's been worrying about making babies, I've been becoming ever more embroiled with Alistair. I message him every morning and am anxious until he responds. We meet at his flat and have sex at inconvenient hours of the day. I lie about meetings out of the office and sneak away from work to go there, or stop off on my way home and tell Tom I'm stuck at an event. I turn down Jules's sympathetic offer of a catch-up so that I can spend time with Alistair instead.

We don't talk much. He's vague when I ask him what he does for a living now, mentioning contracts and odd jobs in an offhand way that makes me feel bad for asking. I look around at his cramped flat and wonder how it must have been for him when Henry Taylor died. I remember his absolute financial reliance on his former boss, how terrified he used to be of damaging their relationship. I imagine how hard it must have been to start again, his entire livelihood yanked from beneath him. It invokes a tenderness in me, an ache, when familiarities emerge in the snatched time we spend together. Unexpected memories begin to resurface that tug somewhere in the center of my chest. The precise way he drinks his coffee, strong and dark, the taste of it bringing back early mornings when the light would fall just right. The birthmark just above his right hip, a mottle of reddening skin that looks almost like a bruise. The way his breath quickens and then stalls completely right before he comes, a tiny teetering moment when it feels as though there is nobody in the world but us, and even the basest of human needs has disintegrated.

I don't need to know what Alistair does for work now, or who is calling him when his phone buzzes from the bedside table, or where he goes when I'm not there. It feels like an unspoken agreement between us, a promise that when we're together the outside world doesn't matter. I know Alistair in a way nobody else does, the most inner and secret parts of him that he only shows to me. None of the rest of it is important.

So I stop asking questions about his life, and in return he never asks about mine. I don't mind. I don't want to talk about Tom, or my work, or my marriage. I don't want to ask him what we are, or where this is going, or if he thought about me as often as I thought about him over the years. I want Alistair to think of me as I was. The girl I was before—hopeful and young and unspoiled by all the terrible things we saw. Sometimes, when I arrive home from seeing him and catch sight of myself in the hallway mirror, I am surprised not to see an eighteen-year-old girl looking back.

I lower myself down onto my bed and pull out my phone. Mum never got round to replacing the single mattress even though Tom and I have been together for years, squeezing our bodies into a thin sliver of space every time we come to stay. The first time we were giggly, squealing about cold feet and weaving our limbs around each other. The last time we were here, we lay back-to-back, and I complained the whole journey home about how badly I'd slept while he snored beside me.

I think of the two years I spent in this bed when I came home from the island, my skin smelling faintly sour as I refused to shower. At first, I had stayed at Jules's house. It was just for a few weeks, until her parents returned from whatever trip they'd been on and I started

to catch Jules longingly looking up flights to places that sounded oth-
erworldly and far away—Costa Rica and Patagonia. I hadn't wanted
to go home. The thought of my parents' house had constricted my
chest. Its ordinariness paled beside the last few months, the stag-
nancy of suburbia already cloying beside the things I had done. But
I had nowhere else to go. I convinced myself it would be temporary.
That it was only a matter of time before Alistair would be back for
me.

I returned with my jaw clenched and climbed straight into my
childhood sheets. I told my parents what had happened in the vagu-
est and most mechanical of words. Facts stripped of feelings as my
mum tried to hide her shock. We didn't talk about it after that. We
were never a family who dealt with the complicated matter of feelings. Dad patted me on the arm and told me it would be OK, his
voice gruff and his eyes not quite meeting mine. We had no vocabu-
lary that could bridge the divide that had formed between us. When
they shut the bedroom door, I heard my mum hiss at him in tones she
didn't think I could hear:

"I told you we shouldn't have let her leave."

They were worried at first, bringing up meals on trays and talking
in low, urgent voices outside the door about whether they should call
the family doctor. They seemed unsure of how to navigate this new
version of me, this changeling child who had replaced their daughter.
When it became clear that I wasn't going back to sixth form, their
sympathy ran out, Mum standing over me and telling me I'd throw
my whole life away, and for what? Some boy? Some stupid mistake I'd
made that we should all just forget about? Their whispered conversations became blazing rows, screaming matches and smashed plates.
I pulled the duvet over my head and imagined island breezes. Hot
dishes of salty squid fresh from the sea. Cold beers. Alistair's arms
around me. It was easier than remembering everything else. Strange
hands on my skin. The metal of medical instruments. A body broken
on the beach. I scrunched my eyes shut and heard waves crashing

onto the shore, and I would feel instantly soothed. Everything would seem all right again.

I must have spent hours lying here thinking about Alistair. Waiting for him to reach out to me. Convinced he would find me when things had quieted down and the time was right. As I unlock my phone and see that he hasn't messaged me, it strikes me how fitting it is to be back here again, still waiting. Sixteen years on and some things don't change. Some things never will.

I place my phone facedown and straighten up to head downstairs. It's a trick I picked up back then, the Schrödinger's cat of modern relationships. As long as my phone screen is out of sight, then Alistair might have messaged me. There's a possibility that when I pick it up again a text will be waiting, tempting and ripe for me to read. I don't remember ever doing this with Tom. His texts have always arrived with a clockwork-like regularity, as reliable as Mum's misery.

As I stand, I catch sight of a photograph on the windowsill, a framed sixth-form picture from that single year I managed to take. It must have always been here, fading into the familiarity of the house so seamlessly I had forgotten about it, but today it catches my attention. The standard-issue cardboard frame, the dark blue flash of a school uniform. I bend down to draw level with it. I have spent so much time over the last few weeks thinking about the person I was back then. I want to look into the face of the girl about to embark on the biggest adventure of her life. I want to see who Alistair fell in love with.

My hair is long and dark, loose and falling in waves over one shoulder. My skin is pale, cheeks slightly pink. My hands are clasped in my lap, bitten fingernails and protruding knuckles. But this can't be right. This must be a different picture. Yet the uniform is unmistakable, the distinctive spotted tie dished out to local sixth-formers. My heart judders, and without thinking I flip the photograph over, facedown like my phone on the white-painted window ledge. There's a sudden and violent urge to get away. To be out of this room, with all its memories. From downstairs Mum calls to say there's a cup of tea waiting for me. I'm calling back down to her without even thinking about it.

"Actually," I say, and I'm surprised by how thin my voice sounds, "I could do with a glass of wine. Do you have any?"

❋

We eat on stools in the kitchen, Mum seeming to have decided the dining table isn't worth setting up for just the two of us. Sitting alongside each other, it's easier not to talk much, and we shovel down sausage casserole in near silence.

"I saw Caroline the other day," she says eventually, our plates almost empty. "At the big Tesco in town."

I don't look up from my food. "Oh yeah?"

"She's married now, you know. Two little kids. They look just like her."

"I didn't know that."

Since our last day together in Greece, I had seen Caroline just once. It had been easy enough to avoid her when I arrived back. She had stayed on at sixth form while I had barely left the house, and when she went away to university exactly as planned, it had been a relief to know she was gone. But one day at the train station, I saw her on the opposite platform, a twenty-first-birthday balloon tethered to her wrist, a gaggle of girls I only vaguely recognized from school surrounding her, brandishing cans of cocktails. She had only seen me just as the train pulled in, and her delighted expression had wavered. By then I had been back for over two years, and I had briefly thought how different I must look, my hair unwashed and scraped back off my face, my clothes not quite fitting properly anymore. When the train drew away, they were gone, leaving behind a trail of confetti, pink and glittering as a breeze blew it along the length of the platform.

Our parents' friendship had faltered after that, dinners at each other's houses transforming into terse greetings at neighborhood watch meetings and pretending not to see each other in the supermarket, Caroline's mum still resentful of me for leaving her daughter to travel back alone. The separation of the two families was cemented when my parents divorced and they could no longer even pretend that we would all have to have dinner again soon, when everyone was less busy.

"People act like it's catching, your husband upping and leaving you," Mum would say. "It turns out it isn't you they want to be friends with, after all. It's the idea of you. Living in a nice house and being friends with other nice couples."

For once I thought her complaining might have been accurate.

"She asked after you," Mum says. "I told her you would be back."

I swallow, the food tasteless against my tongue.

"She wouldn't want to hear from me," I say. "Not after all this time."

After the dishes are cleared away, we move to the living room. Glasses of wine are finished and refilled, and Mum already seems slightly less upright as she perches in her favorite armchair, the stiff-backed one that leaves little room to relax. There's some talent show she likes on television, and I'm grateful for something for us to stare at until it's an acceptable time to go to bed. On an advert break Mum asks me if my dad has called, the much-practiced question sounding painstakingly casual. She purses her lips in satisfaction when I say that he hasn't. It's easier to be abandoned when you aren't the only one who has been left behind.

More aspiring stars take to the stage: dancing dogs, singers, pre-pubescent dance troupes in tight, sequined leotards with brightly painted faces. Their tiny bodies fly up in the air, a sequence of am-bitious flips and acrobatics that make them look like neatly choreo-graphed rag dolls. I think of the photograph upstairs again. Mum's face is glowing in the light of the screen, an approving expression on her face. She's utterly absorbed by the circus of it all.

"Mum," I say.

"Mmm?"

"I wanted to ask you something."

"Go on." Her eyes are still glued to the television set.

"About that year. That time when I got back from traveling. You remember?"

It's enough to get her attention. Her head turns sharply. "Not . . . you're not talking about *that* time?"

I nod. "Yes."

"Well, I don't know about that." She is immediately flustered, unscrewing the wine bottle and then realizing her glass is still almost full. She puts it back down again, her fingers fluttering. "It was a very long time ago."

"I know," I say. "I know it was."

The judges announce their scores and Mum waits for me to say something else.

"What did you think of it all?" I ask. "When I got back. When I told you . . ."

She raises her hand. It's an empty gesture, and it seems almost as though she is trying to stem the tide of the past rather than stop me from speaking. It's hopeless, of course. That summer was more of a deluge than a drizzle.

"It was the right thing," she said. "Why are you bringing this up now, Rachel?" I can see that she's turned slightly pink.

"The right thing?"

"Well, yes. You were too young to . . . you know. To be a mother. A silly mistake. These things happen, don't they?"

"And what about all the rest of it?" I ask. "Not just the baby. What about—"

"Don't," she says. "We don't need to talk about it."

"Someone died, Mum."

I say it quickly. It's the only way I know how. A rush of words, a release of unspoken things that have settled between us. There's a stiff silence, a stunned air to the atmosphere. Mum is the first one to break it.

"Rachel, please." She closes her eyes and presses the heel of her hand against her forehead. "I wish you'd never told me, Rachel. Don't you think I've thought about it? Don't you think I've wondered whether we should have told you to go straight to the police? Why do you think me and your dad used to argue so much?"

Her voice is high-pitched and hoarse. From the television there's a burst of applause. It seems very far away. Neither of us speak, and then she's pulling her palm away from her face and taking a deep breath.

"You got mixed up in something that you shouldn't," she says levelly. "It was very unfortunate, what happened. But I believed you, Rachel. I chose to believe everything you told me. Do you know how terrified I've been that one day you would come back and tell me it wasn't true?"

She turns to face me, and her eyes are pleading. I know now why she wants me to hold on to Tom so badly.

"Please don't tell me you've changed your story, Rachel," she says. "Not after all this time. I couldn't bear it."

I look back at her and I know I couldn't bear it either.

"I'm not," I say. "I was telling the truth."

Her face collapses in relief. "Well then," she says. "Let's not speak of it again."

After that, I tell her I'm tired. She doesn't mention that it's not even nine o'clock yet. She just nods, her eyes still fixed to the television screen, and tells me there are fresh towels in the bathroom, if I want them. I shut the living room door behind me and trudge up the stairs, still wallpapered with a nineties-style print and lined with carefully spaced photographs. There are none of Mum and Dad. There's only me, again and again, aging as I climb up toward my room. Me as a toddler with a blunt and mousy fringe. Me on a beach, my bare legs stretched out beneath me. Me with Tom on our wedding day, him looking at me as though I am the most beautiful thing he has ever seen and me looking somewhere else entirely. You can see me grow up along these walls, a lifetime traversed in the time it takes me to reach the landing. I feel exhausted by myself, the same solemn expression in every picture, the same eyes looking out with no idea of what is to come. But there's one photograph that I can't help but look at again.

Instead of turning over my phone to see if Alistair has been in touch, I find myself flipping my school photograph, still facedown where I left it. Since we started sleeping together, I've thought a lot about who I was when we first met. I've imagined my toned stomach, my tanned limbs, the irresistible bends of my body and curve of my hip. I've remembered my face before it started to show thin lines around my eyes, before I started to stockpile expensive skincare products that promised to ward off the threat of time. When I'm with Alistair, I feel myself becoming more confident, sexier, less inhibited. When his lips touch my skin, I can close my eyes and see myself how he must have once seen me. That perfect intermingling of youth and womanhood. The tantalizing mix of knowingness and naivete.

Yet as I look at this picture, taken just months before I met him, my memories of who I was back then shift. I remembered myself looking older, more experienced. The chiseled cheekbones of my twenties and the wry arch of my eyebrows that I developed later on. Instead I find that the girl looking back at me is almost child-like. There's a shadow of puppy fat still lingering in the slope of her cheeks, an awkwardness to the way she holds her limbs. She looks uncertain and small. I was seventeen, and for the first time I realize how young I was. How young I must have seemed, fresh out of my school uniform. With a lurch, I remember that Alistair would have been about the same age as I am now.

I lower myself down onto the bed, the photograph still clutched in my fingers. So many things were said back then. So many accusations. So many things lost. Yet I had still believed in us. I had believed in Alistair and me with a conviction that had made everything else seem like it didn't matter. When I told Mum I was telling the truth, I wasn't lying. Back then I really believed I was. But as I stare down at myself, I wonder if perhaps the only person I had lied to was myself.

THEN

When Jules has a few weeks left on the island, she borrows a car from her employer's housekeeper. It is dusty and loud, the clutch making a creaking noise of protestation every time she changes gear. The battered dashboard doesn't have any indication of air-conditioning, so we wind the windows down, a hot breeze pummeling us as Jules deftly snakes the steering wheel around sharp corners in the road. I've grown used to Henry Taylor's vehicles, the artificial coolness of leather seats, Alistair waiting for me at the end of every journey. The fresh air on my skin feels like a release.

The island is a great arch of land, the flat edges of the sea rising up into mountains and then sharply back down again. Trips to the other side mean tightly turned roads that edge up the sides of hills, vertiginous drops and lone houses that cling to steep inclines. We climb toward the sky, the world opening up to us, and for a few tantalizing minutes we are at the very top with nothing around us but the vast blue broadness of the heavens. Then the road drops off and we plummet downward, gravity carrying us back toward the sea. The tarmac turns into gravel roads and then winding slips of dirt. This side of the island is almost completely uninhabited. You can only find where you want to go if you already know the way.

The twisted route makes my insides turn and I find myself gripping the side of the seat.

"Are you OK?" Jules asks.

"Fine," I lie.

Jules seems to accept my response. Recently, I have been spending even more time with her. I have found myself avoiding the other girls, finding excuses to turn down invitations to Henry Taylor's regular gatherings whenever I can. The place feels different from when it was just Alistair and me occupying its long hallways and cavernous rooms, the clamor of strangers only serving to remind me of how much I long to be alone with him.

When a message comes from Henry Taylor that he needs girls tonight, often delivered by Agnes or in a text message from Alistair, I have started to say that I am tired. That I will cover the late shift at the bar again. That I have plans. Instead I drink bad coffee on Jules's doorstep and watch the pale sliver of sea visible from her door glittering in the moonlight. We take beers down to the beach and lie flat on the sand as we try to capture the last traces of heat. We light a fire and sit in its flickering warmth, our faces opalescent and vivid with light. We have ambling and circular conversations that seem to go everywhere and nowhere. With Jules I have discovered another side of the island, one that feels peaceful and safe. If Henry Taylor and his bar are the heart of the island, then Jules is its breath, a slow and rhythmic counterpoint to his magnetic and forceful pulse.

Today we are heading for a cove right at the far side of the island. Jules came here once on a day trip with the family she works for and told me about it breathlessly.

"It's perfect," she said. "Completely cut off. Empty. It's beautiful."

Even as she spoke, I felt the tight muscles in my shoulders uncoil. Emptiness feels like exactly what I need right now. Somehow I haven't been able to escape the buzz in the back of my mind recently, a spark of irritation at other people. I need quiet. I need to be away from everyone.

The house has been anything but quiet recently. A slim rib of tension has permeated the corridors, erupting into snipes and arguments without warning. It started with Priya. A night when I came home late to raised voices in the kitchen, Priya standing at the sink with her hands on her hips, Kiera at the kitchen table.

"What do you mean, you're staying?" Priya's face was flushed, her dark eyebrows knitted.

I hovered in the doorway, unsure whether to intervene.

"Everything OK?"

"It's fine." Agnes was sitting back in a chair, brushing a knot out of her hair, seemingly unconcerned.

"It's not fucking fine." Priya pointed accusingly at her friend. "We're meant to be going. On Saturday. And now Kiera says she's staying here."

Kiera's eyes flickered between Priya and Agnes, her mouth a tight line.

"You're staying?"

"Of course she's not." Priya's voice was thin and exasperated. "Kiera? We're leaving, aren't we? We've already been here for longer than we meant—"

"Priya, *chill*." Agnes's voice was cool. "This is what traveling is like, yeah? You find a place you like, you stay for a bit. You meet new people, you go off with them. Whatever."

"*This* isn't like that," Priya said. "You know it isn't like that."

Agnes shrugged. "I'm just working," she said. "I don't know what you girls get up to on your holidays."

She said it casually, but her words dripped with meaning. For the first time I saw us as Agnes must. For her, this is her life. A way of earning as much as she can until the slipping of the seasons forces her to move on, before coming back next year. She'd been living with us for months, but all of a sudden I realized that we were totally different.

I'm not like them either, I wanted to tell her. *I want to stay here too. This is my life now.*

"Kiera," Priya said. "Kiera, please. This is a bad idea."

"She wants to stay," I heard myself saying. "She can stay here if she wants to."

"Rachel—"

"Priya." I heard my voice coming out stronger. "Let her stay. What's so bad about staying here anyway?"

For a moment Priya seemed lost for words, her mouth gaping open slightly and then closing. When she spoke again, her eyes were wet, her voice tight from trying to hold back her frustration.

"This fucking place . . ." she said. "You're crazy. All of you. Why the fuck would you want to stay here?"

She's wrong, I tell myself as Jules parks the car. *Look at this place. Just look at it. Why would you ever want to leave?*

We have to clamber down a fragile spine of steps that clings to the cliff face, worn fragments of rock that need to be sought out by our feet, each drop an indeterminable height until you take it. We edge down one section backward, our hands gripping onto the step above us. When the decline gradually levels out and we can twist around again, the sea is nearer than I imagined it might be, brilliant and blue, as though the island planned a grand reveal just for us. The cove is small and sheltered with great boulders rising up on either side to frame it. The air feels sharper, the smell of salt and sea unbroken by people and houses and boats emitting the scent of petrol. The sand is damp beneath my feet, a lingering reminder of the slip of the tide, the gentle patterns of life here.

We lay towels out on a broad, flat rock elevated up above the beach. It has been baked by the morning sun, and as I lie back against it, my muscles seem to release, and warmth spreads throughout my body.

"You know," Jules says, her voice interrupting my thoughts, "I'm going to South America for winter. You could come with me."

Waves crash down below us.

"What?"

"Come with me." Jules is completely still as she talks, stretched out on her back so that we are both looking at the sky rather than at each other. "You don't have any other plans, do you?"

She says it so easily, but she doesn't understand how deeply this place has burrowed beneath my bones. How deeply Alistair has burrowed beneath my bones. Inadvertently I run my hand along the ridge of my stomach. Am I imagining that it's slightly swollen?

"I can't afford it," I say.

It's partly an excuse, but there's truth in my words too. With the fees for our accommodation taken out of our wages, for the drinks we have while we're on shift and food that Alistair drops off at the house, there barely seems any money left by the time we are paid. Alistair dishes out cash loosely and informally, and often we have to remind him it's due. Sometimes, when we add up what we owe, we find that we've burned through our pay before we've even been given it. Alistair jots down our debts in a notepad kept in the back room, long pencil columns I try not to think about.

"Don't worry," he says. "There's always a chance to make it up."

And there always is. Money is handed out indiscriminately for attending Henry Taylor's parties or for going to help out at the house, notes stacked into slim wads and passed over the next day. We count our cash surreptitiously, glancing side-on at each other to try and calculate who has been handed the most, whether what we have made is enough to erase Alistair's scribbled-down figures.

"I could pay for your flight," Jules says. "You can get a job once we get there. You did it here, didn't you?"

It was only a few months ago, but it feels as though I was an entirely different person. Going somewhere else and starting again feels unimaginable. People would see through me. Without Alistair's approval I would just be the same shy girl who left England.

"I already have a job here," I say.

"You don't want that job," says Jules.

I roll onto my front as though to tan my back, hoping the conversation will be over.

"I don't want to talk about it," I say. "OK?"

For a moment she stays still and I think she's going to say something else. Then there's a rustle of movement as she stands, clothes dropping next to me, the sound of her tread as she jumps down from the rock. I rest my chin on my forearm and watch her go, walking down the sand toward the sea. She makes me think of sea nymphs, her cascading hair wound into braids and her long body naked. The sea foams up to meet her, and she reaches her arms high and lowers herself beneath the waves. I remember what she said to me the day I bumped into her on the beach. *Be careful of that place*, she had told me. *The locals say it's bad news.* Since then she'd screwed up her nose each time I mentioned going to the bar and suggested elaborate ways I could skive off from my shift. I once invited her to visit, thinking that being there in person might change her mind, that she would fall in love with it the way I had. Instead she had shaken her head vehemently and told me she wouldn't be seen dead there.

"And neither should you," she said.

I had pretended she hadn't said anything. I like Jules. Our friendship has been unexpected and refreshing. I don't want to spoil it with the one thing we seem to disagree on, a dislike that feels irrational and overblown to me.

As I watch, Jules's head breaks through the surface again, her hair fanning out around her. She bobs up and down as she begins to swim, short, sharp strokes carrying her farther away from me. *Be careful of that place.* I find myself thinking of the night I woke up in Henry Taylor's bed, not quite remembering how I had got there. The room was bright with early-morning sun. Something felt ugly, and the light hurt my eyes.

"You had a bit too much to drink last night, didn't you?" he had said.

My heart was beating too quickly, and I felt horribly, disgustingly sick. I had to crawl into Alistair's bed and spend the day there. When my eyes were shut, there were vague flashes from the night before, intangible and amorphous things like shadows behind a screen wall. Alistair asking me to go and drink with Henry Taylor. Feeling impossibly tired. Then a strange, slicing movement in the darkness, a blurry shape in the dimmest corner of my mind. It was something jarring, something awful. Something that made me want to curl up in a ball and sleep it off at the same time as wanting to clamber out of the bed and get away. It didn't matter where—just anywhere I could run to.

I tried to focus, tried to pinpoint what went wrong and when. I didn't understand it. I'd never been so drunk that I'd blacked out before. I remembered how Kiera had looked the night we had last been at Henry Taylor's together, her eyes wild and her jaw clenched. Could I have taken something when I was drunk? Could something have been put in my drink, perhaps in the single beer I had at the bar, or in the whiskies I had sipped by the pool? But then Alistair was so sweet, bringing me coffee and water and climbing into bed next to me, that I felt terrible for even thinking it. I had had too much, that was all. I was still no good at holding my alcohol, and I wasn't really used to whiskey. It was unforgivable of me to even think anything else.

Alistair was especially gentle that day. He didn't rush me to leave like he usually did. He told me that Henry was out and it was his day off.

"Plus you're not well," he said. "I wouldn't leave you when you're like this, would I?"

I didn't answer. Instead I leaned back against him, the smell of his aftershave making my head hurt.

"I'll miss you," he said. "When I'm gone."

My stomach tightened. "Gone?"

"Yes. Didn't I tell you?"

The effort of moving to face him made my insides swirl. "No?"

"I'm going back to London. For a business thing. Not for long, but I'll be gone a couple of weeks."

"You didn't say . . ."

"I must have forgotten. Hey, don't look like that." He reached down to lift a strand of hair, damp with sweat, from my face. "I'll be back before you know it."

"Don't go." My voice sounded more helpless than I expected it to, the blurry edges of the night before making me earnest. "Stay. I'll miss you."

"Hey," he said. "I'll miss you too. I love you, after all."

And just like that, nothing else felt important.

"I love you too."

It was the first time I'd said it to a man, even though I'd imagined it enough times. At first it felt like playacting, like some overblown line from a film script, so I said it again even though the effort made my head ache.

"Maybe you could come too," Alistair said. "To London, I mean."

"Really?"

"Well, I'll have to ask Henry, obviously. And we'd be working— you'd have to help out, be useful. Make it worth him taking you over there. But you could do that, couldn't you? And there'd be money in it—good pay, probably. It could be good for you."

I find myself smiling in anticipation of the trip. Ever since Alistair and I met, I have felt uncomfortably young in comparison, my work at the bar vapid and flimsy compared to his adult job, his grown-up life. London feels like a chance to prove that I can be a part of it. The sun is caustically bright, and I lift one hand to shield my eyes. At first I can't see Jules, her figure lost to the endless expanse of sea. And then, in the distance, I see her body rise out of the water, one arm extended upward, and then she is gone again. It takes me a moment to recognize it. The flail of her movements. The ungainly swipe of waves hinting at the cut of a current. I clamber to my feet just in time to see her surface, her open-mouthed fear, her limbs spinning in a hopeless gesture of panic as though she could cling to the air to save herself. She disappears again, a woman turned into the tide, a body lost to the swirl of the sea.

I'm running to the shore before I can even consider the stupidity of my actions, tearing off my T-shirt and dashing into the shallows. My dad used to religiously drive me to lifesaving lessons every Thursday night, a tick box for university applications that I never thought would translate into reality. I remember recovery positions and treading water in chlorine-logged pajamas, scenarios designed to prepare you for a rescue that you half imagine you will never need to make. But I never could have anticipated the whiplash of waves against my body, the saline taste of the sea, the sting of salt water in my eyes as I swim toward Jules, the white flash of her body barely visible above the swell of the tide.

My body collides with hers before I expect it to, an entanglement of limbs beneath the surface, her arms scrabbling for mine. I can feel the drag of the current, a forceful pull of the sea as it draws tight around our bodies.

"You have to relax," I shout over the roar of water in my ears. "You can't fight it. You have to relax."

Her body is hard, her limbs taut as they struggle toward the shore.

"Relax," I say again. "Like this."

I lift my legs to lay my body out flat on the waves. Jules is wide-eyed and trusting, bobs backward to try and imitate me, and loses herself again beneath the slope of the current. She emerges spluttering, her eyes screwed up, her arms windmilling.

"Like this," I say.

I reach out to support her head and pull her backward. She trembles and then leans into me until we are both belly-up, the sun a brilliant white pinprick, the sky flat and peaceable above us.

"Breathe," I command.

I hear her suck in damp, salty gulps. I crane my neck to look toward the shore. We're not so far out, even though the tide has drawn us away, pulled us gleefully into its grasp. I vaguely recall being told to swim along the shoreline, to ride with the riptide, and tentatively kick my legs. Jules is still enough now that her body comes with me, her trust in me infinite.

"Breathe," I say again, simple commands seeming like our only option.

I'm amazed at how calm I am, how careful. I kick again and find that we're moving, gentle motions that seem to ease the drag of the water. I focus on the methodology of it, the scissoring motion of my feet, the weight of Jules's body. As the suction relents, she flips onto her front and paddles with me, her eyes still wide as we swim parallel to the shore, maneuvering our way back toward the beach with slow, careful strokes.

We could have been out there for hours or minutes. Time becomes slippery, the only thing that tethers me to it the laborious in-and-out motion of my lungs, the strokes of our arms, the count of each kick. When one foot collides with the rocky ocean floor, it is as though everything speeds up again, the sound of the sea becoming louder, a survival instinct sending me scrambling to stand. I clutch at Jules's arm and we stagger to the shore, collapsing in the shallows with our bodies tangled together. Jules is crying, the tears on her face indistinguishable from seawater. We lie with our backs flat on the sand, air raking our chests as we gasp for breath. Neither of us say anything. We are stunned by our survival, empty of the power to speak. Beside me, Jules's face is bloodless, her mouth fighting to replace the air she lost. It takes a few minutes for her inhales to turn into words, raspy and half-formed syllables that mimic the juddering beat of my heart.

"Thank you," she is saying over and over again. "Thank you. Thank you. Thank you."

I reach out and take her hand, cold and puckered, as though the sea has soaked beneath her skin.

"It's OK," I manage.

We lie there until our bodies have recalibrated to land, our lungs adjusting to a plentiful supply of oxygen, and then we lie there for longer. It doesn't feel like any words are needed, so I'm surprised when Jules rolls over, her face earnest.

"You saved my fucking life," she says. "I thought it was over for me."

"You're being dramatic," I say, even though I'm not sure she is. "You would have been OK. You were just panicking."

"No, really." Jules pulls herself to seated. "I owe you one. Seriously. If there's anything. Literally anything . . ."

"It's fine," I say. "Really. You would have done it too."

There's a moment when we are silent, our breath synchronized with the fading crash of waves against sand. Then I look at her face and I remember the bite of her words earlier, the relief that I will see Alistair again, the terror in her eyes as she broke the surface of the water.

"Just . . ." I pause, wondering if I'm being ridiculous. "Can we not talk about the bar again? About . . . well, whatever it is you think you know. It doesn't matter. I don't want to talk about it. All right?"

Her forehead puckers into a frown. "I don't know, Rachel, I—"

"Please. Just trust me. I know what I'm doing."

She pauses and then nods. "Of course," she says. "Whatever you want."

Then we lie back and listen to the sea sweep out, our bodies heavy against the sand, the beating of blood in our necks and wrists an affirmation that we are alive.

NOW

The train can't get back to London quickly enough. A couple of nights at my mum's, and I'm already itching for the city. For the welcoming lights of a Pret at the train station, the tired warmth of a late Sunday afternoon, the slovenly emptiness of the tube before it packs back full of commuters in the morning. But more than that, I'm desperate to see Alistair. The picture in my childhood bedroom has unsettled me. As the countryside thickens into the dense suburbs of the city, I scrabble to pull together my recollections of that time. With a jolt, a memory surfaces, one left tucked away and forgotten about for years. How, the first time we had sex, he had leaned in and spoken about my youth with a lust-bloated reverence. It used to feel special, a compliment I had done nothing to deserve. Now I remember it and feel slightly sick.

I've already messaged Tom to tell him I'll be back late, my suitcase waiting in the hallway for the 2 p.m. train. Then I flicked into a parallel conversation, messaging Alistair to tell him I'm on my way over, surprised at how easily the words form on the screen. I'm not used to being so decisive with him. He was always the one to make decisions. When he texts back to ask me if everything is OK, I don't respond.

In the end, I decide to take a cab to his place. The backseats of taxis are always such wondrously anonymous places, dark enclaves sliced briefly with passing streetlamps, easily silenced with a few withering responses to inquisitive drivers. I settle back into a far corner and pull out my phone. There are a few emails from work, a text from Tom asking if I want dinner when I get in, and a new Facebook message. I click to open it, knowing who it will be.

Just landed! reads Helena's message. Are you free this week?

I had almost forgotten our plan to meet up. Perhaps I was half hoping she would decide against it, a silent pact between us to leave the past in the past. I wonder how well she remembers me from back then. She recognized me in the bar straightaway. Did she expect to see someone much younger too? Some ghost of a schoolgirl barely grown into her body?

I'm free whenever, I type, and then slot my phone back into my handbag.

When I ring the bell for Alistair's flat, he buzzes me in at once. The familiar thrum of excitement at the thought of him waiting for me is ridged with a new and terrible anxiety. It sits in my chest and takes up too much space, pressing down hard on my lungs and constricting my throat. As I climb up the narrow staircase, an industrial strip light flickering at the top, I find myself wondering if Alistair is really who I think he is.

He's holding the plywood door open for me when I get there. I turn my face when he goes to kiss me, and instead his lips land on my cheek, dry and awkward.

"Hey," he says.

I can see that his eyes are searching my face for clues.

"Are you OK? Your message sounded . . ."

"I need to talk to you," I say. I haul my jacket off and sit down on his sofa without waiting to be invited.

"O-kay . . ." He elongates the word, the stretched-out vowels sounding wary.

"It's about when we first met."

He exhales heavily, a puff of air that sounds as though he has been waiting to release it. "Is this about—"

"Please," I say. "Just let me talk."

He raises his hands in a gesture of mock defeat and then lowers himself down onto the sofa beside me. He's so close I can feel the heat of his leg next to mine, and in spite of myself I feel a faint pulse of longing. I'm instinctive in my response to him, all the parts of me that control my desire finely tuned to his body. I cross my legs to create space between us.

"I need to know if it's true," I say to him. "All the stuff that happened back then. The stuff Agnes said . . ."

His face collapses, crumpling in disappointment.

"Are you kidding?" he says. "You're not bringing all that up, are you? It was years ago."

"It's just . . ." I immediately falter, scrabbling against how upset he looks. "I protected you. I need to know . . ."

"Of course it wasn't true," he says. "I can't believe you're even asking."

"But there were things that happened," I say, my voice wavering. "Remember London . . ."

"You're not still thinking about London?" he says. "Rachel, you can't beat yourself up about that."

He squeezes my hand, and I can't quite muster the nerve to tell him that's not what I meant.

"I knew you'd be worrying about this," he says. He reaches out and covers my hand with his. It's large and reassuring, and I want to believe him so badly. I want him to tell me it's all OK. "I knew this would come up again. Of course it was going to. It's not something you can forget about that easily. But I promise that you did the right thing."

"But didn't you think I was too young?" I say. It comes out too quickly, a jumble of words that have been building since I saw the photograph. "Back then? You were older . . . didn't you think I was a bit young to be . . . to be . . ."

"Rachel." He's smiling now, that silky sideways lift of one side of his mouth that always used to make my heart turn somersaults. "Are you kidding? Is *that* what's stressing you out?"

He moves his hand to my leg, one thumb stroking my thigh.

"I get it. Nowadays it would seem like a big gap. I know there's been so much talk about that kind of thing. But it was different back then. I mean, do you remember anyone thinking it was weird? It was just how things were. Besides, look at us now." The pressure of his hand is growing. "Some people are just meant to be together. All these years later, and I still feel the same about you. Age isn't import-ant. We're still the same people we were back then."

In spite of myself, I feel a warmth pulse from the base of my spine and extend out through my entire body. Through all the physicality of the last few weeks, we haven't talked about what we are or where this is going. I haven't dared to let myself dream it might be more than sex for him, a convenient throwback to long-ago days. But now he's looking at me as though I'm something precious and perfect and he wants to consume me in my entirety.

"But I looked young, didn't I?" I say weakly.

"Rachel . . ." His voice lingers on each syllable of my name, and he shakes his head in disbelief. "If you could see yourself back then . . . you were so self-assured and beautiful. You knew exactly who you were. Of course, I wouldn't have usually gone for someone so much younger, but you weren't like the others, were you? You were already who you were going to become. You already knew exactly who you were, not like most eighteen-year-olds who are still so busy trying to figure themselves out. And you were so *sexy*. Do you think that if you'd have looked like a kid I'd have gone anywhere near you? No. If anything, I was intimidated by you."

Pictures can be misleading, of course. A one-off trick of lighting and angles. And the school uniform wouldn't have helped.

"Really?"

"God, yes. This is so like you though. You could never see it, how beautiful you were. You'd find anything to put yourself down. But trust me, you looked incredible. And you were so mature. Anyone would have been mad not to see it. And I loved you, you know. So much. We were never like that. We were special. Still are."

I feel a tension ease slightly in my chest. He is right, of course— I've never quite been able to believe that someone could want me the way he did. Maybe I am just looking for excuses. Looking for ways to tell myself he never loved me really, that there must have been some kind of other explanation for how he was. How we were. I've never been good at accepting attention.

"Nothing's changed, you know." His hand moves more slowly now, tracing up my thigh. "If anything, you're even sexier now. I've never wanted someone this much for this long. Sometimes I don't think you'll ever know what you do to me, Rachel Evans."

I don't correct him, even though I haven't been Rachel Evans for years. It feels like a relief to let him kiss me, to let him take me to the bedroom and undress me, to wipe away everything with the familiarity of his hands against my skin. When he's inside me, he brings his mouth close to my ear, and for the first time in over sixteen years he tells me he loves me, and it feels exactly like it did the very first time. Just for a moment I really believe that it was us all along. Just for a moment I let myself believe that it always will be.

THEN

When we land in London, the weather is dismal. The sky is slate gray and blank, the flashing lights of the runway only emerging from a turgid sheet of cloud seconds before we land. I peer out of the window, still patterned with the tiny flecks of ice that formed up in the clouds, and can't believe that it is already October. I should have already been weeks into college by now. The promise of the Christmas holidays would be glittering just out of grasp, the only respite from the unremitting grind of A-level history and remedial computer studies. Summer would have slipped away from us already, a hazy memory of sunscreen and ice cream vans in the park as an autumn chill slipped between increasingly dense layers of clothes. Instead the air outside the arrivals gate feels crisp after the heavy Greek heat. I haven't brought a proper jacket with me, just a thin cardigan borrowed from Helena to ward off the increasingly cool island evenings. In the car to the hotel, the heating is switched on and the slowly circulated air feels strange and scratchy, an artificial lung pumping warmth into a stifled space. I already miss the faded heat of the end of summer, how the breeze feels like a blanket being slipped around your shoulders.

"Are you OK?" Alistair asks me.

I just nod. I'm slotted in the backseat between Helena and Kiera, with Alistair as the front passenger. I had thought it was only me who had been asked to London and had been vaguely disgruntled to learn that Kiera and Helena were coming too. But now that we're here, I'm glad they are with me. It feels surreal to be back, with the car making a slovenly stop-start progress through the traffic-clogged arteries of the city. The familiar smell of Kiera's cheap perfume grounds me slightly as high-rise buildings and great glass office blocks loom around us. I've only ever been to London on school trips before, or on the occasional family outing when Mum and Dad would march me around museums. It feels grown-up and terrifying to be here as someone with work to do. Not a tourist, but part of Henry Taylor's entourage. Alistair has already briefed us on the boat to the mainland. There are going to be business meetings, long dinners, nights out. As we disembarked from the plane, we all prickled with excitement, the city feeling a thousand miles from our parents' suburban homes and the slow peace of the island.

"You know the drill," Alistair said. "If we keep them happy, then Henry's happy. Got it?"

Helena demands that we turn the radio up, and Kiera stares out of the window, her jaw set and unmoving when Helena squeals as her favorite song comes on and starts to wriggle her hips against the leather seats. Alistair rolls his eyes, but I can see that he's smiling, glancing at Helena as she sings along tunelessly.

"Turn it up!" she insists again.

He reaches for the volume control, and it feels like we are friends on our way to a party. The rain starts to come down heavily, a clatter against the roof of the car creating a hypnotic beat to Helena's dance. Around us the city slips into night, and I feel ready to be brought to life.

※

That evening, Henry Taylor is entertaining clients at a nightclub, and we are supposed to be meeting them. We get ready in our hotel room, sharing a bottle of vodka as we sluice on lipstick and pass around outfits to be tried on. I settle on a tight black dress that Kiera offers me. It has thin straps and a square neckline, and when I glance at myself in the mirror I'm surprised to find that I look good.

"I love this," I breathe.

She shrugs. "Henry gave it to me," she says, in a way that suggests she doesn't care that he did.

I feel the same stab of jealousy I do when the other girls make more money than me. Henry Taylor has never given me gifts.

"You can have it," she says, and when I go to thank her, she is already turning away, shrugging off my words.

Kiera has seemed listless recently. Over the last few weeks she has shaken her head anytime anyone has invited her to the beach, and the deep bronze of her skin is beginning to pale. Even though we are dressing up to go out, her hair looks unwashed, clotted at the roots. She pats it with talcum powder from the bathroom instead of washing it and fluffs clouds of white with her fingertips until its usual golden hue returns. Against her scalp a trace of silvery residue remains, and she tucks and untucks one rogue strand behind her ear over and over again.

As we layer on coats of mascara and tease hair dried out from salt water and sun into submission, I am reminded of getting ready with Caroline for the first party at Henry's house. I look back at myself in the bathroom mirror and feel like a different person entirely. If the girls at school could see me now, they wouldn't be able to believe it. Before I turn away, I spot a bruise on the back of my thigh, its deep purple heart fading into shades of yellow. I press against it with my thumb and feel the hard resistance of flesh. I somehow can't remember how it got there.

"Ready?" Helena asks.

She's wearing a bright red dress with her lips a matching shade of burgundy, her hair straightened and her eyes lined with thick black kohl. She looks completely different from the Helena I know. Being in a city has sharpened us and made us into slicker versions of our island selves.

"Ready," I say.

※

It's after midnight by the time we arrive, a queue snaking around the outside of the club. Somehow we're waved to the front. Somebody says Henry Taylor's name and a bouncer steps aside to let us in. It's my first time in a real nightclub. The floor seems to vibrate with a pulsing, throbbing bass line, and beams of light flash and glimmer like stars. We're taken to a table up above the dance floor, leather seats and a bottle of vodka in an ice bucket, unfamiliar bodies crammed into a booth. They are mostly men, older and sharp-suited, although there are a few women I don't recognize too. They're all beautiful—willowy and thin with long glossy hair. I immediately feel dumpy and young, even in Kiera's dress. Henry Taylor gestures at me to sit, and I feel the same unidentifiable revulsion that I recognize from the day I woke up in his bed. The music is loud, and I turn my face toward Helena so that she can hear me speak.

"Where's Alistair?" I ask.

She doesn't hear me at first, frowning and shaking her head, gesturing at her ear for me to speak up.

"*Where's Alistair?*"

She takes my face in her hands so that she can bring her mouth close to me. Her breath is wet against the side of my cheek.

"He's not coming tonight," she says. "Didn't he say?"

I shake my head.

Someone is lifting up a bottle of vodka, and it's so large it takes two hands to hold it. They beckon Kiera over, and she bends down so that they can lift it up above her head and pour it straight into her mouth. She splutters, and then it's my turn.

"Just a bit," I say, but nobody really seems to be listening.

I have to wrench my neck back so that the neck of the bottle meets my lips, and they pour so much I almost choke on it. The liquid is cold and strong, my eyes stinging as I try to swallow. Helena is laughing and demanding to go next. She takes it much more easily, wiping her mouth with the back of her hand and grinning when somebody half-heartedly cheers her.

"Come on," she says to me. "Let's dance."

I turn to head toward the dance floor, but Helena pulls me back.

"No," she says. "Here."

It feels awkward at first, dancing in the roped-off area without the pulse of the crowd around us. I'm used to dancing in the bar back on the island, bodies pressed up on all sides, always too many people to fit into the tiny space. Instead we dance in front of Henry's table. His guests barely even look up at us, too busy with their own conversations, their hands cradling their own drinks. Helena weaves her fingers through mine and pulls me close, her hips swaying. I look for Kiera and see that she is seated between two men, accepting a glass from one of them, looking down at the table as they talk across her.

"Shall I get Kiera?" I shout over the music.

Helena shakes her head. "She's fine," she says. "Don't you want to dance with me?"

She's laughing as she says it, her eyes glittering. I know she's taken something. Since the first night I saw Kiera high at Henry Taylor's house, I've realized that drugs are passed around the circle easily and with an expectation you will take them if they are offered to you. It seems to come with the territory: a slim line of white powder on a table, somebody talking at you with their jaw clenched as you nod and pretend to keep up. Last time we went up to the house, I tried it, rubbing the powder into the seams of my gums and becoming convinced I was dying when my heart started to pound.

"You're just coming up," Helena had said, her own eyes almost entirely consumed by her pupils. "Just enjoy it, babe. Relax."

Even though I wasn't sure if I really wanted it, I had been surprised at how good it made me feel. Being back in Henry Taylor's house had been a strange sensation, as though I had done something terrible and was waiting to get caught. I felt restless perched on his vast sofa, my body twitchy as I suppressed an unmistakable urge to leave. But the drugs made me forget. They made me feel like I was powerful and perfect, like everyone was good, even when a tense sliver of doubt clamored to tell me otherwise.

Helena and I go to the toilets, and she hands me a sachet of powder balled up in thin paper meant for roll-up cigarettes. We chink them together solemnly as though they are glasses of champagne and throw them back with mouthfuls of beer. When I come up, it feels incredible, far better than the last time. The music is heavy and perfect, and the lights are a thousand times brighter and more brilliant, and everyone should feel like this all the time. I tell Helena that I love her, and I don't think she hears me because she just reaches out and smiles and strokes my hair. I wish Alistair were here so that I could tell him too. But then everyone is standing up and Henry Taylor is telling us we're leaving, and the thought makes me want to weep. I want to stay here. I don't want to clamber into a taxi and go back with him. I can't imagine sitting still.

We go to Henry's hotel suite, all of us in a motorcade of London cabs that slip through the city as I fidget against my seat. Helena and I end up in a different taxi to Kiera, and the world seems to slide by slowly, the streetlights that slice through the darkness too bright and the music from the car stereo too quiet. Helena strokes my hand as I look out onto the city, and at one point we cross a bridge and I feel as though my heart could give out with the beauty of it all. I've been anxious for the last few weeks, an unsettled sensation embedded into every day. I worry about my missed period, pushing the possible implications to the back of my mind. I worry about everyone leaving, about exactly what happened that night I can't quite seem to remember. But then there are moments like this when it all feels worth it. When I know I will never be able to go back to my life as it used to be. I look across at Helena and find that we're beaming at each other, the hum of drugs in our system making us ecstatic. In this moment I can't quite believe that only a couple of months ago we had never even met. I feel as though the island has drawn an unbreakable bond between us, an experience that nobody but us could possibly fathom.

The hotel room is a vast space with enormous glass windows. We're so high up that London stretches out all around us, sparkling and dense with possibility. If Caroline could see me now, I think. If they could all see me now, all those people from school who thought I was strange, or, worse, didn't think about me at all. If they could all see me now. Someone is snorting something off a shiny glass table, and someone is putting music onto a sound system.

"Can I have some?" I ask a man who is scraping out lines.

He pats the spot on the sofa next to him. "Sure."

He smells good, a sweet sharp fragrance that makes me want the island badly. It takes me a moment to realize it's because he's wearing the same aftershave as Alistair, a scent that now evokes an involuntary, almost innate reaction in me. I glance sideways and notice he's good-looking. A bit older than Alistair maybe, with sandy blond hair and a square jaw. When I bend down with a rolled-up note in my hand, he places his palm on my back and I find that I don't really mind. Every inch of my skin is telling me it wants to be touched, reminding me how good it feels to be close to people. Really, we're all hardwired to be social creatures. It seems ridiculous that we're all so straitlaced, so careful to keep our distance, to confine touch to relationships. It feels good to let him stroke the small of my spine as I sit beside him, his hand movements slow and rhythmic and calm.

Later on I forget about him. I want to stare at the skyline with Helena beside me. I want to dance on the sofa. I want to find Kiera, but nobody knows where she's gone. People are starting to disappear, calling taxis and pairing off. The music gets turned down. Don't they know it's still early? Helena has started talking to a man I don't recognize, but I know I want to keep on moving. I don't want to listen to her flirt and pretend to laugh at something some guy is saying. I pour myself a drink. I wander into one of the bedrooms. That's when I see him, the man wearing Alistair's aftershave.

"Hi," I say.

He's stretched out on the bed, and I dive down next to him. I feel silly and uninhibited. Exactly as I've always wanted to be, but never quite managed.

"Go and shut the door," he says.

I notice for the first time that he has an American accent. I'm not sure I've ever even met an American person before in real life. It's sexy and glamorous, so I do what he says.

"Now come back here."

"O-kay." I stretch the last syllable out, faux-American. He doesn't laugh.

I lie down next to him. He isn't smiling at me like he did earlier. He looks slightly bored, as though I'm a tiresome child he needs to keep entertained.

"So," he says. "I hear that you fuck."

"I . . ." I sit up. "I'm sorry?"

"That you fuck? Right?"

"No," I say. "That's . . . I don't know what you're talking about."

He pats the bed next to him again impatiently. I slowly, stupidly lower myself back down again, carefully laying my body next to him as my heart thrums.

"OK . . ." he says. "So, you haven't been sleeping with Alistair?"

"No," I say, too quickly.

"No?" he says. "That's not what I heard."

I don't reply. There's a tension stretched between us, the kind that makes me unsure whether I should be getting up and leaving or staying to hear what he knows. The fact that my relationship with Alistair is supposed to be a secret has been drilled into me ever since we started seeing each other. I've never told anybody, and I'm certain he hasn't either. Beside me, the man raises one hand. Slowly, idly, as if he couldn't care less that my breathing has sped up and that my body is braced to leave, he lets it drop down atop my wrist and slide back and forth. He's stroking me as you might a dog, gently and carefully as though to calm me, but the weight feels like a restraint, like hand-cuffs pressing me down to the bed.

"I don't know what you're talking about," I say, but I still don't move and his hand stays where it is.

He laughs. "Sure you don't," he says.

His hand slides across from my arm and toward my torso. He presses one thumb into the ridge of my hip bone so hard that it hurts, a deft prod that feels almost as if he is testing me and how much my body will relent to his touch.

"I'm not . . ." I sit up, struggling to make my words form into a sentence. "I'm . . . sorry. No. You must be mixing me up with some-one else."

I want to be back in the vast living room with Helena and Kiera. I want to be back in the nightclub, clinging to Helena's hand and singing along to songs I only half know the words to. All of a sudden, for the first time in months, I want to be back at my parents' house. I wonder, with a shocking and terrible clarity, what I'm doing here at all. What I've been doing all this time. It's Saturday night. I should be with Caroline, stretched out on one of the twin beds in the room she shares with her sister, watching a bad film and sipping a single sneaked Smirnoff Ice. I should be finishing up schoolwork tomorrow, exercise books spread out over the kitchen table. I should be asleep in my bed, my parents snoring in the room next to me. The man sits back with a shrug, his eyes languid as he looks me up and down.

"That's a shame," he says. "It would be really bad for Alistair if Henry found out. I would really hate for him to lose his job over this."

There's a horrible moment when I realize he's leaving the choice in my hands. When I know that I could leave if I wanted to, or I could stay. The decision is the worst part.

Wordlessly, without looking at him, I lie back down and I shut my eyes. When he leans over me, I imagine I am somewhere else. I am asleep in my parents' house, I think. I am waking up next to Alistair. I am back on the island. When he touches me, I can very nearly taste sea air.

✳

Afterward I wonder if I did want it, after all.

I dress quietly and slip out of the penthouse suite. Almost everybody seems to have left. I tiptoe past Helena using a coat as a blanket, her dress riding up to the curve of her thigh. I walk out into the bleak autumn air without a coat and remember the vague thrum of attraction I had felt earlier on in the evening. The quick pulse of lust that man's familiar scent had sent through me. Throwing myself down on the bed, giggly and excitable. Perhaps even flirtatious. Afterward he had smirked as he pulled his boxers back on.

"I knew you wanted it," he had said, and I had squeezed my eyes shut and tried to pretend his words hadn't sent a visceral shock of horror through me. Maybe I had. Maybe I had made him think I did.

The streets are still wet from last night's rain, puddles pooling at curbsides and bright red buses plowing grimy water onto the pavement. I don't try to dodge them, getting soaked as a car cuts through a flooded pothole. The cold shock of the water feels good, a momentary distraction from the numbness that has overtaken my body. It's as though I'm not here at all, as though I'm floating above the ground. I'm surprised people don't walk straight through me. I think of Alistair and then stop myself. What will he say when he finds out? We had something precious and perfect. Of course I had to spoil it. Of course I had to mess everything up.

I walk aimlessly at first, even though I know what I'm searching for. I step out into a road without looking where I'm going, and a cyclist swerves and swears at me. I imagine how I must look, still in my dress from last night with my makeup smeared down my face. It's that surreal time of morning, early enough that night workers are sleepily making their way home while others wait at bus stops to open up coffee shops, or to relieve colleagues from their dawn shift. The in-betweenness of it feels vaguely reassuring, as though I could slip right in around these people with places to go and things to do without them noticing me. As though I am part of yesterday while they head toward today.

I go into the first chemist I find, a lit-up shop on the corner of a concrete boulevard. The pregnancy test is kept within a plastic container to deter shoplifters, and I have to wait with my eyes cast down at the floor as a teenage shop assistant summons her manager to open it. I wonder how desperate you have to be to steal a cheap pregnancy test, how terribly things must have gone wrong for you, and then I remember I only just have enough money to pay for it myself. Somehow Alistair hasn't seemed to get around to paying me recently, and I haven't bothered to chase. I hurriedly try to calculate how much Henry Taylor must owe me, but then realize I haven't been keeping track.

I walk until I find a McDonald's. The familiar scent of wilting Mc-Muffins and coffee reminds me of when Dad would sometimes take me for breakfast on a Saturday while Mum did the shopping. I slide past the already growing queue: harried-looking mothers still in their night-shift uniforms herding children into booths, and construction workers dressed in high-vis jackets clutching paper bags as they head out to their first jobs of the day. The floor is littered with *Wet Floor* signs, and a disgruntled cleaner attempts to mop away the remains of the night. A girl still dressed as if going to a party sobs into her hash browns as her half-drunk friend pats her on the back.

"He's not worth it!" I hear her declare as I edge around their table.

I weave through the bustle of customers and hope that nobody notices me as I make my way to the back of the restaurant. No one demands to know where I'm going as I push open the bathroom door, or asks to see a receipt. One of the basins is stained with streaks of vomit, a half-digested cheeseburger clogging the plughole. I hold my breath as I enter one of the cubicles and tell myself it will only take a second. That I can leave as soon as this is done. I pull down my underwear and squat above the toilet bowl, and as I do, I try not to think about when I put them on. How I had scrabbled to find them on the floor, desperate to cover myself back up. I hadn't taken my dress off the whole time.

My hands are shaking as I read the instructions. It seems simple enough. Pee on the stick and then wait for my life to change, possibly forever. I have to break it down into digestible parts, relaxing my body enough that urine trickles out, wiping, pulling my panties back up, placing the stick down onto a sanitary bin. Just one thing after the other, tiny tasks that I can focus on individually to block out the enormity of what is happening. To block out the dank and awful feeling of last night. I crouch on the ground while I wait for the result, my back pressed up against the toilet door. Outside the cubicle a mother enters the restroom with a chattering child in tow. She responds exasperatedly to her high-pitched questions, and urges her daughter to hurry up. From my vantage point I can see the lower half of tiny legs clad in bright pink tights swinging cheerfully from a toilet that is too big for a little girl.

I wait until they have washed their hands, the girl exclaiming gleefully about the now-putrid vomit, before I look. I lift the test up between two fingers and hold my breath. I already knew what it would say, but I thought I would panic when I saw that pale line of confirmation. That I would feel sick or scared or terrified. Yet instead a dull glimmer of hope sparks somewhere inside me. Here, in a McDonald's bathroom, amid all the things that have happened over the last twenty-four hours, is something pure and perfect and hopeful. It is as though somebody is handing me another chance.

NOW

Helena and I arrange to meet after work, and all afternoon I am nervous. I have worksheets to put together, and I sit behind my screen clicking through formatting options and graphics without really seeing them. Instead a summer unfolds before me. Helena with her hair falling loose and her head thrown back with laughter. Jules tracing the ridges of my palm and reading my future with the tips of her fingers. Alistair, always there, always with his hands on me, his body molding into mine, the salt-sweet smell of sun cream and sweat as my skin became indistinguishable from his. The soft curve of my stomach against a summer dress as winter edged toward the island, a blossoming amid the cooling sea and darkening skies.

Instinctively I reach up to touch my waist, my hand falling flat where a tiny bump once was. It's a body that's seen a thousand things since, that's reformulated itself as I became a different woman, filled out and grown up, yet I will always remember how it felt back then. I thought of myths of swanlike women impregnated by gods and felt vast in my power, the possibility of creation, the strange sensation that we had turned the fleeting act of sex into something tangible. I remembered diagrams of wombs drawn out on blackboards in my classrooms, triangular and alien-like, and wondered that something so scientific could suddenly seem so magical.

My body felt like an entire universe even though its gradual expansion would have been barely noticeable, a dilation of sinew and flesh that only made sense with a litany of missed periods, and the fact that Alistair and I had hardly ever used condoms. It felt better that way, I told myself, closer. And he liked it like that. That's what he had wanted.

My phone lights up and I fumble past piles of paper to reach it. I want it to be Alistair so badly it hurts, and my disappointment at seeing Tom's name is sharp.

We should talk tonight.

I glance at the glowing numerals at the top of my phone screen. It's already half past four. I wonder how long he's spent agonizing over sending me those few words, worried about how I'll react. For a moment I think I could tell him. He would make me dinner and pour me a glass of wine, and over our gleaming countertops I could share everything with him. The person I used to be. The things I saw. The packet of pills hidden upstairs in the bathroom cabinet. I could finally make us into the fantasy of marriage I'd had years ago, the sharing of our every crevice, the slow revelations of one person to another until Tom knows me as well as I know myself.

He'd be shocked, yes. But then he would reach out and take my hand and tell me it's OK. That I've told him now. That we can figure it all out. There's always been something so reassuring in how Tom approaches problems that it blinds me, takes the breath out of me with relief. It makes me want to curl into him and close my eyes while he makes things better at the same time that it makes me feel sick with myself and my reliance on him. I leave the message on read with the kind of satisfaction that simultaneously makes me feel powerful and makes me wonder who I even am. How I became the kind of person who takes a love like that and wrings it out until both hearts are bloodied and battered.

Instead I tap into my conversation with Helena.

Still on for tonight?

She reads it at once.

100%. You?

My thumbs hover above the screen for a moment, just long enough to let the fantasy of crawling home and allowing Tom to take all the hurt away to dissipate.

Of course, I type. Looking forward to seeing you.

I had found myself surprised by the bar she chose, somewhere seemingly anonymous in a London suburb that I have to look up to figure out the best route.

Are you staying around there? I'd asked her when she told me, and she took a few hours to respond.

Something like that.

The unfamiliarity of the journey gives me space to distract myself, to focus on tube maps and on calculating how long it will take to get there. It's only when I'm a few stops away that I allow myself to remember where I'm going. Who I'm going to see. My last meeting with Helena was suitably single-minded, my eagerness to contact Alistair narrowing my vision. But this is a woman who was there for that brief window of summer, who had slept in narrow beds alongside me and cleared up my vomit when I'd had too much to drink. The person who had seen my transformation from shy schoolgirl to woman, ushering it along with beers beneath sunsets and secrets whispered into salt-thickened air. She had been as much a part of that time as

Alistair, as dominant a figure in the fracture that would eventually cleave my life in two. Before and after. Rachel then and Rachel now.

The bar is tucked down a side street a short walk from the station, and I spend a few minutes hunched over my phone, pacing back and forth as I try to determine which direction the indecipherable digital map is taking me. By the time I find it, I'm late, flustered from the heat of the tube and from navigating unfamiliar streets. It's an unseasonably warm day, the air vibrating with the unexpected delight of a late-season heat wave. I wonder if there are sweat patches on the pale blue fabric of my dress. If Helena, accustomed to the Mediterranean sun, will spot them and wonder how I became so depressingly English again. I scan the room and then realize I hadn't needed to hurry. The bar is sparsely populated, a couple sharing a bowl of chips in a booth and a cluster of women about my age huddled around a table. Helena must be as terrible at timekeeping now as she was back then.

Bolstered by the thought that I have time to cool off, I make a beeline for the bar, the promise of a cold glass of wine already making my head feel clearer. But before I can order, someone is calling my name. One of the women crowded around the small table is standing up, a hand suspended in the air as she tries to attract my attention. It's Helena, dressed in a denim jacket and sensible skinny jeans. She looks as suburban as I do, aside from the long hair that still cascades down her back and the hint of a tan. A clutch of faces have turned toward me, their eyes expectant.

They are all so ordinary-looking that it takes me a moment to recognize them. They could be a book club, or a group of university friends catching up over coffee. They have practical haircuts and wear the kind of clothes that suggest they've come straight from the office. Over the last two decades I never imagined them aging. I never thought the same complaints that corresponded with the gradual slipping away of youth would be bothering them too. In my mind they were all still eighteen or nineteen, perfect and untouchable, women who worried about where you could get the cheapest beers instead of marriages and careers and children. To me they had been eternal, frozen in time, but here they could be anyone. They could be me.

I notice Priya and Eloise first, their necks craning to take me in, their hair cut into short, tidy bobs. It takes me a few seconds to recognize Agnes, heavily pregnant and cradling her belly as she smiles tentatively. I feel a pull deep inside me, a familiar surge of emptiness as I become aware of the stillness of my womb where once there was the tiniest and most hopeful hint of life. All four of them are motionless, waiting for me to say something. Instead I turn so quickly that my handbag swings and hits me sharply in the hip. My body is moving before my thoughts can catch up, a primal urge to escape seizing control of all my limbs and propelling me away from their stares.

I push hard against the heavy bar door, the heat of the day immediately dense again. The street seems to swim past, my legs moving mechanically. I realize almost at once that I'm going the wrong way, that I'm heading away from the station instead of toward it, but I don't turn around. I emerge onto a busy street packed with people. Someone is playing music from an old stereo and bars have flung open their front doors, setting tables out in the street to catch the last gasps of summer. I weave around teenagers clutching cider cans on the curb and colleagues who have escaped from the office to head to the nearest park with carrier bags crammed with M&S picnic food. I catch the shoulder of a woman emerging from a shop holding a stack of disposable barbecues, and she shouts after me, her voice furious.

"Watch where the *fuck* you're going!"

The flimsy magic of a hot day in the city is broken, and it's too crowded, the air too muggy, the warmth rising from the pavements suffocating. I hear someone call my name behind me, her voice thin against the whir of traffic and the hum of a restaurant sound system. In desperation I pull out my phone, stabbing at the touchscreen to try and find a map, but before the app can load, a hand has grasped my shoulder.

"Rachel—don't run off. Please."

Her voice is different, deeper without the inflections of girlhood that used to linger in all our throats.

"What the fuck?" I say. "Eloise and Priya . . . *Agnes*, for God's sake. What were you thinking?"

Helena shakes her head, a muscle twitching in the indent of her jaw.

"I didn't mean to spring it on you . . ."

"What is this then? Why did you ask me to come here? You made me think I was just meeting you."

"Would you have come if you'd known?"

"Would I have—" I break off in disbelief, my words trailing into the early-evening hum. I turn my attention back to my phone before Helena can start to speak. The connection is sketchy, and I stab at the screen as directions resolutely refuse to load.

"Rachel, please," she says, her voice scattered by nerves and noise. "Come back inside. Just hear us out. You're here now. We're all here. We can't just go home without—"

"Without *what*?" I thrust my phone back into my handbag in exasperation. "What's the point of all this? What's it all *for*? What do you think you're all here to achieve?"

For a moment Helena doesn't respond. When she does, her voice is soft and sad.

"I know you're hurting, Rachel. We all are."

"I'm not hurting," I shoot back. "Don't make this about me."

"But it is about you," she says. "Please."

I'm just turning to go when she calls after me, a plea ribbing the edges of her voice.

"I know you've been seeing him," she says. "He told me."

Her words stop me still, a judder in my chest. "He told you?"

"Yes. He did."

"You still talk to him?"

She nods. "Come inside and I can explain."

"He said that he . . ."

She's shaking her head before I can finish. "He lies. He always did. He still does. To both of us."

I follow her back inside then, one hand pressed against the place where my phone sits in my bag, its rectangular bulk reassuring. When I leave here, I'll message Alistair, I tell myself. Maybe I'll even call him and we'll commiserate about how ridiculous this whole thing is. How these women are unable to let go of the past. How they've shored up tiny grievances until they are something much greater, something they've let consume them.

Eloise, Priya, and Agnes shift around the table when they see us, a flurry of activity as they make space for the past. I notice that a chair has been left free for me. A smattering of coffee cups sit half drunk on the table, bright white saucers spattered with flecks of spilled drinks.

"Can I get you anything?" Priya asks, half climbing to her feet.

I shake my head and lower myself down. A coffee machine shrieks with steam behind us. They're all turned toward me, their hands balled up into fists, bitten lips and tacit glances between each other as though they wish they'd agreed on what to say. I think again of Tom at home waiting for me, two wineglasses set out on the kitchen counter, and wish I'd never come. Whatever these women have to say has brought them across seas and borders to a small bar in South London. They don't even have to speak for me to know how much this means to all of them.

Helena picks up her coffee cup and holds it close to her chest without taking a sip.

"I'm sorry that I lied to get you here," she says. "I knew you wouldn't come otherwise."

"Just say it," I say. "Let's get it over with. Tell me what this is about."

Helena glances at Priya. She used to have long glossy hair that shimmered like water and would wear crop tops that showed the hard flat of her stomach, toned by youth rather than exercise. Now she looks polished and smart, her cheeks perfectly contoured, her body hidden behind a crisp button-down. It occurs to me that for Priya that summer would have been transient and fleeting. She would have neatly packed away her tiny denim shorts and sun lotion as soon as she landed. But for me it was everything, seawater and sand seeping down until they infiltrated every crevice of my life.

"It's about Kiera," she says. "Her parents tracked me down. They reached out to me. They've been trying to find people who were there that summer. They want to know the truth."

Mugs are clattered and milk steams somewhere that feels very far away. I have spent years trying not to think about Kiera. Kiera, with her eyes wild and her jaw clenched. Kiera sitting on top of those cliffs and staring out to sea. Kiera, who never came home.

Priya is waiting for me to respond.

"It's been so long . . ." I start.

"Not for them," says Helena. "They never moved on. Rachel, you should see it. Their house . . . I've been there. Her bedroom is still exactly how she left it."

I try to imagine what Kiera's bedroom might have looked like, and it strikes me how little I really knew her. Would it have been girly and pink, plastered with posters of her favorite boy bands? Or sparse and simple, her childhood cleanly packed away, ready for her to embark on an adventure, one from which she would never return?

"That's sad."

Priya nods. "I hadn't thought about her for years. I've tried not to. We all have." She glances at the others and something passes between them, a look that lets me know they've been planning this conversation for a long time. "But it's time now. We need to talk about that place."

The way she says it is scorched with bitterness, the words making her lips purse. Hearing the island spoken about with such venom curdles something deep inside my abdomen, a discomfort I quickly quell before it can consume me.

"We need to do this," Helena says, her voice urgent. "For Kiera."

"Do what?"

More glances, more silent exchanges on whose turn it is to speak.

"When Agnes went to the police all those years ago, they got away with it," Priya says at last. "But a lot has changed since then. And Helena and I have been tracking everyone down. People want to speak out. People want justice."

"Justice for what?"

"Are you *serious*?" Agnes finally speaks, her palm still pressed protectively over her bump. "After all this time, you're still pulling that shit?"

Helena reaches out and places one hand gently on Agnes's arm to quiet her.

"It's OK," she says to no one in particular. "Everyone's on their own journey."

"I'm not on any journey," I say. "I know what this is about. I thought it was ridiculous then, and I think it's ridiculous now. Don't you remember how much they did for us? And you just threw it back in their faces, Agnes."

Agnes snorts. "They didn't do shit for me," she says.

Her hand is stroking her belly now, rhythmic, mechanical, rapid.

"You were an adult," I say. "We were all adults. You can't go back and accuse people just because you didn't like how things turned out. Maybe you wish you'd made different choices. But you could end up ruining someone's life."

Agnes stands up then, her chair clattering back against her legs in her hurry. Her stomach is stretched like a vast orb, her face splotchy and scarlet.

"I can't do this," she says to Helena, her eyes intently fixed away from me.

"Agnes, please—"

"No." She shakes her head, looping a satchel over her shoulder, her voice brisk. "I don't need to hear this again. I'll call you later."

There's a silence as she leaves, navigating carefully around the tightly packed tables toward the exit. I stare down at her half-empty coffee cup, waiting for someone to speak.

"Rachel." Priya's voice is gentle, as though cajoling a child. "I understand. You're not the first person I've spoken to who's reacted like this. It's not easy to confront what happened."

"What happened, then?" Despite the anger in my voice, I can feel the spike of tears in my eyes, a childish desperation to prove them wrong. "Go on. You tell me what you think happened."

Priya surveys me carefully, her eyes sad.

"Henry Taylor was a rapist," she says evenly. "He abused women. He used his influence to coerce them into doing things they didn't want to do. He shared them around his friends, as though they were things he owned instead of girls. Girls who worked in his bar and lived in his house. But it wasn't just him. And it's time for someone to be held accountable."

"Priya's a lawyer now," Eloise chips in.

Priya nods. "That's why Kiera's parents came to me," she says. "They managed to track me down, on my firm's website. Not that I'm going to be working on the case, of course. That wouldn't be appropriate—"

"Henry Taylor's dead now," I say, before she can finish. "You got what you wanted already."

Priya nods. "I know. That's when Kiera's parents reached out. When they heard the news. It wasn't just him though, was it? I'm going to make sure that those men get brought to justice." She pauses, seeming to weigh up her next words. "All of them. And that includes Alistair."

I stand up then, the room suddenly feeling too small, my senses claustrophobically sharp.

"Don't bring him into this," I say. "Look, I'm not completely naive.

Stuff happened. Of course it did. We were young, and we were acting crazy. People do when they're eighteen. Maybe lines were crossed. Maybe people have grown up and don't like some of the things they did. But Alistair had nothing to do with this."

"Rachel, I know that this is hard to hear . . ."

"We were in love," I say, my voice cracking. "We should have been together. These stupid rumors ruined my life, and now you come back and want me to—what? Back you up? Go to the police?"

"You were right in the middle of it," she persists. "Close to Alistair. You would have seen things. Your testimony could be important . . ." She takes a deep breath. "And you were here with them. That time in London? That means we can actually bring a case here. It could change everything."

"This is crazy," I say.

"Rachel," Priya says. "You know, don't you? You know how Henry Taylor died?"

The instinct to leave is so strong that I can't even form words. I just turn and walk away. I wait to hear Helena chase me again, but there's nothing, just the street and the heat and my legs moving beneath me, my feet landing so heavily on the pavement it sends reverberations up through my body. I need to see Alistair. He can tell me I'm not going mad, that they're the ones who have twisted things. That I'm the one who sees it clearly.

I loved you, I hear him say again, *so much*.

The warmth of the memory sweeps over me, edging away some of my fear, calming me. Once, when Tom and I were first sleeping together, I had surgery on my back, an old injury from when I had fallen from a climbing frame as a child flaring up and keeping me awake at night. I still remember the hot relief of the morphine pump they installed next to my hospital bed, the way the drug swept through me, taking away the sharpness of my pain. Thinking about Alistair feels the same. It dulls the rough edges of the past, the unpleasantness we had to go through to get here. The things that Priya said. I remember waking up from my surgery and being told that a man was waiting outside. For a moment, confused from the anesthetic, I had thought it was him. When Tom walked in, looking unsure behind an enormous bouquet of flowers, my heart had broken as if it was the first time.

Tom. I glance at my phone and see missed calls, increasing in frequency as it grows later and later. I tuck my phone back into my bag. I need to go home. I need to see my husband and pretend that everything is all right. Yet on the tube, as I try to focus on the rattle of the carriage against rails, the anonymous faces surrounding me, I hear Helena's words. It is impossible to exist in the present when the power of the past is so strong. I close my eyes and I see Kiera.

Somewhere, from all those years ago, her presence is demanding to be felt.

THEN

Kiera is quieter than the rest of us.

On the island our lives are filled with noise. The beat of music playing in the bar that soundtracks our days. The clink of bottles against each other. Someone calling out a name down the corridor as they try to figure out who is on shift. And then there is Kiera. Kiera, who needs to be drawn out of herself. Who only gets talkative when she's taken something slipped to her across a bar or in a bathroom stall. Who seems able to spend an entire day off with her knees drawn up to her chest at the kitchen table, waiting for someone to speak to her. You don't notice her at first, as you might with someone like Helena. You have to look at Kiera a bit harder. At the way her fringe sometimes brushes against her eyelashes. The smattering of freckles that dusts her cheekbones. How she stands as though she is always unsure of the space she takes up in the world, as though she might disappear at any second.

Sometimes, I think I recognize myself in her. In another world, another lifetime, we might have been the kind of people who would become lifelong friends. We would have bonded together at the sides of a playground and visited each other's houses on a Friday night when we weren't invited to the right parties. Yet here, by some colossal fluke, we've both found ourselves becoming a part of something much bigger than ourselves. Tiny slivers of a team that seethes with noise, a group where there are so many bold personalities that we all blend into an indistinct mass of burgeoning adulthood. It sometimes feels that it doesn't matter how quiet you are, or how uncertain of yourself. You can be whoever you like when nobody is looking at you particularly closely.

Kiera is characteristically closed off the entire flight back. We travel just the three of us, Alistair having been called to the island on some vague and undefined business a few days earlier. Helena seems on edge, unable to sit still, flipping the plastic window blind open and shut until I offer to switch seats so that she can stretch out her legs in the aisle. She doesn't seem to catch my irritation and clambers across me, hooking one knee up over an armrest. She plugs headphones into a portable CD player and taps her fingers to some inaudible tune. I notice that her foot is bouncing out of time, an anxious and rhythmic twitch that seems to mirror the pulse of my own heart.

There is a week's worth of alcohol and excess sweating out of me. It makes my stomach turn and my jaw clench. I kept taking anything that was offered to me, even after the pregnancy test. At first I promised myself I wouldn't. It was a fresh start. A chance to make things right. But when Henry Taylor told us to get dressed up to go out again the next night, I found myself accepting Helena's offer of a shot to lubricate the jagged edges of our hangovers. The first night in London settled like dirt against my skin, a visceral and ugly sequence of events that occupied so much space in my chest I wasn't sure how I was ever supposed to breathe easily again. Every time I closed my eyes, I saw him. Felt the weight of him against my body, the feel of him inside me. All I wanted was to claw him out of me, to take the person who had done those things and crumple her up into a tiny ball, like a scrap of paper easily disposed of. I made it through the rest of the trip by clinging to the thought of returning to the island. Of being alone with Alistair, alongside the peace of the sea. Then I'd remember I'd have to tell him what I had done and my insides would feel as though they were rotting away. Nothing would ever be the same again.

I look across at Kiera and see that she is staring past me, out into the great expanse of cloud. Below us, the thick coils of gray will gradually thin out, tempering into white and then a pale and perfect blue until we are almost home again. With her skin scrubbed clean, Kiera looks tired. There are shadows beneath her eyes, as dark and as purple as fresh bruises, and a smattering of acne just below her jaw that hadn't been there when we left the island. I had noticed that she was taking more than the rest of us on nights out in London, never saying no to the bright white lines Henry Taylor's friends offered to us, disappearing into toilets and emerging starry-eyed. She must have barely slept since we left the island.

"Are you OK?" I ask her.

She nods. "Just looking forward to being back in my own bed."

We're both quiet for a moment, watching the gentle, shifting shapes of the world below us. From her aisle seat Helena taps one hand urgently, her body seeming unwilling to stay still.

"Did you tell anyone that you were back?" I ask. "Your parents or anything?"

Kiera looks surprised that such a thought would even occur to me.

"No," she says, shaking her head. "I haven't talked to them much since I've been out here, to be honest."

It has been unspoken but accepted that although we were in London, none of us would be visiting home. My nondescript town felt dangerously provincial beside the glamorous nights out in Mayfair and Soho, and besides, there was always somewhere Henry Taylor wanted us to be, people to meet. It seemed laughable to imagine I could traverse the impossibly vast gap between his penthouse suite and my parents' staid semidetached house. Sip cups of tea at the kitchen countertop with the spike of party drugs still lingering in my system. I assumed the others felt the same, even though we rarely discussed where we came from. Our new lives offered us something a million miles away from what we had left behind, something enticingly adult and dangerous and inviting.

"We actually fell out," Kiera says. "Over me taking a gap year."

"Oh?"

It's a surprise to hear I'm not the only one who had to battle parents to come out here. I always imagined the others were meant for traveling, some exotic breed built to journey the world. Until I found Alistair, I felt like I was pretending, getting henna tattoos and wearing colorful clothes in an attempt to blend in with girls who made the entire planet their home. But Kiera nods.

"Yeah," she says.

She doesn't volunteer any more information, turning her head toward the window and away from me.

"Have you heard from Priya?" I find myself asking. Helena's movements are making me nervous. "Since she left?"

"No," she says. "No, I don't think I'll be hearing from her again, to be honest."

"She's still pissed off with you?"

"Something like that."

At first I think that's the end of the conversation, but then Kiera glances back at me.

"It's easy for someone like Priya, you know?" she says. "She's so smart. And her parents are crazy rich. She'll go to uni and she'll smash it. End up being a doctor or something mega-brainy like that. She doesn't get what it's like to not just ace everything you set your mind to."

"You're smart too," I say. "You'll be fine at uni."

"Maybe." Kiera shrugs, looking past me out of the window again. "I don't know. I don't know if it's for me, really."

"Uni?"

"Yeah." She shifts in her seat, and I notice how tired she looks. "My mum and dad really want me to go. They never had the chance to, and they were just so thrilled when I got in. They were furious when I deferred a year. But I dunno. I'm not that academic really. I'm not book-smart, like Priya is. I think I was sort of hoping I wouldn't get in, actually. That would have made things a lot easier."

"You don't have to go," I say. "If you don't want to."

"Yeah," she says. "That's what Henry says too."

"He said that?"

Kiera nods. "He says he can help me out. Get me into business, if I want to. I kind of felt I had to go to uni, if I wanted a good job. But he's got connections. He says he can set me up."

"What kind of business?"

"Well, he does all sorts, doesn't he?" she says vaguely. "That's why I stayed. I just need to prove myself to him. Show him I'm a hard worker. And hopefully next year . . ." She trails off, biting her lip, surveying me carefully as though wondering whether she's said too much. "Agnes told me he gets stuff done, Henry Taylor. He knows people. He looks after people who look after him. She reckons that if I stick around, then it could be big for me. He could do a lot for me. Priya just didn't get that, you know? She doesn't need the help. She didn't really understand that some of us do."

I think it's the most I've ever heard Kiera speak. There's a hint of urgency in her voice, and she looks at me as though she needs me to agree, to tell her she's right. That everything is going to work itself out for her. That she made the right choice.

"Yeah," I say. "Yeah, it sounds like she didn't get it."

Kiera's nods, sinking back into the seat as though my words have come as a relief.

"He's such a good person to know," she says. "I'm so glad I stayed."

✳

We settle back into island life as though we were never away from it. It feels as though I could wash everything that happened in London away with the sea. I begin to feel a tinge of optimism again, a gleeful glimmer of hope, when I start to wear a T-shirt on top of my bikini so nobody can see that my waist is beginning to widen, my breasts starting to swell. I find myself toying with baby names, testing out the shape of words in my mouth and imagining how they would fit with Alistair's surname. I like floral names best—Violet and Daisy and Lily. A small patch of roses grows outside Jules's apartment, and she tells me that in Greece they are associated with Aphrodite, with love and passion and beauty. She tells me a story about how when Aphrodite's lover Adonis was killed, red roses grew out of his blood and her tears. She tells me that Aphrodite was born from sea foam, rising out of the waves to meet the land. Here, surrounded by sea, it feels right. In my head I imagine a daughter named Rose, a child so pure and perfect that it will be as if she came from the ocean. It helps to keep the other thoughts at bay—thoughts of what happened in London and of what Alistair will say when he finds out.

It should have been difficult to hide my pregnancy from Alistair, yet he seems too busy to see me, always distracted with something. It's been weeks since we slept together. I try not to mind. He seems stressed on the sporadic occasions I spy him across the bar, hinting at work Henry Taylor has him doing that keeps him away from me.

"It's crazy right now," he says over and over again. "We have a massive deal going through. Big money."

The full-moon party that has been months in planning is only a few days away, and every night the bar seems to be taking deliveries—crates of beer and decorations. There's a frantic energy, and Alistair doesn't seem to be able to fit me in around everything.

"Soon," he tells me, in text messages and when we cross paths on my shifts. "I promise. Soon."

Even though I'm desperate for him, there's a tiny part of me that is glad. Every day I don't see him is another day I don't have to think about what happened, another few hours for me to focus instead on the tiny life growing inside me. When he finally messages, two words lighting up my phone screen, I know I have to tell him the truth.

Free tonight?

I tell him that I am, and then I press my hand against my stomach and make a silent promise that it will all be OK.

I go to Henry Taylor's house late. Alistair lets me in. He holds his finger to his lips as soon as he answers the door and nods toward the staircase.

"Henry's here," he says. "We need to be quiet."

As we tiptoe to his room, I feel as though time is slowing down. Ever since the night I blacked out, I've found being in Henry's house discomforting. Alistair doesn't turn any of the lights on as we tiptoe upstairs, and the rooms are all long shadows and dark corners.

"What's the matter?" Alistair asks as I perch on the end of his bed. "You look like something's up."

And then, all in one go, I take a deep breath and tell him about that night in London. He sits beside me and I can feel his body tense as I explain what happened. The drugs, the way I had stumbled into the bedroom with no idea of what I was walking into. I try to talk it away, but it's difficult to describe exactly how I ended up in someone else's bed, how I had lain back and let those things happen to me. I had been over it myself so many times now, trying to calculate how something I hadn't been forced into could feel so violent and terrible in hindsight. I had heard about rape victims before, in newspaper headlines and talks that police officers delivered in school assemblies. I imagined them being hollowed out and ruined by their experience, women who would perhaps never forget the brutal things that had happened to them. I hadn't really wanted to sleep with that man, but it had been nothing like that. I had flirted with him, after all. I had let him touch me, even when I had every chance to leave. The door hadn't been locked. I hadn't been held down or forced to do anything. It felt wrong, but in an ugly and inconvenient way I couldn't quite articulate. A sensation I couldn't possibly explain away to Alistair.

I had wanted to create a fresh start before telling Alistair about the pregnancy test, to start a new part of our lives together with my guilt rescinded and forgiven, but as I speak, I know it's impossible. This is all wrong. He looks at me with horror, and I can't bring myself to try to turn this into a happy occasion.

"He knew," I say, my voice pleading. "He knew about us. He told me he'd tell Henry. I had to—"

Alistair stands up. "How did he know?" he says. "Who have you told?"

I shake my head. "No one," I say. "I haven't told anyone."

"You must have done." He reaches up his hands and runs them through his hair. "You must have done. How else could anybody know?"

"Maybe he just guessed?" I say weakly. "We've been spending a lot of time together . . ."

"No. No, I've been careful. Never paid you any special attention around the others. Never singled you out. No. You must have told someone. Or maybe you acted differently when you were talking about me? In front of the other girls?"

"I don't think so . . ." I'm tearful now, my voice thick. "I mean, I don't know. Maybe I did."

"Think, Rachel." He sounds exasperated. "This is important. This is my job. My life."

"Maybe I did . . . But . . . I didn't mean to. I didn't think I had . . . I didn't mean to let anyone know, I promise."

"You know that if this gets out, then that's it for us?" he says. "I'll lose my job. I'll have to leave."

"I'm sorry." I reach up to scrub my tears away. My skin feels raw beneath my fist. "I didn't mean it."

"We can't be together if Henry finds out, Rachel."

"I'd come with you. We could leave together."

He snorts, a short, sharp sound that reminds me how little I know about the world. How little I understand his life, his work, what Henry Taylor means to him.

"You don't get it, do you?" he says. "I don't have anything without Henry Taylor. No job. Nowhere to live. My entire career, gone. It's not all about you, Rachel. Some things are bigger than the both of us."

I'm desperate for him to believe I can do this, that I understand what is at stake. He is putting his entire life on the line for me. All I have to do is keep my mouth shut. Keep Henry Taylor happy.

"I know," I say. "I understand. I'm sorry."

"If it's out, then we need to stop it getting any further," he says. "We need to make sure it doesn't get back to him."

He reaches out and rests his hand on top of mine.

"You did the right thing," he says. "It kills me to think of you with anyone else, but you did the right thing. You did it for us. Didn't you, Rachel?"

I nod, too choked to speak.

"But I mean, I guess now you might have to do it again?"

I look up quickly, not quite understanding what he means.

"We have to prevent Henry from finding out," he says, his hand now gently stroking mine. "We have to keep Henry happy. And who knows who else has caught wind by now?" He pulls his hand away. "Word's obviously out about us. And you didn't exactly hide it from that guy either, did you? Who knows who he'll have told. No. You did the right thing, keeping him quiet. So, if anyone else says anything . . . well. I think it's best that we just play along, right?"

"You . . . do you mean . . . ?"

"I mean, only if you have to. You know I would never want you to, right? But since you let people know about us, we have to do damage control. We have to make sure nobody can say a bad word against us." He reaches out for me again, trailing his fingertips up and down my wrist, calming and smooth. "It won't be for long, I promise," he says. "We'll tell Henry eventually. We can be together properly.

It's just . . . right now . . . I mean, I have to do what he says, Rachel. You've never worked for someone like him. You'll understand one day. But right now . . . I need this job. You can help me. You'd do that for me, wouldn't you?"

I find myself nodding, even though I can't quite seem to shake the image of that man, the strangeness of unfamiliar skin against mine, the mechanical motion of him pushing in and out of me. Alistair reaches out to stroke my hair.

"It's for us, Rachel," he says. "It's so we can be together eventually. You know that, don't you? You know how much I love you?"

I say it back and he nods, as though I've finally done something right.

"Anyway." He stands up. "We should get some sleep. I've got so much shit to do tomorrow."

He's a different person at once, businesslike and efficient.

"What's happening tomorrow?" I ask blearily.

He looks at me as though he can't believe I'm asking.

"The full-moon party. I mean, I'm regretting coming up with it now, to be honest, the amount of work it's been. And for what? Henry isn't really keen on the idea. But it's too late—it's happening, the place will be rammed tomorrow. Everyone's coming from the bar, aren't they?"

"Yes. I mean . . . I don't know. I haven't asked."

"You haven't asked?" He shakes his head. "Rachel, this is going to be massive. I thought it'd be all you lot were talking about."

"I don't know," I say. "I'm not sure if I'll go."

"What do you mean, you're not sure if you'll go?"

"I just . . ."

I can't imagine dancing and having a good time right now. I just want to be curled up in bed. I want to have Alistair's arms wrapped around me and to feel utterly safe in how much he wants me, like it was a few months ago. Now when I look at him, I can see that his mind is somewhere else. It feels like being balanced on the edge of a precipice right before somebody pushes you off.

"You have to go, Rachel," he says. "This is going to be a big deal. Trust me. You're going to want to be there."

So I nod and tell him I will. Then, as if the conversation never happened, he turns the lights off and we lie down alongside each other in bed. He falls asleep quickly, but I stay awake, my body completely rigid against his, and feel as though I must have made up the entire thing. I must have misunderstood. Through the thin curtains the moon casts a silvery light over the bed, its brilliance a reminder of the full orb we have been promised tomorrow. I close my eyes, wishing I could sleep my way through its cycle, that tomorrow could come and go without the party that seems certain to rupture the peace of the island. I am beginning to realize just how fragile its gentle rhythms are. How easily the waxing of the heavens and the lull of the tide can turn into clouds and storms.

NOW

know that something is wrong as soon as I arrive home.

I was expecting Tom to be angry with me. He would be waiting in the front room, ready for the click of the door to ask me why I hadn't responded to his messages. I had steeled myself for it all the way home, feeling too exhausted to really care. My heartbeat has barely slowed since I stormed out of the bar, shrill pulses of adrenaline still rushing through me.

I almost messaged Alistair as I sat on the tube, relieved to find a seat amid a clamor of bodies. I reasoned that I should warn him they were after him. That after all these years, he still wasn't safe. I needed him to tell me how ridiculous they were being. That it was all a lie. That what had happened to Kiera had been terrible, but that none of us could have done anything about it.

Yet when I pulled out my phone to type a message, I found that a heaviness in my chest stopped me. It stilled my hands and compelled me to tuck my phone back into my handbag. *He lies*, Helena had told me. *He always did*.

I'm already calculating ways I can avoid another argument with Tom, but when I arrive home, the house is dark. I unlock the front door and call out his name. He doesn't answer. At first I think he's not here. That he got angry enough to go over to his mum's, or to one of his brothers' places to open a beer and let me wonder where he's gone. Then I notice a faint light coming from upstairs, the almost indistinguishable hum of a bathroom fan.

"Tom?"

It's not like him to ignore me. Tom doesn't blow hot and cold. He's reasonable and straightforward, a big believer in the power of communication. I suppose it comes from having had functional relationships before, a steady parade of semi-long-term girlfriends with nice hair and good degrees throughout his twenties. Alistair was my only boyfriend before him, but I had thought the instability of it all was one of the best things about us, the overblown passion and the wanting and the missing. I remember how Helena looked at me earlier with a sad urgency and feel slightly sick.

"Tom?"

The light is coming from our en suite bathroom, the one that was on our nonnegotiable list for a forever home. He's sitting on the lowered toilet lid with his head in his hands. He doesn't even move when he hears me push open the bedroom door.

"What are you doing in here?"

He finally looks up at me.

"Rachel," he says. "What the hell have you been doing?"

For a moment I think he has found out about Alistair. My mind scurries to try and calculate what evidence I might have left behind. I haven't exactly been careful, throwing out lies that could easily have been uncovered with a phone call to Jules or a scroll through my recent messages. But I've had my phone with me all day today, and I haven't even seen Alistair since Sunday. Before I can figure out what hints I've inadvertently dropped, he lifts something up from the side of the sink and holds it out for me to see.

"Were you going to tell me about this?"

It looks so small in his hand, the slim foil packet with its tell-tale tears. The last one was made only this morning, the printed days of the week beneath each empty cavity telling my husband how many times I have lied to him.

"They're old," I say automatically. "I just never chucked them out . . ."

For over a year I had convinced myself that simply not telling him wasn't the same as telling a lie. Not really. But as he shakes his head, I can see it doesn't matter.

"You know," he says, "I was hoping . . . I really thought . . ."

He stands up to wrench open the cupboard beneath the sink and pulls out a piece of paper, crumpled and forgotten about. I don't need to look at it to know what it is, the neatly typed print and scrawled signature.

"I must be mad," he says. "I really thought, you know what, if she comes home and just tells me the truth, if she tells me what's going on, then maybe we can talk about it. Sort it out. But you're still lying. Even now. Even with the evidence right in front of you."

He jabs the piece of paper.

"It's the prescription," he says. "I thought I must have got it wrong when I found it, that the dates were messed up or something. But then I found the pills and . . ." His voice catches in his throat. "Two months ago, this is from. Two months ago, Rachel. When we were already talking about seeing a doctor. You must think I'm a mug. You must think I'm a complete bloody mug."

There's nothing to say back to him. No defense that can make this right. For the last year we've been trying, tracking my temperature and counting the days between periods. It didn't feel so bad at first. I just needed a bit longer. A couple of weeks to get used to the idea. But then weeks became months, and Tom seemed more and more fixated on a baby.

"I didn't mean . . ." I begin weakly.

"You didn't mean *what*?" Tom brandishes the paper, and it doesn't feel like he really wants an answer. "All this time, Rachel. All this time I've been excited about us starting a family. Worrying when it didn't happen straightaway, like we thought it would. And all this time you've known, and you never told me."

"Tom, please," I say. "I can't do this right now. Can we not talk about this? Can we talk about it tomorrow when—"

"Rachel, are you serious?"

It's the first time I've ever heard him raise his voice, and the sound is utterly unfamiliar. Tom, my Tom, my usually calm and patient Tom, is looking at me as if he doesn't know who I am.

"How can this wait? How can anything be more important than this? This is our entire future, Rachel. Our *marriage*. And you want to talk about this tomorrow?"

"I just . . ." I start, but my voice wavers and fades to nothing.

Behind him I catch a glimpse of us in the mirror. We both look exhausted, pale and tense as we face up to one another. It strikes me that I can't quite remember how we got here, how tiny unsaid things and insignificant secrets became entirely different realities. When did I stop looking forward to seeing him after a long day of work, or assuming with a breathtaking simplicity that we would be together for the rest of our lives? When did I start thinking more about the past than I did about the present, more about a man I was in love with when I was eighteen than about my own husband, more about an autumn day sixteen years ago than about today? Small distances between us had hardened and stretched, an ever-thickening wall that made it impossible to reach him. I always assumed it would be easy to disassemble, that I was just tired at the moment, worn out from work, feeling old and nostalgic. We would be OK again when we both started trying. When we started to make time for each other. I'd decide that I did want a baby after all, and I'd shelve Alistair back in the past where he belonged.

Perhaps I should have known that Tom and I were in trouble when I never quite managed to muster the energy to try. The couple in the mirror don't look like two people on the brink of a potentially marriage-ending argument. There are no tears or desperation. No pleading to make it right. When I look at us, I just see two people who are too broken to fight. I see two people who are moments away from giving up.

"Just tell me," he says. His voice is level and he isn't meeting my eye. "Was it the whole time? The entire time we've been trying? Did you ever stop taking it?"

I could lie to him now. Maybe it would save us. I could tell him it was just the last couple of months. That I'd had second thoughts, that I'd made a stupid mistake. But instead I breathe in and say the words I know will break his heart.

"No," I say. "I never stopped."

He exhales slowly, a long, defeated breath that seems to seep out of his very core. I think of how well I know his body, how many times I've rested my head on the rise and fall of his chest as we doze on a Sunday morning, how many times his breath has tickled the hairs on the back of my neck as he spoons me on the couch.

"OK," he says. "OK then. In that case, I think you should leave."

Outside the unexpected heat of the day has broken, the sky rumbling and a sheen of rain, dense and fine, dampening the world. I haven't brought a coat, and I drift to the tube station with my hair slicked to my face. People tumble past me still in summer dresses, laughing and squealing at the absurdity of the weather, holding handbags above their heads as if they are foolishly delighted by their own ill-preparedness. I feel as though I am in a fever dream, the world sighing and shifting around me, seasons hurtling past and people wearing shorts and sandals in a downpour. Alistair loves me. Helena and Priya want me to go to the police. Tom has told me to leave. All these things are facts, and yet my mind feels blurry when I try to connect them. They are slippery and incomprehensible and just out of reach. The rain feels warm and the air is thick and heavy. Water collects in my eyelashes and pools in the pucker of my mouth. Like seawater, I think. Like swimming on a hot summer's day.

I message Jules on the tube, pools forming beneath my fingertips and obscuring my words. The carriage is hot, steam rising from damp skin and condensation forming on the grimy windows.

I need somewhere to stay, I type. I'm coming over.

Then I rest my head back against the matted fabric of the seat cushion and close my eyes. Of course, it's not the first time I've run to Jules in a crisis. The last time still rests somewhere between the warm and gentle parts of our relationship, the endless cups of tea at each other's houses and dinners squeezed in between trips across the world. It's the memory of a flight where I was sick in a flimsy paper bag. The thick pads the clinic provided that seemed to need changing so often they became my only grasp on time. Jules holding my hand in a waiting room that smelled faintly of antiseptic as we tried not to meet the eyes of the other women seated in similarly clinical plastic chairs.

I've tried to avoid thinking about that baby. I've told myself it was a blessing in disguise really, Alistair disappearing when he did. I was too young to have a child. The abortion was the right thing for all of us. Whenever Tom talked wistfully about future children, painting an entire family with a hopeful sideways look at a pushchair with a bundled-up baby peeking out, I tried to swallow the ache that threatened to choke me. I smiled and nodded and cooed and pretended it didn't make me feel as though my insides were crumbling every time I saw a tiny human strapped to someone's chest. I acted as though I didn't still find it hard to sleep sometimes, didn't still look at myself in the mirror and wonder what kind of person could get rid of a child she wanted so badly. The child of someone she had loved. Still loved.

In my most hidden and secret fantasies, I imagine another baby. It's exactly how I picture the baby we lost, with my upturned nose and Alistair's eyes. I imagine undoing all the things I did back then. Making amends with the child we left behind. It's always Alistair's baby I dream about making. In fact, I'm never quite sure if it's really a new baby at all or a perfect re-creation of the baby that was never born, a reincarnation of all my regrets.

I remember when Tom and I agreed to start trying. We were on holiday, this time in Italy. We had drunk limoncello all day, sipping sugary spritzes that cast a sticky and magical sheen over the fairy-light-hewn glow of the square where we had dinner. It had blurred the edges of how irritated I'd been that morning, picking up a damp shirt Tom had discarded on the bathroom floor. We were sitting at a table with legs that wobbled against the uneven cobblestones and resolutely refused to stabilize, no matter how much I giggled at almost-spilled glasses of wine and how many times Tom tried to fold over a napkin, shaking his head in bafflement every time he wedged it beneath an errant leg to no avail. I ordered pasta stuffed with ham and cheese, and he ordered pizza in broken Italian. A waiter came around and lit a candle on our table, and we stayed so long that it drizzled into a disfigured lump while we ordered another bottle of wine and diners drifted back to their beds. I gazed at Tom in the dizzy brightness of the night and thought how handsome he looked. It wasn't all that often that it occurred to me. It wasn't as though Tom was tear-your-clothes-off sexy, or the kind of person you worried about other women flirting with. He was just Tom. But then I thought how lovely he looked, how familiar, how safe.

A couple weaved through emptying tables, young and enviably attractive, her in a floaty black dress and him with a smattering of evening stubble. She wore a sling that ensconced a tiny baby, a round head and sleepy-looking eyes just visible against her chest. Tom glanced at them and then back at me.

"What do you reckon?" he said.

"Reckon about what?"

"You know," he said, and he nodded toward the couple. "About that. Us. Don't you think it's about time we made a go of it?"

"What you mean—"

"Babies," he said. "Well, one baby, specifically. At least to start with. I know it hasn't felt like the right time. But, well—maybe it doesn't ever. And we've always meant to one day, right? Maybe the right time is actually now."

My eyes followed them as they retreated toward a winding alley-way, back to a hotel or perhaps to their home, some trendy and baby-proofed apartment somewhere out of sight. As I watched, the woman ducked her head to plant a brief kiss on her child's cheek. Her partner reached out his hand as though he didn't need to think about it and touched her lower back, a tiny circle of safety sketched around the three of them. I looked back at Tom, his eyes slightly bleary, and found that I could almost imagine it. The two of us. A baby. A tiny version of us that we could take care of and protect. A chance to put things right. The thought felt irresistible. Strange and crazy, of course, but irresistible. We could do it, couldn't we?

"OK," I said. "OK, yes. I think we should."

Tom's face split into a grin. "Really?"

"Really," I said. "Why not? We've got the house now. And you just got that promotion. We could definitely afford it."

"Exactly!" Tom lifted the half-empty bottle and refilled our glasses, splashing red wine onto the pristine white tablecloth in his enthusiasm. "That's exactly what I was thinking."

"And you never know, do you? I mean, we could start trying now and it's not like I'd get pregnant right away, is it? I mean, it would take a while anyway, wouldn't it?"

"Definitely." Tom nodded. "It took Danny and his girlfriend six months."

"Right. And six months is plenty of time to . . . you know. Get ready for it."

"Exactly."

Tom reached across the table and grasped my hand.

"God, I'm so glad we're on the same page, Rachel. I've wanted to bring it up for ages, but I didn't want to rush you . . ."

"No, you're right," I said. "If not now, then when?"

We went back and had sex as though it was the last time, with a rhythm that made me feel as though every part of me was perfectly attuned to him. The next day I woke up feeling sick, a sour mixture of wine and limoncello churning in my stomach.

"You won't be needing these anymore," Tom said cheerily, pointing at the packet of pills that I had left at the side of the sink.

I smiled and nodded, and we went out for strong Italian coffees and talked about baby names and local nurseries.

We flew back to England and I finished the packet of pills just because it seemed silly not to. And then I found myself booking a doctor's appointment and requesting more.

"Have you thought about more long-term methods of contraception?" the GP asked, and I shook my head and said something vague about maybe trying for a baby sometime, although I wasn't sure when.

"Well, it can take a while for your body to get back to normal," she had said in response. "You might want to think about coming off the pill a little bit before you start seriously trying."

That night I lay next to Tom in bed and imagined the child Alistair and I had somehow created. It would have been a teenager now, almost as old as I had been when I got pregnant. What was I thinking, telling Tom I was ready for a baby? I couldn't be trusted to look after a living, growing thing. To nourish a life within the shell of my own body. While Tom imagined all the babies that could exist in our future, I thought about the baby that had been in my past. The baby that had almost been. The baby that would have been right now, if I had been strong enough. My Rose, a tiny cluster of cells and yet a colossal and unwieldy creature of my imagination.

Beside me my phone vibrates. Jules has replied to me already.

Of course, I read. Are you OK?

My hands falter before I type out my response.

I'm fine, I type. It's just . . . I think Tom and I might be over.

Then I tuck my phone away. As the tube trundles toward my best friend, I close my eyes and remember what Helena said. When I should be thinking about my marriage, I find my thoughts filling up with that summer. That last day. That one night when our tiny world imploded. I take a deep breath and I can almost feel the white heat of fire, the cold sharpness of the sea. As the carriage clatters a hard and rhythmic beat against the rails, I could almost swear that it is drumming Kiera's name.

THEN

The beach is a dreamland. Alistair has made sure of it. There are fairy lights strung up on wooden sticks and tiki lamps flickering in the breeze. There are firepits and makeshift bars painted with bright colors. Henry Taylor has arranged boats from the mainland, and they arrive in slow fleets throughout the day, partygoers wearing bikinis and floral headdresses deposited barefoot on the sand. They congregate on the shore as the sun lowers, waiting for the night to begin. A sound system is set up and the locals shutter their windows. Someone is making cocktails in buckets, and someone hauls themselves up onto a podium to dance alone. It is going to be the biggest party the island has ever seen.

As the sun edges beneath the horizon, the beach begins to glitter and pulsate, the slow deposits of partygoers starting to stir. People move to dance close to a fire, clutching bottles of beer as they circle the flames. More boats arrive, more travelers eager for a drink. Soon the crowds are thick and the beach splits into distinct spaces. A spot where people lounge on the sand and share plastic cups. A dance floor made out of flattened sand. A stretch of sea where the waves come in shallowest becomes a place for people to strip down to their swimwear and paddle, shrieking and laughing.

Against all odds, I manage to convince Jules to come with me. We get ready back at her place, daubing day-glo paint onto our cheekbones and glitter along the indents of our temples. She is due to leave tomorrow, and as much as she seems to dislike the bar, she grudgingly agrees that she doesn't want to spend her last night on the island indoors. We drink sour-tasting wine sitting on the stoop outside her apartment, me making one tumbler last. Over the past few days I have found my hand drifting down to my stomach and resting protectively and unthinkingly over its slight swell. Jules catches me doing it, and I see her eyes narrow slightly. Then she drains her cup and suggests we head down to the beach.

Alistair has arranged for most of us to be working, manning small bars built from driftwood and handing out trays of brightly colored shots.

"You take the night off though," he said to me. "You deserve it."

He had been cheerfully normal this morning, as though our conversation last night had never happened. He told me Henry wanted me up at the house in a few days to host some friends he had visiting, and I had agreed, unsure exactly what he meant by it. What would be expected of me. When he dropped me back at the house, I had asked him if everything was all right, and he had looked at me as though he had no idea what I was talking about.

"Of course it is," he said. "Why wouldn't it be?"

"Are you OK?"

Jules's voice brings me back to the present. We're close to the beach, and in the half-glow of fairy lights and flames she is beautiful. Jules always looks like a Greek goddess, with her mermaid-esque hair and her radiant smile, but the trail of glitter that highlights her face and the reflection of fire in her eyes makes her look even more mystical than usual.

"I'm fine," I say. "Come on. Let's find the others."

I haven't introduced Jules to any of the girls yet. They are two spheres of my life out here, gently orbiting but entirely separate.

Jules has never seemed interested in meeting any of my friends from the bar, and somehow, I've never mentioned her to Helena or Kiera.

We find Helena close to the water, manning a shelf of bottles with Eloise, arranging drinking games and body shots on a trestle table dragged close to the shore.

"Rachel!"

She shrieks when she sees me, clambering up onto a log that is being used as a bench to wave me down. I take Jules's hand and we weave through the crowds toward them. I can't believe how many people are here. I feel a familiar glow of pride, a possessive pleasure that they have come to our island. My island. I want to tell everyone who has only just found this place that I live here. That the man who arranged all of this is mine. Helena falls on me as soon as I reach her, throwing her arms around me.

"Can you believe it?" she says breathlessly. "I didn't think anyone would come. And look at this! It's incredible."

I find myself laughing.

"I know," I say. "Helena, this is my friend Jules. She's been working on the island as well."

"On the island?" Helena says. "I didn't think there was anywhere else to work on the island, apart from the bar."

Jules shrugs. "The locals seem to manage it pretty well," she says, her voice clipped.

"Oh yeah, the locals." Helena rolls her eyes at me. "But I mean people like us."

"Where's Kiera?" I say quickly, before Jules can shoot something back.

Helena shrugs and turns to pick up a bottle.

"I haven't seen her all day," she says. "She must be here somewhere. Drink?"

"Sure," I say. "But she's working tonight, isn't she?"

"She must be." Helena pours generous slugs of vodka into red plastic cups. "There's so many people here though. It's impossible to keep track."

I can tell that Jules is getting riled by Helena's easy energy, so I suggest we go and sit by the water. It's quieter down here, the crowds thinning out as we approach the sea. Somebody has dragged another log into the shallows, and we perch on top of it, the waves lapping against our feet. A cluster of girls strip their clothes off and run into the sea naked, their pale bodies illuminated by the moon as they shriek and splash each other.

"We should stay here," I hear one say. "I could stay here forever."

We watch them for a moment, their easy joy making me feel sad. There will be new girls who come here every year, fresh-faced and looking for work. Everyone will leave eventually, first Jules and then maybe Helena and Kiera. This summer has already slipped away, as impossible to hold on to as sand in a clutched fist. The magic that at first felt as though it would never end has shifted, almost as if it wasn't real to begin with. The excitement of these girls seeing the island for the first time is distant and unfamiliar. Even though I hadn't really planned on drinking much, I take a long swig of my vodka. We left before Helena had time to track down a mixer, but the strength of it feels good.

"Does it feel weird?" I ask Jules. "To be leaving?"

She digs her bare feet into the sand, a wave sweeping water out around us.

"No," she says. "It feels right."

Even with the beach lit up, you can see stars, great sprawls of them clustered against the sky. A plane passes overhead, silent, the only sign of its existence a lazily flashing light moving across an entire universe of stillness. I wonder about the people on board, where they are going to and where they have come from. I wonder if they'll look down and see the blaze of the beach, and try to guess who is thousands of feet below them.

"What about you?" Jules says. "Do you feel like it might be time?"

I shake my head. "No," I say. "I feel like I'm exactly where I need to be."

Just then one of the girls in the water shrieks and falls, her body crumpling into the waves. Her friends splash around her, panicked and reaching out for her arms as they try to pull her from the dark clutch of the sea. She's gasping and sobbing, her face contorted. Before we even have time to stand up, Alistair is there. He wades into the water and helps to lift her out, shouting for someone to fetch help. The girl sobs as she's lowered onto the ground, and I see that her foot is bloodied and torn, her face pale. Her friends surge around her, pulling their clothes back on, urgent and afraid. One of them catches sight of the deep slash and immediately vomits on the sand.

"Shit," Alistair is saying. "It must have been a broken bottle or something. Why can't people be more fucking careful?"

"We should help," I say to Jules, but she's shaking her head.

"What can we do?" she says. "They've got it. We should stay here."

The girl wails as somebody binds her foot in a T-shirt, and Alistair is urgently giving commands.

"We'll get her to a doctor," he says. "She needs stitches."

The girl is wrapped carefully in a towel, nobody seeming to want to risk helping her back into her shorts, and lifted up again. Her friends look lost, gathering clothes from the beach and debating whether they should all go with her as she is carried into the crowds, or if someone should stay behind. Jules turns to the ocean and throws back her drink.

"Something's not right about this party," she says. "I have a bad feeling about tonight. Something isn't right."

After that, the breeze picks up into wind. Suddenly, everyone seems to be trying to secure drink stands and stretches of cloth. Somebody declares it isn't safe to be in the sea, and the music becomes heavier and more trancelike. Jules decides she's going back, and I find myself alone on the beach. There are people everywhere, but I don't recognize any of them. It's surreal after months of living here, of occupying a tiny circle where everyone's life seems entirely entwined with mine. I spot Eloise weaving her way through a crowd of people, but when I flag her down, she looks harried.

"Have you seen Kiera?" she asks.

I shake my head. "No. Helena said she's working. Why—"

"If you see her, tell her we're looking for her," she says. "She didn't turn up tonight."

Then she's gone again, hurrying away. Her urgency seems misplaced. We're not really accountable to anyone out here. That's the whole point. Kiera is probably having fun somewhere, making new friends and finishing up drinks. I imagine her dancing like she did that night at Henry Taylor's house, intoxicated and uninhibited, her arms stretching up to the sky. I imagine the light of a fire flickering against her skin, livid and bright. Kiera will be fine, I tell myself. She always is.

Instead of looking for her, I drift back down to the water. I take my shoes off and wade until the waves lap over my ankles. I follow the pull of the ocean until the sounds of the party fade away. I wonder if anyone can see me, a shadow slipping away with the sea. The crash of waves breaking over my bones is louder than the thrum of a bass line. The moon is brighter than the lanterns that speckle the shore. I turn my face skywards and breathe in the cool sea air, and as I do, I think of how badly I will miss this place. Realize that my time here will eventually end. I am an oracle, I think, a Cassandra. I can see premonitions and curses. I know now what is coming for us.

Then I hear the scream. It's an animalistic howl, a noise that cuts through everything, the sound of someone's heart breaking over the pounding of a sound system. I spin back round to face the shore and see a crowd gathering. A woman bent double on the sand. Someone stops the music, and the noise of the party is urgent, a rising tide of voices. Some people are moving, heading away from the crowd, running toward the cliffs. Someone else is herding people back, shouting at everybody to get off the beach. Something is very wrong.

I stumble as I start back toward the shore, falling forward in my hurry and finding myself on my knees in the water. As I lift my head, salt water in my eyes, it feels like watching a scene on a stage, a tableaux of figures that I can't make any sense of. I clamber to my feet, and my hands are thick with sand. I start to run, but I can't seem to get back to the shore quickly enough.

"What's happened?" I shout, but nobody is paying me any attention.

Somebody is crying, a red-headed girl I don't recognize crouched on the ground. I see Alistair pleading with people to leave the beach, but the crowds seem unwilling to disperse. Everyone is turned toward the cliffs, wide-eyed and open-mouthed. I see Agnes sitting on the sand, her head in her hands.

"What is it?" I say.

I drop down next to her and she just shakes her head.

"Agnes." I prize her hands away from her face. "Agnes, it's me. What's happened? What is it?"

In years to come, I will remember that moment and wish I could take it back. That I could never hear it. As though it was Agnes's words that made it real. Agnes's words, instead of the terrible, awful thing that happened. Instead I ask again, and Agnes turns her face up to look at me. It's then that I see she is pale and shaking, her eyes dazed.

"It's Kiera," she says. "Rachel, it's Kiera."

NOW

Jules gets up late every morning while Eli leaves first thing, the click of the front door sounding as streetlights outside still beam. Autumn has arrived, the edges of the day becoming ever more blurred into night and darkness encroaching on light. On a weekday I always get up and make myself a coffee so that I can leave while Jules is still snoring behind a bedroom door. It's been three weeks since I turned up, and I've been surprised by how adaptable people really are. How quickly we slide into an easy routine and rhythm, as though I have always been here. As though the life I have spent the last decade pouring all of myself into never happened at all.

The weekends are hardest. Without work to get up for, I stay in bed late, even though I wake just as sunlight is easing through the thin curtains of Jules's spare room. I open them and lie still so that I can see the sky. The windows are single-paned, and they gather condensation overnight. Droplets form and lace the glass, and I watch them fall down to the wooden sill below, already beginning to darken with a shadow of damp. I hear Jules and Eli stirring in the room next door, murmurs and the gurgle of pipes as they shower. Footsteps on the stairs as Jules goes to make tea, and the clatter of saucepans as Eli starts breakfast. The easy sounds of coupledom, the smell of toast and Sunday morning tunes on the radio. I wonder what Tom is doing, whether he'll have found something to fill his time without me or whether his day will follow the same pattern it always used to. A cup of coffee in bed. Pastries and breakfast television. A walk to the shop for the weekend papers. Then I remember we haven't been like that for years. That our weekends were more often taken up by temperature checks and lying side by side, scrolling through our phones.

I always get dressed before I go downstairs, a weekend uniform of jeans and a jumper even though Jules and Eli will both still be in their dressing gowns. Eli offers to make eggs even though their plates are already waiting to be washed up in the sink, and I shake my head and tell them I'm going out for a walk and that I'll grab something on the way home. As I pull on a coat and trainers, I can sense their silence in the kitchen, the noise of bated concern and unsaid things. I know that as soon as I'm gone they'll talk about me. They'll worry about what I do for all that time outside the house. Eli will ask Jules if she knows what happened yet. They'll wonder if I've spoken to Tom.

In truth, I don't do very much at all when I'm away from the house. I buy coffee from a chain shop on the high street. I wander around the neighborhood until my legs ache, circling past the same houses and wishing time away. I mostly just think, my mind somewhere else entirely as I waste the afternoon into evening. I sometimes leave my phone back at the house, eager not to be distracted by the motions of everyday life. Alistair has messaged me multiple times since I saw Helena, and I have yet to respond. Our relationship is balanced somewhere between fantasy and reality, that irresistible space where I don't have to act on his growing presence in my life. But suddenly, it all feels real. Suddenly, seeing him would mean decisions; it would mean choosing to draw him closer. It would mean asking him about what Helena and Priya had to say.

I've spoken to Tom, of course. It was easier than I imagined. If I had ever considered how things might be if we broke up, I would have envisaged a sea of rage and hurt. Complicated conversations that stretched for hours and fights that left us more bloodied than when we began them. Perhaps he would have pleaded for me to stay. Perhaps we would have fought over who got what. Instead the breaking down of our marriage has been breathtakingly simple. Frustratingly civilized. We've texted like concerned friends, checking up on each other and delicately stepping around the business of what we would do next. I went back to the house a few days after I first left to collect some things. He was there to see if I wanted any help. He offered to leave, to give me space to sort everything out. I told him he didn't need to. I would take as little as I could and come back for the rest later.

He made me tea, and we sat at the kitchen island where we had imagined eating dinners and pouring late-night glasses of wine for years to come.

"I think the first thing we need to do is see someone about valuing the house," he said. "And once we've done that, we'll have a better idea of where we stand. I don't think we need to rush into all the legal stuff yet for . . . you know."

He treads so carefully around the word that you would think it was caustic.

"For the divorce?" I said.

He winced so slightly I almost didn't catch it.

"Yeah," he said. "Yeah, for that."

Neither of us fought against it. We didn't talk about whether there was anything left that was salvageable. We both had an air of exhaustion and acceptance, steeling ourselves for the careful unraveling of a life together. We both still wore our wedding rings.

"I want you to know that I didn't mean to do it," I said, the dregs of my tea cold in my cup. "Hurting you like that. It sounds stupid, but I really didn't think about what I was doing. It just happened."

He smiled sadly.

"It's OK," he said. "In some ways it was for the best. We hadn't been right for a long time. It's just that neither of us had the guts to admit it."

Before I left, he pulled me into a hug, standing on the doorstep of the house where we had planned to build a life.

"Do you know what you're going to do yet?" he said. "I'm worried about you, you know."

"I think I just need some time," I told him. "I've got a lot of thinking to do. I just need to stay still for a bit so that I can do it."

Yet instead of staying still, I find myself compelled to keep moving. I walk up and down the same streets. I dip into parks and walk in ever-expanding circles around their paved paths. I find hills to climb, urban plains that stretch up into the sky until London falls down below me. My usual place to go to is Hampstead Heath. I even have a favorite bench that I trudge to at the top, always hoping to find it empty. It usually is, the damp chill of the season keeping enough walkers moving, hurrying back to the warmth of their homes. I sit still, my lungs heaving from the short sharp climb, and dig my hands into my pockets for warmth. I look at the same view through sheets of rain and tentative winter sun and early-evening mists. I find myself faintly marveling at the years I have spent in this city, the places where I met Tom and got my degree and saw Alistair again for the first time all within view. By the time my breath has slowed, I am entirely caught up in memories.

For the first time in years, I have thought about that night in London. About what Alistair said to me when I told him. They used to feel like such small details, fragments of a time that was chaotic and had too many parts to put together. But now, I find a restless unease gathering in the pit of my stomach. Now, I go over what Alistair said to me. What he was asking me to do. It used to feel like everything he did was to ensure that we could be together. Now, I'm not quite so sure.

One day, when I'm waiting for it to get late enough to go back to Jules's, my phone vibrates. At first I ignore it. Nobody calls me on a Saturday. But then, a few minutes later, it starts to hum again, stoic and insistent against my leg. I pull it out of my pocket and see that it's him. Still, after all this time, his name makes my heart leap. Almost instinctively I swipe to answer it.

"Rachel," he says. "Thank God."

"Hey." My voice sounds weak, and I realize it's the first time I've spoken all day.

"Where have you been?" Alistair asks. "You haven't been answering my messages. Are you OK?"

At first, I feel a familiar warmth, a small secret pleasure in knowing that he cares. I always used to view him as a kind of protector, someone who looked out for me. For us. Then I remember Helena's words and the glow fades. For the first time, I wonder if he isn't really concerned about me. Perhaps he's more worried about himself. After all, I'm an adult woman now. Perhaps he's been asking himself what my silence means.

"I'm fine," I say. "I'm . . . yes, I'm OK."

"So what's been going on?" he asks. "Why have you gone all quiet on me?"

"I . . ."

In the distance the city still seethes: a hum of sound, distant car horns and faded sirens. I imagine him out there somewhere, his phone clutched to his face, scared that I am going to disappear.

"It's nothing," I say. "I'm sorry. I've just had a lot on."

"Anything I can help out with?"

"No. No, nothing like that."

"Well, can I see you? Soon?"

In spite of myself, I feel a gentle thrill, an excitement at being wanted by him. At being missed by him after spending so long missing him. I feel as though having him back in my life has invigorated me, woken up parts of me I had assumed belonged to teenage years and first loves. I think of Tom and the blank slate of my life that stretches out ahead of me. Then I think of Alistair, and it all feels easier. How good it would be to go to his place and drink wine and eat takeout. To be able to fall asleep in his bed and wake up there. Maybe to plan the life together that I thought we had lost.

"Yeah," I say, and it feels like relief. "Yeah. I'd like that."

Down the line I hear him exhale.

"Great," he says. "Message me and let me know when you're free?"

"I will," I say.

"OK. I love you, Rachel."

There it is again, that twinge of relief at hearing him say it.

"I love you too," I say, and then the phone rings off.

THEN

After the party, everything changes.

Agnes is gone the next day, taking a boat to the mainland alone. Without any kind of discussion, the bar is shuttered up. Hurriedly, and without saying goodbye, people leave. Every day the house feels quieter, a vast empty belly of what it once was. You never used to be able to walk through the front door without hearing music bleeding out of somebody's room, or the sound of drinking games radiating from the kitchen, or somebody pounding down the stairs late for their shift. Now, when I come back from the few trips outside that I take, the house is silent. Occasionally somebody pads down the hall to the bathroom. Even more infrequently the front door will click, although you are never sure whether it is somebody coming home or somebody leaving for good.

The door to Kiera's room stays shut. It seems to have developed a magnetic force that both draws and repels us. We tiptoe past, our eyes firmly cast away. We don't mention it when we pass each other in the corridor. We don't suggest going inside to sort through her things. But there's no amount of avoiding Kiera's room that can stop her absence from keeping us awake at night. That can push her out of our thoughts as we pace the corridors and try to focus on anything else.

Her room is the potent center of the house, a dark and omnipresent force that bleeds down the corridors and creeps into our dreams. An innocuous door that none of us can bear to open. A space that remains untouched, even though all we can think about is the girl who should be sleeping inside.

It was Agnes who found her. I've heard what feels like a thousand versions of the story now. A hundred recollections told in hushed tones around the kitchen table or muttered in disbelieving fragments as we try to piece together something that feels utterly senseless. Dozens of parts of the same night told in different ways: *I was just queuing for a drink. I was just looking for Alistair. I was just helping to carry some bottles. And then I heard the scream.* It's always the same climax. The same sentence that makes us all flinch. That shared moment when everything we knew ended. The animalistic cry that changed things forever.

This is what we know.

Agnes was looking for Kiera. They were both supposed to be going up to Henry Taylor's house. He was holding an after-party, and he had asked for them to arrive early. But Agnes had been worried about Kiera all day. Somebody had heard her say something that morning. Or perhaps it was that somebody had heard somebody else say it. Nobody is sure, and yet we try to pull strands of the story together, try to make whole parts out of imperfect pieces. Yes, we're certain that Agnes was worried about Kiera. No, nobody really remembers why, and Agnes wouldn't say. She wouldn't say a word to anyone, after it happened. She just sat on the sand, her knees clutched into her chest, staring out to sea.

Agnes had realized that Kiera wasn't at the party. She had decided she would go up to the villa anyway, slipping up the path at the side of the beach to avoid the crowds. That was when she saw her.

It was dark. The cliff face was only partially illuminated by the glow of the party. At first Agnes had thought it might be a pile of old clothes bunched up on the rocks. It wasn't until she drew closer that she saw what it was. Who it was. That at some point, while we had all danced beneath the bleached white glow of the moon, Kiera had climbed to the top of the cliffs and then let her body fall into the sea below.

Her shattered body was caught in a gully of rocks, cradled between boulders and rock pools. The tide had washed over her, just deep enough to ring her with seaweed and shells. While we paddled and splashed in the shallows, the sea had been toying with her, slowly and secretly slipping away to leave a body ravaged by the ocean. The figure that Agnes had found wasn't Kiera, but a tattered and sea-swollen shell of our friend. That freckled skin I had once admired would have been bruised and bloodless. Everything about her was drained away with the drawing out of the sea. I saw how pale Alistair was when he came back up the beach. He didn't look at me, but I saw him shake his head and speak to someone else.

"Don't go over there," he said. "It's not good."

The next day I take a bath, absentmindedly trailing my fingers against the surface so that the very tips are damp. It doesn't take long until they are pale and wrinkled, puckered from the water. I imagine what hours of submersion would do. I think of Kiera's bronzed skin and imagine it white and waterlogged, her slim limbs bloated by the sea and her honey-colored hair matted with salt. The rocks battering her face beyond recognition. I imagine how it would feel, those last few seconds when the land is no longer beneath your feet, the breathless plummet toward the ground, and then nothing. I pull out the plug and sit on the bathroom floor for hours. After that, I stay away from the shore. The blank blue expanse of ocean, once so promising and beautiful, feels as though it is laughing at us. As though it is punishing us for underestimating its power.

They find her things up on the cliff top, in the same place where we had all sat and shared beers and played music the night that felt like forever ago. A pair of cheap plastic flip-flops. A mobile phone.

Scraps of a life left behind for us to find. There is no note or explanation, nothing left to tell us what had happened to her. Police come from the mainland to take her away, and I am struck with the blunt and terrible realization that when we arrived together we had no way of knowing that one of us would never leave. I consider reaching out to Caroline, but I can't stand the thought of a clipped silence down the phone line or trying to put into words everything that had happened since she left. Those nights up at Henry Taylor's house suddenly feel singed with the threat of what was to come. Could we have seen it? Could we have done anything? Could I have changed things if I had left that night with Kiera when she asked me to? If I had paid more attention to how bad Kiera's drug use had got, or how withdrawn she had become? If I had listened to Jules when she had warned me to stay away from Henry Taylor's house, would Kiera still be alive?

When Jules hears, she cancels her flight. She turns up at the house and immediately draws me into a hug.

"Me and Jack are still here," she says. "Come and stay with us. You have to get away."

I just shake my head. "No," I say. "I want to stay."

I know I can't leave here without Alistair. Not when I haven't even had the chance to tell him I'm carrying his child. It is as though everything stopped the night Kiera died. As though we are suspended in some dazed and intangible place where it is impossible to move forward or look back. Instead I drift around the house and wander the streets of the town, taking the same alleyways over and over again and carefully avoiding the beach. It is still scattered with the remnants of the party, blackened firepits and discarded bottles. Nobody wants to go and clean it up. Nobody wants to go there at all.

※

A few days after Kiera falls, Alistair comes to see me. He is twitchy on the doorstep, shaking his head when I ask him in. He has stopped inviting me to Henry Taylor's villa, Kiera's death seeming to have written new rules. He seems restless, and when I reach out to take his hand, he brushes me away.

"People might see us," he says.

"Does it matter?" I say. "Really? Now?"

The last few days have made me feel desperate, as though everything is fragile and could easily be snatched away. Everything here is over—that much seems clear—and yet Alistair still looks sidelong at me as though I am speaking another language.

"Of course it does," he says. "Don't you get it? It matters more than ever."

We end up walking to the edge of town, the road dusty and the houses around us run-down. Without the ocean pulling us toward it, the undulating beauty of sea and sky, I notice how ragged this place is. How the streets the locals live on are slightly grimy, the paint on their houses cracked by the sun. I hadn't looked closely enough before.

"Did she talk to you?" he says. "Kiera? Did she say anything to you? Anything that might make you think . . ."

I'm already shaking my head. "We didn't really talk that much," I say. "She didn't tell me anything."

For a second I think I see something resembling relief, a slight crease of his forehead, a relaxation at the lines of his jaw. Then he sighs and looks away.

"It's sad," he says. "The poor girl. Who'd have thought she would do something like that?"

I don't say anything because I am thinking about Kiera. About how she seemed quiet at first, overshadowed by her noisier friends. How easily she seemed to be pulled into life out here. But then, within the last few weeks, something had changed. That time I saw her sitting up on the roof alone. The things she had said on the plane back from

London. The drugs. Henry Taylor. I knew she was getting drawn in more deeply than the rest of us, that the flesh was melting away from her limbs and the tan she had acquired out here was fading from her skin, even though the days were still warm and bright. She would be agitated and jittery at night, listless and absent by day. We had stopped seeing her in the mornings, shut away in her bedroom with the blinds lowered or staying at Henry Taylor's house long after the rest of us had left. Perhaps we should have thought. Perhaps we should have known.

"I know," I say. "I still can't believe she's gone."

We walk back in silence, and he gives me a chaste and hurried kiss on the cheek before I go inside.

"Oh, and Rachel?" he says just as he turns to go. "Do you know where Agnes went, by the way? I heard that she left."

"Yeah." My key is already in the door. "Yeah, she did. The next day."

"You don't know where?"

"No. Should I?"

"Not really, just . . ." He seems to survey me carefully, as if weighing up what to say. "Just tell me, OK? If you hear from her. It's just that there'll be some people who want to talk to her, you know? About what happened."

His voice is level, but one hand is drumming an incessant beat against his thigh.

"Of course I will," I say. "I'll let you know."

"You do that," he says. "You make sure that you do."

NOW

I arrange to meet Alistair on a Friday night. It's effortlessly easy to see him now without the need to construct a careful excuse about where I'm going. Jules doesn't seem particularly interested in my plans, probably just pleased that she and Eli will have the place to themselves for the night, and too busy calculating what takeaway they will get and where they'll have noisy sex to worry about where I'm going. I'm surprised by how lonely it feels to be untethered, without Tom to wait up for me or wonder when I'll be home. I thought it would feel like freedom, but instead it feels like loss.

For once, I choose the bar and the time, messaging him before he has a chance to do so. As I leave the house, I have to swipe away a string of missed calls from Helena. I thought she would have given up trying to contact me by now, taking my silence as an answer. Last night I listened to a voicemail she left, the volume turned down low.

"Please, Rachel, just give me another chance to explain," she said, her voice muted and distant. "We shouldn't have sprung it on you like that, I know. But I really think you need this. We all need this."

I arrive at the bar before him. I remember mine and Alistair's first meeting, how he was waiting for me with a bottle of champagne, a deliberate flattery and imitation of the past, and don't want to be flustered and unprepared again. Seeing the others has hardened something inside me. I want to be in control of this situation. I want to show them that I have a choice. That I always had a choice.

I order a glass of wine and take a seat at the bar, high up and on show to the entire world. Alistair and I can be a normal couple now, a decades-old love story that we don't need to hide. I swill my wine around its oversized glass without taking a sip and watch the crimson liquid stain the sides. Would the person Helena described go out for a drink with a woman he's in love with on a Friday night? Do victims sit and enjoy the company of their abuser and think about how their entire lives have been building up to this? Of course they don't. Helena thinks this is the end of something, but really it is only the start. This is the beginning for Alistair and me. We've waited long enough. I set down my wineglass and notice that my hand is shaking.

I feel him before I see him. After all, I've spent my entire life on hold for this man. I turn around at exactly the right time to catch him walking toward me. It's just another thing that reminds me we are meant to be together, that he's the meaning of it all. Everything we've been through was so that we could finally have this.

He deposits a dry kiss on my cheek, and then there's a brief moment of logistical fuss as he flags down the barman and asks what they have on tap. As he nods along to a list of beers, I'm reminded of a time when Tom and I came here together. It must have been early on, in that precarious space where we were balanced somewhere between sex and a relationship. We had sat in a booth and ordered a bottle of wine. At one point his hand had strayed over and rested on top of mine, cautious and respectful, and I had found myself liking it. I suppose there are different kinds of love stories, the ones that take your breath away and the ones that creep up on you quietly.

"Let's go and sit somewhere else," Alistair says, glancing around the room distractedly. "I hate feeling like I'm on show."

I find myself nodding, and all at once the control is taken away from me like wind cascading out of sails. Alistair always was the decision maker. I always did what he wanted me to.

He chooses a table tucked away in the corner and checks his phone as he slots into his seat.

"Sorry," he says. "Work stuff."

It occurs to me now that I still don't really know what he does as a job or who he works for. Perhaps there's another Henry Taylor out there somewhere, typing out commands and getting Alistair to do his bidding.

"It's fine," I say, even though it's not, not really. Really, I just want him to look at me properly. To tell me it's going to be all right. I want him to say something that will dispel the spiky seed of doubt that has settled somewhere in the center of my chest.

"I need to ask you something," I say.

He looks up at me over his phone. "Go on then," he says. "You can ask me anything."

There it is, that confidence, that intimacy. I feel myself relax slightly. Of course I can ask him anything. This is Alistair, after all.

"How did Henry Taylor die?" I ask. "He can't have been very old. What happened to him?"

Alistair lets out a long exhale. "Do we have to do this?"

"I want to know," I say.

For a moment he just looks at me, as though considering his words carefully.

"It was suicide," he says at last.

"Did you still know him at the time? Were you still close?"

"I mean, we weren't *close*. I worked for him, Rachel. You know that. He was my boss. It's not like we were best mates. But yeah, I was still working for him. Why are you interested in what happened to Henry Taylor all of a sudden?"

"I met up with the others," I say. "Helena, Eloise, Priya . . ."

I pause, the weight of the next word almost stopping my mouth from moving.

"Agnes."

He's immediately attentive. I see a muscle tighten in his jaw, and he sets his pint glass down just slightly too hard.

"You what?"

"I saw them. I didn't mean to. I thought it was only going to be Helena. But I turned up and then—"

"Rachel, what the hell . . ." He's running his fingers through his hair, urgent, tense. It's a gesture I recognize from some long-ago time that I can't quite place. "I mean . . . why? Why would you meet up with them now? After all this time."

"Alistair, please." I reach out to touch him, but he bats my hand away. "You have to listen to me. They're going after you. This is important."

"Well, of course they fucking are." He shakes his head disbelievingly. "They never did get what they wanted, did they? And you're telling me you've been getting mixed up with all that?"

"I'm not," I say. "I swear. I'm not getting mixed up with anything."

His lips are tight, a muscle spasming gently at the base of his neck.

"So, what?" he says. "What did they want? What did they say to you?"

"It was . . ." I pause, unsure how to explain what they told me. "You know. The same as before. About Henry. About what he was like. But this time . . ." I take a deep breath. "They're after you. They think you should be in trouble for it."

"Fuck." He leans back in his chair and weaves his hands together behind his head. "Seriously? Again? People need to let go of this crap and get a life."

"I know, I know. I told them it was stupid. I told them that—"

"I mean, really." He lets out a half laugh, a noise of disbelief. "Did I get arrested for anything? Charged with anything? Of course I fucking didn't, even with all those police sniffing around the place. We had to leave. Start again. They ruined everything once. Jesus. What more do they want?"

"I know, I know," I say. "Obviously I believe you. I'm on your side . . ."

"Are you though?"

I stop short, taken aback by the question. "Of course I am."

"I mean, you can say you are, but what were you doing meeting up with them?" His voice is accusatory. "How do I know I can trust you?"

"You can trust me." I lower my voice. "Remember what I did? What I did for you? I protected you."

"Give me a break, Rachel." He releases his arms to fold them across his chest. "All you did was tell the truth."

"It wasn't all the truth." I can feel that I sound strained. "You know that. You know I lied for you."

He doesn't say anything at first. He sits back in his chair, his eyes fixed on me. He goes as if to lift his drink and then seems to think better of it. His hands coil back to his head again, a gesture of fear in spite of the bravado. I've never said it out loud before. Never admitted that I lied, barely even to myself. But as though my words make it real, I am filled with a dim sense of horror. A realization that what I said back then could have changed everything. That perhaps I was protecting the wrong person.

"Well," he says, his voice unsteady. "Maybe you shouldn't have done. Maybe the truth would have been enough."

"It wouldn't," I say. "It wouldn't and you knew it. If the truth would have been enough, then why did you leave? Why did you go if you thought it was going to be OK?"

It's the first time I've ever asked him. For years I've been telling myself I didn't have to. That I could trust him. A part of me had to believe he didn't have a choice, and yet now, with him sitting opposite me, his hand clutching his glass, I have to hear him say it.

"Are you serious?" he says. "You know why I had to leave. The police were everywhere. The things Agnes was accusing us of . . . it was only a matter of time before it all came down on Henry and me. It didn't matter whether it was the truth or not. You've seen what it's been like over the last few years, all these women making accusations about men. You only have to say a few certain things and it's a witch hunt. The truth doesn't matter anymore. It didn't back then, really."

"Maybe we should have told the truth anyway," I say, my voice unsteady. "Let the police do their job. You could have cleared your name. We could have been together."

He exhales then, a long and frustrated sound.

"You can't be changing your mind, Rachel. Not now. Not after everything."

"I'm not," I say, but even as I do, I realize that maybe I am. Maybe Helena is right. Maybe there were things I didn't understand back then after all.

He stands up abruptly, his chair scraping back against the floor.

"Fuck this," he says. "This isn't what I need tonight."

"Alistair . . ."

"No." He bats my hand away again. "Call me when you've realized how ridiculous this whole fucking thing is."

Then he leaves me, his beer barely touched, alone in that bar where Tom's hand crept onto mine all those years ago. I don't follow him. My head is spinning, unbidden parts of the past coming back to me like driftwood floating back in with the tide. I remember Kiera that night at the party she had wanted to leave, her eyes frenzied and her voice desperate. I remember Alistair asking me to keep his secrets, no matter what I had to do. They feel like parts of the same puzzle, lines from the same song, chapters of the same story. Fragmented things that I had never thought to put together before, feeling suddenly sharp and solidified.

I pull my phone out of my bag, and for the first time, I type Henry Taylor's name into my browser. The internet connection in the bar is bad, and at first the page remains blank, results refusing to load. And then, in one heart-stopping instant, I see it all in one go. Headline after headline. *Property magnate dead. Henry Taylor dead from suspected overdose. Friend to the rich and famous Henry Taylor found dead at his home.* I hold my breath as I click open an archived news story from an American website. I skim it, knowing exactly what I will find.

> Henry Taylor, who controlled a significant property portfolio, was facing charges relating to human trafficking and sexual exploitation. Taylor, whose body was discovered in his New York apartment, had recently been accused of crimes including rape and sexual assault. Investigations were ongoing after eight women came forward to claim that Taylor had abused and trafficked them over a period of several years in the late nineties. The women, who reportedly went to police after reconnecting on social media decades after the alleged crimes took place, have not been publicly named.

Without meaning to, I remember the women who had surrounded Henry in London, blank-faced and anonymous. I remember Helena telling us about friends she had met in Athens who had visited the island before us. The late nineties. Ten years or more before I had met Henry Taylor and Alistair. To me those months had been special, magical, a once-in-a-lifetime summer. With a lurch, it occurs to me that I must have been just one of dozens of girls who had visited Henry Taylor's home, a parade of women who swept in and out with the seasons. There could be hundreds of us, all with our own stories, our own interpretation of what happened to us. If Henry Taylor had been alive, then he probably wouldn't even remember me at all, just another teenager who drank his drinks and entertained his friends.

I think back to that night in London again, as though I'm watching it unfold in front of me for the first time, strange hands on my body, my teeth gripped so hard my jaw ached. I imagine it replicated over and over, another faceless girl arriving in the city and feeling stupidly grateful for Henry Taylor's generosity, thinking she had to do exactly what she was told. It was a night that had been impossible to shake, a few hours that had stayed somewhere dark and vicious inside me for years. What if it had been entirely forgettable for the man who was inside me? If I was just another girl, another Saturday night, an experience he and all his friends had come to expect from their friendship with Henry? What if Alistair had known exactly what he was taking us to?

I swipe the article away without reading any more, and before I know what I'm doing, I'm typing out a message to Helena. As soon as it sends, I tuck my phone away in my handbag, as if I could hide the things I have seen. I take a large swig of wine and try to steady my breath. I wait to feel surprised, to feel a sense of horror at what I have discovered. When it doesn't arrive, I wonder if perhaps I knew all along.

Helena responds as I'm walking to the tube, the two glasses of wine I've now drunk on an empty stomach slightly softening the edges of the evening. She sends me an address which I immediately look up. Somewhere in South London, not far from Jules and Eli's place.

I'm so glad you want to talk, she writes. I was hoping you would.

I haven't changed my mind, I reply. I still don't believe that Alistair was involved.

After that it takes her a while to respond, a silence that stretches into days. When she does, her message is brief. It arrives late at night as I sit awake listening to the sound of cars purring past, unable to sleep. I never seem to be able to sleep much anymore.

I understand that, she writes. But there are some things you still need to know.

I take a deep breath, and I find that I'm typing the words before I've really thought them through.

OK, I write. I'm ready to hear it.

THEN

When Agnes comes back, the news spreads like a bad rumor, a sickness that threatens to strike us all down. Like Pandora opening her box and releasing all that is bad upon the island.

Eloise finds out first. She goes down to the bar one afternoon to see if anyone has opened up yet. To see if there's any sign of life beginning again. She comes back breathless, bursting into the kitchen as Helena and I are silently navigating around each other, both making paltry lunches and studiously avoiding the other's eye.

"The police have come over from the mainland," she says, her eyes bright and wide. "Loads of them. And Agnes is with them."

Helena sets a knife down with a clatter. Her face is drawn when she turns around.

"Agnes?" she says.

"Yes."

Helena inhales sharply. "I'm sure it'll be nothing," she says. "They probably had to come again. Procedure, or whatever."

She leans back against the counter, and we all stand still, suspended, each waiting for someone else to speak. The police have already been here once, the day after Kiera died, an overweight local officer who asked vague questions and oversaw arrangements for her body to be taken to the mainland.

"But . . ." Helena breaks the silence first. "Maybe we should go and take a look. Just to see. Just to make sure that everything's OK."

Helena and I barely seem to have spoken to each other since Kiera fell. The thing I interpreted as friendship seems to have vanished, like water evaporating from skin. She arrived here with Kiera and Priya, the three of them thrown together by some distant quirk of circumstance. Plane tickets booked to the same place. A night scheduled at the same hostel. There is a discordance in the realization that we can never know when we meet somebody exactly what part they will play in our lives. Who will be there at the very end.

We stride down to the dock together. We are silent and determined, not daring to vocalize what we are all thinking. If the police are here, then perhaps they know something. If Agnes is here, then perhaps she has told them.

Not that any of us think anyone has done anything wrong. Not really. Kiera jumped. Nobody could have stopped her. But there are things that won't look quite right. Things that might sound strange coming from Agnes's mouth. Why a young girl, on an adventure and with her whole life ahead of her, would climb to the top of some cliffs and let herself fall. The parties at Henry Taylor's house. The drugs. There are fragments of our life out here that won't make sense from the outside, even though they are woven into the fabric of our everything. Even though we know there's nothing wrong with them. And yet every now and again, late at night when I'm unable to sleep, I remember Kiera sitting up on the roof, her eyes cast down, her silhouette dark against the sky.

It's not difficult to find the police who have descended upon our island. We are so used to the order of this place, to the people who live here and the tourists who roll in off boats, that any slight disruption is immediately apparent. You can feel them before you see them. In the woman who stands in her doorway talking tersely to her neighbor in Greek. In the shop owner who sometimes gives us free pastries dense with syrup glaring at us as we pass. The air feels thick with tension and knotted with fear. There's a sickness that doesn't feel like a side effect of my increasingly apparent pregnancy. It's been almost a month since I took the test, and I have deliberately dressed in my baggiest shirt to avoid any questions.

They are clustered around the dock, wearing uniforms that look far too heavy for the midday heat. Even now that it is almost winter, the air feels claustrophobic, clotting in my lungs and tightening around my neck.

"Where's Agnes?" Helena asks.

Eloise shakes her head. "She was here," she says. "I saw her."

We don't go down to speak to them. We watch for a few moments, uniformed men teeming like ants in the slender street that lines the beach. To me, their presence threatens to rock everything we have built here, a weight that tips the delicate balance of our island lives. I want to see Alistair badly. I want him to tell me this is normal, that the police have to look into this kind of thing. That they're only doing their jobs. But there are so many of them their presence feels stifling. And Agnes brought them here.

※

I don't need to wait long to talk to Alistair about it. He calls me early that night as I am stretched out on my bed waiting for the day to end. The vibration of my phone makes me jump, loud and violent against the thick quiet of evening.

"Hey." He speaks before I do. "I need you up at the house. Don't tell anyone you're coming."

Alistair comes to pick me up and we make the journey in silence. As the car traverses familiar terrain, I feel a growing anxiety tighten

my chest. I want him to tell me it will all be OK, but I can sense
that he's as nervous as I am. His hands grip the steering wheel so
hard that his knuckles turn white, and he takes corners too quickly,
distracted and frequently glancing in his rearview mirror. I find myself resting my hand on my stomach as though I could protect the
scrap of life growing inside me, even though I'm not quite sure what
from—its father's terrible driving or some other looming and indefinable disaster.

The lights are off in Henry Taylor's house. Alistair flips them on
and goes straight to the kitchen to pour a drink. I wonder vaguely if
this could be my chance to tell him about the baby, perhaps refusing a
whiskey with a knowing smile, but he replaces the bottle cap without
offering me one. He throws his own drink down straight, and that's
when I notice the state the place is in. The house is usually pristine,
all shiny white surfaces and mood lighting. For the first time it looks
as though somebody actually lives here, as though the living room is
more than just a backdrop for glamorous parties. There are piles of
dishes in the sink, an empty bottle on a coffee table, a lingering smell
that is almost muddy, like unemptied bins and the outdoors. Alistair
pours himself another whiskey and paces to the sofa. I've never seen
him like this before, frantic, his limbs twitching as if he doesn't know
what to do with them. He pats the space next to him, and I lower myself down. The sofa cushions are scattered with crumbs that scratch
the back of my bare legs.

"Have you heard?" he says.

"About the police?"

He nods, his mouth set grimly straight, and runs one hand through
his hair. It's a gesture that's new to me, and it looks almost like a nervous tic.

"I saw them earlier. Eloise said Agnes was with them."

Helena, Eloise, and I haven't talked about what we saw. We walked
back to the house without speaking and went straight to our respec-
tive rooms. We all had to pass where Kiera had slept on the way up,

our steps slowing as we neared her door, our feet arching into tiptoes as though there was anybody inside that could hear us.

"Fuck." Alistair takes another gulp of his drink. "I knew it. They've been here today, asking questions, poking around. I should have known it was Agnes."

"What did they want?"

"What did they *want*?" He shakes his head disbelievingly. "They think there was a reason that Kiera jumped. I mean, of course there was. She was ill. Not right. But they think something else is going on. They think she was in some kind of trouble. And they think Henry had something to do with it."

"How could . . . how could Henry have had anything to do with it? He wasn't there."

"Of course he doesn't have anything to do with it. It's all a load of bollocks. Horseshit. But fucking *Agnes*."

He says her name as though it tastes bad in his mouth, and it seems to necessitate him taking another swig of his drink to wash the dregs of it away.

"She came here, you know. The day after Kiera died. Demanded to see Henry. He wasn't here, so I said she could talk to me. Look, Henry is a rich guy, right? A lot of people want something from him. You know what it's like. People try to take advantage. And Agnes is smart. She saw what happened. And she saw it as an opportunity."

He reaches out and his hand grips my thigh. It's not sensual, like it was the first time he touched me in this very room. It's urgent, desperate.

"Look, you know what we're all like out here, don't you? Everyone comes here to have a good time. Get pissed. Take stuff. Have sex. Everyone's just having a good time. Kiera did. Agnes did. But now . . ." He exhales sharply. "Agnes told me she wanted money, and if she didn't get it, she'd go to the police. Tell them that Henry was running . . . I don't know, some kind of ring of girls. Taking advantage of them. Forcing them to sleep with his friends. I mean, it's bullshit. I obviously said no to her. Henry isn't paying to shut someone up when he didn't even do anything. But now . . ."

He trails off, and I think back to the night I blacked out. The sick feeling I hadn't been able to shake afterward. The vague shadowy memories that made something inside me coil and sour.

"I mean . . ." My voice is shaky. "Is it true?"

"Is it . . . ?" He emits a short bark of laughter. "Rachel, are you serious? How can it be true? You've been here the whole time. You've seen it all."

"But there was . . ." Somewhere shapes are shifting, memories reformulating and slotting into different forms.

"Look, we're all adults here, aren't we?" Alistair interjects before I finish my sentence. "Did you ever see Agnes or Kiera look like they weren't having fun? Like they weren't flirting with the guys, going off into bedrooms alone with them, enjoying themselves?"

I find myself shaking my head.

"I mean, if Henry is doing what Agnes says he is, then don't you think you'd have been brought into it? That he would have . . . I dunno, told you that you had to do something you didn't want to do? Agnes is a slag. She's slept with all these guys and now she feels guilty about it. She's probably got a boyfriend at home or something, who she's going to have to explain it all to. And she's probably thinking she can get a nice bit of cash into the bargain too. It's fucking bullshit, Rachel, that's what it is."

I cast my mind back to the parties. Agnes draped over some guy, laughing, drinking. Kiera dancing in the middle of this very room, her face split open into a smile.

"So what's going to happen?" I ask.

"Well, this is why I wanted to talk," Alistair says. "They're going to want to ask you questions too, obviously, all the girls still here. You don't really have to do anything. You just have to tell them the truth. That there was nothing going on here. They're not going to listen to me, Rachel. But they'll listen to you."

He reaches out and takes my hand.

"I love you. You know that. But right now, I'm really fucking scared. If they believe Agnes, then I'm going to jail, Rachel. Henry too. Probably for years."

"But it had nothing to do with you . . ."

"They won't think that though, will they? Given how close I was to Henry. My name will be the first one they know about. Look, I've been thinking. About us. I have been for a while. All this life here . . . the partying, working for Henry. Ever since I met you, I don't know if I see the point in it anymore. I just want us to be together. Away from all this."

"What do you mean?"

"We can go, Rachel. Get away from here. Find somewhere to live, just the two of us. Start a life together. All this sneaking around . . . I've had enough of it. I want to be able to show the world that I'm with you. I want us to be together, properly."

In spite of myself, my heart jumps. It's all that I want. It's everything I've longed for him to say. I imagine us as a family, in a white-painted house somewhere indistinct and sunny. I let my fingertips drift to the slight curve of my belly again and feel the warmth of my skin beneath my shirt. It's as though our child is somersaulting in my stomach, glowing at the chance to have a new life. Then, I imagine the alternative. Alistair in some Greek prison. Me having the baby alone. Perhaps having to go back to my parents and living through their disapproval every day, the shock of my former classmates when they hear I'm a single mother with the father locked away. It's unimaginable. And what Alistair said makes sense. We're all adults. We all made choices.

"I want that too," I say.

"Thank God." He leans over and kisses me hard on the mouth. "I knew you would. I knew I could count on you. So, you'll do it? You'll tell the police it's all lies?"

I nod. "Of course I will. It's only the truth, isn't it?"

"It is," he says. "But if you have to lie . . . if they ask you anything uncomfortable. Anything that might look strange from the outside. Things they wouldn't understand. You'd protect us, wouldn't you, Rachel? Just a few tiny white lies. You'd do that for me?"

And I don't even have to think about it, because just now, just in this moment, I don't think there is anything that I wouldn't do for him.

✳

The next day the house turns into a makeshift station. Without anywhere else to take us, the police transform our kitchen into an interview room. They tell us all to stay upstairs and that they'll come and get us when it's our turn. I sit on the floor next to my bed and hear knocks echoing down corridors, footsteps down halls. It's haunting how many of the summons remain unanswered, how many of the girls I once considered friends have by now caught flights far away from here. It started the day after Kiera died, a slow emptying out of the house that reminded us nothing could ever be the same again. First Agnes, then Amy. A girl who had only recently arrived to take Priya's room, horrified by what she had seen on the beach that night. I lean my head against the crumbling plaster. I remember what Alistair told me yesterday and then push the thought from my mind. Everything is going to be different now.

They call me down last, two officers who walk me to the kitchen in silence. If Agnes had been telling the truth, you would expect sympathy. Perhaps a kindly female officer offering cups of tea and concern. Instead I sit opposite blank-faced men at the kitchen table. Someone places a glass of water down in front of me and I feel distinctly as though I am the one being accused. I think of how it must be for Alistair, up in Henry Taylor's house waiting for all this to come down on him. I hate imagining him scared.

"There are some things we want to ask you about," one of the officers says. "Some parties that have been happening."

I see Kiera again, shivering in the corridor, her expression frantic. My throat tightens, and I feel a dampness start to form beneath my armpits and in the small of my back. I wish somebody would suggest throwing open the window, stirring the stillness, giving us all a chance to breathe sea-spiked air.

I hope it will all be over quickly, but their questions are long and slow. Every time I speak, they pause to take notes. They talk in thickly accented English, sentences occasionally broken by inadequate phrasing, words lost in the thick mist of translation. I find myself reciting what I've said in my head, imagining how it will look in their looping black scrawl, how it will sound as they sift my responses into their own language. I peer at their notebooks but can't figure out from across the table whether they're writing in Greek or English. I wonder how my responses will render across the obvious language barrier. I try to make sure they are deliberate and uncomplicated, closed off to interpretation, immune to confusion.

"No," I say over and over again. "No, I never saw anything like that. I was there the whole time."

They ask me about London, and I skim over that night, the things I did, how withdrawn Kiera had seemed. They ask me about the night I saw Kiera panicked and alone in the hallway of Henry Taylor's house.

"Did Alistair invite you?" they ask.

I shake my head. "No," I lie. "It was Henry."

Alistair would be furious at me for implicating his boss, but better Henry than Alistair. Better Henry than us. The men are both writing, their pens poised above paper.

"But he invited Kiera, didn't he?" one prompts. "You were surprised to find out she was invited?"

"No." The lies are coming easily now. I'm too eager for this to be over, too eager to be out of this room and away from its oppressive heat. "No, I wasn't surprised. Because I invited her."

More twitching of pens. More empty seconds as I wait for the next question.

"And did you see Kiera that night? Did you see her talk to anyone?"

I look straight at him this time. His gaze is unfaltering, his eyes almost aquatic.

"Of course I did," I say. "She talked to lots of people. Before she left early."

"She left early?"

"Yes," I say. "She had a couple of drinks with us in the living room. And then she went home."

"Back here?"

"Yes."

"On her own?"

I nod. "Just her."

"And did you notice Kiera spending a lot of time up at the house? Did she ever used to go up there on her own?"

"Never. We were almost always together here. I would have known if she did. I would have gone there with her."

The weight of words can be astounding sometimes. You can never really know the power they have, how long they will follow you for. I have to steady my breath to keep my composure level when all I want to do is scream, leave this room, run back to Alistair. The single kitchen window is closed, and even though it's nearing winter, the room feels breathless, stifling. I watch a bead of sweat form on the forehead of one of the policemen and make slow progress from his temple to his jaw. He swipes it away just as it starts to pool against the blade of his neck, pregnant and threatening to drop down onto the table.

"I think that will be everything," one says.

And I know I will never be able to take back what I have said.

NOW

I t turns out that Helena isn't staying anywhere near where we last met. Instead I find myself at a suburban townhouse on a quiet Balham street. She smiles apologetically when she answers the door.

"Sorry to drag you here," she says. "It's my sister's place."

I try to remember if I knew Helena had a sister. It occurs to me that the friendship we all used to feel was mostly an illusion, a closeness forged from being thrown together at a time when everything felt new and exciting. I suppose we didn't really know each other that well at all.

It's a bright day, the sun beaming white and stoic against a crisp blue sky. There's a hint of frost in the air, a turning of autumn into winter, but the house is warm and inviting. Helena takes me through to a kitchen with beams of light filtering through leaded windows and stacks of brightly painted crockery piled in glass-fronted cabinets. A plant hangs from the ceiling in a suspended clay pot, its long, green tendrils cascading over the edge. Helena looks surprisingly domestic as she potters about making tea, a ginger cat coiling lazily between her legs. She invites me to sit at the kitchen table and asks if I take sugar, another intimacy lost to time or perhaps never known at all. A window looks out onto a conservatory where the same teenage girl who served me back in the bar all those months ago lolls in a wicker chair, headphones firmly clamped over her ears as she plays with her phone.

"You remember my daughter?" Helena says, gesturing vaguely toward her. "Astraea?"

I nod.

"She lives here in term time," Helena says. "And I come back a lot. My family weren't that bothered that I decided to stay out there, but they were dead set on Astraea going to school in London. It's been good for us actually, me and my sister. We got a lot closer again."

She fishes a tea bag out of a striped mug and carries it over to me. As she sits down, she blows on her own drink, and I feel an unexpected jolt of familiarity. Perhaps we used to know these things about each other after all.

"I'm sorry for springing it on you like that the other day," she says. "Priya said you wouldn't come if we'd told you."

"I wouldn't have," I say. "Probably."

Helena nods. "Priya's smart like that."

Her fingers are drumming against the side of her mug, tapping out a rapid and urgent beat. Her nails chink against the handle, and the pale brown liquid trembles.

"So . . ." she says. "What do you think? Now that you've had time to . . . you know . . . consider it all."

"I want to hear it," I say. "I left without giving you a chance to explain the other day and . . . I want to know what you think happened. What you're planning to say."

Helena surveys me carefully over her mug.

"Rachel," she says. "You're still seeing Alistair, aren't you? After I gave you his number?"

"That doesn't matter."

"I knew it." She turns her head and looks out of the window, into the room where her daughter sits. "I knew I shouldn't have given it to you."

"So what if I am though? Seeing him? What difference does it make?"

"It makes all the difference." Helena stands so quickly that tea sloshes over the edge of her mug and spatters onto the table. "I know what he's like. It makes all the difference."

She goes over to the window, her hands resting on the countertop. For a moment we're both silent. There's the noise of a distant clock chiming, the gurgle of the boiler, the padding footsteps of the cat as it hurries away down a hallway.

"Look, Rachel," she says. "If I talk to you about this, you have to promise not to tell him, OK? You can't talk to him about any of this."

"I don't know if I can promise that," I say.

Helena half laughs, a dark and despondent sound.

"I thought you might say that," she says. "You always did protect him. But honestly, Rachel, once I tell you this I'm not sure you'll ever even want to talk to him again."

She turns to face me, and our bodies seem to square up to each other, suspended in a moment between what we know now and words that could change everything forever. I look into her eyes and I see summer. I see the island as it used to be, its enormous peace and the promise of a future. I still see Alistair, even now, reflecting back in everything.

"I want you to tell me what you know," I say. "I need to hear it."

"Fine," she says. "Fine. I think it's time that you did."

And then, there in the peaceable quiet of a London townhouse, she takes me back sixteen years. I am seventeen again, and we are newly arrived in paradise. Yet now, through Helena's eyes, I see that she remembers everything differently. The bright blue stretches of sea are where she lost her friend. The white sands are where she would stand and wonder if she should leave. The island crumbles and sours as she starts to talk. It is a place of fantasy and illusion. A place of secrets and hurt.

"I bet you wonder why I stayed," she says. "It's in me, Rachel. It's everywhere. I couldn't get away from it. I didn't know who I was when I wasn't there. And I think you feel the same."

Helena's words skirt around the edges of my memories. She talks about familiar places and her mouth forms familiar names, but beneath her tongue they buckle and warp. She describes a different world from the one I remember, one that is tinged with darkness where I saw magic. Instead of a businessman, Henry Taylor was somebody nobody really knew much about, a man who had acquired his money through dubious and unclear means and had ugly and twisted appetites.

"His parties were famous," Helena says. "But not among the kind of people you'd want to know. He was powerful. He could do whatever he wanted. And he knew that."

She tells me that the bar was a recruiting ground for girls, barely even an operating business. We would turn up in our droves, and Alistair would cherry-pick the ones Henry Taylor would want. Usually they were the girls who were most desperate—people like Agnes who needed the money or who were untethered like Kiera, unsure if she really did want to go to university and wasting a year while she worried about what to do with her life. Others would pass through never visiting Henry's house or seeing the side of the island that we did.

"But he knew what he was doing," she says. "And Alistair was a massive part of that."

She tells me Alistair did Henry Taylor's dirty work. It would be him in the bar, spending time with the girls and deciding which of them he would bring up to the house. Once they were there, he was their friend, a confidant who would tell them what to do. Give them drugs. Sort out money for them.

"We all ended up reliant on them, in one way or the other," Helena says. "He'd make sure we were financially dependent on him—I mean, they were paying for where we lived, for God's sake. Then there'd be the drugs. You saw what happened to Kiera. Breaking us away from every other part of our lives until we couldn't imagine leaving. Making sure we were so indebted to them that we couldn't tell anyone what was happening."

When she talks about the sex, she stares down at her feet, only speaking in the most clipped of terms.

"When it started, I thought I was in control," she says. "I was having fun. I was getting drunk and taking whatever anyone gave to me. You'd go to these parties and some guy would want to touch you and you'd think, whatever. We were that age where you feel powerful. You're just making sure everyone has a good time. You're keeping Henry Taylor happy. You think it's such easy money. You'd think what a total idiot the guy was, whoever he was, thinking you actually like him. And then it's happening more and more. And then you look around and realize it isn't really a choice at all anymore. You realize it probably never was."

Helena sighs, and there is a shudder to her breath, as though she has been holding it in for a long time.

"Afterward I tried to forget about it. I pushed it all down for years. I think I even convinced myself it hadn't really happened like that. It was easier than confronting what it had really been like. What I'd done. I'd feel sick with myself if I even thought about it. I once told an ex-boyfriend that they had been my 'wild years.' Can you believe it? I used to brag about how many guys I'd slept with. All these crazy parties we'd go to. That time we went to London. It was easier that way. I think, if I told it like that, I could pretend I'd had a normal time as a teenager. Sleeping around. Having fun. I could pretend I had wanted it." She stares out of the window again, and her eyes are steeped with sadness as she looks at her daughter. "She's almost sixteen now. Just a few years younger than I was when I went out there. Mad, really. As she's got older, it's made me think. Made me remember what I was like at that age. Made me imagine the same thing happening to her. I've had to confront it, Rachel. I've had to face up to what really happened back there. And I want to do everything I can to stop the same thing from happening to her. To other girls like her."

She takes a deep breath.

"Seeing you back at the bar made my decision for me. I could see it so clearly. How you still believed them. How much of an impact it's had on us. On all of us. It's our responsibility now. Alistair was as much a part of it as Henry Taylor was. And we protected him. But now we have to stop him. We have to make sure that people are held accountable."

"No."

Even as Helena talks, I'm not quite listening. Somewhere deep down inside me, the island is the same, even though her words erode some of the corners of it, invade some of the brightest spots with a gray and thickening fog. That place has been my whole life. Everything I thought I knew about myself was constructed in those few months I spent within touching distance of the sea. Everything I am is because Alistair loved me. My dreams have always been tied up in him, even after he left, even after I married Tom and talked about building a life with him. I always wanted Alistair. I wanted to have his children. I wanted to wipe clean everything that happened after we went to London and start again. If only I could make it right with him, then I would have another chance. If only the island could stay as it always had been—pristine and perfect and pure—then I could still believe in him.

"It's not true," I say, my voice sounding far stronger than I feel. "Not about Alistair. Alistair loved me. You're trying to turn me against him. He wouldn't have done anything like that. Not to me. Not to anyone."

"But think about it, Rachel," Helena says. "Did he? Did you even spend much time with him? Did you really even know him at all?"

A memory surfaces then, bloated and ungainly. Always waiting for Alistair to call me. Hoping to catch him at the bar when I was working. The odd hours we had together always feeling something like snatched time. It didn't seem to matter back then. I'd never had a relationship before, and Alistair was older. He had a real job. Things he had to do. I had polished the memories of the time we spent together until they dazzled, shining so brightly that it made it impossible to see anything else. But Helena's words chime somewhere. They make the memories in between raise their head a little and demand to be seen.

"Of course I did," I say, but I can hear my voice waver with uncertainty. "We spent time together. You just didn't know about it. We couldn't tell anyone. We had to keep it a secret."

Helena snorts. "Of course. A secret. You didn't ever wonder why that was?"

"Because of Henry Taylor. Alistair could have lost his job . . ."

Helena is shaking her head. "You think Henry would really have fired Alistair for having a relationship? Seriously? Alistair was lying to you, Rachel. It would have been convenient for him if he wasn't allowed to tell anyone, right? If none of us were able to say anything to each other? If we couldn't all talk to each other behind his back? Henry Taylor knew what was happening. Henry Taylor was the one making it all happen. They were in it together."

It's strange how quickly a truth you have believed for years can seem ridiculous the moment it is said out loud. Helena's voice is scathing, bitter, the drawn-out weight of her words pulling apart the fragile seams of my past.

"Why do you think he's seeing you?" she says. "After all this time? Don't you think he could have found you before now if he wanted to?"

"You don't know anything about us," I say, my voice thinning.

"But I do. Did you tell him you'd seen us? Tell him what we told you? Did he act surprised?" She shakes her head. "He knows, Rachel. I know he does because I told him. Months ago. And then who should come along but you? Someone who's always protected him. Someone who could be a really important witness if we ever did manage to make a case against him. Someone who, if he plays it right, might still be in his corner, even now."

"No."

"I bet he didn't want to see you at first, right? And then all of a sudden . . ."

I'm shaking my head vehemently now, but I can still remember the very first message he sent. Before he knew that I hadn't spoken to Helena, or Priya, or Agnes yet.

How did you find me?

"He did," I say. "He wanted to, right from the start. I'm not like the rest of you. Alistair and I were together. He loved me."

"OK, fine," Helena says. "He loved you. Sure. But I can prove that things weren't quite how you remember them."

"How?"

Helena sighs, and I can see lines of pity sketched out on her face.

"We knew about the baby, Rachel. I know you thought that you were doing a good job of hiding it. You were in such a dream world about Alistair. We all used to take the piss out of you. I know it was cruel of us. But you just seemed so innocent. So naive. You'd come back from seeing him and think nobody knew where you had been. You'd walk around all dazed and happy. And when you started throwing up in the mornings, we all noticed. And you were showing, weren't you? When Kiera died? I could see it that night on the beach. Just a little bit, but we all already suspected." She pauses to check my reaction. "Did you get rid of it? Was it after he left?"

"I don't want to talk about it."

"No, of course you don't. I get that. That's fine. I won't mention it again. But you weren't the only one, Rachel. I'm sorry. It wasn't just you."

"What do you mean?"

"Me and Alistair." She sounds as though she is forcing the words out, as though they are thick as treacle, distasteful as mud. "We were . . . we were together. I don't think he buttered me up as much as he did you, to be fair. I didn't really need as much of it. All the romance shit. But I slept with him, that first night we went to the party at Henry Taylor's place. You remember? After you went back to the hostel?"

I try to remember the end of that night, but my memory falters. I remember my white dress. The feel of Alistair's skin on mine. The fizz of excitement and longing when he took me outside to talk. I don't remember going home, or Helena staying. I didn't have to. The edges of my recollection were so sharp, so perfect, that I hadn't spent much time examining them. I had just relived the best bits, a highlight reel of Alistair and me on repeat.

"I had a shit childhood, you know that. Daddy issues, as Kiera used to say. It didn't take much for me. A bit of attention, a bit of special treatment, and I was obsessed with him. I knew he was sleeping with other girls. I knew he was sleeping with you. And I didn't care. I'd do whatever he wanted."

She takes a deep breath as if to steady herself.

"I used to let men treat me like shit then. I'd been homeless before, you know that. Sleeping on people's sofas. Sleeping with older guys so they'd put me up. I was perfect for them. I was exactly what Alistair was looking for. You were harder work. At first, we didn't think he'd bother with you. You weren't the usual type. But then you were so . . . so crazy about him. So pliable. Don't you see, Rachel? It was easy for him to manipulate you. But I was even easier. I did what he wanted. What would keep him happy. Get him in Henry Taylor's good books. He used to say that to you too, right? That you had to keep Henry Taylor happy? That we had to do whatever he wanted."

There's a grim tug of recognition in the pit of my stomach, and when my voice emerges, it sounds wounded, strangled.

"No," I say. "It wasn't like that. Not with us."

I push my mug aside, and it tips over on the table, a clatter of porcelain against wood, a pool of tea cascading out.

"I don't believe you," I say. "He's not like that. He wouldn't have—"

"If you don't believe me, then believe Astraea," she says.

"What do you . . . ?"

"Look at her." Helena grasps my arm and pulls me toward the window. "Look at my daughter. I can lie, but biology doesn't. Her face doesn't lie."

Trembling, I lift my gaze and look, really look, at Helena's child. When I saw her back on the island, I saw Helena in her every move, in her long dark hair, her playful gait. This time I look at Astraea, and my whole world tumbles down around me.

I've imagined the child Alistair and I might have had more times than I care to admit. It's been impossible not to. For the first few years, every baby could have been her. I always thought it would have been a girl without any real logic behind my suspicions. I would see tiny swaddled bundles in prams and imagine dark tufts of hair like Alistair's, his olive green eyes wide in a minute face. I'd see a toddler taking ungainly steps in a playground, and my heart would ache for our lost child, a daughter with my mouth and his smile.

As time passed, my image of her became blurrier. She would get old enough to have her own personality, characteristics that were beyond my imagining, likes and dislikes I was unable to fathom. Perhaps she would have grown up on the island and love the sea. She would dream about being a marine biologist or a mermaid, both occupations equally as feasible in a childishly unconstrained mind. Perhaps we would have come back to London, and she would go to school in a neatly ironed uniform and join netball teams, and have unrequited crushes on boys who her dad would threaten to beat up. Her dad. It was always painful to imagine what we might have been, how the roles of parenthood would have redefined us and shaped us into something wholly new together. Everything that had happened after Kiera's death had taken that away from us, and yet I had hung on to the hope that the daughter I dreamed about might still be born one day.

And now here she is. Not my daughter, but undoubtedly Alistair's child. Everything about her is somehow also him. The slant of her cheekbones. The shape and color of her eyes. The way her body lounges back in the chair, relaxed and yet ridden with the same kind of confidence I thought I would one day grow into, the same certainty of her place in the world. Now that Helena has pointed it out, I am amazed I haven't seen it before. But then it seems that I have become an expert in only seeing what I want to.

"She's his," Helena says, as if I needed her confirmation. "Astraea is Alistair's daughter. We were both pregnant when Kiera died. But I kept her. I stayed on the island, and I had my daughter. I had Alistair's child."

THEN

Alistair is gone. He is gone, and I feel as though my entire world
has fallen apart.

I lie on his abandoned bed and I am utterly lost. All the
hours spent waiting for him on the beach have blurred into nothing,
time feeling inconsequential. I press my face into his pillow until it is
sodden, grasping at explanations for why he would have gone without me. What terrible events took place here last night that meant
Alistair took off just hours after he said goodbye to me, promising me
he would meet me this morning. I mutter Agnes's name like a curse,
not believing that she would have gone to the police after everything
Alistair and Henry have done for us. She has torn everything we
knew apart, and I will never forgive her.

"We'll go," Alistair had told me last night, just hours after I had
spoken to the police. "Tomorrow. You and me."

I had gone back to the apartment block with my heart singing even
as the world closed in around us. When I woke up this morning, it
had felt like the first day of the rest of my life. As I packed my things,
I could have almost sworn I felt the baby move, a tiny flutter in the
pit of my stomach, an affirmation that I was doing the right thing.

Eventually I gather myself enough to leave Henry Taylor's house, perhaps for the last time. I walk barefoot all the way back to town, hardly noticing the heat of the tarmac beneath my feet, the dirt beneath my soles. I walk without knowing where I'm going until I'm already there, standing on Jules's stoop.

"He's gone," I say to her when she opens the door.

Then I'm on the floor, my palms flat against the tiles of her doorstep, my knees bloody against the concrete. I'm sobbing, noisy tears that come from deep down inside me and make my chest heave. Jules drops down to reach her arms around me. She's making soothing, hushing sounds as though I'm a child having a temper tantrum. She pulls my hair out of my eyes and asks me what happened. There aren't the words to tell her. I feel sick, my swollen stomach heavy, my heart torn in two.

"Come inside," she says. "You need to sit down."

She guides me into her apartment and pours me a glass of water from a spluttering tap. My lips are dry and cracked, my throat sore from crying.

"Tell me everything," she says.

And I do. I tell her about Alistair and me. The pregnancy. The fact that he had gone without saying goodbye.

"He wouldn't have left me here unless he had to," I say over and over again. "The police were coming for him. There was nothing he could do."

Jules doesn't say anything, just pours me another glass of water.

"He'll be back," I say, taking a sip. "He has to be."

※

After a week, Jules books us flights home. I've spent the past seven days sharing her bed, lying awake with my phone on the pillow beside me waiting for it to light up. I call him over and over again, the same mechanical intonation of his voicemail chipping away at my hope each time I hear it. I start to jump at the smallest sound, and dark hollows form beneath my eyes from lack of sleep. I hardly dare eat or go to the bathroom, terrified of missing a call when I'm not properly listening out. Even as my pregnancy progresses, I find that weight is falling from my limbs and face, bones sharpening at the corners of my joints.

"You can't wait here forever for him," Jules says eventually, her voice level. "You need a plan."

She asks me where I want to go. I shake my head hopelessly. The thought of turning up back at my parents' house with them still furious and barely speaking to me after dropping out of college is impossible to endure. I imagine the disappointment on my dad's face, the horror on my mum's when they see my distended belly, the arguments that would fill up the kitchen and make being back home unbearable. The defeat of returning to the shell of my former life, torturously ordinary beside the world I have constructed out here, the future I have imagined with Alistair. Jules hovers, her fingers above the keyboard of an internet café computer. She chews her lip and then clicks the mouse, changing the number of plane tickets to two.

"OK," she says. "It's fine. We'll figure it out. You can come home with me."

"I can't," I say.

"Yes, you can. It'll only be for a few weeks. Just while you're getting sorted. I owe you one, remember?"

I vomit in the small toilet of the plane, the stench of artificial cleanliness putrid against the acidic taste of bile. A voice intones that the "fasten seat belt" sign has been switched on, and I rest my forehead against the cold metal of the sink and wish I were dead. I imagine Alistair and I flying somewhere together, anywhere together. He would know about the baby. He would loop his arm protectively around me at passport control. But instead it's Jules who asks me if I'm OK when I slot back into my seat beside her, my eyes still stinging. Jules who chases our backpacks at the luggage carousel and books trains and taxis to her parents' place. Jules who shows me where I'll be staying, an attic room at the top of an enormous and isolated country house. I never imagined that Jules's family might be rich or that she would have grown up somewhere like this. But then, I had never really imagined life away from the island since I had arrived there. It subsumed me so entirely that nothing else existed outside it.

"My parents are away a lot," Jules tells me. "You can stay as long as you need."

My new bedroom has one window that spans all the way up to the ceiling. The bed is beneath it, and when it rains the single sheet of glass seems to buckle beneath the weight. The sound is colossal: a thunder of droplets, a symphony of water. It always seems to be raining back here. There is a tiny gap in the wooden frame, and a spatter of liquid lands on the sill. Old houses, Jules says, are always imperfect. It feels like an unfamiliar concept after the magic of my summer, those fragile and bewitching months when I imagined Alistair and I had a future. I spend hours sitting on my new bed, looking out of the window onto the gray flatness of fields that span around the house. I miss the view of the dusty street outside the apartment block, the way the sea seemed to emerge at the end of every alleyway, the taste of salt in every breath. I miss sitting on the stoop outside Jules's place and feeling the sun warm my skin. And I miss him so badly my bones ache. So badly that I swear I can feel my heart for the first time, its furious weight in my chest pulling me back toward him. I sleep with my arm cupped around my belly, clinging to the last trace of him. Now that everything has fallen apart, I almost feel as though I have imagined the entire thing. Only the gentle rise and fall of my stomach reminds me that it was all real after all.

"It has to be your decision, at the end of the day," Jules tells me over tea and toast, crumbs scattered across the bedsheets. "Nobody else can make it for you."

But it isn't really. It can't be. I lie awake as my hand makes rhythmic circles across my belly. Alistair will be back, of course, but for now he is gone. It strikes me with a vague horror that I don't even know enough about his life to be able to start to track him down—who his family are, or if he has any friends outside of the island. Back there it didn't feel like those things mattered. We existed in our own orbit, our own world. Now I'm forced to confront what would happen if I tried to bring this baby up alone. How it would look if anyone found out I was pregnant. I had told the police that Alistair had never touched me. Would they track him down if they found out I had lied, my whole testimony in tatters? Would *I* be arrested for protecting him? By the time the room starts to brighten, I have made my decision.

"I know what I'm going to do," I tell Jules.

And she nods as if she has expected it all along.

"It's up to you," she says.

But it never really was. The Fates have spoken. Alistair and I couldn't possibly have a baby, not now, not with everything that has happened.

Jules arranges everything swiftly and quietly. All I have to do is let it happen to me. Let Jules drive me to the nearest town in her battered car. Let the receptionist check my date of birth and give me forms to sign. Let the doctor examine me, take blood from my arm, explain the procedure in level and gentle tones.

Afterward, I tell Jules that she should sleep in her own room for a bit. I want to be alone. I close the curtains and switch off the lights and lie on the bed until the sheets start to smell sour. Above the bed hangs a framed cross-stitch, pink and embossed with tiny teddy bears and ballerina slippers, *JULIET* woven into aging fabric. It occurs to me how little we really know about even the people who we think we are closest to.

I hear on the grapevine, through occasional texts from some of the other girls still on the island—Helena and Eloise, hanging around the house and hoping that everything will go back to normal—that the investigations against Alistair and Henry are eventually dropped.

Everyone on the island is talking about it, the delicate peace of the place rocked by swarms of police officers and rumors that swirl in the ocean breeze.

Tell me if he comes back, I type out to Helena.

She doesn't respond.

I briefly hope this is it, that he will go back to the island looking for me, that a message will come from Helena any day now. When it doesn't arrive, I fall back into despair. He doesn't know where I am, I tell myself. He has to keep a low profile for a bit. He'll be back. I'm sure of it. I just have to give him time.

Jules brings me food and gently asks me if I want to take a bath, or go for a walk. The thought feels utterly pointless. Everything I had imagined my life would be is gone. I'm no longer Alistair's girlfriend, or an expectant mother with the name Rose already picked out, or a traveler, or even a student destined for university. I don't know who I am or what I am supposed to do. There is only this room, this bed, this house, suspended in a state of before and after. Leaving it would feel like the end of everything. It would mean figuring out what is next. It would mean beginning my life without Alistair. So instead I lie still and I listen to the rain. I listen to the rain and tell myself that he is coming back.

NOW

When I leave the house, it feels as though the entire world has shifted. The streets feel narrower and the air feels denser. Alistair fills my mind, but my memories of him are suddenly claustrophobic and warped. I think of his lopsided smile, the smell of him, the taste of him. I think of him touching my skin and kissing me as recently as last week, and I feel slightly sick. I have to stop at the side of the street to vomit, retching onto a scrubby patch of grass. From across the road, a woman regards me warily as she grips the hand of a small child, unsure of whether she should cross over and offer to help. She seems to think better of it, glancing back at me as she hurries away. It's the right thing to do. I feel that something inside me has buckled and soured. People must be able to sense it. It must radiate from me like a sickness. I feel as though anybody who looks at me might see it.

I know that Astraea isn't my daughter, of course. I know she isn't the same child I chose not to have back when I was eighteen. Yet when I looked at her, I could only see what I'd done. I saw Alistair and Helena and the slight glances between them that I would put down to Helena's nature, always overly intimate with everyone. I saw parties with closed doors and older men. I saw nights that blurred into drinks and dancing and watching the sun come up. And I saw Kiera. Kiera swaying in time to music as eyes watched her from across the room. Kiera begging me to leave with her. Kiera, her body broken at the bottom of the cliffs.

Jules and Eli aren't there when I arrive back at their house. It's still late morning, but I go straight to the kitchen and pull open cupboards and drawers. They must have a spirits supply here somewhere, dusty bottles and Christmas presents put away to be regifted. I find a case of whiskey and pour a dark brown measure into a mug. I toss it down and then immediately throw it back up into the sink, acrid bile churning in my belly as my insides burn. I haven't drunk whiskey for years. Perhaps not since that night I slept in Henry Taylor's bed. The smell of it always brought something back, something rotten and ugly. I told myself I just never liked the taste, but now the back of my tongue remembers something salty and unfamiliar. Something slipped into a drink. A glass dropped on the floor. Even as I gag again, my body bent over the sink and tears hot in my eyes, I hold the taste in my mouth. Smoke and sugar. The shadow of it stale against my tongue as somebody moved above me. The utter revulsion I'd experienced the next day. My head is spinning, and I rest it down against the cold countertop and squeeze my eyes shut.

In the past the thought had come to me, fleetingly and infrequently, that Agnes might have been telling the truth. I would be half drunk on red wine or lying awake while Tom slept next to me, and my mind would spark like a furnace igniting, a fire I would dash to put out.

But what if he lied? it would hiss.

I would screw my eyes shut and try desperately to think of something else. If Agnes had been telling the truth, then Alistair was a person I couldn't recognize. *I* was a person I couldn't recognize, someone shaped and sculpted by a mess of half-truths and hurts. I inhale deeply, attempting to steady the heavy thud of my heart. I think back to that day with the police, the cold lines of their mouths, the things I said. Things I haven't thought about for years. Lies I can't quite remember. For years I had been proud of how I had protected Alistair, wearing the things I had said as though they were proof of how much I loved him. Helena's words have awoken the very worst fear in me, and I wonder how much my insistence that that summer was perfect and golden and magical has hidden a terrible truth. If Agnes was telling the truth, then I had protected *them*. If Agnes was telling the truth, then I was complicit in it all.

I unscrew the whiskey bottle and slowly and methodically empty the entire thing down the sink. I watch the dark liquid slip away, slowly and neatly swirling in the cold metal of the basin and disappearing, and as I do, I know that everything is about to change. Nothing can ever be the same again.

LATER

'm at work when Priya calls me.

I have to scrabble under my desk beneath an increasingly accu-mulating pile of boxes dragged here from mine and Tom's house, part of the slow process of dismantling a life together. I'm still staying at Jules's place, an unfortunate quirk of the drawn-out mechanisms of divorce that keep us from selling our marital home until solicitors have pored over and picked apart our life together. At first, I thought I'd only be there for a few months, just until I was no longer paying off a mortgage on a house I couldn't stand to be in and could afford to rent somewhere. I insisted on still paying my share, even though Tom wouldn't have minded helping out.

Yet somehow a month had turned into over a year, and I had started to spend my lunch break scouring property websites and growing increasingly despondent at the sight of decaying bedsits and houses shared with students. In the meantime, my office creaks at the seams, towers constructed of cardboard and plastic bags stuffed with things to take to charity shops, a life that took years to build boxed away and crammed into corners. It means that I only just catch the final trill of my phone, clawing to answer and breathless from hoisting an armful of discarded clothes aside.

"Hi! Hi, hello."

"Rachel, hi." Priya's voice, almost always calm and level, is edged with excitement.

I know why she's calling before she even speaks, can anticipate the high-pitched flurry of words she's waited for years to say. I hear her take a deep breath. It's the sound of her steadying herself, slowing herself down to savor this moment.

"It's happening. He's in for questioning. Rachel, we did it."

There's a tremor of emotion in her tone, and I wonder if she's trying not to cry. Maybe I should be trying not to cry too, this call the climax of months of hurt.

"Rachel, did you hear me? The police went to his place this morning. It's finally happening."

"I heard you," I say. "I heard."

It's been almost a year since Helena told me about Astraea. In the weeks after our meeting, she messaged me over and over again. I would lie flat on Jules's spare bed ignoring the insistent whir of my phone, my eyes fixed straight up at the ceiling. I didn't want to talk. I just wanted to remember. I wanted to bury myself so deep in the memories of that summer that they suffocated me. To untangle the parts of myself that were finally starting to make a strange kind of sense. How I was a seventeen-year-old girl caught up in the attentions of a much older man. How I had wanted to believe him so badly that I would turn a blind eye to everything. How, when he asked me to protect him, I had done so willingly. How I convinced myself I had done the right thing because the alternative was utterly unimaginable.

"They probably won't charge him straightaway," Priya is saying, her tone becoming businesslike. "We're expecting them to release him under investigation later on today. And obviously these things sometimes come to nothing. You know how it is. Someone's word against someone else's. But I'm hopeful. I think we can all be hopeful."

"OK." I feel as though somebody else is speaking, as though I have departed my body and a more reasonable remnant of Rachel is responding for me. "OK. Well, keep me updated."

"I will," Priya says. "I'd better go, I still have to tell Eloise. Talk to you later, Rachel."

And then she's gone, leaving me in the deadening quiet of my office. I put down my phone and push my chair away from the desk. If this is what I wanted, then why is the room spinning? If this is what I was working for, then why do I feel like my heart has fallen out of my chest?

It took me a long time to come to terms with Helena's revelation. Months of late-night conversations with Jules and tentative coffees with Priya.

"It wasn't your fault that they weren't ever charged," Priya had told me. "The only people they interviewed were the girls still left on the island. The ones who were still loyal to Henry. Of course you all protected them. And besides, nobody really cared back then. They just thought we were idiot girls who'd got ourselves in too deep. And Henry Taylor was too powerful to mess with. They would have got away with it anyway, even without what you told them."

I only half believed her. The sticky sensation of needing to put things right was always there, deep and unsettling. It had been Helena who had made my mind up for me. I had called her when she was back on the island, and it felt like connecting to another time. She told me what had happened the day Kiera died, details gleaned from Agnes many years later. Kiera had gone to speak to Henry Taylor on the morning of the party, to talk to him about leaving the island, and what he could do to get her on her feet. She had done so much for him by then, so many things, and she was exhausted by it all, broken by the thought of keeping it up for much longer. She had believed him when he told her he wanted to help her out. But she had caught him in a bad mood about the party he had never wanted to throw.

"He laughed in her face," Helena said, her voice hard as she repeated words it had taken her months to come to terms with herself.

"Told her that the only job she was any good for was the one she was already doing."

The line crackled and I heard her voice stall.

"He never intended to help her, of course," Helena continued. "He just told her what he needed to make her stay. To keep her doing what he wanted her to. And by then it was too late for her to go home."

When I first went to the police, I had no idea that these things could take such a long time. No indication of how crippling and all-consuming the process could be. How many times I'd have to go over the deepest hurts I'd ever known. How it would feel to sit across from someone and tell them about the worst thing that has ever happened to you and to know they don't believe you. Not really. I would see the flicker in their eyes and recognize the same doubts, the same questions, that I had held on to for years. Silly little girls growing up and regretting the things they had done, things they had wanted at the time, things they had asked for. And now, Priya is calling to tell me it could all be about to be over. That people are listening to us, believing in us. That the past might be about to catch up with Alistair.

I walk without knowing where I'm going, my legs carrying me down corridors and out into the high-ceilinged swoop of the museum. I could navigate this place with my eyes closed, my body sailing through long galleries and past tucked-away exhibits that anyone else could only stumble upon by accident. The rooms on Greece are almost directly above where my office sits, three floors up. They are dimly lit with carefully positioned lighting, long white benches, immaculate glass cases. Nothing that could touch on a thousand years of history.

I feel my breathing slow before I even reach the gallery. Couples link arms and tease each other about tortured pronunciations of ancient names, and a cluster of schoolchildren sketch serious drawings of broken vases. A woman walks alone, captivated by a mural, the colors less brilliant than they once would have been. A model of the Acropolis, pale and faintly illuminated, dominates the center of the room. It's been years since I saw the real thing, but I've often marveled at this perfectly scaled rendering, imagining myself at seventeen standing in its crumbling shadow. I remember how I used to come here after closing time, how I would see scenes of terra-cotta islands and faded seas and immediately feel calmed. I would hear his name between the lines of typed-out stories of gods and imagine how we might visit here one day, point out our favorite sculptures and talk about how we met, each retelling more gilded than the last. Perhaps we would even bring our children here, mythical creatures with palms sticky as they pressed up against the glass. They would smell of talcum powder and sea salt.

I try to summon the vision, but it fails to materialize. I can't capture the phantom feel of Alistair's hand in mine anymore, the image of daughters with his dark hair. Priya's words seem to have taken some essential part of my imagination from me, snatched away a future I'd fantasized about so many times it almost felt like reality. Here, among hundreds of stories and thousands of years of mythology, it hadn't seemed so difficult to memorialize my own past, to carefully carve it into something as perfect and pristine as the neatly labeled statues, their shape transcending time. Somehow I had put my memories of Alistair into their own glass boxes, flatteringly lit and painstakingly preserved.

I lower myself onto a seat and stay there until the gallery empties, a slovenly trickle of stragglers slowly vacating. A security guard casts me a sidelong glance and then clocks my staff lanyard and sidles away. With each person who leaves, I feel my lungs open up a little bit more, my body relenting, the race of my mind slowing.

I didn't take the decision to go to the police lightly. But somehow, I hadn't considered how it would feel if he was arrested. If all these years of wanting him would end up with me destroying him instead. Alistair is not the man I thought he was. He was never going to walk this room with me or reminisce about a past that means something completely different to him. Yet in the pit of my chest, a dull ache refuses to acquiesce. How can you stop loving someone after all this time? How can you let go of a dream you have let define you, shape the very contours of your life, hollow out a great space within you to allow it to exist? I imagine myself in a courtroom wearing scratchy tights and a too-tight suit, taking to a stand, testifying against him. The thought makes my stomach shudder.

I wait until the lights are turned down, a final reminder that it is time for everyone to move on. That space I had left for him seems to caw and clamor, to beg for something to fill it. I have to clench my hands into fists to control it, so tight that my fingernails dig bloody crevices in my palm.

✳

'm alone when he calls me. It's late, but I'm still awake, an open bottle of wine on the coffee table, a half-drunk glass clutched in my hand. My phone buzzes on the arm of my chair with a slovenly and mechanical hum. After Priya's news, I've been expecting a call all evening. Helena perhaps, or another update from Priya. The last person I expect it to be is him.

"Hello?"

There's a brief pause, a whisper of him breathing from somewhere across the city. Then he speaks, and he sounds just like he always did.

"Rachel," Alistair says. "I didn't think you'd answer."

"You shouldn't be calling me," I say.

My voice comes out stronger than I expect it to.

"I know." His voice is cold. "But I had to. I had to talk to you."

There's a brief moment when I wonder whether I should hang up. To disconnect from him and everything he still means to me. To switch off my phone and finish my glass of wine in the dense quiet of Jules's house, with her and Eli out for the night.

"What the fuck are you doing, Rachel?" he says, before I can will myself to move. "What did I ever do to you?"

I close my eyes and try to steady my breath. His tone is accusatory, frustrated, yet he's only asking me the same question I've asked myself an infinite number of times. His voice is a reminder that he is still a person, not just words tripping off Priya's tongue, potential crimes he could be tried for, translations of all those things we did into evidence. When I hear him say my name, my heart still judders, even though I try hard to shake it.

"Rachel?" he says. "Are you still there?"

He'll be at his flat now, temporarily released from questioning, perhaps feeling as though the world is closing in around him after all this time. I see him on his sofa, his body hunched over, a glass of whiskey clutched in his hand. Then I remember all those hours of interviews. The endless exhaustion of being second-guessed. Helena's daughter, long-legged and with Alistair's eyes. I feel a new dart of revulsion cut through the still-perceptible love.

No. Not love. Reliance. Addiction. Desperation. I grip the stem of my wineglass slightly tighter.

"You know exactly what you did," I say, but my voice comes out thin and sparse, barely even a whisper.

Down the line I hear him laugh, disbelieving and disapproving.

"Rachel, Rachel, Rachel," he says. My name in his mouth still sounds saccharine. "I thought I knew you, that we knew each other. I thought you were better than the other girls. Smarter. But you let them get inside your head, didn't you? You ended up just like the rest of them."

I close my eyes. His words still spark something inside me, some desire to be special, to win his approval. I remember champagne and steak. Sipping whiskey out by the pool at midnight. The way his hands pressed against me on the dance floor. All the tiny things he would do to draw me in before he would pull away again, leave me wanting him, leave me willing to do anything he asked. I've never quite managed to marry up the things I've said in interview after interview to the reality of him—to the taste of him, the smell of him, the sound of him. I've never been able to articulate the *how* of it all—how he altered me to my core. I'm not sure I ever will.

"You got inside my head," I say. "For years. You lied to me."

"I loved you, Rachel," he says. "I really did. And you betrayed me."

"You manipulated me. You made me think you loved me. Then you used me."

He laughs again, dry and erratic. His voice is slurred, and I can tell he's furious with me, his sickly disguise slipping too easily now. Fear has chipped away some of his glossy veneer, eroded some of his act.

"You were so fucking stupid, Rachel. Don't forget how involved you were. You were happy to be used at the time. To bring your friends up to the house. To tell the police whatever you had to, to make sure you got what you wanted."

Something inside me sparks then. Some deep and unsettling need to tell him. I had always let myself believe that Alistair knew me better than I knew myself, that he saw me more clearly than I saw myself, but there's always been one thing he doesn't know. One vast and endless fact that shaped the outlines of our relationship and weighted every time that he touched me, every time he said my name. After we reunited, it sat between us whenever I saw him, a great orb of possibility and promise. A matter of biology that welded itself to my heart and made it impossible for me to scrub him from my mind. A simple fact that might have changed everything, if only he had known. If only things had been different.

"I was pregnant," I tell him. "When Kiera died. I was going to have a baby. I was going to have our child."

There's a silence. At first I think I have caught him by surprise. That I have taken the words out of him for the very first time. There's a fragile moment when I expect him to finally feel something. A glimmer of hope that he might regret everything. Perhaps he will finally share a small sliver of the hurt I have been carrying around for all these years. The phone crackles, and I hear a slight intake of breath, static and mechanical.

"I know you were," he says. "I always knew."

That's when I know I have done the right thing. The moment when the last tiny part of my eighteen-year-old heart that still secretly wanted her first love to have loved her back, even in spite of everything, flickers and dies.

"Rachel?" he says. "Rachel, are you still there?"

"This will be the last time we ever speak," I say to him.

And I pray to any god who might be listening that I am right.

※

It feels as though it should rain the day I am called to trial. I want gray skies to match my mood, for the heavens to open and provide some imitation of relief, but instead it is sunny. The pavement outside the courtroom is warm beneath the soles of my most sensible shoes, and I'm relieved I wore a jacket to cover up the whisper of sweat staining my freshly ironed blouse. A small crowd of journalists are gathered outside, coats discarded on the ground and sunglasses perhaps hastily dug out of drawers. Henry Taylor was enough of a minor public figure back in the day, the type of man who was rich enough to garner corners of gossip columns and occasionally be photographed beside some nameless model, that a trial attached to his name still attracts interest. There had been whispers for years apparently, long before we even met him, rumors we were too young to hear about or understand. Anyone who knew anything was too close to him to come out and say it. It was left to people like us, women who had grown up and gathered the strength to hold his memory to account.

I'm surprised by how much of the trial consists of waiting. We're not allowed to watch the proceedings until we are called to give evidence, and so we spend the first few days familiarizing ourselves with gray walls, plastic chairs, a coffee machine that dispenses stale-tasting liquid into thin cardboard cups. I almost forget he is in the same building. For years it has been as though my body belongs to him, and now I feel nothing at all. I search for that invisible thread I always thought tied us and find only an empty space in my chest.

The holding room doesn't have air-conditioning and so I use a sheaf of notes as a fan, uselessly stirring the sluggish air and lifting damp strands of hair from the pulse of my throat. My chair is positioned directly opposite Agnes, her stomach now soft, her new baby at home with her partner. It's only recently that I learned it was she who brought everyone back together, in the end. When Priya had first tried reaching out to a few people, to try and track down decades of women who might have been harmed by Henry and Alistair, she had been met by resistance. After Henry's death, nobody had wanted to revisit that time or remember the things they had done. The women who had initially gone to the police to report Henry Taylor were too jaded and disappointed by the lack of justice they had received the first time around. Nobody wanted to go through the whole ugly process again.

"Even me, at first," Helena had told me. "I mean, me and Alistair had barely talked for years, of course, but we were still in touch. We still shared Astraea. He was a pretty crap dad, on the whole, but he'd send money every now and again. Birthday cards. We'd try to see him, if I was back in London. Not that he showed up half the time. Even then, I didn't want to hear it. He's still the father of my child, after all. And can you imagine, having to tell Astraea what he was like? Even if they never had much of a relationship, who wants to hear that about their dad? To know *that* was where they came from?" I heard her voice break then, a quiver that told me how hard this had been for her. "But then Agnes called. She talked about Kiera. That's when I knew I had to do something."

I had always known Agnes wasn't like the rest of us, but I hadn't quite understood how different her trajectory had been. Helena told me she had first come to the island as a fifteen-year-old, brought there by Henry Taylor. By the time we met her, she had spent seven

seven years of being abused by Henry and his friends, worn down from the outside in. Every summer she girls arrive and know exactly what we were there for, were too young and naive to see it ourselves.

Helena told me that Agnes's mother had been a drug addict; her father had never been around. She had met Henry in Athens during a summer she had spent working there, waiting tables and picking up badly paid odd jobs in an attempt to escape her life back home. Henry had been her way out. He paid her a little extra to keep an eye on us all, to tell him if we were talking to each other about what went on up at the house. Kiera had trusted her. She had gone to her the first time she was raped, hoping that Agnes, far more worldly than the rest of us, would know what to do. Agnes had told her it was OK. That she had nothing to worry about. That it wasn't so bad really, was it, to have sex with these men in exchange for getting what we wanted? Some cash, some adventures, some connections? But then Kiera had gone to speak to Agnes the day she died, to repeat what Henry Taylor had said to her.

"I just told her I was busy," Agnes said to me when we met for coffee, months after I went to the police. "I told her I would talk to her tomorrow."

For years, all my rage had been directed toward Agnes. It had been she who had gone to the police after Kiera died, who had told them there was something terrible happening on the island. Things she didn't have the language to articulate or define, but that she knew were wrong in some deep and awful way. She had sat in a police station on the mainland and the last seven years of her life had poured out of her. The parties. The sex. The trips abroad to be passed between men. When Alistair and Henry had fled, she was arrested herself, the police unsure of what to do without a suspect to detain. They had toyed around with potential crimes, attempted to pin Agnes with conspiracy to commit sex trafficking and sexual assault, but were unable to decide if she was a victim or accomplice. Eventually the entire case trailed off to nothing. With no trace of Henry or Alistair and no one else willing to speak out against them, it was decided that the investigation should be dropped. Agnes came to England for a while and ended up addicted to the same drugs her own mother had wasted away on.

"I'm clean now, obviously," she had told me, her hand circling her then-straining belly. "But the whole thing destroyed my life. I never stopped thinking about it. When Priya contacted me, I knew I had to do something. I knew I had to make the others listen."

In the waiting room I catch her eye, and she attempts a smile, her lips hard and tight. She was lucky, in a way, that the police understood. The contours of victimhood seem to have changed since the last time she went to the police, sculpted out with fresh nuances, new ways of understanding abuse. I wasn't angry when I found out how involved Agnes had been. After all, I'd been in Henry Taylor's world myself. I understood how intoxicating it could be, how quickly you could feel as though there was nothing else but the island, his house, our tiny and strange universe. After seven years, nothing would have felt real. It would have been the easiest thing in the world to convince Kiera that nothing was wrong. It would have been the hardest thing in the world to forget. Today means so much to Agnes. It does to all of us.

When they call my name, it's as though I'm watching myself from above, as if I'm observing from outside my own body as I walk down the corridor to the courtroom. I had imagined dark wood panels, an imposing room like the kind on television crime dramas, but everything is surprisingly bare and modern, a wall of faces turned to look at me. It takes me a moment to locate him. I can feel his eyes on me even without turning to meet them. In a room full of people, it could be only me and him, just like it always was.

It turns out that historic cases are slippery and difficult to prosecute, especially when they involve international crime, different borders and countries, crimes that nobody quite knows how to define or explain. I've lost count of the number of times someone has looked at me from across the table and frowned when I told them that yes, I was in a consensual relationship with Alistair. Yes, I was the proper age, acted in a proper way, did proper things that adults decide to do. Most of the charges we had initially hoped for slipped away within the first few months of going to the police. We didn't know the names of Henry Taylor's friends or how to find them. Our lawyers were unable to fit most of the things that had happened to us into the rigid requirements that defined their crimes. Once, one of them told Helena that perhaps she hadn't exactly been abused, not really. Not if she was happy to take the money for it. Not if sometimes, just sometimes, she said yes.

It was the London trip that did it in the end. Our accounts of that week meant that Alistair could finally be arrested, accused of trafficking. Our words against his, each of us prepared to take the stand to tell the world what had happened. When Agnes first went to the police, she had been alone—now, there are multiple voices speaking up about what we saw, what we experienced. An entire body of evidence that what Alistair and Henry Taylor did was wrong. Before I start to speak, I close my eyes tight for a second and hope for the thousandth time that it will be enough.

The words come out easily. Yes, Alistair arranged it all. Yes, he was there. Yes, we all had sex with people. I remember that interview with the two Greek police officers all those years ago, the lies heavy and caustic on my tongue. It feels like a relief to finally undo them, unpicking the threads of a story that let Alistair and Henry walk free, their names unblemished. Not this time though. Not anymore.

I don't look at him throughout my testimony. I only turn toward him once I am off the stand, permitted to take a chair in the gallery to watch the remainder of the trial. For a second, that familiar feeling rises up in me, the instinctive sense of hope I always had for him, an ache of affection deep in my bones. How many times have I looked at that face and seen the world unfurl around me, at the same time that it narrowed down to just the two of us? How many times have I stared into the depths of his eyes and imagined an entire future constructed from bloated promises and half-formed hopes? I remember the jut of his clavicle, the flat certainty of his sternum as I laid my face against his chest, a body I used to know by heart. He looks slighter than I remember him now, his face shadowed by afternoon stubble. For the first time I see how much older he is, in his fifties, with hair that is starting to gray and thin. There's a stoop to his spine, as though defeat is already wrought onto his bones. When I catch his gaze, I remember where I am. Why we are here. I feel myself flinch, decades of memories condensed and dissipated by the disappointed look on his face.

I stay for the start of Helena's testimony. I know that the last few months have been hard for her. Although Helena told her daughter about the police investigation as gently as possible, Astraea had taken it badly. Priya told me that she had refused to talk to Helena about it at first. She had always hoped to develop a relationship with Alistair and was furious that her mother might jeopardize that possibility. In a way, Helena has taken a greater risk than all of us. She has risked losing her daughter.

I sink low in a wooden seat as she relives those months. It was worse for her. When they ask her how many men Alistair had arranged for her to have sex with, she ducks her head.

"I don't know," she says. "It was always a lot."

I don't stay to hear any more than that. I already know the rest. Nor do I want to stay for the verdict. Hearing the things we did translated into a legally binding judgment would only make it real. It would solidify that summer to a time full of terrible secrets, turn me into the victim I was always scared I might become. It's better to go before anything else is said. Better to go with the weight of the past slipped from my shoulders, if only for a few hours.

I ask if I'm free to leave, and a bespectacled receptionist tells me that I am. The idea of being free feels unfathomable after everything.

I know the relief of telling the truth won't last long. Instead I will lie awake all night, the answers I recited re-forming on my lips, encircling my throat. But for now I feel light. My feet speed up as adrenaline bleeds out of my system and the weight of having dozens of eyes fixed on me lifts. Outside the unexpected heatwave has broken and the pavements are damp. People scuttle to the tube with newspapers stretched out above their heads, a flimsy attempt to fend off the forces of the sky. I reach my arms wide and lift my face upward, and for a second, it is as though I am swimming. As though I am being pulled by some unrelenting current again, and when I surface, I will be back in my eighteen-year-old body, kicking toward the shore.

✳

Helena messages me the day I move into my new flat.

At first, I ignore the gentle buzz of my phone, muffled somewhere amid piles of boxes and rolled-up rugs. I've been still for a few moments, sitting on the floor with my head resting against the living room wall. The light at this time of day is warm and beautiful, and I want to enjoy it, just for a moment. My eyes are closed and my face is lifted toward the long windows that line the room. From outside I can hear the faint rustle of trees, a child careening past on a scooter, the sleepy sound of birdsong. It was one of the things I'd liked about this place the first time I came to see it. It's a tiny flat, a cluster of ramshackle rooms at the top of an old terrace house, but I loved that you could see the very tops of trees just outside my window. I had imagined the pictures I would hang and the bric-a-brac I would buy from the vintage fairs I could visit at the weekend. It would be completely different from mine and Tom's place. Cheap kitchen units instead of polished islands. Brightly colored curtains instead of muted tones. A bed, all to myself, where I could stretch out and sleep off the last two years' worth of worries. I'm almost drifting off into a dream of my new life here when my phone vibrates again.

My arms are aching from moving furniture all day, and I groan as I stand. When I see that the message is from Helena, I feel a strange shudder of the past pass through me.

You should come and visit, now that it's all over, her text reads. I know you loved this place as much as I do.

I stand in the middle of my packaged-up life, boxes waiting to be opened and a world waiting to start again, and think of the last time I saw her. She had been disappointed by how everything had turned out.

"It took up years of my life, and it almost feels like it was all for nothing," she had said to me after the verdict.

He got six years in the end. We gathered at Priya's house afterward, all of us clutching our wineglasses as though they were life rafts. I remember everyone looking slightly lost, as if now that we had arrived here none of us were really sure what to do next. It was a strange, solemn kind of party. There was no music or laughter. Just sadness and relief.

"I'm sorry he didn't get more," Jules said to me.

It sounded as though she was consoling me for a loss. Perhaps she was.

"It's OK," I told her. "I did what I could."

I felt endlessly grateful for Jules, who had always suspected, perhaps always known, what had been happening up at Henry Taylor's house but had never pushed me to say more. Yet when I had eventually felt ready to tell her everything, to explain that what I had always framed as a summer romance gone awry had actually been so much more than that, she had just listened, held my hand, promised me she would be there every step of the way.

Helena had caught my eye from across the room and raised her wineglass. We both lowered them again without taking a sip. Throughout the trial and the terrible year that had preceded it, we had formed a tentative friendship. Helena was back in the UK a lot, and I was eager to be out of Jules's house as much as possible. At first our meetings were awkward. The things that had once bonded us had evaporated over time. Now all that we shared were the darkest and most difficult parts of ourselves, a trauma we were both only just coming to terms with. Our rebuilt relationship felt fragile and strange, ridged with the remnants of a past we were both trying to forget. I still struggled with the existence of her daughter, a newly assigned grief counselor prodding me to come to terms with my feelings about the abortion frequently enough that Astraea's very existence felt like an open wound. I had demanded to know Astraea's date of birth and counted backward, a terrible sense of foreboding growing as the months got closer and closer to that summer, until they confirmed the thing I had been most afraid of. That she would have been conceived at almost exactly the same time as I fell pregnant. That her existence represented a parallel life I might have had, a vivid and real-life reconstruction of all the things I had dreamed of. I could accept that Alistair wasn't the person I thought he was, but I couldn't quite let go of the world I had carefully created around us. I wasn't ready for that. Not just yet.

It wasn't until Helena asked me to come to a support group with her that things started to make sense. Sitting in a circle of women, I realized that perhaps we might be good for each other. After all, we were going through something that so few people could understand. When we left, we sat on a car park curb and shared a cigarette, the first I had smoked in years.

"It's an unusual name, Astraea," I said.

It was the first time I had said it out loud. Acknowledged the existence of Alistair and Helena's child. It felt that by defining a new space to talk about our past we had freed up other parts of ourselves to share with each other, enclaves that were present and real and hopeful.

Helena smiled at the mention of her daughter's name. Things had improved between them since the case had gone to court. She had mentioned in the support group that they were rebuilding a relationship shattered by the revelations of the past year.

"It's been hard," she had said. "But it's worth it. Knowing that she'll grow up in a world that's a bit safer for girls like her."

Now she passed me the cigarette, the paper drooping slightly. She always was terrible at rolling.

"It's the name of a goddess," she told me. "I mean, I just chose it because it was pretty, at the time. I only found out what it meant a few years ago."

"Oh yeah?" I said.

When I turned to look at her, I saw that she was smiling, a wistful and mischievous lift of her lips as though she was waiting for me to catch a punch line.

"It means justice," she said. "Astraea was the Greek goddess of justice."

When she spoke, I found myself feeling a tiny surge of gratitude for Astraea's existence. Without her, we might not have been here. Without her, I might never have given up on Alistair.

I look down at Helena's message, an invitation back to a place I have thought about every day for the last two years. A place that used to be my entire world. Then, I take a deep breath and tap my phone to respond. I type rapidly, and as I do, I swear I can almost feel an island breeze.

OK, I write. I think I'd like that.

And then I put my phone away and I prepare to unpack for a new beginning.

A re you ready?" Helena asks.
I nod. "I'm ready."
The sun is beaming down on us, and she smiles as she looks back at me. I'm surprised at how good it feels to be on the island again. I went down to the sea this morning and paddled, the waves shockingly cold against my feet. I am beginning to remember that

the sun was sometimes too hot, the sea sometimes too cool. Every day here erodes a tiny bit of the magic I attached to this place, at the same time as I feel a tiny bit of my love for it return. Yet when Helena suggested that we come up to the cliff top, I had been reluctant.

"Isn't it a bit . . ." I had pulled a face to articulate my unease. "Morbid?"

Helena had shaken her head. "Just trust me on this," she told me. "You need to see it."

Now she glances down, her face split by a grin. She's fitter than me, the island keeping her strong and wild.

"Keep up," she laughs.

As we climb, I realize how much time has changed us since we were last here. My knees complain at the uneven terrain, and I feel a heat in my chest, a thinning out of my breath, an ache in the base of my spine. Did we really used to clamber up these cliffs as though they were nothing? Helena turns back toward me again, and I notice the laughter lines that crease her skin, the gentle give of the flesh on her upper arms. She looks happy, wholly and vibrantly alive. She looks more beautiful than she ever did back then.

I take a particularly ambitious leap to avoid a precarious rock and find that these steps feel familiar, even now. That my feet find indents in the soil like they belong here. I am so different from the person I was when I last climbed this hill. So much stronger. So much surer of myself. I think of my flat back in London and remind myself that my new home is the first thing I have done that is entirely for me. Not because somebody else wanted it, or because somebody else suggested it. Not because I was placing my entire life on pause for somebody else. Not because every decision I made was guided by a specter of the past. By a child who was never born. A relationship that had only really existed in my mind.

I went back to the house Tom and I used to share right before I flew out. It was under contract at last, and there were a few final things to divide between us before the sale went through. I had let him keep almost everything we owned together: the sofa that we'd picked out of an online catalog and wineglasses we had been given as a wedding gift. He could get rid of anything he didn't want. It was part of another world now, another time when I was somebody completely different. And after all, he had more need for things than I did now. He had met somebody six months after I had left, a woman from work with red hair and a wide smile, if her social media was anything to go by. Of course I'd looked her up. I would have been mad not to. She beamed out of pictures with her arm looped around Tom. They looked better together than we ever did. He looked happier.

"I've got something to tell you," he said as we stood at the same kitchen counter where we'd neatly broken down our marriage. "About Kate and I."

I knew what it was before he said it. I could see it in his face: the bashful smile, the new radiance that had never been there when we had been together.

"Is she . . . ?"

He nodded. "We're having a baby."

"Tom, that's . . ."

"I wanted to tell you. You know, before you heard from someone else. I know it's a bit weird, but . . ."

"No, it's great. It's great news. Really. Congratulations."

It turns out that divorce was the thing that had uncomplicated our relationship, that had untangled all the resentments I had carefully woven over the years. He looked relieved, his shoulders visibly relaxing.

"Thanks, Rachel. That means a lot."

"I'm happy for you," I said. "Honestly, I am."

It wasn't until I was striding away from the house, the same walk I had done so many times before to get to the tube, that I realized I meant it. I'd hurt Tom so much. This was all he'd ever really wanted. He deserved a chance at happiness. We all deserve that much.

Helena's hair is starting to blow in the breeze. As we edge higher and higher, the world shifts and changes just as I remember it used to. The sounds fall away and the crashing of the waves seems to grow louder, even as we rise farther away from them. The sky widens and heightens at the same time, a great ceiling of blue that spans out all around us. It is so perfect up here. So peaceful.

As we reach the highest point of the cliffs, I expect to see a familiar sight, a place I have thought about a thousand times over the years, a broad stretch of flat ground and then the world falling away around us. Yet instead I see a cacophony of color. A chaotic, sprawling symphony of flowers. A patch of irises, named after the messenger of the gods. Larkspur for Ajax, and violets for Io. A border of poppies and a footpath marked out by wild orchids. A spiral of roses, the flower that Aphrodite created with her own tears. Tiny saplings bravely protect them from the sea air. At the edge closest to the cliff there is a white-painted sign. I go to read it, but find that the words are stuck solid in my throat. Then Helena is beside me, and she takes my hand just as her mouth forms the words that mine won't.

"Kiera's garden," she says.

I find that my eyes are blurring with tears, the bright details becoming one beautiful blend of color.

"You did this?" I manage.

Helena nods. "You found your peace by going to the police. This is where I found mine."

I turn outward toward the sea, and all of a sudden I am eighteen again. Memories like this are coming back more frequently now, tiny inflections in the narrative of my life, days I had long forgotten about rising to the surface like pockets of air beneath the sea. I remember that we stayed out all night and then came here just as the sun rose. Helena, Kiera, and I. We would have perched up here, feet away from where Kiera would fall just a few weeks later. We would have rested back on our elbows and closed our eyes, the sun warming our faces. The sea always seemed enchanted at that time of day, the bright white of the sun glittering against the edges of the tide. It was the only way you could ever tell it was a living, moving thing. From this far away, it would always look still and flat, a blank expanse waiting for us to write the day out onto it. I remember Kiera turning her face toward me and smiling. She had tied her hair up and her shoulders were bare. Across the ridge of her nose you could just make out freckles, a tiny smattering of sunshine on her skin.

"I could stay up here forever," she said, and her voice was so dreamy, so blissful, that I really thought we would.

Memories like this have become a strange feature of the past year. Revisiting everything that had happened back then was hard at first, the gradual casting of all my best recollections in an entirely different light. Yet slowly, gently, happier parts of my past have also begun to surface. Things I had forgotten about, or perhaps had never wanted to remember. Things that didn't fit in with the narrative I had woven about my life back then, or that had paled beside the blindingly bright picture of Alistair I had so adamantly created. Yet they had still always been there. They had been more powerful than I had imagined. The past has a way of making its way back to me.

"She loved it up here, didn't she?" Helena asks.

I nod. "She would have loved this," I say. "She would have loved what we did for her."

Then I take Helena's hand, and we walk to the edge and sit. We don't say anything. We don't have to. We stay still until the sun sets, just like we did the first time we all came up here, a golden glow casting shadows over the sky. Kiera's garden is most perfect just before the horizon darkens. The flowers seem to absorb the last traces of light, and they are at their most brilliant and bright. Then the sun tumbles from the sky and empties out the day. The flowers become shadows of themselves and the world softens into night.

As the sky darkens and the sea continues to stir, I vaguely remember legends and ancient stories of sea demons and water goddesses. Tomorrow I will go home, and all of this will be a memory. Another day that helps me to rewrite a past that the last two years have wiped clean. We all tell stories, just like they did back in ancient times. The tales we whisper to ourselves just before we fall asleep and the songs that structure our lives. We may not believe in goddesses anymore, but we make our lives part fairy tale all the same. Sometimes we need to remember what is real.

※

It's too hot to be outside for long, but just today, I can stand it. Just today, I don't mind staying here, sweat dampening the backs of my legs, my skin starting to pinken and sting. It's been almost twenty years since I sat alone on this beach and waited for Alistair to come and find me. I used to wake up in the middle of the night and imagine it was happening all over again. That he had only just gone. It always felt as fresh as it did that very first day, a scar that never quite healed. In some ways, it still does.

The boat is beginning to board, a slow line of tourists on the dock migrating toward it. Everything always did move slowly out here, a viscous and heavy quality to each day, sticky and sweet as honey. As all-consuming as air. I already know this is the last time I will ever come here. The last time I will sit on this beach and taste the sea in every breath. I wish it could be the last time I will think of him, but I know it won't be. It takes a long time to train the mind, to undo the thoughts that have lingered there for so long they have embedded grooves in my brain, deeply woven patterns that my imagination follows even when I try to smooth them away.

"Are you ready?" Jules asks.

Ready feels like such a strange and indefinable word. Her question is purely logistical—whether my bags are all packed and I've said goodbye to Helena—but it feels as though she is asking me something else entirely. A bell clatters, a peal of sound warning us that the boat is about to leave. I rise to my feet and brush the sand off my hands.

"I'm ready," I say.

We're the last to board, having to dash down the dock and shriek at the boatman not to leave without us. It means that by the time we embark we're flustered, giggling, collapsing in a heap on one of the long benches that line the boat's edge and pretending not to notice the disapproving glances of people tired and thin-lipped at the end of their holiday. I remember that this was exactly where Jules and I first met, and I'm overcome by gratitude toward her for coming back with me again. For still being here, after all this time. After everything.

The engine splutters and emits the greasy scent of petrol. Ropes are tossed in the elaborate rituals of passage that are enacted here every day. People arriving and leaving as sure as the sea sweeps in and out. The sun is starting to lower, shadows lengthening across the shore. Jules reaches out and squeezes my hand.

"Are you OK?" she asks.

I nod. "Yes," I say. "There's just one more thing."

I reach down into my rucksack and pull out a single rose plucked from Kiera's garden. It is crumpled and frayed by transit, petals shedding on the wooden boards of the boat. It doesn't matter anymore. I have carried the thought of the child Alistair and I might have had with me until she became almost real, a force that kept me bound to him for over a decade. But now I know it was never real. Rose never really existed, not in the way Astraea does, vivid and vital, a life-altering force. With a kind of ceremony that should feel overblown and ridiculous, I reach over the side of the boat and drop the single flower into the waiting waves. It falls into the whirlpool spun by the boat's engine and scatters, stems and petals hemorrhaging outward into the sea. I watch them spiral along the hilt of waves as the lurch of the boat drives them away from us, crimson scars on the surface of the water fading into sea foam. I imagine that some of them will wash up on the shore, wilted and waterlogged and yet still bright. I hope somebody will find them, a broken bouquet on the beach that will make them believe in the magic the island still holds. Jules squeezes my hand again as I lower myself down beside her.

"It'll be OK," she says, and even though we have no idea whether it will be, her words still spark a kind of relief.

Then we turn toward the island and watch until it is a scrap on the horizon, a tiny inflection of darkness in the place where the sea meets the sky. I squint until I'm not sure if I can see it anymore or if it is just my imagination, an imprint of that place in my mind, a swell of sun, a trick of the eyes. The boat picks up pace, the roar of the engine too noisy for me to formulate any more thoughts, any more fears, any more memories of that place. I close my eyes, and I find that I can still taste the sea.

ACKNOWLEDGMENTS

The majority of this book was written during the first UK COVID-19 lockdown in 2020 and finished in early 2021. I didn't tell anyone that I was attempting to write a novel, so in some ways this was the most solitary piece of writing that I have ever completed. But in many ways, this book is also the product of so many people, friendships, and support networks without whom it would have been a very different project.

Thank you to Ariella Feiner at United Agents for sending the email that changed my life. You were the first person to read *The Girls of Summer*, and I will forever be grateful to you for taking a chance on me. Thank you also to Molly Jamieson and Amber Garvey for all your help throughout the process, and to Amy Mitchell for coming up with such an excellent title.

Thank you to everyone at Transworld for loving, shaping, and cheerleading this book. Your belief in my writing has been completely life-altering. Tash Barsby was the first to fall in love with *The Girls of Summer*, and I'm eternally grateful to her for deciding to publish me. I have the tremendous good fortune of having both Frankie Gray at Transworld and Sarah Cantin at St. Martin's Press as my editors, and their insights have been fundamental in bringing this book to its full potential. Frankie—your faith in this project has genuinely made all of this possible. Sarah—your vision helped make this book what it is, and I'm thrilled to have someone as thoughtful and insightful as you on board.

On the publishing side of things, a phenomenal amount of hard work goes into bringing a book into the world. At Transworld, thank you to Sarah Scarlett, Imogen Nelson, Tenelle Ottley-Mathew, Kate Samano, Claire Gatzen, Phil Evans, Laura Garrod, Emily Harvey, Tom Chicken, Gary Harley, Louise Blakemore, Sophie Dwyer, Laura Ricchetti, Natasha Photiou, and Irene Martinez. In particular, thank you to Transworld's brilliant marketing and publicity teams—especially Vicky Palmer, Sophie Bruce, Becky Short, and Hana Sparkes—for your tireless efforts. At St. Martin's Press, thank you to Jennifer Enderlin, Lisa Senz, Anne Marie Tallberg, Tom Thompson, Kim Ludlam, Sallie Lotz, Drue VanDuker, Allison Ziegler, Katie Bassel, Lisa Senz, and Paul Hochman. Thank you also to my foreign publishers and translators for bringing this book to a wider audience and helping me to share this story with the world.

In my own life, I'm extremely lucky to be surrounded by women of not just summer, but of every season, who inspire, encourage, and support me every step of the way. I am particularly thankful for Bethany Leslie and Eloise Stoker-Boyd, whose unwavering friendship has been a shining light in my life since we first met. You are both incredible women, and I am very lucky to know you. Thank you also to Johanna Van Der Straaten, Cass Brown, Harriet Keen, Siân Jamison, Anna Shannon, Rachel Goldsworthy, Kathryn Ferguson-Leitch, Ruby Maxfield, Amy Watson, Audrey Chikasha, Cat Stringer, and Cathryn Steele for your friendship, encouragement, and good conversation throughout the writing and publishing process. I am grateful to have such awe-inspiring, kind, smart, and brilliant women in my life.

My family, and in particular Karen, Kevin, and Nathan Bishop, have always been an unwavering source of support. To my mum and dad—thank you for teaching me to love to read, for encouraging me to write, and showing me that you are never alone as long as you have a book. The endless trips to the library were all worth it. Also to my grandparents, Beryl and Michael Hurl, and my grandma, Dorothy Farquhar, who sadly passed away within the first few weeks of my starting this novel, but who always encouraged me to be myself and is deeply missed by us all.

Thank you to everyone who read and engaged with my writing along the way, particularly those who were kind enough to read my first attempt at a novel. Thank you to the editors whom I've worked with throughout my journalism career who taught me the power of a good story. Thank you to the Davies family, for making me feel so welcome during the time that I was working on this book and beyond. And thank you to all the women who have shared their stories with me over the years. This book is about Rachel, but it is also about and for all women who have not been believed, who have endured indignity and disrespect, who have spoken out, and who haven't yet been able to speak out. Your strength and power are beyond measure.

And finally, to Joe Davies. There's no one I'd rather go on this journey with, and I am extremely lucky to have found you. Thank you for always challenging me, believing in me, sense-checking me, and being my best friend. And thank you, most of all, for explaining Chekhov's gun to me. This book, quite literally, would not have existed without you—or would at least have been a whole lot less interesting. You are the story of my life.